THE HEALER of FOX HOLLOW

"The wound is the place where the Light enters you."

Joan Rose Leonard

THE HEALER *of* FOX HOLLOW

JOANN ROSE LEONARD

FIRST EDITION: July 2012

Published by Vantage Point Books
Vantage Press, Inc.
419 Park Avenue South
New York, NY 10016
www.vantagepointbooks.com

Manufactured in the United States of America

ISBN: 978-1-936467-35-8

Library of Congress Cataloging-in-Publication data are on file.

0 9 8 7 6 5 4 3 2 1

Cover design by Victor Mingovits

For those who yearn for healing

For those who bestow healing – a bowl of soup, a smile, a sharing of time and talent

And for those who have found healing.

As Mark Twain says:

Truth is stranger than fiction, but it is because Fiction is obliged to stick to possibilities; Truth isn't.

PROLOGUE

RAIN – two weeks of relentless downpour – and for the second Saturday in a row, I was cooped up indoors, going crazy.

There was no way to walk outside without stepping on drowned earthworms, their waterlogged bodies scrawled across the landscape in hieroglyphic shapes that seemed, if only I could decode them, like messages from the underworld.

I could have gone into town with my parents, but what thirteen-year-old wants to get out of bed early to go grocery shopping? I wasn't in the mood to do homework or chores and when I tried to read, everything was so clammy – the pages in my book, the furniture, my clothes, my skin – I kept jumping up, wishing for a way to wring out all the dreariness. I was pacing from room to room when, out of the sodden recesses of my brain, an idea mushroomed – an umbrella-shaped impulse perfectly suited to the day. I'd go to the attic for a change of scenery.

On tiptoe, I pulled down the folding stairs from the ceiling, climbed up the metal rungs, and with the rain drumming on the roof just above my head, groped for the light cord. My eyes did their magic-camera trick adjusting to the single lightbulb and I began rummaging around in the dusty hodgepodge.

Chairs, wicker baskets, and backpacks hung from the rafters. Cardboard boxes and old suitcases bulged with books, clothes, and stuff saved for "who knows what" and "who knows when," but nobody had the heart to throw away. I opened a box full of just such examples – jammed with manila folders containing handmade valentines, old school projects, and drawings I'd made from kindergarten on up. Underneath the folders was the tail feather of a sharp-shinned hawk and a tiny fluff of down from the warbler it dined on, years ago, while I watched horrified from our kitchen window. And farther down, a child's fossilized handprint splayed in yellow plaster of Paris.

Even though the folders seemed twice as big as when I took them out, I managed to wedge everything back in, wrestle the box flaps back into their four-fold puzzle, and continued to poke through enough junk to create a separate universe.

Wide-stepping over a metal laundry tub of plumbing parts – maybe to equip an ark if the rain kept up – I lost my balance and bumped smack into my old baby cradle. The creaking rockers thumped back and forth on the gritty floor as if a ghost were trying to make contact. Suddenly, the musty air felt more claustrophobic than the closed-in house below. As I headed back to the stairs, walking carefully so I didn't trip again, I noticed something in the shadows.

Behind a row of twine-bundled magazines was a faded shoe box, the word *Sears* barely legible. Curious, I edged over to the box and lifted the lid, expecting to uncover an old pair of dad's work boots. Instead, I found a sheaf of yellow-tinged newspaper clippings. My heart stopped when I saw the very first headline from the *Smoky Mountain Gazette*. FAITH HEALER VICTIM OF VIOLENT ATTACK.

I gripped the shoe box, inched closer to the light, and began to read.

By the time I finished, I was barely breathing. I read every word again, trying to make sense of it all. "Area residents in a quandary... Sheriff postpones investigation... Emotions running high...A sin not to..."

But even after reading the articles a third time, I still couldn't make whole cloth out of them. Too many unanswered questions. Too many missing pieces. I needed to know *more.* Especially, the biggest question of all. *Why has this story been kept a secret?*

Knowing how hush-hush everyone had been, I was certain it wouldn't be easy. But in the attic, I made a decision. Or rather, the decision was made for me by my *other* self – the one inside me who is stronger and smarter, and can figure out what to do better than I can.

In that deep silent place, I made a vow. No matter how long it took, no matter how many people I had to talk to, no matter how much wheedling and prying it took, I wouldn't stop searching until I found out what really happened. Until I uncovered the truth.

PART I

TAKEN

CHAPTER ONE

SOMETIMES five-year-old Layla had night terrors and woke up wailing. But tonight, it wasn't really a scream that roused her father from sleep as much as a staccato shriek.

"Havin' a bad dream, Ducky?" Ed called out as he shuffled down the hall to Layla's bedroom, rubbing his eyes and blinking hard to clear away the blurriness.

Just hours ago, when Ed tucked his daughter into bed and kissed her good night, Layla was in good spirits, her cheeks still rosy from chasing fireflies.

During the summer, capturing lightning bugs was a bedtime ritual for Layla and earlier this evening, her blue-flannel nightgown billowed out like a bellflower as she swooped and twirled against the darkening sky.

"I caught one!" Layla said, cupping her hands over the pulsing glow. She scampered across the grass and up the wooden steps to the porch swing where her father sat, swaying.

"Look, Daddy. Look!" She opened her hands ever so slightly. In the dwindling light, Ed Tompkin nodded and smiled.

Often, when Ed watched his daughter, a miniature of her mother in looks and temperament, he had the strange sense that, five years ago, fate snatched his wife with one hand, and returned her with the other – offering a glimpse of what she might have been like as a little girl. The same eyes, blue as forget-me-nots. Catlike curiosity. A smile that could uncurdle cottage cheese, but, when provoked, stone-faced as Mt. Rushmore's Washington. Yet little Layla, who was named for her mother, had plenty to call her own too. Among the most noticeable differences was the child's predilection for texture. She often skimmed her fingertips along furniture and walls – even the bark of the chestnut tree – as if she were reading embedded Braille messages.

Also unlike her mother, Layla's littlest toes curled inward, underscoring selfhood from the moment she was born feet-first.

"Fireflies are your mama coming back to light up the sky with a thousand candles because she was so glad you were born," Ed told his daughter. The mercurial child jumped off the porch and pursued the winking lights that floated up from the grass and into the sky until she couldn't tell stars from lightning bugs.

Ed yawned. "Time for bed now, Ducky."

"Just one more, Daddy. *Pleeease.*"

Lean and laconic, even before life threshed him, Ed smiled. "One. But that'll be all," he said, knowing that as the daylight hours got longer, his sleep got shorter.

After Ed put his daughter to bed, he turned on the radio to hear Friday's forecast and sat down at his desk in the living room to pay a few bills.

"...Cold War tensions mount. U.S. officials continue to dismiss Soviet accusations that the downed U-2 pilot was involved in espionage. And that's the news for Thursday, June 23, 1960..."

At 10:30, Ed closed his checkbook and filed the bills in one of the cubbyholes of the rolltop desk. Before bolting the back door, he peered out into the impenetrable dark that enveloped their log home and the surrounding woods of Fox Hollow. A hoot owl called from down in the valley: A sure sign, despite the clement forecast, bad weather was on its way to their part of eastern Tennessee. Owls over weathermen every time, Ed mused.

The weary father peeked in on Layla, sleeping sweetly as a spaniel pup. He tiptoed over and gently brushed back a strand of blond hair that fluttered near her eyelid. Through the open window, a light breeze ruffled the spring-green curtains his wife had made in a whirlwind of sewing for their coming child.

Without bothering to change into pajamas, Ed collapsed on top of his bedspread. Weekdays, Ed's alarm was set for 5:00 AM. Barely enough time to feed and water the barn animals; shower, slap on some Old Spice aftershave, which was an annual Christmas gift from his sister-in-law; wake his daughter, who was a slow, sometimes grumpy riser; get breakfast ready; pack his lunch; drive the rutted, mile-long road to deliver his daughter to the babysitter; and continue eight miles down the mountain to Addison's Lumber Mill, just outside the little town of Wayland, in order to punch in by 8:00 on the dot.

Avis, the older sister of Ed's deceased wife, might disapprove if she knew her brother-in-law went to bed without undressing, saying it didn't set a good example for Layla. The babysitter, Ida Mae Yeagley, who was a stickler for rules, certainly wouldn't consider it proper. But with no one to spoon with in his empty bed, the tired father viewed it as just another willing economy he made for his daughter.

The piercing screams from Layla's bedroom intensified as Ed, now fully roused, hurried down the hall. Hearing his daughter gag between shrieks, his mind raced. It wasn't the right season for the grippe and too early for eating the wrong kind of berry. Tainted food, maybe?

When Ed switched on the light, he could hardly process what he saw: Layla's arms flailed wildly, her little body convulsed as blood – frightening amounts of blood – spurted from her mouth. Ed stood frozen in the doorway as his eyes searched for a possible cause of all that blood. A tumble from bed? An intruder?

"Ducky!" he cried, as he rushed toward his daughter. "What happened, Ducky?" he asked, as he swept up Layla in his arms.

Blood gushed everywhere as Ed sped down the hall carrying his screaming child. He snatched some towels from the kitchen to staunch the bleeding and stopped only to jam his feet into his barn boots by the door. Blindly, he managed to unbolt the back door, shove open the screen, and get his thrashing daughter into the truck. With his left hand, Ed steered down the dark mountain at breakneck speed. With his right hand, he pressed a towel to Layla's mouth.

For whatever good it did, Ed struggled to keep up with the moving target of his little girl as she jerked and twisted, her screams barely muffled.

"It's gonna be all right, Ducky," he said, willing it to be so; praying it to be so. "It's gonna be all right."

Summoning composure from God Almighty, who must know how much help he needed, and from his gut, already toughened by a low blow from his wife's death five years before, the distraught father kept repeating, "There, there, Ducky, it's gonna be all right. It's gonna be all right."

For eight miles he kept up the mantra, hoping to comfort Layla, trying to assure himself, as he threw one blood-soaked towel after another to the floor of the truck and repositioned it with a clean one.

With Layla gasping for breath and writhing in his arms, Ed rang the bell, then pounded on Doc Fredericks' door until the porch lights went on. A sleepy voice inquired, "Who's there?"

"Ed Tompkin. Layla's bleedin' bad."

The broad-faced doctor led them into the clinic at the side of the house, tying his bathrobe with the efficiency of a warrior girding for battle. When the physician removed the bloody towel, Layla screamed so loud the room rattled.

"Open your mouth wide as you can, sweetheart," Doc said. "Ed, try to hold her still."

In between her choking, Doc deftly maneuvered a tongue depressor and the beam of his flashlight. "Do you have the piece of tongue she bit off?" he asked.

Ed was as dumbfounded as if his own tongue was taken.

"Tongue?" The shocked father paused. "No. I didn't know it was her tongue."

Doc Fredericks pressed a big wad of gauze on the

wound to stop the bleeding and the pain made Layla scream even louder. "We could get her to the hospital in Petersburg and see if there's the possibility of reattachment," Doc said, weighing possibilities out loud.

"I didn't see anything layin' on her bed, but then I wasn't lookin' either," Ed said. "Do ya' think she swallowed it?"

"It's doubtful she could swallow that big a piece," Doc said, setting a container of gauze pads on the examining table. "Ed, you hold this gauze tight on her injury. Add a new wad on top of the first piece and, soon as it gets soaked, change it. Keep up the pressure till the bleeding stops."

Doc Fredericks took out a glass vial from the cabinet and a syringe from a covered metal pan. "I'm going to give Layla something to ease the pain. Then I'll call the emergency room and see how we should proceed."

"Layla," the doctor said, holding up the syringe to the light and squirting out a few drops, "This is going to make the pain go away. I know you hurt, honey, but try to hold still for just a minute."

He pushed up the flannel sleeve of Layla's blood-soaked nightdress, swabbed her with alcohol, pinned down her flailing arm, and stuck the needle into her vein.

"Good girl," the doctor said, as he steadily pushed down on the plunger.

Doc Fredericks excused himself to call the hospital

and when he returned, Ed knew the news was not good. Doc looked somber. Funeral somber. He had a heaviness about him that made everything weigh more, even the air.

The doctor pulled Ed aside, out of Layla's earshot, though he didn't need to bother. Layla's head buzzed with the loud hum beehives make; the whole room swirled round and round like she'd spun herself dizzy.

There were times Doc Fredericks wished he were made of sturdier stuff than flesh and blood – something easier to steady for the task at hand. Nevertheless, Doc looked the desperate father in the eye and began. "I just talked to a surgeon at the hospital who said he was experimenting with ways to reattach parts of a body that have come off. But the surgeon said by the time you went back to home and found that piece of tongue to sew it back on, and an ambulance came and got you and Layla, and then drove eighty-five miles to Petersburg, it'd be too late for all the vessels and muscle parts to take to each other and grow back properly. Best thing to do, he said, was control the bleeding, treat for infection, and get therapy for how to carry on afterwards. I'll call a specialist in Petersburg after things settle down."

Ed nodded.

"Let's see how you're doing, sweetheart," Doc said, looking at the pile of bloody gauze next to the drug-dazed child. Doc checked inside Layla's mouth, cautiously lifting the gauze. "Looks like the bleeding is under control now. But just to be safe, I want you to stay the night." Doc Fredericks carried the sedated little girl, soaked crimson, to a vinyl couch in the clinic's waiting room.

From her bedroom on the second floor, Eileen Fredericks had heard the racket. Heard that it was the crying of a child. The distressed wails triggered a womb-deep alarm that pulled Eileen out of bed, into her chenille robe, and down the stairs. In the briefest moment, Eileen performed a visual triage.

Please do whatever you can, her husband's eyes said, in the wordless code that passes between long-married couples. Eileen looked at Ed, who hovered near his blood-drenched child and saw a man whose stoic demeanor now asked for help; for remedy; at the very least, for some baling wire to bind his daughter to life.

The doctor's wife hastened to the linen closet and dug through it for the softest cloth she could find. Then she took the large metal basin usually reserved for Epsom salt footbaths after a hard day, filled it with warm water, and carried the sloshing liquid to the couch.

With a mother's dread concealed in the ample cheek-folds of a reassuring smile, Mrs. Fredericks removed the little girl's sopping nightie and began to clean the child's stained, drug-limp body.

Unhurried as if she were performing a holy rite,

Eileen dipped the cloth in water, wrung it out and, as she cleaned blood from one area at a time, soothed the child with a nursery song adapted to the task at hand.

This is the way we wash your arm, wash your arm, wash your arm...

Afterwards, Eileen eased the almost-sleeping child's arms into the sleeves of an old pajama shirt that belonged to their only child, Brian. Hoping to follow in his physician father's footsteps, Brian was in his second year as a premed in North Carolina.

Swimming in Brian's pajama tops, swathed with a large terry-cloth towel bib, Layla was propped up on several pillows so she wouldn't choke.

Mrs. Fredericks went upstairs and brought down a comforter that she handed to Ed as if she had personally stuffed it with feathers and hope. Ever so gingerly, Ed tucked the quilt around the pint-sized body of his daughter.

Doc offered to bring the shaken father a folding cot to sleep on, but Ed declined. He pulled over a straight-backed chair and sat next to his daughter. Meanwhile, Eileen brought Ed a cup of tea and some homemade nut bread, but when he failed to reach for it, she set it on a nearby end table.

"I'll leave the hallway light on," Eileen said in a hushed voice, glancing at the sleeping child whose gaped mouth trickled red from the corners. "That way you can see how your little one is doing and find your way to the bathroom if you need to use it. I put a clean set of towels in there for you."

"Appreciate everything you've done for us," Ed replied, leaning forward on the chair to cautiously dab blood with one of the gauze squares the doctor supplied.

"Here's a container for the waste," Eileen said, returning from the kitchen with the aluminum pail she toted to the garden when she snipped flowers for the house. "Let us know if there's anything else you need. That's what we're here for."

Eileen went to put her hand on Ed's shoulder but thought better of it. He was so taut she thought his thin body might snap in two.

After Mrs. Fredericks went back upstairs, shadowy forms began to coalesce and dissipate in the murky darkness. At least that's what it looked like to Ed. Not given to many things he couldn't hammer together or pry apart with his skilled hands or practical brain, Ed dismissed the grainy movement as fatigue and focused his eyes on the only thing that mattered: his daughter. But just as murky were the unanswered questions that loomed in his mind. What caused Layla to bite off her own tongue? Did she have a nightmare that terrible? Or had some evil entered Layla's room through the open window and instigated an injury so out of the ordinary that it even confounded Doc Fredericks?

None of it made any sense.

The ticking grandfather clock in the corner of the waiting room chipped the night into unending splinters. Ed adjusted himself in the chair and watched his daughter, attentive to every breath, leaning forward at every gurgle. During his sleepless vigil, Ed's mind began to play trickster. Echoes. Memories. Dull lurkings.

He barely blinked as he stared at his drooling child with the same bludgeoned shock he had five years earlier on the day his wife, Layla, died from complications minutes after their daughter was born feet-first.

Ed drove his wife to the doctor near the end of her pregnancy. That's when Doc Fredericks tried, one more time, to coax the baby to turn in the young woman's slim body. Although Doc had successfully ushered dozens of breech babies into the world, he recommended that Ed and Layla go to Mercy Hospital in Petersburg for the delivery.

"Complications in a healthy woman like you are minimal," Doc said. "But in the off-chance you need help, Mercy is well-equipped to handle it."

After his wife hemorrhaged to death, Ed, with eyes as glassy as the nursery observation window, gazed at his daughter. The infant slumbered peacefully, unaware of any loss.

"Layla," he thought. "I'll call you Layla, after your mama."

"Ed. Ed," his sister-in-law Avis said, trying to tow him from the depths of grief. In shock herself, Avis had just returned from the phone booth in the lobby of the hospital. The euphoria over the birth of her niece and becoming an aunt for the first time was eclipsed by the impossibility of her younger sister's death.

Avis, however, being a mother whose minor emergencies with three children gave her daily practice, was better prepared to operate on autopilot. "Ed, come over and sit with me for minute," Avis said, prying the new father away from the nursery window where he stood in a trance.

She guided her brother-in-law to a lounge area, as far away as possible from an expectant father who flipped through the pages of one magazine after another. Avis and Ed sank into the butt-sprung cushions of the waiting-room couch.

"Ed, I know how much..." Avis couldn't finish.

Looking at the gaunt, unshaven face of her sister's husband, sapped of its usual outdoor burnish and as vacant as an abandoned house, Avis could barely breathe. She retrieved a hankie from her pocket, pressed each eye and gave her nose a vigorous, head-clearing blow. In an attempt to squeeze her crumbling composure back together, Avis clutched the balled-up fist of one hand with her other and began again.

"Ed, I know how much you loved my sister and how much she loved you. And I know you want to do right by what your love created...that precious little baby.... We all do. But with you working all day and then some... well, Franklin and I...we want to help take care of little Layla."

Avis knew that Ed didn't have other relatives who could help lend a hand. His closest kin was his chronically ill mother, who lived with her sister in Vicksburg. Avis paused, giving Ed a moment to process what she proposed.

"You know we'll love her just as much as our own three."

With no response from her brother-in-law, and to address any uncertainty, Avis added, "You can visit as often as you like. Take your daughter home whenever you want. And if you get married again or have a change of mind, we'll bring little Layla straight back."

Ed, captive at the bottom of an airless ocean, sat unmoving, trying to weigh the best course of action in his unhinged mind. Finally, he mustered a broken voice. "No. I can't lose both my Laylas. That'd be more heaviness than I could bear."

Avis unclenched her fists and reached over to pat the knobby knuckles of Ed's hand.

"You know we'll help any way we can," Avis said. "And if you change your –" She knew better than to deepen a hole once she hit bedrock.

"I know you'll figure things out, Ed. My sister always sang praises about you. 'Ed's like gold,' Layla used to say. 'Aboveground you wouldn't know the shine that's buried beneath.' Said there wasn't a thing you couldn't set right or get to work. Made it sound like you could turn back a tornado."

Tears sprung up in Ed's eyes. He, like Avis, was struggling to stay afloat in the tsunami of grief. It didn't seem possible *or fair* that his Layla could be gone. But he knew she was because, before the doctor drew the sheet over his wife's head, Ed kissed her. Her forehead, her cheeks, her unresponsive lips, her honey-colored hair. And even though she was still vaguely warm to the touch, Ed knew that all her sunny energy, all the vitality that made her as buoyant and as full of wishes as a dandelion puffball, had blown away. The quicksilver of her brain, her joy about the baby, the spooky way she knew what he was thinking, sometimes before he did, the secret of where she hid pin money to buy birthday or Christmas gifts – everything that made Layla, Layla – had vanished from her body as swiftly as her blood. She was as empty as a discarded cicada shell.

For Ed, every moment delivered a new wallop of *never agains*. But hearing what his wife said about him to her sister caught him off-guard and filled him with a new kind of anguish. One that was almost too selfish to admit. In addition to losing all the ways he loved his wife, he'd also lost all the ways that she loved him.

The way she beamed and said, "Ed, you're a wonder," when he did the simplest thing, whether it was bringing the canning jars up from the cellar or re-splicing a frayed clothesline. The way that, nestled together after they made love, she wrote with her finger on the inside of his arm, whispering as she traced the letters, *you are my one true love.*

Memories flailed like a film reel jumped from its sprockets until Avis's voice broke in. "If only we didn't live so far away," she said. "A hundred miles seems like an eternity when I wish I could hug that baby fifty times a day. But we'll come often. You know we will."

"Thank you, Avis. Layla always said there wasn't a better sister in the world than you."

Avis smoothed her skirt. "What about arrangements? Do you need help, Ed?"

"No. Like we talked about, she'll be buried at home. The funeral will be soon as possible. Don't want Layla pumped full of chemicals. She liked things natural."

They both fell quiet.

"Well, I better head back home," Avis said, shaking herself into action. "I promised my neighbor I'd pick up the kids before supper. See you about six, then? We'll have a bite to eat and I'll make up the front room so you can get some rest."

"Can't, Avis."

"It's not more than twenty minutes to Shady Grove. I clocked it."

"I know." Ed sighed heavily.

"Well, where are you gonna sleep?"

"Don't matter. Couch here is fine. Soon as the doctor checks the baby over in the morning, I want to take off."

"I just hate to leave you this way, Ed."

"Don't be worrying. You've got plenty on your own plate, Avis. Besides, I need some time to work things out."

Avis and Ed stood and hugged. Feeling the warmth and pressure of living flesh triggered another ache. One more loss.

The next morning, with only a fitful catnap or two on the hospital's lumpy couch, Ed – now widower Ed – sagged with fatigue and the long road ahead. The only good thing about his exhaustion was that it took the edge off his grief. He'd spent the night pacing, making to-do lists in his head, gazing at his daughter through the nursery window and taking note of how the nurses diapered the infants, blanket-wrapped them, fed and burped them. One of the nurses had motioned the widowed father in and led him through the various tasks, step-by-step.

"Picture of health," the doctor announced after examining baby Layla.

When the nurse handed the tiny newborn to Ed, he was so fearful of dropping her he thought his knees would buckle. But he steadied himself and headed back home carrying a gift bag from the hospital containing booties, baby powder, rash ointment, a pacifier, his swaddled daughter, and a ragged hole where his heart used to be.

❧

Dong. Dong. Dong... In Doc Fredericks's waiting room, gray morning light filtered through the venetian blinds as the grandfather clock chimed 5:00. With a trembling hand, Ed leaned forward to dab a trickle from his tongueless daughter's slack-jawed chin, her gurgling respiration punctuated with small, unnerving gasps.

Ed heard footsteps slowly making their way downstairs.

"Long night." Doc said, putting a hand on Ed's shoulder.

Ed nodded.

"Let's have a look," Doc said, opening the drowsy child's mouth and shining his flashlight around. Layla began crying.

"There, there," Doc said. "I'm going to give you something for the pain and then you can go home. Sound good, honey?"

Layla nodded, unconvinced.

The doctor, heavy with lack of sleep and the burdensome knowledge of what lay ahead, gave Ed tubes of salve, a bottle of peroxide for Layla to rinse with, and some morphine for her pain. "Keep a close eye on her for seizure. Sometimes a severe head injury like hers can precipitate one. I'll come check on her this evening," he told the nervous father.

"Appreciate that," Ed said, almost as numb as his re-drugged daughter.

"Till she's out of the woods, I'll come by every day," Doc said, patting Ed's back with what little comfort he could offer.

"Injuries to the mouth bleed more than most because there's so many vessels there," Doc Fredericks told Ed. "But the wounds heal fast for the same reason."

Ed called into work and took the week off. Before they headed up the mountain, Eileen Fredericks brought Ed a cup of strong coffee to drink and filled an ice bag for Layla's throbbing mouth.

Once they were back home, Ed perched Layla on the sofa and with a wary, roving eye, went straight to her bedroom, shut the window and locked it tight. After a few moments, he emerged, ashen, and headed to the kitchen.

He rooted in the cupboards and came back carrying a piece of wax paper and a metal mixing bowl. Once again, Ed entered Layla's bedroom and, shortly after, came out.

From the sofa, Layla saw her father put the bowl on top of the refrigerator, proceed to the linen closet, take out fresh sheets, and return to her bedroom.

Layla was pretty certain that her father found her

tongue and put it into the mixing bowl. And because it was her tongue, she had a powerful urge to see it.

Full of the morphine Doc Fredericks administered earlier that morning, Layla felt wobbly when she stood. The room undulated. Furniture bobbed and floated as she teetered into the kitchen, bracing herself along the walls as the room tipped one way, then the other.

Not tall enough to reach the mixing bowl, Layla pulled over a kitchen chair and stood on tiptoe, but the bowl was still too far away. Looking to extend her height and reach, Layla eyed a broom propped against the wall by the back door. She managed to heft herself and the broom onto the chair and with unwieldy jabs, maneuvered the bowl closer to the edge.

In a flash, the bowl tumbled off the refrigerator, Layla fell off the chair, the broom went flying, and the room whirled and went pitch-black.

The next thing Layla remembered was her father calling her name and frantically patting her arm. When she opened her eyes his anxious face hovered above her.

She tried to say, "Daddy, I'm sorry." But what came out was more moan than anything else: *"Aaee ahm arreee."* Ed grabbed up his daughter in a hug.

They both spied it at the same time. On the linoleum floor a foot away from the overturned bowl laid the graying, severed flap.

Layla started to cry and Ed sat on the kitchen floor

and cried with her. With stifled heaving sobs, he rocked Layla in his arms back and forth, back and forth.

Never having seen her father cry before, Layla cried even more. Now she was doubly scared. Scared for herself and scared for her father. Scared for how she was going to say she was scared. Or say anything.

After a while, Ed took a few shuddering breaths, swallowed hard and said, "It's all right, Ducky. We're goin' to pull ourselves together and figure out what's the best thing to do next. And after we do that, we'll figure out the next thing. On an' on like that. We'll make our way forward figurin' it out as we go."

Ed notified the babysitter, Ida Mae Yeagley, that Layla wouldn't be coming for a while. By noon Ida Mae had broadcast what happened to everyone she knew. And by evening, the news about Layla's terrible injury reverberated like thunderclaps up and down the mountainside.

CHAPTER TWO

FOLKS came bearing poultices, soup and ginseng tea for the tongueless child. And to keep the father's strength up, heat-and-eat tuna or ham casseroles.

Dixie Kessling brought her famous pecan pie. It was no secret that Dixie was sweet on Ed Tompkin ever since her husband, Holt, ran off with the organist from the Baptist church. Holt, whom some folks renamed "Bolt," had worked at the mill with Ed and their families got together at the annual Fourth of July picnic that Mr. Addison threw every year for all his employees.

After Holt ran off, Dixie, a perky bottle-blonde with hair sprayed into a flip, began to drop by with baked goods for the unfortunate widower. Ed tried polite discouragement. He thanked her but never invited her in, apologizing for always being busy, which he was.

With frosted pink lipstick as luscious as her cake icing, the undeterred woman persisted in "popping by." So Ed resorted to means as thumb-blunt as squashing a bug. The next time Dixie appeared with oatmeal raisin cookies, a lunch-box favorite at the mill, saying, "Don't you worry about the plate, now. I'll pick it up later," Ed stepped out onto the porch.

"Dixie, you're a good-lookin' woman and a good cook but you're barkin' up the wrong tree. By the time I finish work, chores and spendin' time with Layla, I just wanna sit on my porch swing and listen to the crickets. You deserve livelier company than that."

With a curt head-bob that sent a jolt to her stiff, upturned hair, the once-jilted woman took her plate of cookies and hurried down the steps.

"Truth is," Ed confided to Layla, "no woman can hold a candle to your mama."

After that, Dixie stopped coming by until she heard about Layla's misfortune. Then, figuring a family in need and a pie full of Karo syrup might be just the ticket to sweeten the pot, Dixie showed up at the Tompkins' door along with many others who came to pitch in with the chores, feed the livestock, and muck out the barn.

Although Ed was grateful for the help, it was too much

commotion for the quiet man who was faced with adapting to his daughter's needs just as he did when, soon after she was born, Layla developed colic and Ed learned to carry his fussy infant, one-handed, in the crook of his arm.

In the evening, Doc Fredericks stopped by to examine Layla's injury and see how she was coming along. He took Layla's pulse and listened to her chest with his stethoscope, transferring the earpieces to Layla so she could hear the thub-dubbing of her own heart.

"Be sure to check her temperature, Ed," Doc said. "If she starts to spike a fever, call right away, you hear? Have to be real careful of infection."

"Y'bet," Ed said, as if he had grown an extra self just to watch over his daughter.

"Open up wide as you can, Layla," Doc said. He shined his light beyond the rim of pearled baby teeth into the swollen, red interior. Layla cried when she had to open her mouth. Too much jaw movement caused pain. The air burned her raw stump like fire.

"Healin' well," Doc said.

After he said that, Layla thought she could close her mouth, but Doc just kept looking. From beneath his unruly gray eyebrows, his eyes stared in puzzlement as if there was a column of numbers at the back of her throat that he was trying to add up.

"You remember anything about what happened last night?" Doc said, switching off his flashlight.

Layla closed her mouth and held her hand over it, waiting for the agony to subside. She glared at the doctor who caused her resurgence of pain and nodded.

"Guess you don't know how to write words yet?" Doc asked the five-year-old.

Layla shook her head.

"Did something hurt you?" Layla nodded.

"Where did it hurt?"

Layla repeatedly thrust her fingers toward her mouth, still closed so the air wouldn't start it on fire again.

"Your daddy says you sometimes have bad dreams. You weren't having a bad dream, were you?"

Layla shook her head and squeezed back tears.

"We're all done, sweetheart," Doc said, not wanting to distress his young patient further. He folded his stethoscope into his black bag and latched the buckle.

"Hmmph...." he muttered. "Unusual."

"Most unusual..."

After the doctor left, Ed carried a glass of milk and the bottle of morphine into his injured daughter, careful not to trip on an oddly placed braided rug in the living room. Months before, when a knot in the floorboard fell out and left a space big enough for a rat to crawl through, he nailed the lid of a giant butter bean can over it and hid the repair under the rug. Now Ed needed to do the same thing for himself and his daughter; find a way to patch together their life.

That night, Layla was so full of pain and drugs, by turns crying out and dozing off, that the worried father carried his little girl to the rocking chair in the corner of her bedroom. Ed rocked Layla with the words of the only lullaby he knew–the one he sang to her when she was a baby.

Hush little baby, don't say a word,
Papa's gonna buy you a mockin' bird...

He remembered how he used to feed his baby daughter in this very rocker, temperature-testing her formula on the ropy tendons of his wrist, and he remembered Avis calling every Saturday morning with a litany of questions.

"How much formula is the baby taking? Are you burping her real good? How long is she sleeping at night?"

Ed was glad for the chance to run things by Avis, checking that he was doing everything right.

"Any way to keep from poking the baby with the safety pin?" Ed asked.

"You're putting your hand between her skin and the part of the diaper you're sticking the pin into, aren't you?"

"Ummhmm."

"Well, nothing is gonna happen except to your own fingers, Ed. You're keeping the pins in soap aren't you?"

"You have to wash'em?"

"Heavens no. Get a bar of Ivory and stick the pins

in. It'll make the point slip through the fabric slick as a whistle."

"You've got more tricks than a magician, Avis."

His sister-in-law's laugh ended on a downturn, the unspoken reason that prompted these conversations.

Ed continued to rock and sing to his injured daughter in the silent house, thinking about all the hopes he and his wife had shared. How they secured a modest bank loan to give their dreams walls and a roof and built this home from the ground up.

As Ed rocked his moaning, restless five-year-old, he recalled his daughter's gift of gab. No doubt, his daughter had a maternal gene for talkativeness since Ed himself, never possessed an overabundance of verbal ease. But once little Layla started to speak, it seemed her tiny mouth was quiet only when she was sleeping or lost in contemplation. With the same zeal that she picked wildflowers, the lively child collected words. *Blumps. Aminal. Umbellabella.* Now, as he remembered her mishmashed vocabulary it sent pangs akin to bullet shots through him.

The words *Hush little baby* caught in Ed's throat, yet he persevered for his daughter's sake, only hinting toward a tune. Periodically, the rocking slowed and came to a halt as both of them, however briefly, drifted into sleep. But by the time Ed got to the last verse, he was oblivious to anything but the overwhelming love he felt for his tongueless child.

CHAPTER THREE

TWO days after Layla lost her tongue Aunt Avis came to help. Avis was harried from hastily made arrangements and worried sick when she entered her niece's bedroom and found Layla half-asleep, doped up with morphine and thoroughly miserable. Because Avis dared not touch Layla's swollen cheeks, she leaned over and planted a gentle kiss in the palm of child's droopy little hand.

Layla's eyes sprung open. She jolted upright, terrified by being touched unexpectedly in the very bed where her agony began. When she saw her aunt, she reached up to embrace her.

"I'm here now, sweetie," Avis said, brushing clumpy strands of hair from Layla's face that Eileen Fredericks's washcloth missed.

Avis smiled. "I brought some homemade raspberry syrup and Borden's vanilla ice cream. Picked it up special for you at the Piggly Wiggly in Wayland."

Instead of the excited response Avis thought the words *ice cream* would elicit, Layla's gaze searched in the direction of her bedroom door.

Guessing, her aunt said, "Abbey, Wolfy, and little Frank didn't come this time."

Layla always looked forward to visits from her cousins. But she was feeling too sick to run around, playing and hollering. She'd already screamed herself hoarse from all the pain. Thinking about her cousins, the five-year-old became even more out of sorts. How would she count out loud when they played hide-and-seek? Or ask riddles? Or tease Wolfy about not being able to whistle now that she couldn't either?

The little girl's troubles escalated too fast to keep count aloud or by any other means. There was the excruciating ache where her tongue had been. And the ache of not being able to tell what really happened.

Layla wanted to explain to everyone that she didn't bite off her own tongue. A snake did. A hissing serpent crawled in through the window, pushed down her throat until she choked, and lightning-swift, sunk its fangs into her tongue until she felt fire. But, unable to talk, there was no way to let anyone know. She felt like yelling and kicking with frustration, but it hurt too much to move, especially her mouth. And even though she was plied with all the popsicles and ice cream she wanted – a wish come true – swallowing was torture and, with most of her taste buds gone, food had no flavor. The only bright spot was having Auntie Avis all to herself.

A selfish sin. That's what Ida Mae Yeagley called that kind of thinking. Ever since she was two weeks old, Layla spent weekdays with the strict babysitter who brined her own eight children in the fear of God so they'd weather the seasons without spoil. As a result, Layla was acquainted with a daunting number of thoughts and actions that constituted sin. But even if coveting her aunt's attention was a sin, it's how Layla felt and Ed raised Layla to be truthful – a virtue Mrs. Yeagley held in high esteem, as well. Ida Mae paddled the truth into seven of her children as regular as a rooster crows. Only seven, because Petey, who was born palsied, never got a whacking. And, after the first time, Ida Mae didn't paddle Layla either. Ed said that wasn't his way. He made it clear that "if Layla does somethin' bad enough to warrant a paddlin' you let me know an' I'll make sure she gets corrected."

Privately, Ed told his daughter, "When you give a lesson to a critter or a child, don't be surprised if they learn it."

As Layla looked up at her aunt, hovering beside her, tears rolled down the child's cheeks. She wanted to say, *Oh Auntie Avis, it hurts so much.* She wanted to tell her aunt how it happened and how frightened she was.

"Come here, darlin'," Avis said, sitting down on the edge of the bed, gently lifting her niece onto her lap and cuddling her in a hug. "You're gonna feel better, soon. I promise you will. You know that, don't you?" The little girl nodded halfheartedly.

Yes, Layla knew without a doubt that Mrs. Yeagley would have deemed her *sinful* for glorying in her aunt's undivided attention. But it was God's honest truth and at the Yeagleys' church, where Layla went on many a Sunday, Reverend Simpson shouted, "The truth shall set you free."

Worried about the lax upbringing of her charge, Ida Mae wondered out loud and often if Ed Tompkin didn't feel a need to be churched or to bring up his daughter in the ways of the Lord. But Ed replied, "The Lord saw fit to take my good wife, leavin' me with a man's work and a woman's too. And if I take off on the Sabbath, how am I to keep to the righteousness of *the Lord helps them who help themselves*? And what better church is there to say your prayers in than God's created world?"

Well, Mrs. Yeagley allowed for some truth to his words, but it didn't satisfy her, so she made special efforts to school Layla along with her own children in the *shalt* and *shalt nots* and in the books of the Bible and the revelations of the prophets.

Once Layla was out of diapers, Mr. and Mrs. Yeagley made it a point to stop by on their way to church and ask Ed if they could bring Layla along.

The first time, Ed said, "I know I shouldn't be selfish about keepin' you here with me, Ducky. Your mama would want you to get more Bible learnin' than I give you."

Weekends, Ed's routine was to plunk his elfin daughter into a wheelbarrow and ferry her from place to place while he worked in the garden and cared for the mule and hog and chickens.

"Here Ducky," he'd say, giving Layla a bean or a brushed-off carrot to chew on. Or he'd set a baby chick or a barn kitten in her lap to play with.

Concerned that Layla might be better served by being exposed to the word of God than a day of farm chores, the conflicted father finally let the Yeagleys take little Layla off to church in their hay wagon full of children. The four boys with their hair slicked back – teenaged Zeb, Petey, bound to his wheelchair with one of Ida Mae's aprons folded into a wide band so he didn't fall out, little Micah, and toddling baby Jake. The four girls – Rebekah, Rachel, Lizzie, and Sarah Jane – in ironed dresses with their hair neatly plaited. And Layla in any old thing she had on, including a pair of shoes stuck on her feet, which were dirty from running around barefoot.

Though Ed had never attended the Holiness Pentecostal church, he knew the members practiced the Bible literally by taking up serpents, drinking kerosene, and faith healing. Ida Mae, however, reassured Ed. "Layla won't be placed in any danger. No. The only thing the young join in is listenin', singin', and prayin'. They aren't anointed to confirm the word of God by handlin' serpents till they're older."

Ed and his wife grew up Baptist and continued that way. But after his wife died, Ed was stretched too thin to go to church or to poke into the ways that other folks chose to pray and praise.

His decision to send Layla to church with the Yeagleys sprang from his belief that "A good dose of hallelujah never hurt anybody."

On the way, Mrs. Yeagley had the oldest of the girls, Rebekah, re-braid Layla's hair and spit-wash the dirt off her face as the wagon headed to the church halfway between the Tompkin house and Wayland.

The old church was in serious need of hammer, nails, and a fresh coat of paint. In the sea of peeling white, map-shaped patches of wood appeared like foreign islands. The splintered door on the formerly abandoned house had a hand-painted black cross on it. Inside, the linoleum bucked and heaved where damp rot had eaten into the floorboards. In those wavy places, the folding chairs that made up the rows became rocking chairs. A long, wine-red velvet mural depicting the last supper of Jesus and his disciples hung behind the plywood platform where Pastor Simpson preached. On the front of the platform were several low, well-crafted wooden boxes. And inside those boxes were serpents. Not every service had handling. It all depended on whom the Holy Spirit moved upon that day.

While Dolly Parks played a gospel hymn on the plingy piano and Ray Runkle strummed along on his electric guitar, Pastor Simpson stood on the platform thumbing through the pages of his battered Bible. After finding the passage he was searching for, the preacher picked up a microphone that trailed a cord long enough to get him all the way down the center aisle to the back row, and called out.

"Sisters and brothers. Are you ready to receive the Holy Spirit?"

There was a fervent response of *hallelujah*s. After the pastor preached a short sermon, he launched into Mark:16.

"And these signs shall follow them that believe!"

Amen! Praise God, shouted the worshipers.

Layla heard Pastor Simpson talk about serpents and she saw them being passed around. But mostly she focused on playing cradles with Sarah Jane, looping string in and out of their fingers, or clapping out music on Petey's leg to "How Sweet the Name of Jesus Sounds" or any of the other hymns the congregation sang. She and Petey were close like that.

When Ida Mae didn't feel that the children were paying proper heed to the service, she goaded them to attention with a finger prod that left an afterburn. Then, Layla and Sarah Jane would jump up amid the tree-tall legs of the men and the swishing skirts of women and, taking their cue from the rapture around them, raise their small palms toward heaven and mimic the words in time to the music. They joined in as best as they could with the stomping, clapping, and shaking, crying out with the others, *Save me Jeeezus*!

After she returned from church, Ed would quiz Layla. He gathered that she liked the music but didn't pay much mind to the service. From what his daughter said, Ed could tell that she didn't understand a good deal of what transpired in the frenzy of singing, tambourine shaking, and calling down the Holy Spirit of God.

As long as Layla bounced back into his arms untroubled and unharmed after being with the Yeagleys, whether it was at their church or their home, Ed was satisfied.

As Layla sat on Avis's lap, the aching and confused child went, by turns, from fidgeting to sinking into her aunt's embrace. "Selfish sin," she thought.

Layla wondered if, to be forgiven for coveting her aunt's attention, she had to shout like Pastor Simpson, "The truth shall set you free," because her silent admission didn't feel freeing at all.

Sometimes, Layla even pretended Avis was her own mother. Then she felt like a thief, stealing Abbey's, Wolfy's, and little Frank's mother for herself. And like a traitor, wishing for a mama other than her own.

Layla's image of her mother was unchanging because of the photograph Ed kept next to his bed. The gold-framed picture of his wife sat on his night table beside an alarm clock, a handkerchief, a pocketknife with a razor-sharp whittling blade, and a bag of Luden's mentholated cough drops to soothe the irritation in his throat and lungs from breathing a decade's worth of sawdust, forty hours a week and overtime.

Except for more flesh and roundness, Auntie Avis looked like she sprang to life from her mother's photograph. Mama, Layla thought, was like a willow tree. Auntie Avis, more kin to a sycamore.

"Be back in a jiff," her aunt said, laying her niece gently onto the bed. A few minutes later, she returned with a bowl of ice cream topped with raspberry syrup.

"Propped up in bed like a princess, now aren't you?" Avis pouffed up the throw pillows commandeered from the sofa.

"Eat this, honeybunch. Got to build your strength

back up and fortify your blood."

Layla took a tiny bite of the syrupy cold. It had no taste, whatsoever. Swallowing was nearly intolerable. And the second spoonful sent her into fits of choking.

"Goodness gracious. Goodness gracious," Avis said, patting her niece's back until the coughing subsided.

Whenever Layla swallowed, it felt like the tricky maneuverings her father used to steer their truck on the narrow mountain road in winter's worst. It was so exhausting she didn't want to eat even though her stomach twisted with hunger. But she knew she had to try because she overheard Doc Fredericks talking to her father when they thought she was asleep.

"Might have to use a feeding tube through her nose if she doesn't start eating more. Wouldn't want to put her through that unless we're out of options. Mighty uncomfortable."

In Layla's mind, "uncomfortable" translated to *hurt* – something she didn't want any more of. So she kept swallowing and choking, hoping to get the hang of it.

The day Avis arrived, she cooked, cleaned, and doctored her niece's injury with ice, peroxide, and salve. Ed tended to chores outdoors and in the barn, and made frequent trips inside to check on his daughter. When Ed encountered Avis in the hallway or in the kitchen, they compared notes.

"Swelling seems a bit less," Ed would say. "She got

down a few spoons of ice cream," Avis reported. Their snatched exchanges were peppered with questions that had them both so head-spun, they couldn't see straight.

"Been able to figure out what happened?" Avis asked, as Ed stopped to pour himself a glass of water from the tap.

"Not yet." Ed gulped down the water and refilled his glass. "My brain's cut to pieces thinking about it. I looked around. Didn't see signs of anyone coming in. But I'm fixin' to put in all the window screens. Meant to get them up when I took down the storm windows this spring. Nightmare's the only thing that makes sense, but Layla says it wasn't that."

"Dreams can seem awfully real," Avis said, filling the ice bag with cubes. "Hard to tell the difference, sometimes."

Ed dared not let on that there were several instances when his wife appeared to him in such vivid detail he was heartsick to wake up.

"Dream or not, I wish she had a way to tell us," Avis said, tightening the cap on the ice bag. "It scares me, I can tell you that...just so horrible."

Ed shook his head and headed back outside.

Layla spent the day drifting in and out of morphine fog, playing in bed with her rag doll, and stringing yarn with the colored macaroni that Mrs. Yeagley brought by earlier that day.

Using a different pattern for each one, Layla made a necklace for Auntie Avis and cousin Abbey and all four Yeagley girls. She considered whether to string one for the bearer of the gift. But Mrs. Yeagley was not a necklace-wearing kind of person, leaning toward the plain and simple like most folks in her church.

That afternoon, Auntie Avis came into Layla's room carrying a shopping bag.

"Sweet pea, I brought a surprise for you."

Layla perked up.

"I've got a special game, here," she said, brushing the hair off Layla's forehead and resting her hand there. Avis's fingertips felt like the winter sun radiating warmth down to Layla's bones.

"Would you like to try playing the game with me?" Her aunt's voice had the glint and bubble of a creek.

When Layla bobbed her head up and down, the throb in her mouth drummed in her ears like a tom-tom.

Avis moved the plastic bowl of macaroni and yarn out of the way and sat down on her niece's bed.

"Here's how we play." First, Avis removed a sketch pad from the bag. Then, a thin metal box. When the box was opened, Layla eyed the colored pencils inside.

"All rowed up like peas in a pod," she thought. There was a red pencil that reminded her of dark, sweet cherries. Another that was baby-toes pink. And three shades of green – one that looked like the scum on Turtle Pond near Addison's Mill. All the colors of the rainbow and more. Her aunt lifted the cover of the sketch pad and plucked up a brown pencil.

"Now let's say I'm thinking about an apple," she said. "So I draw a picture like this."

"That's not an apple," Layla tried to say. Only it came out, *"Ehhh uh a aaaauu."*

"Hold on a minute, sweet pea," her aunt said.

Puzzled, Layla looked closely as Avis drew a round circle with a butter bean at each side. Suppressing a smile, her aunt penciled in more lines. But it wasn't until a tail, eyes, and a nose were added that Layla could tell it was dog.

"Do you like my apple?" Auntie Avis asked with a twinkling voice.

Shaking her head, cautiously this time, Layla laughed. It was the first sound since she lost her tongue that wasn't distorted.

"Then why don't you draw me an apple to like?"

Smiling, her aunt held the box of pencils so her niece could choose one. Layla drew a red circle and colored it solid, slipping from the lines only once. And then for good measure, she added a brown stem and green leaves poking from each side of the stem.

"Why Layla Grace Tompkin," her aunt said, "you're a real fine artist. But then why wouldn't you be? You're a whizbang at everything you do." Avis rubbed Layla's back in proud little circles.

"Would you like to play some more?"

Layla nodded.

Desperately casting about for a small avenue of communication, Avis pondered a moment before she spoke. "Now if I said, 'Supper's soon. What would you like to eat, Layla?' Show me what you'd draw."

That question stumped Layla. She never imagined she'd get tired of eating sweets. Though her father could mix up a passable corn bread, he didn't have the know-how or time for making cakes or baking cookies, a void Dixie Kessling eagerly tried to fill. And Mrs. Yeagley was a firm believer in only eating natural sweets. Come noon-time dinner, Ida Mae served up desserts of plums, cherries, watermelon or whatever was in season. Occasionally, she allowed bread with jam.

But eating nothing except ice cream left Layla hungering for crisp, streaky bacon or beans with salt pork. Jets of warm saliva gurgled in Layla's mouth and trickled out as she picked up a brown pencil and drew a circle to represent a bowl. She filled the bowl with little round beans and held the picture up for her aunt to see.

Avis scrutinized the drawing. "A hamburger? Is that what you have a taste for? A hamburger?"

Layla's insides plummeted. It was the same feeling

she got on the rope swing that hung off the maple tree when she was as high in the sky as humanly possible and the swing started dropping back to earth, carrying her stomach down with it.

"No? Not a hamburger?" Momentarily, her aunt's expression sagged. "Don't be discouraged, punkin." Avis smoothed back Layla's hair. "Getting to guess till you get the answer is part of the fun. Now turn that frown upside down," her aunt said, gently tracing a smile on the little girl's face with her forefinger, wiping away dribble in the process.

"Hmmm...I've already guessed hamburger and that's not it. So see if you can think of a way to put me in mind of what you mean."

Layla stared glumly at the round circle. Slowly, she began to see what her aunt saw. It did look like a hamburger. So she heaped up more beans in the bowl and put a spoon beside it.

"Beans? Are those beans?" Auntie Avis asked, her soft brown eyebrows lifting hopefully.

Layla beamed.

"Well, let me see what I can do." Avis stood up and tugged down her blouse over her belly.

"You know, Doc Fredericks said you weren't to have anything that needed chewing till you saw the specialist in Petersburg. But I've got me an idea to mash those beans up real good. Mash 'em into puree. There'd be no chewing whatsoever. So then you and Doc Fredericks would both have satisfaction. Sound good to you?"

Layla nodded, basking in her aunt's shine.

"Okay, sweet pea, you draw some more pictures while I start fixing supper." She leaned over and kissed Layla's forehead with lips light as butterfly wings.

"Oh Auntie Avis," Layla said in her mind, as she looked deep into the blue pools of her aunt's eyes. "I wish you could stay here always."

As surely as if she'd heard her niece's words, her aunt gave Layla's shoulder a squeeze.

"I wish we didn't live such a distance, sweet pea. I miss you something terrible when we're apart just like I miss my dear sister." Avis had a faraway look in her eyes. "Draw some more now," she said, as she hustled off to the kitchen.

Staring at the white expanse of paper and the row of colored pencils, Layla thought about the world of things she could draw. Gradually, like the morning sun rising from behind the mountains, an idea emerged.

Layla could draw a snake and show it to her aunt. She couldn't think of a way to show the terrifying hiss the snake made but she could draw her tongue in its snaky jaws. With a burgeoning eye for precision, the diminutive artist surveyed the pencils and determined the shade of pink she could use, but she didn't know how to fully depict what happened.

How could she show the snake slithering in while she slept? Show how it sneaked in through the dark and thrust itself down her throat until she nearly choked to death. And then, before she could scream, grasped hold of her tongue and yanked.

How could she show how it felt? The fire. The hot thickness gushing from her mouth and down her throat. How she was so desperate for air she couldn't catch her breath to scream. Along with agonizing pain, that's what Layla remembered most. Trying to get air.

She reasoned that if she drew a snake, the triangle of her tongue protruding from its mouth, she could point to the picture and then point to the stub in her mouth. When the curious little girl peeked at her tongue in the bathroom mirror after she peed, the stub looked like strawberry jam. Gooey red. She wished she could show her tongue-flap but it was nowhere to be seen. Her father buried it in the backyard after it fell out of the bowl in the kitchen.

Drawing the snake would be easy. Layla had seen her share of snakes at the Yeagleys' church and slithering through the underbrush alongside the road and sometimes sunning themselves on rocks. But her father taught her to leave them be, especially when snakes were in molt, peeling themselves out of their old skin. Layla understood how losing your skin could make you ornery. The summer she was four, the fair-skinned child sunburned so badly, blisters as big as fish eyes boiled up on her nose and shoulders. Layla didn't want to be touched any more than a shedding snake did. Even when her father dabbed on vinegar to soothe the burn, she was none too friendly.

By age five, Layla had seen her share of snakes up close and personal, mostly on account of Zeb Yeagley. Zeb, the oldest child of Clay and Ida Mae, had a passion for capturing snakes. He caught any snake he saw. Long, short, thick or skinny. Ones that could kill you with their poison, and ones that kept the rats from overrunning the barn. Zeb would hold the snake up by the tail as it whip-snapped its body this way and that, riled up and hissing like water on hot oil.

But better than capturing them, Zeb liked to scare the little kids with snakes. He'd stick the serpent right up to their faces – even to chair-tied Petey, who couldn't do a thing to move away – hold the snake's writhing body within biting range and swing it backwards just before fangs touched flesh. Early on, Layla learned that if she didn't flinch, Zeb moved on to someone else. Someone who ran or hollered.

When Mrs. Yeagley saw Zeb tormenting the children with reptiles, she'd take the paddle out from behind the kitchen door and go after him.

"Zebidiah Yeagley," she shouted in a fearsome voice. Sure to follow was the lecture heard a thousand times, the consequences of sin, and the trials that the put-upon mother had to endure.

"You're not too old for a lickin' to put the fear of God back into you. I've used up half the breaths in my body and all my patience tellin' you to stop. Now let that serpent loose an' bend over."

"*Why?*" Zeb would say, even though talking back to a parent was a strict *shalt not* at the Yeagleys. "I'm just getting the kids used to serpents so they won't be a'feared in church."

"There's a powerful difference between prayerful handlin' and terrifyin' your brothers and sisters. 'Sides, not one of you is anointed to handle till you get older. And then not till the Holy Spirit tells you to. Now bend over while I give you a remindin' you won't forget."

The night the snake bit out her tongue Layla couldn't see its actual color. She was unable to determine if the reptile had any pattern of diamonds or stripes. Remembering the shroud of darkness, the little girl selected the black pencil. Because she didn't want to be misleading, she judged black to be more accurate than a wild guess. With great care, the budding artist made a long, wavy line from one side of the drawing tablet to the other. Then she fattened the line until it had some thickness to it. She added a head and sharp fangs projecting from its wide-open mouth. And even though Layla knew that snakes heat-sensed their prey and smelled with their tuning-fork tongues, she drilled the pencil point into the paper for the snake's eye so it could see in the dark.

Next, she chose a red pencil the color of the climbing roses on the porch trellis and drew a good amount of blood coming out of the pink flap of her tongue between the snake's jaws.

"Looky what I brought you, sweet Layla," Auntie Avis said when she returned bearing a tray with a bowl, a spoon, and a glass for rinsing with peroxide after eating.

"A cold bowl of stirred custard, smooth as silk, that Mrs. Gilly carried over for you." Avis set the tray at the foot of the bed.

"Did you draw something for me to see?" Her aunt's cheerful countenance reminded Layla of spring daffodils. Sunny and welcoming.

When Avis leaned over to see her niece's drawing, her cheerfulness vanished. She sank down on the side of the bed, took the drawing tablet in her hands and began to study the picture.

"Layla, honey," she said, hesitantly. "This here looks to be a picture of a snake. Did I guess right?"

Still mindful of not being too rambunctious, Layla nodded slowly.

"Is the snake eating something?"

Again, Layla nodded, eyes urgent with the message she was frantic to convey.

"What's the something that snake is eating?" Avis

lifted the tablet up higher and looked as intently as if she were threading a sewing needle. "Is that snake chewing on a chunk of ham?"

Excited that her aunt was giving voice to what she was bursting to say, Layla shook her head – shook it so fast the throb started up again. But Layla didn't care. She opened up her mouth and pointed to the where her tongue used to be. *"Ehh, ehh,"* she said, gesturing over and over.

"Your tongue?" Auntie Avis whispered. "The snake is eating your tongue?"

"Uhhhuh, Uhhhuhh, uhhuhhh." Layla nodded.

"That's what happened? A snake?"

Layla pointed to the open, screenless window and mimed the reptile slithering through it and then straight into her open mouth.

"The snake bit you?" her aunt asked, in disbelief.

Yes, Layla nodded. She repeated the same action she did for the doctor, thrusting her fingers, over and over, toward her mouth. Then, with her hand positioned as if she were going to make a shadow puppet of a snake's head on the wall, she opened the jaws and snapped them together.

Avis gasped. "Oh, my poor, sweet Layla." She gave the agitated child a long hug. "You're *sure* that's what happened?"

Layla nodded and nodded with little, almost

imperceptible head bobs.

Avis moved the tray with the custard onto Layla's lap and whisked up the drawing tablet.

"You eat on that now while I go do something. I'll be back quicker than a wink. If you need anything before, give a shout. You still have good lungs and a lot of sound left, honeybunch. Don't ever be afraid to use 'em."

While Layla ate the bland custard, smooth like Auntie said it would be, she heard the screen door bang shut and her aunt's shouting, "Ed. Ed..."

"What? What's the matter?" Ed, frantic, came flying out of the barn. "Is it Layla?"

"Look at this, Ed," Avis said. She held up the picture for Ed to see. "Layla says this is what happened. A snake! Crawled in through the window and bit out her tongue. She showed me how it happened."

Ed stared at the drawing while Avis repeated every detail.

"Now that just doesn't make sense, Avis," Ed said, shaking his head. "Doesn't make sense at all. How big was the snake?"

"She didn't say. But it had to have had a strong bite. Oh, Ed...she seems so sure."

Ed shook his head, deeply troubled. "No sense at all," he said. "But I better go see." Avis took the lead as they started toward the house.

When he got to her room, Ed settled on the edge of Layla's bed. "This true, Ducky," he asked, holding out the drawing.

Layla answered his questions exactly as Avis had described. Despite the bizarre story, the look in his daughter's eyes and her obvious distress, whatever the cause, told Ed he needed to pay attention.

"We'd better check every inch of the house," Ed said. "I'll start in Layla's room. Avis, you start in the kitchen."

Ed knelt down on the floor and looked under the bed. "Nothing here." He opened the closet, shoved hangers aside, raised shoes up off the floor. "Nothing here." He opened each drawer of her bureau, lifted out the clothes inside. Took the drawers completely out and looked into the empty framework. He removed every one of the books and toys from her bookcase and replaced them.

"No snake anywhere, Ducky. I'll make sure there are none in the rest of the house, either," he said, closing the window and locking it. "And I'll make sure there's no way for one to get in." He hugged his daughter and left.

A few minutes later, her aunt returned. Avis measured out morphine in a dropper and held the glass while Layla rinsed with the peroxide. Then Avis dabbed antibiotic salve on the amputation.

"Let's wash you up a bit, sweet pea." The shaken woman went to the bathroom and returned with a damp cloth.

"Round and round the garden, marched the teddy bear," Avis recited as she carefully circled her niece's swollen, blotchy face, hoping to comfort with long-past rituals. "*Up the path, down the path,"* she chanted, spiraling behind Layla's ears, *"tickle her under there."* Ever so gently, she wiped beneath Layla's chin.

"You'd best get a nap now. When Doc Fredericks comes later, I want you to be rested so you can show him your picture just like you did to me. Think you can do that?"

Layla nodded, then yawned. Trying to communicate without speech was exhausting. So was having pain that reeled her in and out like a hook-caught fish. It was tricky to find a relaxing position with the many bolsters and pillows that were needed to elevate her head. But her aunt adjusted a little this way and a little that way until there was a cushiony nest.

Avis tucked the wan child in, pulling up the patchwork quilt her pregnant sister had so carefully stitched together. Luckily, it hadn't gotten bloodstained like the sheets. It was so warm on the night of Layla's accident, her father draped the quilt over the back of the rocking chair.

"Here, honeybunch." Avis handed Layla her rag doll. "You have a good nap, now."

She kissed her niece's forehead, took the tray with its barely-eaten custard and headed out of the room.

Just as she closed her eyes, Layla heard sounds outside of her window. *Rustling.* The terrified child jumped out of bed, shrieking.

"Layla!" her aunt yelled. Avis flung the tray onto the sofa and rushed back into the bedroom, hands outstretched to snatch Layla from the jaws of danger. She found her niece plastered against the wall next to her bed, screaming. Commotion came from the window. Avis looked over and saw Ed frantically knocking on the pane. "What's going on?" he shouted.

"Layla, honey," Avis said, unlatching the window and raising it up. "It's your daddy. It's okay, sweetie," she said, returning to rub the petrified child's back.

Ed hoisted himself in through the window into the room. "You okay, Ducky?"

Layla nodded, shaking. She pointed to the window and mimed a slithering snake.

"No snakes, Ducky. Just me. I'm putting screens in all the windows and going around to every rafter and overhang in this house to make sure there are no chinks or holes. Not so much as a gnat will be able to get through when I'm done."

He lifted Layla up from her bed and took her to the open window. "See. My hammer and nails are down in the brush. Didn't mean to scare you, Ducky."

Trying to reconcile what she thought she heard and the actual cause of the noise, Layla took a shaky breath.

"You're safe and sound, sweet pea," Avis whispered, as she took Layla from Ed's arms and carried her back to bed.

"Just a little more racket and I'll have everything squared away," Ed said, easing out of the window. "Won't be much longer."

Avis set the child down but Layla popped back up and ran toward the bathroom. The scare made her have to pee. Holding her crotch, she called as she ran. "*Pee pee.*" Only it sounded more like *Beh beh.*

❧

When Layla woke from her nap, she saw three faces staring down at her. Her father, Auntie Avis, and Doc Fredericks. Doc was holding the tablet open to the page with the drawing of the snake. Everyone was smiling but, to Layla, it was the sort of smile that covered up what was underneath. Like a patch over a hole. Or tape holding together something that was ripped in two.

"Hello, sugarplum," Auntie Avis said. She wiped red-tinged drool from the sides of the sleepy child's mouth. "Let's prop you up on some pillows." Avis wedged the sofa cushions behind her niece's warm little body and gave her a sip of water. "Are you ready to play the drawing game we played before?"

Layla nodded, blinking the sleep from her eyes.

"Only this time," Avis said, "Your daddy and Doc Fredericks are going to play with us."

"This snake you drew is black. Did it have any of these other colors?" Ed asked, pointing to the row of pencils.

Layla shrugged.

"Does that mean *no*?" Doc Fredericks asked. "Or *maybe*?"

Layla shook her head.

"So it didn't have any other markings?" her father asked.

Layla shrugged again.

"Can you show us, honey?" Avis said, holding out the drawing tablet.

Layla took the black and scribbled all over the page.

"Night? It was too dark to see? Is that what you're saying?" Avis asked.

Layla nodded.

"Did you see anything else?" Doc asked.

Layla looked puzzled.

"Remember how you play charades sometimes, honeybunch?" Avis asked. "Can you think of something it sounds like or looks like?"

Layla shook her head.

"Did the snake speak?" Doc Fredericks asked.

Yes. But Layla had no way to hiss. "*Hhhhhh,*" she breathed, exhaling.

"Like *sssssssss*?" Avis coached.

Layla froze. *Yes*, she nodded.

Doc pursued. "The snake crawled in your mouth?"

Layla nodded and once again thrust her fingers into her parted mouth that she dare not widen fully, and once again, in imitation of the snake's mouth, opened her fingers and clamped them tight.

"Did you feel that snake touch you anywhere else, Layla?" Doc asked.

No, Layla shook her head.

"Do you remember smelling anything?"

No. No. Layla kept shaking her head until the throb in her mouth felt like a ball being pitched from one side to the other. Like a tire stuck in the mud, the story kept coming around to the same place it started without going forward. Layla thought everybody would be glad to know the truth of what happened. But it seemed that her father and Doc Fredericks just couldn't grasp what she was telling them.

Layla knew that Auntie Avis believed her. Her aunt offered encouragement, squeezing Layla's hand, patting her back, and putting a protecting arm about the little girl's shoulders. Especially when Doc started asking some of the same questions again.

"I know this is hard on you, Ducky," Ed said. "But it's real important for you to remember best as you can."

Tears ran down Layla's cheeks. The wound hurt her mouth. The questions hurt her head. The doubt that hung in the air seemed smothering and accusatory.

Avis pulled a kitchen towel from the waist of her apron and dabbed her niece's tears. Seeing how distraught her sister's child was, Avis rose from the edge of the bed, maternal instinct outweighing deference.

"Ed. Doctor," she said, giving the bottom of her blouse a firm yank. "There's a good-looking crumb cake in the kitchen that Zoella Hawkins brought over and coffee to go with it. Why don't we take our conversation out there?"

"Sweet pea, we're gonna let you have some quiet for a spell. I'll bring you a popsicle and you can string up a necklace or color or do any ol' thing you please. Sound good to you?"

Layla nodded.

Layla heard the scrape of chairs on the kitchen linoleum, the freezer door thump shut, and her aunt's brisk steps on the wooden floor of the hallway. Avis handed Layla half of a twin pop in a bowl.

"Now you give a hoot and a holler if you need something, won't you, sweetheart?" She kissed the child's forehead to make sure a fever wasn't brewing.

Layla nodded.

"The beans'll be ready pretty soon. You still want some beans?"

Layla nodded again.

As Avis went back to the kitchen to serve up crumb cake, Layla let the popsicle rest inside her mouth until she couldn't stand the pain anymore. Before, she used to get excited about choosing cherry or a grape. But it no longer made any difference. They all tasted the same. Cold.

At the bottom of Layla's drug haze, anxiety brewed. After finally being able to tell what happened to her tongue, her father and Doc Fredericks didn't seem to believe her. If she could only talk, she knew she could make them understand.

What can I do to show them? The question banged around inside her head, over and over, but she couldn't get her brain to think straight.

What can I do? she fretted.

What?

CHAPTER FOUR

ED and Doc, relegated to the kitchen by the protective aunt, finished eating crumb cake while trying to digest unsettling answers from a five-year-old. And not just any five-year-old. One that was well-schooled in truth-telling. Dubious nonetheless, Doc parted, promising to return the following afternoon to check on Layla's progress.

When Doc got back to Wayland, Effie Parks was in his waiting room, her crochet hook tunneling in and out of an afghan square.

"Be right with you, Effie," Doc said, his resonant voice a healing balm all by itself. But instead of donning his white coat so he could administer Effie's monthly iron shot and check her blood pressure, he went into his office, closed the door, picked up the telephone receiver and dialed.

"Just doesn't smell right," he said to Sheriff Dones. "I've heard of snakes coming into a tent and crawling up for warmth in a camper's sleep sack. I've seen dozens of snakebites. But nothing even close to resembling the way this little girl's tongue looked. Of course, if her peculiar story is partly true, maybe she clamped down with her own teeth out of sheer terror. But how that all would happen, especially from the look of the wound, so clean-cut ...well, it seems pretty unlikely, in my opinion."

"Sounds like you're suggestin' foul play, Doc."

"Not suggesting anything in particular. Only thing I know is it doesn't add up."

"I'll check it out, Doc," the sheriff said. "With the fire over at Tommy's Bar and Grill and all the complaints about folks gettin' lickered up at the Rib Fest, things are jumpin'. But I'll get over to do the preliminaries soon as I can."

"Appreciate that," Doc said, and hung up the phone. The doctor wished the sheriff shared his own sense of urgency to solve the cause of Layla's bizarre injury.

❧

That evening, Layla sat at the kitchen table and ate bean soup – her first meal out of bed since losing her tongue.

The soup was flavored with fatback and had the saltiness the little girl longed for.

Auntie Avis apologized. "I know the soup's on the cold side. But Doc Fredericks says you're not to eat anything hot for two weeks or else the bleeding could start up. Will you remember that, sweet pea?"

Layla took another sip and nodded. Getting food to go down the right way was arduous. Manageable bites were so miniscule it hardly seemed worth the messy trouble of swallowing. No matter how careful she was, some dribbled out. She had to keep a cloth nearby just like Petey, whose drool rag was tied to the arm of his wheelchair.

In the Yeagley household of ten, no one was too young to pitch in with the never-ending chores, even if it was only to tickle the baby's toes so he'd stopped wailing or wipe the slobber off poor Petey's chin.

Ida Mae, who sang while she went about her work as if her arms and legs couldn't budge without the rhythm of God songs to move them, would often stop mid-verse of "Softly and Tenderly Jesus is Calling" or "Blessed Redeemer" as she mashed potatoes and milk together, and say, "Layla, catch that spittle of Petey's with the rag 'fore he wets his shirt bib." When Petey wasn't in bed, his mother kept him close by so she could keep an eye on him.

Even when she was three, Layla scooted over and with a practiced gesture, stopped the stream of saliva from the bottom up, ending with gentle dib-dabs on the boy's mouth.

In an attempt to make contact with the head-slumped eyes of the palsied seven-year-old, Layla bent sideways, peering up as if she were checking the flue of a chimney to see if Santa might be making an entrance the same way she had, feet first.

"Peeteee, Peeteee," she'd say, trying to cajole a smile from him. "Want a story? The bear one?"

Interpreting the boy's not unhappy moan as a "yes," the petite storyteller frequently regaled the boy with whatever rhyme or song or story was freshest in her mind.

Thinking about Petey, Layla, on the verge of tears, wiped away her own drool. Avis seemed to read her niece's mind. "Lots of things'll seem different for awhile, sweet pea. But you'll get used to them. I know you will."

While Ed and Avis passed corn bread and ate leftover chicken and dumplings, Layla noticed her father eyeing her with that kind of lizard-like glance parents use when they suspect something is afoot. But the sound of a car chewing up the driveway gravel and a motor shutting off diverted everyone's attention. Ed blotted his mouth with his napkin and rose from the table.

"Sheriff's car," he said, looking out the window. "Wonder what he wants."

Ed opened the door for the officer, whose shirt buttons strained over his sizable abdomen.

"Sorry to be bargin' in at suppertime, Mr. Tompkin. "Ma'am," he said, nodding at Avis. "Is this the little girl that had the accident?"

"Yes, sir. Three days ago," Ed replied.

"Terrible thing. Terrible. Mind if I ask you a few questions and maybe take a look around? I'd like to start outside while we still have light."

"Whatever suits you," Ed said, clearly with questions of his own. "Avis, you and Layla go on and finish up eatin'."

Ed and the sheriff went outside. "I'm guessin' you must have heard the particulars of the story," Ed said, as the sheriff removed his flashlight from a holster that hung from his belt, snapped it on and made slow, sweeping arcs as they walked around the house.

"Well, you know how news spreads quicker than a case of chicken pox around here. This here the window to your daughter's bedroom?"

"Umhm." Ed nodded.

Sheriff Dones bent down to examine the trampled brush on the ground before inching the flashlight beam slowly around the window frame. "Don't seem to be any pry marks on the screen."

"No, sir. I just put that up. It wasn't there the night it happened."

"Was the brush all broken like this when you put the screen up?"

"Nothing noticeable. I looked around long and hard before I put down my tool bucket, thinking somebody might've come in through the window. The quack grass was bent here and there. But there are plenty of coons and other critters that come around at night. And seein' that my daughter is sure it was a snake, far-fetched as it sounds, I figured there wouldn't be too much sign of it."

"Kids play here?"

"Nope. I never got around to clearing away the brush back here. Kids play out front and over to the side, but not back here."

The sheriff started back around the house. "Anyone else you know come to this side of the house?"

"It did cross my mind," Ed said, after a moment. "Every now and again, the older Jeeter brother, the one who limps, comes around. Lyman, I think is his name. You know... those two that've lived in the old shack off Rattle Snake Pike for a number of years now. Keep to themselves mostly. Occasionally, Lyman'll ride his bike over to use the phone. Some nights he comes so late we're already in bed and he'll come 'round to the window and tap at it. Sometimes, mine. Sometimes, Layla's. Gives me a start when he does. I told him not to do that. 'If you have to come after dark,' I said, 'knock on the door.' He's done that, ever since.'"

The sheriff took a bandana out of his hip pocket to catch an explosive sneeze. "Pollen gets to me this time of year," he said, blowing. "Would it be all right if I take a look inside, now?"

"Suit yourself. Somethin' in particular you're looking' for, Sheriff?"

"Just routine," Dones said, stuffing his bandana back into his pocket.

Sheriff Dones nodded to Avis and Layla as Ed escorted him through the kitchen. "Won't be much longer, ladies," the sheriff said.

Avis and Ed exchanged puzzled looks. Layla's foot swung back and forth, kicking the chair rung, a habit Ed repeatedly tried to break. "None of that, now." His voice was terse with fatigue and niggling anxieties prompted by the sheriff's visit.

The sheriff peered out of the window at the far side of the living room. "Was this open that night?"

"Everything was closed up but the window in my bedroom and the one in Layla's," Ed replied.

"Your little girl's room is down the hall?" the sheriff asked, leaning out of Ed's bedroom window and shining the beam of his flashlight in a methodical, sweeping motion.

"Yes, sir."

"You a heavy sleeper, Mr. Tompkin?"

"Not much wakes me 'cept my daughter."

"Don't see one of these every day," the sheriff said, holstering his flashlight and picking up Ed's pocketknife from the night table. The barrel-chested officer unsheathed the blade and looked it over with keen attention.

"Sharp," he said, rubbing his big thumb over the blade.

"I use it to whittle."

A few minutes later, the sheriff and Ed returned to the kitchen.

"Alrighty," the sheriff said, flipping a pocket notebook closed. "Might have a few more questions down the road. Again, sorry to be buttin' in on your meal. Thanks for your time." The two men shook hands.

Ed sat back down, picked up his fork and knocked the tines slowly against the plate.

"Gonna finish your chicken, Ed?" Avis asked.

"No. Appetite's gone. Too much commotion."

Avis set a big wedge of apple pie in front of Ed and a sliver for herself. "Maybe a little dessert'll whet your appetite. Then, after supper we're all gonna sit down together and make out a remembering list."

The yearn for the flake of pie crust and cinnamony apple filling traveled toward Layla's stomach.

"There's so much to be done," Avis said. "It'll be a good reminder to have it all written down. 'Specially since I'm going back home in a few days and you'll have more to do when I'm gone. Wolfy and little Frank probably have their dad fit to be tied by now."

Before the sadness of that news could take hold of Layla, her aunt set a bowl of applesauce in front of her.

"Just like pie without the crust," Avis said. To maximize the mouthwatering aroma, Layla stuck her face so close to the bowl that she got a dab of sauce on the tip of her nose. "I'll lick it off," she thought before remembering she didn't have a tongue. She and her cousins used to have contests to see whose tongue could reach the farthest.

Wolfy boasted, "My tongue's so long I can pick my nose with it." And he could...almost.

One more loss.

"Sure be nice if we could make that list out on the front porch," Ed said. "Gotta make the season last while we can."

"Ed," Avis said, "if it weren't for winter and a warm bed, I don't think you'd ever go inside a house. Angel face, are those sauced apples tasting good?"

Layla nodded. She didn't want to hurt her aunt's feelings, but really, they didn't taste one way or the other. Just more painful swallowing to get through.

"Tell you what," Avis said, gathering up plates and silverware. "Let's leave these dishes soak in the sink and go on out. It's been a trying day for you, honeybunch, and I'll bet you'll tucker out sooner than later."

Ed lifted the still doped-up child off her chair and opened the front screen. The metal springs complained as her father carried Layla out and lowered her onto the porch swing. Ed sat down next to her.

Avis followed, quickly gathering up writing material and an old flannel shirt of Ed's that hung on one of the coat pegs by the door.

To make sure she sat next to her soon-to-be-leaving aunt, Layla scootched over on the swing to make room. Avis took up more space than father and daughter put together, Ed being stringy as a pole bean and Layla, growing more toward her mother's willowiness than her aunt's sycamore spread. But seating posed no problems because Avis's soft body, comfy as a well-upholstered easy chair, squashed in to accommodate whatever was next to it.

Layla still hadn't dressed in clothes since the accident so Avis wrapped Ed's flannel shirt around the child's thin nightie and they all swayed quietly, the throb in Layla's mouth surging with each to and fro of the swing.

In the waning light, the five-year-old snuggled into Avis's warmth and gazed up at her beloved aunt. Avis's face was smooth except for a line on either side that curved from her nose to her smiling lips. Not like Ed's face, which was so full of lines he looked like a rumpled shirt someone forgot to iron.

Ed's tanned forehead had furrows deep enough to

plant lettuce seeds. There were creases on either side of his mouth too, and his nose had a scar at the top where the mule clipped him.

"The mule an' me had a difference of opinion," her father said, the night he came in holding a rag to his nose.

On more than one occasion, Avis said, "Ed, you're a handsome man but you've gotta eat more. Your belly's such a cave a bear could take up residence."

Ed laughed, causing the lines at the corner of his eyes to deepen.

As the trio sat swinging, Ed said, "I'd rather be lookin' at the scrawniest sapling and listen to the scratching of a varmit than be inside. Especially in front of a television watching somebody speechifying about nothing in particular."

Avis tapped the pencil on the tablet page where the list was going to go. "Mighten be such a bad idea to think about getting a television, Ed. There are programs for kids that teach good values. *Lassie. Leave It to Beaver. Father Knows Best.* Might be a good thing for Layla."

Layla, who watched television with her cousins in Shady Grove, struggled up from somnolence. *"Eeee aaaeee..." Please, Daddy,* she tried to say, nodding in agreement.

Ed pointed around at the trees and the sky. "Best television in the world."

The three swung, physically and emotionally drained.

It was the time of day when everything seems full of inertia. When day creatures slow down for sleep. And night creatures begin to wake up. There were silent stretches between the evening sounds – gaps separating one cricket chirp from another. A quiet period after the call of a bullfrog as it waited for a lover's gravelly reply. The momentary pause when the metal grind of the chain that held the swing stopped to change directions. It was the first time Layla paid much attention to silence.

There was the heavy quiet that held the words Ed and Auntie Avis were not saying. And there was the hurt silence holding all the words the frustrated child, sandwiched between those she loved best, wanted to say but couldn't.

"Well," Auntie Avis finally said, "I reckon we'd better get busy before our brains start to doze off."

At the top of the page Avis wrote in bold, neat lettering: *Important Things to Remember*. She underlined the words on the page with the same emphasis as her voice.

"First off, let's write down everything Doc Fredericks said to do. Like," Auntie Avis wrote as she spoke, "rinse your mouth with peroxide every time you eat. That's real important so you don't get infection.

"Since you're such a good artist, sweet pea, maybe you could draw some brown peroxide bottles. We could cut 'em out and paste the pictures up in the kitchen and the bathroom to help you remember. Think that's a good idea?"

Layla nodded and nestled further into her aunt's cushiony recesses.

"Make sure to put lots of salve on after you rinse. And, twice a day, mix in those vitamin drops Doc Fredericks prescribed. And you be sure to let someone know right away if something starts to feel worse than better." Avis locked eyes with Layla to make sure the little girl understood the importance of her words.

"Well," Avis said, when no other "remembers" came to mind, "it's all down in black and white. The writing helps, but it's the doing that counts." She started to hand the list to Ed.

"Oh," she said, taking it back. "One more thing." She smiled as she wrote. "Every night, say your prayers. Right, sweet pea?"

Layla nodded.

But in the dusk, as rising fireflies flashed their inscrutable Morse code, confusion moldered in the child's sleepy, medicated mind. For one thing, Layla wondered if God could hear prayers if you didn't say them out loud. She knew how deafening the praying got in the Yeagleys' church. So it made her wonder if the louder you got, the more God could hear you.

Layla knew God took her mother to heaven. That's

why she'd jump from the swing on the maple tree just when the rope was stretched so far up all she could see was the sky.

Every time she jumped, she scraped an elbow or bruised a knee, or both. But every time, just after the thought of *don't* came into her head she heard a louder thought.

DO! DO IT! This time you'll fly straight into the heavenly clouds and into Mama's arms. Then you'll soar right back to the top of the tree where the robin builds her nest every year and lays little blue eggs the color of Mama's eyes in the framed picture on Daddy's nightstand.

Another puzzlement had to do with her tongue. Layla was quite certain that a snake took her tongue. But if God made the world and everything in it like Mrs. Yeagley said, didn't God make snakes too? And if snakes were a Godly creation, wouldn't her dead tongue go to heaven?

With no heavenly access as yet, Layla doubted she'd be able to confirm her tongue's whereabouts. But silently, she prayed that when she died, she and her tongue would be reunited at the Pearly Gates. Then she'd be able to say all she'd been waiting to tell her mama. And she'd ask God why He let her mama die.

But until then, how was she going to get along without a tongue?

⁂

That evening, after returning from the Tompkins', Sheriff Dones wrote up a report of his findings. He slugged down the cold dregs of his latest cup of coffee before dialing Doc Fredericks. "Still some things to check out, but the little girl and the aunt are convinced it was a snake."

"The wound is too clean. Got to be something else," Doc said.

"We'll keep investigating, Doc. But too many people are talking snake to discount it. Frankly, it's got quite a few folks pretty spooked. Wouldn't be doing my job if we didn't look into it."

The next day, the sheriff, his deputy, and several men from the area scoured the Tompkins' property to make sure that the offending reptile – which grew to mythical proportions in the ethos of the community – wasn't still lurking there. The hunting party bagged a few nothing-to-speak-of varieties.

"Several garters," Sheriff Dones later reported to Doc Fredericks. "A small hognose. A rat snake. Ruled out the timber rattler...it wasn't too sizable. Besides, the little girl would have probably remembered hearin' its tail shaker. And the king snake, though it was a big 'un, was a constrictor not a biter – docile as a house pet.

"The father did mention that one of the Jeeter fellows

comes by now and again so I paid them a visit. Isn't clear if they've up and left or what. Not hide nor hair nor word about their whereabouts from anyone. We'll keep checking. But at this point I don't know what more I can do."

Doc didn't know what more he could do either but keep his eyes peeled and his ear to the ground.

CHAPTER FIVE

Five mornings after her injury, Layla woke up later than usual. Her father had finished his coffee and toast, both of which he liked black.

"That's why you stay so warm all winter," his wife used to tease him, as she kissed the back of his neck and served him his purposely-burnt bread. "You have enough char built up inside to keep you on a slow burn."

Avis had already done two loads of laundry rewashing, for the fourth time, the bloodstained sheets that she soaked in bleach.

"Good mornin' glory," her aunt said. She set down the laundry basket to hug her niece and kiss her forehead. "Cool as a cucumber. How's your mouth feeling today? Better?"

Layla nodded.

"Let's have a look."

As Avis checked for signs of infection – increased redness, swelling, pus – her smile stayed fixed but the whites above her blue eyes widened at the sight that took her aback every time.

Avis patted her niece's shoulder. "Your healing up fine and dandy.

"Looky what I made for you, sweet pea." Avis dished up yellow porridge from a pot on the stove. "Cornmeal mush. Nice and soupy so it'll be easy to swallow and just barely warm so you don't burn your – so you don't burn your pretty lil' mouth. And there's maple syrup on the table. Now eat up while I hang these clothes out on the line."

Avis hauled the laundry basket onto her hip. "You can go on and get dressed if you finish before I do."

The screen door screeched open and banged shut.

Layla loaded soft butter into her bowl and drizzled amber into the yellowy puddles. It looked so luscious and she was so hungry – starved for fat and sugar like a winter-roused bear. She scooped up a small bite that barely filled the teaspoon, but along with her anticipatory jets of saliva, it proved too much. Choking and gagging, trying to swallow and regurgitate by turns, everything leaked: Gruel from her mouth, tears from her eyes, mucous from her runny nose. And for all that struggle, not one taste of sweetness – only the burn of acid at the back of her throat.

After breakfast, Layla rinsed with peroxide and headed to her bedroom to get dressed. She put on clean underwear daily because Mrs. Yeagley said that's how it should be.

"Cleanliness is next to Godliness," Ida Mae stressed, as if her tongue were a throw pillow cross-stitched with the saying.

What stumped Layla was why make such a fuss about being clean when it was God who created dirt in the first place.

Having enjoyed the airiness of a nightgown for the last several days, Layla was in the mood to wear a dress. So she dragged a wooden chair across the floor to the closet. But before she took hold of the chair that sat by the window, she examined it for scales and sniffed for rankness in case the snake slithered over it the night she lost her tongue.

Layla studied her hand-me-down dresses from Abbey that Auntie Avis arranged according to size.

Ever since the tragic death of her younger sister, Avis and her children came three times a year to visit and brought all the still-good clothes and shoes from cousin Abbey, who was five years older than Layla.

Little Layla could always go to her closet and see what she had to look forward to. On occasion, she'd take such a fancy to a particular blouse or sweater that she wore it like a dress, all baggy and down to the floor.

Whenever Layla showed up at the Yeagleys wearing some outlandish outfit, Ida Mae spoke to Ed about spoiling a child by letting her do whatever she had a notion to do. Not to mention looking so unusual.

"She's wearin' out awfully good clothes 'fore she gets enough size to wear 'em proper," Ida Mae cautioned in her "thus sayeth the Lord" tone.

But Ed would just smile and say, "Wait for tomorrow an' tomorrow may never come. Best enjoy today."

Suddenly light-headed as she stood on the chair, Layla steadied herself on the closet door frame, leaning over to look at the skirts and tops that her aunt organized next to the dresses. One blouse caught the little girl's eye, though it was clearly too big. Cherry red with ruffles. The red color would save Auntie Avis the trouble of scrubbing, since bloody drool was a continuing problem. Everyone – Ed, Doc Fredericks, and especially Layla – hoped the slobber would subside as the stump healed.

Layla managed the middle buttons, but the top ones and those down by her ankles were hard to coax through the narrow slits.

Avis, returning from hanging laundry, knelt to assist.

"Whatever possessed you to wear this big ol' blouse, sweet pea?"

"*Oouuu.*" Layla smiled.

"Oouu?"

Unable to explain, Layla pointed to her aunt.

"Me?" Avis asked. "You wore it on my account?"

Her niece nodded.

"Well, why ever you wore it," Auntie Avis said, lifting Layla's hair that was caught inside the back of the blouse, "with your yellow hair and blue eyes and red blouse, you look like a flower. Did you rinse your mouth out?"

Layla nodded.

"Aren't you the big girl today!"

Avis rolled up the blouse sleeves that were covering her niece's little hands. "Would you like to draw those pictures of the peroxide to keep reminding you to rinse? The ones we're gonna cut out and hang up?'

Layla nodded again, eager to improve her artistry since drawing was turning out to be such a powerful form of communication.

"I'm going out to the garden," Avis said, taking Layla's hand as they walked to the kitchen. "Pick some peas to puree into good soup for you," she said, smiling. "Be back in a jiff."

The five-year-old was at the kitchen table, clutching a brown pencil, intent on getting the likeness of the peroxide bottle, when there was a knock at the screen door.

"Hello. Hello. Anybody home?"

Layla knew the voice well. She climbed off the chair and went to the door where Ida Mae Yeagley stood with a covered dish in her hands. There was a man there too, though Layla couldn't quite place him.

"Layla. I'm surprised to see you up and around," Mrs. Yeagley said. "You remember Pastor Simpson?"

Layla nodded, even though the preacher looked different standing there in the doorway. Kind of squatty like a baked ham. In church he seemed taller, waving his arms around and shouting and calling on the Holy Spirit of God.

"I brought over a bowl of mashed potatoes that everyone could enjoy," Mrs. Yeagley said.

Layla opened the door.

"Is your father or aunt about?" Ida Mae asked, as she and the pastor came into the kitchen.

Layla pointed outside.

"Would you mind if we waited for them?" Ida Mae put the foil-covered bowl on the kitchen counter.

Unsure about the "waiting" part, the red-clad child led the guests into the living room to sit on the couch, which contained only half the normal number of seat cushions, since the others were in Layla's room to bolster her up in bed.

"Layla," the preacher said, removing his hat and settling himself on the sofa next to Mrs. Yeagley, "we heard tell that a serpent took your tongue. Is that true?"

Something about Pastor Simpson's voice made Layla feel like a trap-caught rabbit. That answering *yes* would lead to trouble. But answering *no* would too. She was still upset from the way Doc Fredericks and her father received the truth about the snake.

Layla wished her father and Auntie Avis were in the living room with her. She was scared to answer Pastor Simpson's question – so frightened her eyes welled up with tears. Head bowed, she nodded.

"Oh, you poor little thing," Mrs. Yeagley said. "Shhh, shhh, shhh..."

Layla's breath stopped. Serpent hiss. The terror of that sound lurked deep in her bones.

"You must be hurtin'," Mrs. Yeagley said. "Shhhh, now. Come here and let me take a look."

Layla was frozen with fear. She didn't know how she could move. But when Mrs. Yeagley said, "come," you came.

Layla didn't know anyone stricter than Ida Mae Yeagley, especially when it came to praying and getting paddled. Ida Mae had a lot of meat on her and when she swung a paddle, you felt it. Yet the mother's voice alone, worn to a stern edge by so many kids, was motivation enough for Layla to obey. The petrified child willed her two stone legs to walk.

When Layla opened her mouth, both guests drew in their breath – an alarming response knowing that Mrs. Yeagley, with eight children, had seen her share of injury and blood.

"Cleaved clean in two," Mrs. Yeagley said. "I'd'a thought fangs would work more at chewin' somethin' off."

"God works His wonders any way He chooses," the preacher replied.

"Can you talk at all, Layla?" Ida Mae asked. "Try sayin' your name."

Layla thought about the words she'd already attempted. *I'm sorry, Daddy. Pee-pee.* And how they came out sounding more like a lowing cow than human speech. Wondering if she could make any proper sounds at all, Layla pronounced her ABC's out loud in the solitude of her bedroom. She could recite the alphabet with well-drilled ease, not from the usual nursery singsong but from a game at the Yeagleys, hopping on one foot to see who could get farthest. She could hop to the letter *X* on her right foot and to *K* on her left.

Alone in her room, the determined child commenced with *a*. Adequate, not perfect, she continued. *B* sounded more like *lamb-bah*. Things went downhill from there. Without her tongue's middle to squish up against the roof of her mouth, she couldn't manage *C, G, H, J, S X*, or *Z*. And without a tongue tip there was no way to tap out *D, L, N, T* or *W*, either. She hoped that when the stump healed and it didn't hurt so much, she'd be able to say more. But until then, she tried not to talk because she hated the sound.

"Go ahead, Layla," said Mrs. Yeagley. "Say your name for me."

With loathing obedience, the little girl mumbled, "Layla Grace Tompkin." Only it came out *Aaya Aaee Ahhmpahh.*

Stunned, Pastor Simpson recognized the voice of the Holy Spirit.

"Glossolalia," he whispered in awe.

He wiped the pink drool from the sides of the five-year-old's mouth with his thick thumb. "Child," he said. "You've been marked by the sign of God. God has cast out your tongue, so you can learn to speak in new tongues."

Even before the preacher began to talk about signs and new tongues, Layla was frightened. Now she was frightened *and* confused. Her eyes shot down to her arms to see if there were marks on them. Then to her bare feet protruding from under the red blouse. Nothing visible. No scratches or pricks like the briar snags she got picking berries. Pastor Simpson saw her confusion. Leaning close to the little girl, he gently began to explain.

"It's in the Bible, Layla. Right there in Mark:16. The last words on earth of our Lord Jesus.

"And these signs shall follow them that believe; In my name they shall cast out devils; they shall speak with new tongues. They shall take up serpents; and if they drink any deadly thing it shall not hurt them."

Devils? Was Pastor Simpson saying she had devils in her? Was that why God let the serpent come?

Thinking about devils and serpents and wondering if getting new tongues was going to hurt as much as losing her old one, tears started to stream down Layla's cheeks.

Mrs. Yeagley laid a heavy hand on each of the child's shoulders, which were as delicate as bird bones. "Don't cry, Layla. It's a blessing. God has showered you with a mighty blessing."

Layla struggled to understand why God swelled her mouth with fire and blood so she could speak with new tongues when she was still trying to learn words with her old one.

She knew she shouldn't fear the Lord's way of teaching what she needed to learn. Especially when God was ridding her of devils. She just wished being God-struck didn't hurt so much.

"Layla. Layla." Auntie Avis called. Layla backed away to run to her aunt's comfort, but the *shalts* and *shalt nots* on Mrs. Yeagley's face stopped her cold.

"Where are you, sweet pea?" Avis called, checking the bedroom and bathroom before making her way into the living room.

"Well, my stars," her aunt said. "I didn't know we had company." She tucked a perspiration-damp wave of hair behind her ear.

The pastor took his hat off his lap, placed it on the sofa, and stood.

"Reverend Simpson," he said, offering his hand. "I don't believe we've had the pleasure of meeting."

"No we haven't, Reverend. Avis Lovell. Layla's aunt on her mother's side. Pleased to meet you."

"We came to pay our respects and confirm God's wonders in this little girl."

"Layla's a wonder. No doubt about that." Avis smiled as she looked over to her niece.

Surprised by visitors in the dimly-lit living room, Avis only now noticed her niece's tears.

"Are you hurting, honey?" Alarmed, Avis bent down, eye level with Layla and clutched both of the child's small hands in her own.

Layla tried to word with her eyes what she wanted to say – entreating her aunt the way a dog pleads to be understood.

She wanted to say, *yes, my mouth hurts. But that's not why I'm crying.*

She wanted to say, *I'm scared, Auntie Avis. Afraid of what Pastor Simpson says about me having devils and marks and getting new tongues. Afraid of Ida Mae Yeagley making me say words that come out sounding more proper to an animal.*

But she couldn't. And that made her crying worse.

Avis lifted up the sobbing child. Layla buried her face in her aunt's pillowy shoulder.

"Pastor, would you or Mrs. Yeagley care for some coffee or sweet tea?"

"No. Thank you kindly," said the pastor. "We'd best get goin'."

"That goes for me too," said Ida Mae. "I left Zebidiah and Rebekah mindin' the other children. But the lil'uns don't heed 'em the way they heed me. I just wanted to bring over a covered dish that would help ease your load."

"That was very kind of you," Avis said, smiling over her niece's head. "I know what a goodness you are to the family, caring for Layla the way you do."

"I'm sorry to be losin' Layla to school in September," Mrs. Yeagley said. "Do you think she'll be goin' to kindergarten at Cumberland or will you be makin' special arrangements?"

When Ida Mae said *special arrangements*, the attempted subtext was as understated as the wart on the side of her nose.

Knowing how much her niece looked forward to starting school, Avis patted the clinging five-year-old's back.

"We have more than two months to figure out what's best. Layla can do anything she sets her mind to do, can't you, sweetie?" She gave the sweet bundle in her arms an affirming bounce.

"Before we go, I'd like to offer a little prayer," the pastor said.

"Of course," replied Avis. "We've all been doing a lot of praying, lately."

Reverend Simpson bowed his head.

"Beloved Lord God, we pray for your healing balm on this family besieged by so many troubles. Especially this precious little girl who suffers so. Suffers like our Lord Jesus suffered. Wash her in the blood of the Lamb. Humbly, we pray for the strength to follow your signs. Make us into your chosen vessels that we may fulfill your destiny for us. Shower your mighty mercy on her family.

We pray in the glorious name of our Lord and Savior, Jesus Christ. Amen."

"Amen," echoed Ida Mae and Avis, raising their heads.

Avis led Pastor Simpson and Mrs. Yeagley to the door. "Thank you for stopping by."

As the screen opened, Layla felt a rush of fresh air. Avis lowered her niece onto a kitchen chair, covered her with dozens of little kisses – giving her "sugar," she called it – and blotted the child's blotched, tear-stained cheeks.

Layla sat for a moment. Then, once more, rotating each arm to check for "marks," she took up the brown pencil and continued to draw the peroxide bottle.

CHAPTER SIX

THREE days later, Avis, with young children of her own, had to leave. When her aunt stooped down for a good-bye hug, Layla clung onto her like a leech.

"Come over here and sit by me on the porch, honey," Avis said, prying the child off with gentle force and a pied piper's lure. "Before I leave, I have something to give to you."

Ed carried his sister-in-law's well-worn suitcase over to her Studebaker and lingered there, watching. He wondered how life always seemed to revolve around Avis like she was the hub of a wheel. Not like some folks who were constantly striving. Or others, so held back with fear and regret, their hunched bodies had to double-step for every one pace forward. Avis's presence and words had weight.

That's why Ed was still thinking about their conversation the night before.

"Ed, you're so busy, you don't have the time to spit twice," Avis said. "And while you manage to see to all the necessaries for Layla, we'd be able to give her a more normal family life. Especially now that she'll need so much extra care."

"I'll find a way," Ed replied.

"You're already as far down to the bone as you can go. Not sleeping. Not eating. You couldn't keep a turnip alive with that kind of neglect. Give it some thought, won't you, Ed?"

"I'll sleep on it," the weary father said, rubbing his forehead.

"Layla could come with me to Shady Grove tomorrow. Even if it's just to give you a break."

Underneath Avis's words, Ed felt his sister-in-law wondered whether Layla's devastating trauma wouldn't have happened if she were living with her aunt. That thought had Ed stirred up and second-guessing himself.

Avis perched on the front step and patted it for Layla to sit down. As soon as the seat of the little girl's overalls settled, her right foot started jiggling. Without speech, all the energy the little girl previously put into talking up a storm, made its way down to her right foot that jittered as if it were motorized.

Avis took her niece's small hand and made it into a

cup. Then she poured tickling strands of gold into it. Layla lifted the chain and saw a heart-shaped locket.

"Your mama gave this necklace to me on my weddin' day," her aunt explained. "Said since I was going off to start my own family, she wanted me to have it as a sign of her abiding love."

With her thumbnail, Avis split open the locket to reveal a miniature of herself on one side and her sister on the other.

"I was waiting to give it to you on your weddin' day, Layla. But I thought you might like it now. Thought it'd be something for you to hold onto in the coming days so you'd remember that both your mama and me are always with you. Wherever you are, whatever you're doing, your mama and I are embracing you in our hearts. Want me to put it on for you?"

Enthralled by shining gold and by something from both Auntie Avis and her mama, Layla nodded.

Avis fastened the clasp. Then she kissed her niece's forehead and fixed the benediction of her eyes on the child.

Layla yearned to thank Auntie Avis and say that she'd treasure the necklace every day until she died. She wanted to tell Auntie Avis how much she loved her. So many unsaid things mounted inside, they ached like fester.

Auntie Avis stood up and smoothed her skirt. Because Layla knew that meant her aunt was about to leave, the little girl burst into tears.

Avis embraced Layla. "We'll be back before you know it, sweet pea. All of us. Abbey and Wolfy and little Frank. Maybe even Uncle Frank if he can get time off from the plant. We'll have us a good ol' time together."

Layla's tears became soft rain – wet but not torrential. But her fierce crying resumed as the car door closed with Auntie Avis inside, starting the ignition's tubercular hack.

Ed lifted his daughter as Avis drove off. He held Layla tightly, torn about whether he made the right decision. As they waved good-bye, Layla bawled inconsolably. In the sliver of mind that was still processing more than her emotions, Layla wondered why she hadn't run dry of tears yet, considering how many she shed in the past week. But she was quickly learning that the body was full of surprises.

"There she goes in their *up* car," Ed said.

Through a blur, Layla looked at her father, puzzled.

"Uncle Frank calls it their *up* car 'cause he says to keep the darn thing up and runnin' he has to grease it up, tune it up, patch it up, and gas it up."

Layla smiled. "Same as our truck," her dad said, lowering the child's feet to meet the ground. He extracted a handkerchief, pinkish gray because, in his usual haste, he didn't always separate the whites and colors as stringently as Avis advised.

"What d'you think, Ducky?" he said, wiping his daughter's flooding eyes and nose bubbles. "Should we call our truck the *up* truck?"

Layla shook her head and made her fish-oil face. Up truck sounded too much like *upchuck* – precisely what a dose of fish oil made her feel like doing. Mrs. Yeagley dosed her eight children every week of the winter and talked Ed into the practice. Her father prefaced the fishy spoonful by saying, "Swallow fast. It'll cure you before you get sick."

"I've got to go out to the barn and do some chores," Ed said. "Doc Fredericks says you shouldn't be runnin' around for a while, so you can't be chasin' after Buttermilk and her kittens. You hear?"

Layla nodded.

"Go in and get your barn boots on, Ducky. I'll meet you out there." Ed headed to the barn.

Instead of going into the house, the five-year-old stood still, blinking in the sunshine.

Ed looked back before he entered the barn and called, "Go on now."

But she couldn't. Her feet felt rooted to the ground.

Her father stuck his head out of the barn and called again.

"Don't you be lollygaggin'."

Layla reached up to her new locket and rubbed the

smooth metal, warm as a newly-laid hen egg. The golden heat traveled through her fingers, got taken up by her blood, and pumped through her body until she glowed.

"Layla Grace Tompkin," Ed yelled. "You go on now!"

Layla's feet came unrooted and she hurried inside to fetch her boots.

With his dreams for Layla in tatters, Ed was smacked with the reality of, once more, getting along single-handedly. Those who had come to help were back to dealing with their own travails.

Ed, beyond exhausted, began to muck out the mule's stall. Stabbing the pitchfork over and over into the reeking straw, he lapsed into mindless ramblings.

With Avis gone, he felt abandoned. Now there was no turning back. Cooking, washing, cleaning, tending to his daughter – all those tasks Avis undertook with such ease – were back on his shoulders. He missed his wife. He missed having a helpmate, a friend, a confidante; the comfort of shared bodies through thick and thin.

Ed thought back to the standout events of their marriage: The day their home loan was approved, carrying his wife through their newly-built entry door, finding out they were going to have a baby. What he missed more, though, were the ordinary days. The ones that used to slip by, comfortable as an old pair of bedroom slippers. Routine days that, despite their ups and downs, ended with the two of them in bed together, the rest of the world locked outside.

When Ed and Layla married, they vowed to become "as one." And they had. In three brief years – four, counting their courtship – day by day, the two wedded hope, purpose, and love into a single entity. An *us*. A *we*. An *our*. Their lives were knitted together from the bone up. They were EdandLayla. LaylaandEd. So when his wife died, Ed discovered that a big part of himself died too.

While everyone mourned the too-young woman who was laid to rest at the side of the house with her headstone in the shadow of the huge, crimson-leafed maple, Ed had to bear death upright. And though he was good at figuring out most problems, he didn't know how to uncouple his mind, his heart, and his body from their deep, abiding connections.

He cherished his memories, especially since his daughter was the fruit of that marriage. Without little Layla, Ed sometimes wondered if he would have found a reason to get out of bed in the morning.

He tossed another pitchfork of foul straw out of the mule's stall.

Long after the period of mourning when most people thought it was high time for the widower to get on with his life, what troubled Ed was that he couldn't think two thoughts without the insinuation of memory.

It wasn't so much the burden of household labor that left him with twice as much work to do, though that was no small hurdle.

It was the small vacancies that continued to knife at his insides. Sitting at the kitchen table and eating half of the banana he and his wife always shared at breakfast. Chilly nights when he placed her cold feet between his thighs to warm them. Her voice chiming "bless you" from the other room when he sneezed. The way she pulled back the covers for him when he returned from peeing in the middle of the night.

Linked together by so many commonplace habits and with the lion's share of their thoughts and actions done in service of each other, the water torture of daily reminders kept her loss painfully alive, even after five years.

Suddenly, Ed was barely able to breathe. Pressure mounted inside his head and chest until he was on the verge of exploding. Light-headed, he faltered, lost grip of the pitchfork and staggered backward. As his vision blurred, Ed fell against the rough slats of the stall and crumpled onto the straw. Filled with dread, his mind raced at the breakneck speed of his heart.

"Layla," he thought.

"What'll happen to Layla?"

⁂

Fingering her locket and with her boots on, Layla headed back to the barn and peered around in the dusty light. Usually, her father called out when he heard the sound of her footsteps on the straw-strewn, dirt floor. She looked up for movement among the stacked bales in the hayloft.

"He must be in the barnyard," Layla thought. She headed to the side door. The mule was switching away flies with his tail, and the pecking chickens looked like her father when he wrote a letter, picking at the keys of the Underwood typewriter with his pointer finger. "Shoulda learned to type," he told Layla. "Or else write more legible."

The hog came over and snuffled at Layla's boot, leaving mucky wet on it, but her father was nowhere to be seen.

Layla saw the tractor, so she knew he hadn't gone out to the fields. He never went without her, anyway. At plowing time, Ed would lift his daughter onto the tractor and carry her on his lap through the fields. Since it was useless to try to talk over the motor's din, the child just sat there fiddling with her father's fingers on the steering wheel and watching the rabbits and groundhogs take off between the rows. Or she watched the black crows scare up out of the corn. Sometimes she closed her eyes against the sun and didn't wake until her father pulled into the barn and turned off the engine.

Maybe he went to the garden to pick peas or get greens. Disappointed because they always did that together, Layla headed out of the barn. As she passed the mule's stall, she glimpsed something humped in the corner.

"Daddy," she gasped. Only it came out, *Ahheeee.* She ran over to his slumped body. *"Ahhheeeee, Ahhheeeee,"* she cried, shaking the shoulder of her unresponsive father. She patted his knees, something he hated because he was so ticklish there. Surely that would wake him up. But he didn't even twitch.

Layla remembered how good a wet cloth felt when she was feeling sick so she dug down into her overall pocket and took out a cloth square, one of a dozen that Avis cut up from remnants in her sister's sewing basket. "In case you need something to wipe your mouth, honeybunch," Avis said.

Layla ran to the spigot where the buckets for the animals were filled and struggled with the obstinate handle. Unable to turn it, she went to the chickens' water trough and carried the dripping cloth over to her father's motionless body. She swabbed his forehead and cheeks, his chin and his neck, and squeezed the remaining water over his head.

Unable to rouse Ed and growing even more panicky, Layla crawled into her father's lopsided lap. She nuzzled her head into the crook of his arm, lay her hands on his chest, and began to sob.

Wake up Daddy, wake up, she wailed. *"Waauuaahheee! Waaayahhheee..."* Her cheeks burned from crying. Her hands too. They felt hot and tingly, the way they felt when she came in from playing in the snow and held them too close to the flames in the living room fireplace.

"Whaaa?" Ed said, slowly coming to.

"*Ahhheeee,*" Layla shrieked, hugging him tightly. *"Ahhheee..."*

"Where ...? Ducky? Where...what's happening?"

Ed hugged his daughter and took a deep breath, remembering the awful terror he'd felt.

"Don't you worry, Ducky. Just had a little scratchy patch there. Let me get myself up here."

When Ed tried to get Layla off his lap, she refused to budge, hugging her father more fiercely.

"I'm okay now," he said, trying to calm her with gentle back pats. "Let's go back to the house and have us a drink of water, okay, Ducky?"

Layla nodded, wiping the tears from her eyes.

Grabbing onto the side of the stall, Ed hitched himself upright. With his shirtsleeve, he mopped off water that Layla dripped onto his head.

Ed took his daughter's little hand in his and they walked out of the barn with measured steps.

"Hand is awfully warm. You're not feverish, are you?"

Ed put his hand to his daughter's forehead. "Nope. Nice and cool. How 'bout we sit a spell on the porch after we get our water? Sound good?"

Layla nodded.

When they got to the house, Layla ran ahead and pulled a chair over to the sink. By the time Ed finished brushing bits and pieces of straw off his clothes, Layla had filled two glasses of water.

"Look at you, Ducky. Regular little mother you are," Ed said, carrying the glasses out to the front porch and holding them while Layla climbed up onto the swing beside him.

"There you go," said Ed. He handed his daughter her water and took a long drink from his own.

Ed looked down at Layla and smiled. She looked up at her father, her pale face still frightened.

"Partners, we are." Ed said, patting her leg. "Go together like hammer and nails. Each one needs the other. Right, Ducky?"

Her blue eyes were so trusting. So full of love.

"Whatever it takes," thought Ed. "I'll do it."

"Whatever it takes, no matter what."

CHAPTER SEVEN

ON a foggy July morning, Ed drove Layla back to the Yeagleys for the first time since the snake took her tongue, three weeks before. On the way, he sipped coffee from his thermos that, in an attempt to beef up his health, was no longer black, but loaded with milk and sugar. After his alarming episode in the barn, Ed was determined not to lose his daughter because of pressure from Avis or anyone else, however good their intentions. So, when Doc Fredericks brought over a protein and vitamin powder to add to Layla's drinks as a nutritional boost, Ed got the idea for spiking his coffee with milk.

Eat more, worry less was his new motto. During lunch

break at the mill, he went to his truck and dozed off for fifteen minutes or so. "Take it where you can," he thought as he tried to hone his routine to a finer edge.

Shortly after Avis left, Layla saw a specialist in Petersburg.

"Here is a list of approved foods," the specialist said, during Layla's appointment. "Liquids, soups, purees. Without a tongue to sweep food from one side of the mouth to the other or to work the food to the right place for swallowing, choking is a danger with anything that requires chewing."

The specialist had Layla swallow different things: apple juice, applesauce, liquid gelatin. He said she did remarkably well. Better than most people who had to be trained to eat without a tongue.

"The majority of her taste buds have been lost," the doctor explained. "Normally, there are about ten thousand. Sweet and sour, for the most part, are gone. A few sensors for salt still remain at the back of her tongue, as well as some receptors for bitter."

As further confirmation of his diagnosis, the specialist clicked off the light on the mirrored disk strapped to his forehead like a miner's lamp, and pointed to various areas on a poster affixed to the asparagus-green wall behind the examining table where Layla squirmed. The large pink diagram bore no resemblance to the things that went missing from her life, day-by-day, hour-by-hour, minute-by-minute. Talking. Whistling. Being able to stick her tongue through the hole when she lost a tooth. Licking her lips.

Layla thought about all the things she'd never taste again. She wouldn't be able to fit the hollow part of a raspberry on the tip of her tongue and burst the sweet beads of juice into her mouth. She wouldn't be tasting the sour of windfall apples plucked off the ground, too good to waste. And though Layla never thought she'd tire of ice cream, without flavor, it tasted no more special than cold water.

Before the visit, Layla prayed that the specialist would fix her so she could talk without drooling, especially since she was looking forward to kindergarten in two months. She certainly didn't want to be slobbering in front of a bunch of new kids, not able to pronounce the *L*'s of her own name.

The laryngologist said Layla would never talk properly so she should learn to write as soon as possible. "The earlier, the better," he advised.

Layla's heart dropped when she heard that. But seeing the look on her father's face made her feel that the news was, somehow, even worse.

The specialist strongly recommended sign language.

"Like the way Mr. Rupert talks with his hands," Ed explained. Layla didn't understand how she had the same needs as the man who lived on the other side of Stony

Creek who couldn't hear a bear if it roared in his ear. The best plan, the specialist said, would be for Layla to attend the School for the Deaf in Knoxville where she could communicate with other children.

Thinking about the long drive in order to visit his daughter, losing weeks and months of their time together, all sacrificed so Layla could communicate with sign language, Ed replied, "I'll think on that." But, young as she was, Layla could tell by her father's voice that he'd done all the contemplating he needed. When Ed was in a considering mind, his voice had a way of opening up. But when an idea went counter to his thinking, his voice became closed in, like a mud turtle pulling into its shell.

Layla and her father left the doctor's office carrying a handful of papers. Directions for what to eat and how to eat it, mouth exercises, oral care, and pamphlets about schools for the hearing impaired.

"Not a thing's wrong with your ears, Ducky," Ed said. "So there's no reason for you to be goin' away to a deaf school. I'm goin' to set up a meetin' with the school in Cumberland and try to get it worked out. That okay with you?'

Layla nearly nodded her head loose.

"How 'bout we get you new shoes for school while we're in the city?"

The five-year-old pointed to the sneakers she was wearing.

Her father winked. "I know you have shoes from Abbey. But you're gonna pick out whatever shoes you take a fancy to."

The shoe salesman made Layla place her foot in a funny contraption. When he bent over to read the measurement, the shiny bald spot on the top of his head reflected the overhead light and looked like the moon landed in front of her eyes.

The salesman disappeared into a back room and returned with a stack of boxes. One by one, he slipped a shoe onto her foot with what looked like a flatish sugar scoop. The scoop was the sole drawback to the thrill Layla felt because it reminded her of the cold metal instrument the specialist used. The doctor had poked the depressor so far back in her throat she gagged. It upset her enough to wish she'd gone ahead and hurled onto his white coat instead of swallowing the bitter gruel back down.

But now, that horrid experience – the ominous smell of alcohol that she learned to associate with the words *this may hurt a little*, the clink of metal instruments, the words she hoped to hear from the doctor but didn't – something along the lines of *you'll be chomping on a turkey leg by Thanksgiving* – all that was eclipsed by the Christmasy flush of opening box after box to see the surprises hidden inside the tissue wrapping. Layla pranced around in each pair of shoes to see how they felt. But as soon as the salesman buckled on the red ones, her heart was set.

Red was Layla's new favorite color.

Because blood didn't stain it. Because it didn't show dirt so badly. Because Auntie Avis said she looked like a flower when she wore it.

Luckily, Abbey liked the same color so lots of the clothes she passed down to her cousin were red. Layla reveled in a world brimming with red: cardinals, skies at sunset, crab apples, partridgeberries and, most of all, Mama's red trellis roses on the front porch.

The salesman said the red shoes cost more because they were *gen-u-ine* leather. But Ed said, "That'll be no problem."

It sounded like it *was* a problem by the way the balding man looked at the sorry state of the shoes that Ed wore.

Still somewhat skeptical, the salesman inquired, "Will you be wearing them home or do you want them boxed?"

"It's bad luck to put shoes back in the box before you wear 'em," Ed replied, not terribly superstitious about common lore, but not wanting to tempt fate, either. "We'll hand carry them."

Again, the moon flashed in front of Layla's eyes as the salesman unbuckled the red shoes. Disappointment taffy-pulled her pale face downward.

"These shoes are for school, Ducky," Ed said. "September'll be here before you know it. Now draw that lower lip of yours back in before a bird comes and perches on it."

The happiness of red shoes and the sadness of not getting to wear them – two such poles-apart feelings – vied for the upper hand at the same time. Bewildering!

Half of Ed's milk and coffee was drunk and the fog was burning off by the time he and Layla arrived at the Yeagleys. Since there was no school, all eight Yeagley children, forewarned by their mother to act natural and not roughhouse, were home to greet Layla, who was still pale from blood loss and the radical shift to a liquid diet. School ended in May for mountain children because every hand, big and small, was needed to help with spring planting, especially vine day, when all the squash, cucumbers, and melons were seeded into the ground.

Samson, the family dog, ran over to welcome back Layla. Samson, who was part collie, part mongrel, but all heart, nuzzled and licked the little girl's hands as she walked to the house. Then, alert to underground scrablings or the scent of musk, Samson took off.

Clay Yeagley was at the canning factory where he had seasonal work on top of his regular hours at the Quincy County Power and Light Company.

Sixteen-year-old Zeb, the only Yeagley old enough and able-bodied enough to help with his father's chores, was on the tractor plowing the cornfields. Rebekah, Rachel,

Lizzie, and even Sarah Jane – who was the same age as Layla, but not nearly as tall – were in the garden hoeing weeds, working horse manure into the soil, and setting in extra rows of beans. In order to plant by the old moon they had to get the seeds in quickly, otherwise the beans ended up leggy.

Layla, still not allowed to run around or get overexerted, remained in the house and helped tend the toddlers. It didn't take much to keep up with Jake, but three-year-old Micah could run faster than a chicken. And of course poor Petey, who was almost nine, had to be watched.

SSSSSSssss!

Layla jolted.

It took her a minute to realize it was the kettle hissing. Mrs. Yeagley was making a cup of tea while she cooked up collards the children harvested earlier that morning, and scrambled eggs and wild ramps to go with the greens. There was oatmeal for Layla and Petey because of their chewing problems.

Suddenly, the door banged open and Rebekah, Rachel, Lizzie, and Sarah Jane came stampeding into the kitchen, yelling.

"*Samsongotrunover, Samsongotrun...*"

"All of you quiet 'cept Rebekah." Mrs. Yeagley held up the big-bladed knife she was using to chop the oniony ramps into pieces.

"Samson's dead," Rebekah said, trying to catch her

breath. "Zeb was backing up the tractor and –"

"He's comin' now," cried Rachel, looking out the back door.

The mother and children piled out the door as rail-thin Zeb trudged up the path carrying Samson in his arms. The ghost-white teen sunk to his knees and laid the limp body of the dog on the ground in front of the family.

"I didn't see him, Mama. I was backing up the tractor and I didn't see him." Zeb's head drooped, his voice broken.

Samson more than earned his keep in the Yeagley family, helping herd the livestock, barking warning at strangers, bears, and snakes, and keeping the deer and woodchucks shy of filling up their bellies in the garden. But Samson was more than a good work dog to the Yeagleys.

The previous summer, on a scorching August day, the children were playing in the creek to cool off. Nobody knew for sure what happened because they were spread out splashing and shrieking.

In water that was little more than knee deep where it ran through the Yeagley property, Zeb was catching salamanders and stuffing the slippery wriggle down the girls' shirts. Samson started to bark and carry on but everyone thought he was just joining in the fun until they saw him drag four-year-old Sarah Jane out of the water by the seat of her pants. Confused and scared, they sped over. Rebekah rolled her sister onto her back, exposing a sizable goose egg on Sarah Jane's forehead – indication that the four-year-old might have slipped on a rock and fallen face-first into the water.

Sarah Jane didn't move. Her body was floppy. Her chest still as stone. Her face and lips, the blue of violets. Screaming, Rebekah hoisted her little sister to carry her to the house. In the process of being lifted, Sarah's knees got folded up to her chest – closed together like a book. The blue child spluttered, coughed, and regurgitated water all over her confounded big sister.

By the time Zeb, the fastest runner, got back with Mrs. Yeagley, Sarah Jane had pinked up and was holding her hand on her lumped forehead, bawling. From that summer on, Samson was no longer the Yeagleys' dog; he was Yeagley family.

Zeb knelt over Samson and moaned. "I didn't mean to. Lord knows, I didn't mean to." Most animals steered clear of Zeb because he kicked them when they got in his way. Or he caught them by any part he could and sent them flying. But Samson was a charitable and forgiving dog and Zeb treated him with grudging regard on account of Samson saving his sister's life.

The stricken family congregated around the lifeless

animal. Mrs. Yeagley handed baby Jake to Rebekah and ordered everyone to hush. She put her hand near Samson's still-wet nose, feeling for breath and, head on his rib cage, pressed her ear against his black-and-white fur.

"He's gone for good. Gone to his heavenly reward."

Sarah Jane started wailing. Everyone patted Samson, shedding tears, saying what a terrible shame it was.

"That's enough, now," Ida Mae stated, stiffly. "Zeb, you best go an' make a restin' place to put Samson in."

Zeb started toward the barn. In her five years at the Yeagleys, Layla never saw him look so sorrowful.

"Not behind the barn, Zeb," Mrs. Yeagley said, firmly. "Not with the other pets. No. Samson'll be buried next to baby Ada in the family plot. Girls, you get busy and make a marker for the grave."

She took baby Jake from Rebekah. "I'm goin' back in the house to check on Petey. Micah, you come along with me. We'll hold the funeral after lunch."

Layla lingered outside after everyone else left. It was so crowded around Samson, she hadn't had a chance to say good-bye. She knelt down beside him and laid her hand on his furry chest.

Halfway back to the house, Mrs. Yeagley turned and called. "Hurry up now, Layla. Leave the poor dog be. I need you to set out cups and plates for dinner."

I have to make this quick, Samson, Layla said, her mind racing. *Even though you can't hear anymore and I can't talk, you're probably already an angel and angels know everything. I want to thank you for how kind you've always been to me. Especially since I lost my tongue. Licking me and telling me with your eyes that you understood all the hurt I've been going through. Soon as you get to heaven, Samson, please go find my mama. Tell her how much I miss her and love her. I hope they have heaps of meaty bones for you in heaven. I'll miss you, Samson. I learned a lot of goodness from you that I'll hold onto always.*

Layla started to get up but stumbled and fell onto Samson's chest. She knew he was dead, but apologized anyway, patting and kissing him before she stood and started back to the house.

Mrs. Yeagley was on the porch clanging a big cowbell to call everyone in to eat. "Dinnertime," she shouted. "Come in for dinner. Dinn –"

Abruptly, the busy mother stopped mid-sentence and clutched her heart. As the steel bell clattered down the porch steps, Layla ran to her, petrified. After what just happened to her father in the barn, Layla was afraid. Maybe Mrs. Yeagley was having a heart attack like old Mr. Gus at the mill. The fingers of Mr. Gus's one hand had gotten sawed off before anyone could get to him. Fortunately, he survived. The shock of Samson getting run over was trying on everyone in the Yeagley household, but Layla, young as she was, knew that the older you got, the more reasons there were for having your heart give out.

Mrs. Yeagley's eyes were frozen open like she was having a cataleptic fit. Her gaped mouth emitted horrible, otherworldly sounds. Layla didn't know what to do so, without taking her eyes off of Mrs. Yeagley, she picked up the bell and started ringing wildly in hopes that Zeb or Rebekah or Rachel would speed up their normal pace. When the distraught child looked around to see if anyone was coming, she practically had a conniption herself. Ever so slowly, Samson wobbled toward the house. Layla dropped the cowbell and ran to him.

She was hugging and kissing Samson when the other kids started to appear. Ida Mae, having recovered her faculties, joined in the patting and hugging. "Hallelujah!" she exclaimed, over and over. "Praise the Lord!"

Finally Mrs. Yeagley said, "Give the dog room to breathe. He's got some catchin' up to do."

"I didn't kill Samson." Zeb's relief poured from every fiber. "Just stunned him real bad."

"That dog was deader than a doornail," Mrs. Yeagley said. "Nary a breath nor a heartbeat. I witnessed it myself."

"Then how's he alive now, Mama?" Sarah Jane asked, kissing Samson for the hundredth time.

"Samson's risen by *pure miracle*," Mrs. Yeagley said.

She fixed her eyes on Layla with such strangeness that the frightened child wanted to run and hide, afraid she had done something wrong.

"Yes, indeed, we've been witness to a miracle. Everybody go wash up now for dinner. Layla, you walk Samson to the house nice an' easy. We'll let him rest an' eat till he's feelin' hisself again."

Layla started walking toward the house. Samson stood up and followed until they ambled together, her hand on his back. The five-year-old wondered why Ida Mae was acting so spooky. Layla didn't understand exactly what was brewing but, like most children, she could feel portent in the air the way wind-stirred trees foretold a coming storm.

Up ahead, Layla heard Mrs. Yeagley say to Zeb, "After lunch you get back to those corn rows."

"Yes, ma'am," Zeb said, in an unusually compliant tone.

"And Rebekah," Mrs. Yeagley said, glancing back at Layla and Samson.

"Yes, Mama?"

"You look after the kids. I've got *important* business I need to tend to."

CHAPTER EIGHT

LESS than a week later, on a July afternoon full of insect hum and the scent of fruits and flowers coming into season, Layla and the Yeagley kids were playing outside. Samson, brought back to life in an event that rocked the church community, was his old, tail-wagging self, and Layla was still trying to figure out why people thought she had something to do with it. The miracle dog romped alongside the children, barking and keeping keen watch with a ready tongue to offer warm, wet affection.

All of a sudden, Rachel tripped on a tree root and pitched forward. "My wrists," Rachel wailed. "Get Mama!"

Rachel was going on eleven and not prone to carrying on. Most of the time she was so mouse-quiet it was easy to forget she was there, so when Rachel cried it meant something.

While Rebekah ran to get Mrs. Yeagley, Layla knelt down beside Rachel. The five-year-old, still tender and mending from her own trauma, wanted to tell Rachel how sorry she was for her. Tell her that she knew what it was like to hurt so badly you cried right in front of everybody, and then had hurt heaped upon hurt because you were considered a baby for crying. Since there was nothing Layla could say, she laid her palms on Rachel's wrists to comfort her.

Ida Mae strode over from the direction of the house, drying her hands on a dish towel and looking none too pleased.

"Move aside, Layla," Mrs. Yeagley said. Supporting her bulk with one hand on the ground, the matron stooped down with an arthritic wince next to Rachel. The injured girl's crying had subsided – not a good symptom. Crying meant a child was alive enough to make noise. And no Yeagley offspring would dare interrupt the orderly routine of their mother's day with an incident not severe enough to cry about.

"Hold out your hands to the front, Rachel Sue. I'm gonna push down but you hold firm. Try not to let me move 'em."

Ida Mae, her worry disguised as a scowl, pressed on the boney parts of Rachel's hands and wrists. She examined the scrape on Rachel's left knee and asked her daughter if she hurt anywhere else.

Rachel shook her head.

"Well I don't know what all the fuss was about, Rachel Sue Yeagley. Rushin' me out here right in the middle of tryin' to get the wash done."

"I'm real sorry, Mama," Rachel said. Her head was slumped and her lower lip quivered until she bit it.

"My wrists pained bad. Truly, Mama, they did. Like somethin' was broke. But then Layla put her hands on 'em and they commenced to stop hurtin'."

"What d'you mean, Layla put her hands on 'em?" asked Mrs. Yeagley.

Layla backed off, wondering what she did wrong and if Mrs. Yeagley was going to tell her father.

"Like I said," Rachel said. "She put her hands on my wrists."

"Layla, come here and show me what you did." Mrs. Yeagley's words had a strange tone that made the five-year-old wary.

"Hurry up now, Layla."

The little girl knelt down beside Rachel and showed Mrs. Yeagley.

"You're sure that's how you did it?" Mrs. Yeagley asked. "Your hands were curled 'round Rachel's wrists like that?"

Layla shrugged because she didn't really remember. She wasn't thinking about her hands, only about Rachel's hurt.

"Oooo!" Rachel said, pulling away. "Your hands are hot."

Layla retreated, frightened she somehow burned Rachel.

Mrs. Yeagley reached over and put her hand on Layla's forehead. "Not a bit feverish." She took Layla's grubby fingers in hers, and quickly let go. Looking at the puzzled child like she was the two-headed calf born at the Lowry farm, Mrs. Yeagley said, "it's a *sign*!"

"Sign of what?" asked Lizzie, who was standing with the other kids looking on.

"She's got the *gift*," Mrs. Yeagley said. "The gift of healin'. *God be praised!*"

After work, when Ed picked up his daughter, the mother of eight related the whole story to him.

"Could be other explanations," Ed replied, uneasy about the implications of Ida Mae's belief that Layla could heal people.

That evening, when they got home, Ed asked, "What's this all about you mending Rachel's wrists, Ducky?"

Layla shrugged. She had no idea why people were making such a fuss.

Ed, remembering the heat he'd felt from his daughter's hands the afternoon he collapsed in the barn, took Layla's palms in his own, examining them front and back. "Do you feel anything different?" Layla shook her head.

"Mrs. Yeagley said your hands were hot as an oven when she touched them. You ever notice that happen?" *Sort of*, Layla indicated with a shrug.

"Hmmmm...." Ed said, gently squeezing her little hands in his. "Somethin' to keep an eye on."

Ida Mae had already spread the word about how Layla had raised Samson from the dead. Now she shared news that the child healed Rachel's nearly broken, maybe even broken, wrists. There was no doubt. With Rachel's recovery, the belief that Layla Tompkin possessed the power of healing was firmly cemented in the mind of Pastor Simpson, the mind of his congregation, and the minds of many others in the community. And like discovering gold, everyone was looking for a way to get some.

Doc Fredericks, however, wasn't buying it any of it. Not the part about healing. Not the story about a snake. He kept after the sheriff, who continued to interview anybody who had contact with the Jeeter brothers in an attempt to discover their whereabouts. The sheriff couldn't dismiss the possibility of Ed's whittling knife having been somehow involved, either.

Ed too remained unconvinced about the snake story. His heart believed his daughter. But his brain couldn't. "Square peg, round hole," he told Avis. "Just doesn't fit."

"Some things never do fit," Avis replied. "Who can explain love? Or why my angel sister died so young? What's true and what's not seems fickle as the weather sometimes. The world was flat. Now it isn't. Don't ask me what the truth is, Ed. Some things just don't make sense."

CHAPTER NINE

IT was Saturday, the morning after Rachel Sue's wrist incident. July's sun made blinding patches on the knotty-pine wall and the kitchen table where Ed and Layla were having Cream of Wheat for breakfast.

"Looks like a hot one today, Ducky," Ed said. Without his daughter's lively chatter, the days seemed as quiet as if the birds had stopped singing. Ed, good at listening but unaccustomed to small talk, was making an effort to fill in the gaps when there was a knock at the door. Somebody's forceful knuckles rapped a lilting rhythm that, if continued, could set feet to tapping.

"Anyone home?"

Wiping his mouth with his napkin, Ed got up and went to the door.

"Reverend Simpson." Ed held open the screen.

"Mornin' Mr. Tompkin, Layla," the pastor said, removing his hat. "Hope it's not too early to be callin'."

"We're gettin' around to breakfast a little late," Ed said. "Layla was a sleepyhead this mornin'. But Doc Fredericks says to let her get all the rest she can. Doc said sleep's as good a nourishment as food for her. Can I offer you a cup of coffee, Reverend?"

"That'ud be mighty nice."

"I'll bring your coffee to you in the livin' room. You can go on in and sit down."

"Please, don't let me disrupt your breakfast. The kitchen suits just fine." Pastor Simpson hung his fedora on a peg by the door, the pinch marks on the hat's crown permanently smudged from being raised in frequent courtesy.

"If you're sure you don't mind, go ahead and have a seat. Do you take your coffee white?"

"Black's fine," said Pastor Simpson. "How you doing today, sweetheart?" he asked, glossing his solid fingertips over Layla's uncombed hair.

Layla lowered her eyes.

"Jesus made you fair as a summer day," the preacher said, patting Layla's head and smiling. Then with that small grunting sigh that those of a certain girth or of a certain age make when they sit, he lowered himself onto a chair.

Ed poured a mug of coffee and set it in front of Pastor Simpson.

Pastor Simpson pondered Layla through the steam rising off his coffee. Still in her nightgown, the little girl stopped eating, embarrassed by drool.

"I trust Mrs. Yeagley told you about what transpired yesterday when Layla helped Rachel? And the week before with their dog, Samson?"

"Yes. She did speak of it," Ed replied.

"I'm not meanin' to pry into your religious beliefs, Mr. Tompkin. That's between you an' God. But I was wonderin' if you were acquainted with the Signs Followers?"

"No," Ed said. "I can't rightly say I am. Just what I gather from Ida Mae Yeagley and from Layla after she's been to one of your services. We're Baptist. But we don't get to church much since my wife passed."

"Lord knows you've been given a hard row to hoe," the pastor said, with sincere caring.

"Layla's mother would've had her to church every Sunday for sure and me right along with 'em. But all I can seem to manage is the everydayness of things. I try hard to raise Layla to be truth-tellin' and righteous. She says her prayers before eatin' and bed, and we read the Bible most Sundays."

"It's the Bible that brings me here today, Mr. Tompkin. At the Praise and Glory Holiness Church we're Signs Followers. We adhere to the last words of Jesus in Mark:

16: *And these signs shall follow them that believe; In my name shall they cast out devils; they shall speak with new tongues; They shall take up serpents; and if they drink any deadly thing, it shall not hurt them; they shall lay hands on the sick, and they shall recover."*

"I've heard mention of the snake handling," Ed replied. "But Mrs. Yeagley assured me that no harm would come to Layla."

Ed glanced at his daughter. "After she'd been to church, Layla used to describe what went on. From what I could make out, she didn't grasp a whole lot."

Layla wished she had some way of telling her father about what happened a few weeks ago when he and Auntie Avis were outside during the pastor's and Mrs. Yeagley's visit. She wished her father knew what Pastor Simpson said so he could ask the preacher what he meant by devils and new tongues and getting marked by God.

"Yesterday," Pastor Simpson said, "when Layla put her hands on Rachel, the pain stopped. We believe what's happenin' are *signs*, Mr. Tompkin. We're witnessin' signs of God manifestin' through Layla. Firstly, the sign of her tongue bein' taken by a serpent to bring forth new tongues. And now the sign of layin' on healin' hands. It's not usual, Layla bein' a child and all. But the Bible does say *a little child shall lead them.*"

"Yes," Ed replied. "The Bible does say that."

"Which brings me to the point of my payin' you a call,"

the preacher continued. "Would it be all right for Layla to come to church Sundays and lay her healin' hands on folks that ail? 'Course you'd be welcome to accompany her."

Ed scratched his cheek. His whisker stubs made a raspy sound. While he was cogitating, he looked over to his daughter for indication of how she felt about the idea. But Layla, unsure what was at stake, sat there blankly, her foot jiggling.

Ed folded his arms across his chest and rested them on the kitchen table. He pondered the remains in the bottom of his cereal bowl. Maybe Avis was on the right track. Maybe he was looking for proof where none existed. And yet...

Ed raised his eyes to meet the reverend's. "I'd not deny anybody the chance for healin' relief," he said. "But it strikes me that the rightful order of things would be for Layla to have healin' first. And I'd be neglectin' the truth if I didn't say that I have powerful reservation about sendin' her to a place with live serpents after all she's been through."

"I can understand your reticence, Mr. Tompkin. Bein' a father myself, I have high respect for your care of Layla. But we owe our heavenly Father obedience above all else. And He has seen fit to bestow gifts of the Holy Spirit on Layla. Is it not a sin and abomination to refuse those gifts?"

"Pastor Simpson, I'd be no match arguin' religion

against you. And I can't say anything false against your words. It's just that somethin' feels amiss."

"We must be wary of our feelings, Mr. Tompkin. Feelings can be easily swayed by Satan."

"I'll think and pray on what you're askin', Pastor. And I'll take it up with my sister-in-law too. That's the best I can say for now."

"Our congregation will pray for you, Mr. Tompkin. For Layla too. Now I'll be leavin' you to the breakfast I interrupted. Good day, to you. And God bless."

"Good day, Pastor."

Pastor Simpson retrieved his hat and Ed let him out the door. The troubled father sat down with a heavy sigh born of neither girth nor age, but of a body running on empty for three and a half of the longest weeks of his life.

Mindful that his daughter was probably as confused by the pastor's visit as he was, Ed voiced his dilemma.

"I know we talked about this before, Ducky, but is there anything at all you remember happening with Samson or Rachel?"

Layla shook her head. *Nothing*, she wanted to say. *Nothing but strangeness about how everyone else was acting.*

"You know, Ducky, you don't have to touch anybody you don't want to. Or let anybody touch you. Not if it doesn't feel right. You hear?"

Layla nodded.

"Sometimes," Ed said, "life throws a problem at you where there's just no good answer. But if my heart says *don't* do somethin', I don't. Not till it says otherwise. Confound if I know who's sayin' the *don't*. Could be the devil, like Reverend Simpson says. Could be God. Could be my own self. But we're gonna sit tight till I get it sorted out. That suit you okay, Ducky?"

Layla nodded. She took a bite of cereal, started to choke, but swallowed hard and managed to get it down.

PART II

SCHOOLED

CHAPTER TEN

EVERY step in her new red shoes pinched as Layla mounted the stairs of Cumberland Elementary on her first day of kindergarten. Ed held his daughter's hand tightly. She held his even more tightly.

Excited children cut in front of the silent pair, jabbering and squealing. Layla was surprised how many kids lived in the gaps and hollows of the mountain. She'd seen some of the children at the Piggly Wiggly, the drug store, and at Praise and Glory Holiness Church. Or when their parents toted them over to the Yeagley house to be healed by the little girl with "God-guided" hands. But most of them eyed her as curiously as she looked at them.

Assured by her father that she'd already know some people – Sarah Jane, Lizzie, Rachel, and Rebekah

Yeagley, for sure – Layla hadn't thought much about how she would be able to make new friends without talking.

For a child's eternity, Layla had been waiting to turn five – old enough to go to school. All that time her mind created pictures from tales the Yeagley kids told about storytime, homework, and playing outside at recess.

As Layla climbed the school steps, reality felt entirely different from her imagination. Her stomach churned so hard that her breakfast milk was slowly turning to lumps of butter.

"You look all growed-up, Ducky," her dad said, smiling down at her. The lines in his face made alphabet letters. *W*'s at the side of his eyes. *M*'s on his forehead.

Rachel and Rebekah Yeagley had been teaching Layla to write the alphabet. And every night, heeding the advice of the specialist, Ed encouraged his daughter to practice. Layla already knew how to print her letters and could spell out her entire name even though the *k*'s and *l*'s sometimes faced the wrong way. She couldn't quite grasp perplexing letters like *J* and little *d* that went one direction and little *b* and big *D*, the opposite – all willy-nilly like a litter of kittens.

New shoes. New faces. And in her backpack, a new box of eight crayons along with a writing tablet and four pencils with brand-new erasers – not like the pencils Layla used to practice her alphabet, their erasers so worn, so smudged with letters taken back, they marked up the page with more than they rubbed out.

And one more new thing. A red thermos with her nutrient-spiked drink in it.

Ed and Layla made their way down the yellowy varnished floors in the hallway of Cumberland Elementary. Framed portraits lined the white wall above the ocher wainscoting; first president, George Washington; current president, Dwight D. Eisenhower; and group pictures of every graduating class from 1936 to 1954.

The school was bigger than a one-room schoolhouse by several classrooms and even boasted a tiny library. The first room to the right of the hallway was a cramped office with a coffeepot, a few shabby lounge chairs, mail cubbies for the teachers, and a desk for the traveling principal, who juggled a split appointment between two elementary schools and a high school.

In the unfamiliar surroundings, Layla's eyes were everywhere at once. Ed, in an attempt to focus his daughter's attention, slowed to a stop in front of the sixth-and seventh-grade classroom.

"See this room here, Ducky? This is where Rachel and Rebekah are. Two doors down is your room."

Layla and her father arrived in the kindergarten-to-second-grade classroom where Sarah Jane and Elizabeth Yeagley waved. Like Layla, Sarah Jane was new to school, while Lizzie, in second grade, was already an old-timer.

Mrs. Phoebe, the teacher in charge of all three levels, twenty-two students in all, shook hands with Ed.

"Good morning, Mr. Tompkin. Nice to see you again."

"Welcome, Layla," Mrs. Phoebe said, kneeling down on one knee, her dark-green skirt pooling on the floor around her like a sheltering forest glen. "We're so glad you're here. I know this is a big day for you, so anything you need; just let me know and we'll work it out. All right?"

Feeling overwhelmed by a strange place and so many new faces, Layla nodded. "Remember," Ed said for the tenth time, "the bus is gonna pick you up and take you over to the Yeagleys' house after school. You stick by Elizabeth and Sarah Jane, you hear?"

For the tenth time, Layla nodded, her own worries intensified by the edginess in her father's tone.

"Okay, Ducky. Learn somethin' good today." He hugged his daughter and turned to leave.

Until her father started to walk away, Layla felt very grown-up. But suddenly she was reduced to a five-year-old, not quite waist-high to most adults who, more often than not, doggie-patted the top of her flaxen head when they greeted her. A child who still needed two hands to carry a glass of water or pull the barn door shut.

Bereft of her father, Layla stood scared and alone,

abandoned in childhood's wordless void – more unutterable for her – as a reliable anchor dredged free and, amid receding landmarks, set her adrift into the unknown.

Mrs. Phoebe took the little girl's hand in hers and smiled. She led Layla to a desk at the front of the classroom and showed her how to lift the oaken desktop.

"You can put your things inside here, Layla. This is where you'll be keeping your reader and workbooks. I'll get Elizabeth Yeagley to show you where to put your lunch and hang your coat. Elizabeth will show you where the restroom is, too. If you need to use the toilet, just raise your hand and do this."

Mrs. Phoebe, who'd been studying in anticipation of her student's unique needs, showed Layla how to make a fist, poking her thumb up between her first two fingers. "This is the letter *T* in sign language. And when you shake your hand from side to side while making the *T* sign, it means toilet or restroom. It'll be our special signal. Can you do that?'

Layla tried.

"You're a fast learner, Layla. I can see I'm going to have my work cut out to keep up with you." She smoothed the child's cornsilk hair just the way Auntie Avis did and straightened the crooked bow that Ed, trying to make the occasion of his daughter's first day extra-special, had struggled with that morning.

Avis had been running up a considerable phone bill with all the *must do*'s that Ed might not think about in preparing Layla for kindergarten.

"You sure you got all her school supplies, Ed?"

"Went to Woolworth's and Layla and I checked 'em off the list as we put each one in the basket. Good thing the Big Chief writing tablet is red. Don't know why, but she wants everything red these days."

"Did you get her one of those little pencil sharpeners?"

"No. Didn't see that on the list."

"Well, it's good to have when their pencil breaks. They don't always want to be trotting to the big pencil sharpener and have to grind away while the teacher is talking."

"Think we have a couple of those around the house. I'll make sure to put one with her things."

"And don't forget the little notes we talked about. Doesn't have to be much. Just an *I love you* tucked in with her lunch. Or maybe a picture of some kind – a flower, a dog. Just a comforting reminder those first days when she might be feeling kinda scared."

"My drawin' would probably scare her more, but I'll think of somethin'."

"Did she get the hair ribbons I sent?"

"She did. Yesterday I mailed a picture she drew for you."

"Oh, and Ed," Avis lowered her voice, almost to a whisper. "Make sure you tuck an extra pair of panties into her book bag. Roll 'em in a paper bag...maybe an extra pair of socks too. You know, just in case. It's awful different being at school. Sometimes they just get caught by surprise."

"I'll do that. Avis," Ed said, though Layla hadn't had an accident since she had been three.

"Give her a great big ol' hug from me. And one from each of her cousins and Uncle Frank."

"Same here, Avis."

After they hung up, Ed slipped the list into his shirt pocket for later. He still had supper to get on the table and then dishes. It used to be when Ed took Layla on errands with him, he felt a sense of accomplishment when he got her out the door with reasonably clean clothes, her shoes on, and her hair brushed relatively free of tangles. School was a whole new ball game. It was dicey business not knowing how Layla would react to this new environment and how other kids would react to her, so it was worth going through all the rigamarole his sister-in-law suggested to help ease the transition. Ed, a woodworker, knew it was often the bit-by-bit efforts – shaving off a hair here and a hair there – that made the difference of a good fit. He was determined to do whatever it took.

❧

Mrs. Phoebe gave Layla's head a final pat before she turned and walked away, leaving behind a waft of lilac.

Again, Layla practiced the restroom sign.

Then, in the desk's hidden compartment that smelled like old erasers and chalk dust, the beribboned kindergartener began placing her supplies in, one by one, guided by the embedded voice of Ida Mae Yeagley: *"A place for everything and everything in its place."*

Layla resisted the idea of ever using her crayons and pencils. That way, they'd never get broken or lose their new smell. And, as her small, unusually clean fingers pried unsuccessfully at an old wad of chewing gum stuck underneath the top of the desk, she knew deep down in the pit of her stomach full of butterflies and butter lumps that she couldn't wait to try them out.

Lizzie came over, pulling Sarah Jane by the hand. "Come with us, Layla. We're gonna show you where to find things." As Lizzie pointed out the restroom, Layla, her hand inconspicuously at her side, practiced the *T*.

"Here's the shelf where you put your book bag. Mine and Sarah Jane's are already on it. We're all close to each other because our name starts with *Y* and yours with *T*. See, it says *Layla Tompkin* taped to the edge."

Escorting Layla around, seven-year-old Lizzie, a child as close as smack-dab in the middle of a family of eight kids as you can get, had an authority, a singular importance Layla never really noticed when they did chores and played together at the Yeagleys'. Lizzie showed Layla the peg for her coat, the sink at the back of the room, and the toilet. Layla couldn't wait to show her father how to make the letter *T* because when he liked something, he would say, "That suits me to a *T*."

So far school was suiting Layla to a *T*.

Mrs. Phoebe clapped her hands. "Take your seats, everyone. Class is starting." Lizzie waved bye and scooted to her desk.

Pinchpinchpinch. Layla ran to her desk, plopped onto the wooden seat, and stuck her legs out to more fully appreciate the fine-looking cause of her discomfort. Being barefoot felt better, but dirty toes didn't look nearly as nice, she thought, waiting for what Mrs. Phoebe would say next.

"Shhhhhh!" The second-graders tried to hush the younger kids. Fear slithered up and down Layla's spine. Suddenly, she had to pee but the urge passed as soon as Mrs. Phoebe started to talk.

"Good morning, students." Mrs. Phoebe's smile made you think she had a wonderful secret. Her eyes pledged comfort and fun and a steady watch on the seesaw outside so that no one would be left sky-thrust and dangling.

"Good morning, Mrs. Phoebe," everyone said back.

"It is wonderful to greet returning students and to

meet new ones. The first thing we're going to do this morning," said their teacher, "is to go through the rules of how we behave in school." She took a yardstick and pointed to a sign that hung above the chalkboard.

Be kind, helpful and respectful to everybody.

"Now let's say that out loud together." Mrs. Phoebe pointed to each word as everyone repeated.

There was no way Layla could articulate any of the words except *be*. She was confused about how to continue. She wouldn't be following the "respectful" rule if she didn't do what the teacher was asking so she mouthed the words as best she could and thought them out loud in her head.

Raise your hand when you want to speak.

Use your inside voices.

A growing concern started to rise inside Layla with all the rules about *speaking* and *voices*. Maybe school wasn't going to suit her to a *T* after all.

Listen to your teacher and follow the school rules.

That rule was easier because, bolstered by her father's decision not to send her to a deaf school, Layla knew she had good ears.

"Nuthin' wrong with your ears," Ed said.

Ever since his daughter lost her tongue, Ed avoided the words *severed* and *amputated*. He chose his words and tone as deliberately as he positioned a board on the cutterhead at the mill, making his daughter's injury sound more like a missing shoe than the serious and permanent loss she had to deal with for the rest of her life. There was no sidestepping the hurdles ahead, but Ed refused to terrify or mollycoddle his daughter. Either extreme, he felt, thwarted her way forward.

Later he said, "Everybody alive has somethin' that makes their life harder than the next person. Some folks have what hinders 'em right out where you can see it, like Mr. Gus at the mill with no fingers on his one hand. Or deaf Mr. Rupert.

"And some folks seem to get more than their share of troubles, like Petey Yeagley. But just because you can't see a struggle doesn't mean it's not buried deep down inside. So don't you get fooled into thinkin' that you're the only one, Ducky. You lost your tongue, but you still have a hundred other things that work just fine. You remember that now."

Layla tried to hold onto her father's words when Mrs. Phoebe announced, "Now we will go around the room and introduce ourselves. Stand up when I point to you and speak nice and loud so everyone can hear."

Layla froze. She tried hard to mask how scared she was. Fear, she knew, made you an easy target. Layla learned that lesson from all the times Zeb Yeagley dangled snakes in front of her. She'd also learned to disguise her fear by watching clever Mother Nature teach her offspring to masquerade like every day was Halloween.

To hackle, hunch up, puff out, slaver, play dead, change color, or like the buck-eyed moth, show so many false eyes you didn't know if it was coming or going. Pretending, just to keep alive.

To Layla, fakery in the service of survival was plain good sense. Different from the crystal-clear sin of falsehood, except for white lies. The five-year-old was still trying to puzzle out what exactly made a lie *white.* Why not mentioning the warty mole on the side of Ida Mae Yeagley's nose was a *good* lie because the truth might be hurtful. And not mentioning that she, herself, hadn't brushed her teeth before bed was a *bad* lie. Wasn't getting your own feelings pummeled with a scolding as keen a reason to tell a white lie?

When Mrs. Phoebe started at the other end of the room Layla eyeballed the other students. None of them, even the shy-seeming ones, looked overly concerned about the introductions. Especially not the freckle-faced boy in the back who was picking his nose and rubbing his stubby finger underneath his desk.

Suddenly, Layla didn't care that she had new red shoes or eight never-used crayons. All she wanted to do was find a hole and curl up into a little ball inside it until school was over.

"Stand up now, Layla," Mrs. Phoebe said, coming over and putting her arm around the mortified child. Layla wondered how she managed to rise; newborn colts had less wobble in their legs. Her shoes were the lone part of her that weren't quivering like calf's-foot jelly.

"Class, this is Layla Tompkin."

"That's *her!*" whispered a little girl in the next row.

"Layla is going to be one of our teachers this year, teaching us a special way of talking with our hands. Layla, show the class how to make the sign if they need to use the restroom."

It was providential that part of the sign for *toilet* was shaking your hand from side to side. Otherwise, everybody would have noticed that her hand was quaking like an aspen leaf.

"Everybody see that?"

"I can't see," booger boy called out.

"Remember to raise your hand, Lon. Layla, let's go over to the sink at the back of the room and you can stand on the hand-washing stool so that Lon and the others can see."

Layla felt twenty-two pairs of eyes boring woodpecker holes into her as Mrs. Phoebe led the way to the rear of the classroom and pulled out a step stool.

"Everybody follow along now and do what Layla's doing. She's going to be learning more signs all the time and teaching everybody how to use them. Layla was injured in an accident earlier this year so she has special ways of communicating without talking. That will help all of us learn new ways to say things. Won't that be fun?"

"*Yes, Mrs. Phoebe,*" said the class in unison.

"You can go back to your desk now," Mrs. Phoebe whispered, patting the back of Layla's yellow-checked dress like she was burping a baby.

As she went back to her desk, Layla heard whispers all around her. "*Snake... No tongue... Mama says not to...*"

"Hush now, class," Mrs. Phoebe said, quick-stepping to the front of the room. "Everybody stand up now. Reach way, way up. Now bend over and shake like a wet dog trying to dry off. Good. Sit back down and get out your writing tablets and a pencil."

Layla's breathing steadied as desktops groaned open and thumped shut. Before starting the copy work for the kindergarteners that Mrs. Phoebe printed neatly on the chalkboard, Layla buried her nose in her writing tablet and nearly stuck the pencil eraser up her nostril, smelling their newness, breathing in the scent of paper and wood and rubber, the trees they came from, and the possibilities they held.

The girl behind Layla leaned forward and whispered, "My daddy says that's what you get from goin' to a serpent church."

Layla, engrossed with pencils and beginning her very first school assignment, halted with surprise. Before she could process the remark, she looked back the same way she would have reacted if she heard an insect buzzing behind her. With one eye on Mrs. Phoebe, the apple-cheeked girl,

Roberta, stuck out her tongue as far as she could and wiggled it. Suddenly, Roberta's face was fixed in a big, toothy smile. Mrs. Phoebe walked over and bent down between the girls. "Does someone have a question?"

Roberta grinned widely and shook her head. "Oh no, teacher. This girl just wanted to see my...my special eraser." She snatched the pink rectangle from her desktop and held it up.

"Well..." Mrs. Phoebe said. "It's nice you girls are making friends." Mrs. Phoebe leveled her eyes at Layla. "You'll let me know if there's anything you need?"

"Yes ma'am," Roberta said, sweetly.

Eyes downcast, Layla nodded.

"Good," replied Mrs. Phoebe. With a steely undertone and a look that showed she wasn't born yesterday, the teacher said, "It'd be a shame to have to separate new friends. But that's just what I'll do if you can't pay attention to your work."

Because of Layla's speechlessness and the strange story surrounding her situation, Mrs. Phoebe knew she needed to find ways for the other students to accept the new girl. But she didn't anticipate the prejudice that some in the area held against the little girl. And what parents talked about among themselves, their pitch-perfect children repeated. With so many students, Mrs. Phoebe was troubled by how she could protect the speechless child and keep harmony in the classroom.

At recess, while Layla stood at the end of the jump-rope line waiting for a turn, booger boy, Lon Randall, came over. When Mrs. Phoebe wasn't looking, Lon shook his fist in her face, making the restroom sign.

"Toilet girl," he said, under his breath. "What'sa matter. *Snake* got your tongue?" With brutal force, he mashed his foot down on the toe of her new shoes. Stunned and hurt, Layla yelped like a bee-stung puppy. Lon took off and was on the other side of the playground by the time anybody looked over to see what happened.

Booger boy Lon probably figured a frog had more chance of flying than the mute girl had of telling on him, so he continued to make Layla's life a misery every chance he got. But even if she could have told, Layla knew that nobody likes a tattletale. She already learned that lesson from Zeb Yeagley.

Layla remembered the time that Zeb, for no earthly reason, slapped her across the face, *hard.* After Zeb did something like that, if anyone tattled on him, he'd always tell his mother, "I was just funnin' with 'em." All Mrs. Yeagley would say is, "You stop that right now, Zebidiah Yeagley."

Afterwards, whoever ratted on Zeb got tormented twice as bad as the first time. Once, when Layla still had her tongue, she squealed on him. Later, Zeb snatched her by the arm while she was playing hide-and-seek and pulled her behind the bushes. He pushed her down and laid the full length of his weight on top of her, so she could barely breathe – and he clamped his hand over her mouth so she couldn't cry out.

"Now you're in for it, you dirty lil' snitch," he said. Rachel called *ready or not here I come*, closer and closer, until Zeb finally jumped up and took off.

But booger boy wasn't Layla's only nemesis. As the days went on, several other kids, on the pretense of talking to Layla in sign language, sidled up to her in the cloakroom or as they passed her on the playground or when Mrs. Phoebe had her back turned. Curving their two front fingers into snakelike fangs, they hissed and ran away, sniggering at the look of fear on Layla's face.

Layla stared down the bullies with her formidable Mt. Rushmore stare. But every morning, when the yellow bus stopped at the bottom of their lane, she'd cry and drag her heels.

"After you learn readin' and writin', things aren't gonna be so hard, Ducky," her father said, thinking she was stymied by lack of speech.

Layla never revealed why she dreaded school. At first there was no way. And later, it seemed plain shameful to be afraid of sounds that hissed.

CHAPTER ELEVEN

EVERY day Mrs. Phoebe taught Layla a new sign and had her demonstrate it to the rest of the class. *Please. Thank you. Water. Want. Friend. Stop.*

And each day after school, Mrs. Yeagley had the child lay her healing hands on whoever in the family wasn't up to snuff. Ida Mae swore Layla could ease the ache in her cranky knees and stop grippe faster than boneset tea. All the more miraculous since the child's pint-sized hands, still dimpled where knuckles would eventually surface, had palms no bigger than the silver-dollar buttermilk pancakes Ida Mae spooned onto a griddle hot enough to bounce a drop of water.

When other folks stopped by for healing, Ida Mae escorted them into the steamy kitchen where one or two pots of something or other – soup or stew – were usually simmering in preparation for the next meal. The stalwart matron would pull out a chair from the long, oilcloth-covered table, glad to relieve Layla from caring for the Yeagley brood in exchange for the jar of apple butter or rasher of bacon that folks brought by way of appreciation.

Layla itched to be racing around with Lizzie and Sarah Jane. Or giggling in the garden while they pinched creepy-crawlies off the plants and dropped them into coffee cans of kerosene. Or pick whatever was ripe. Instead, Ida Mae made the child sit quietly, using her "gift" until Layla felt she was turning into a tree stump.

After the five-year-old's healing powers became known, Ida Mae would phone on Sunday morning inquiring, "Is Layla wantin' to be picked up for church as usual?" More often than not, Layla balked. In no uncertain terms, she shook her head in refusal. And if the Yeagleys' wagon rumbled up the gravel drive "to make sure she hadn't changed her mind," Layla suddenly became as invisible as a no-see-um. She disappeared to the barn or hid under the bed, pushing the dust balls together into life-sized bunnies. Full of pent-up, not Pentecostal, energy, she wanted nothing more than to run around in the shine of her father's adoration.

But, if the weather was foul and her father was

nose-deep in paperwork, Layla opted for church and being with the Yeagley brood as less boring.

Ed, however, was conflicted. He felt guilty about the religious education his wife would have wanted for their daughter. Yet he was equally concerned about Layla being called upon to heal folks and also occupying the same room as serpents, even though Ida Mae promised she'd sit the children well away from the handling. The strict mother added to Ed's conflict by saying, "How's Layla supposed to learn the ways of God without goin' to church? Especially since you see fit to spare the rod."

When Layla went to church with the Yeagleys', she felt a certain odd pleasure as everyone vied for her hands on their body. But, not knowing what she was supposed to be doing, in the end, it wasn't worth the stew of uncomfortable feelings.

Out of everyone whom Layla was called upon to heal, there was only one person who was wholly repulsive: Zeb Yeagley. There were the unavoidable times when Ida Mae barked, "Go on now, Layla. Find Zeb an' put your hands on him." Times when Zeb had been caught in some act of menace he couldn't wheedle out of. Like the time he dangled screaming Sarah Jane by one arm from the barn's high hayloft. Or when he put a dead rat into Rachel's lunch box. The aggravated mother, beyond wit's end, would say, "I don't know how Satan found my boy an' filled him with so much venom. Use your God touch on him, Layla. Draw the poison out."

When Mrs. Yeagley shooed Layla outside to find Zeb, experience warned the child to keep at a safe distance because whenever he got a chance, Zeb forced kisses on her and groped her private places. So early on, Layla learned to stick close to the other kids whenever he was around. Or, if she were by herself, she skirted around him like he was a pasture full of fresh cow patties.

But sometimes Ida Mae cornered Zeb in the kitchen and ordered Layla to lay her hands on him. As soon as the young healer's hands touched on the teenager's greasy skin, her body walled-up. Adding to Layla's repugnance, Zeb gave her the hairy eyeball and said things she didn't understand but that made her feel sick. He'd put his mouth close to her ear and whisper, "Want a lollipop? A big red one?" Then he'd smile.

Zeb threatened the little girl every chance he got. "Just you wait. I'm comin' to get you," he said. "Just you wait." Or he made twisted faces that no one except Petey could see.

Mrs. Yeagley instructed the child to "lay healin' on Petey" as well. Ever since the incident with Samson, Ida Mae said, "make Petey's feet to walk and his mouth to talk."

As much as it hobbled Layla's coltish energies, healing

Petey was a protection from Zeb. And in a peculiar sort of way, the little girl wanted to be with Petey. Nobody at the Yeagleys' had time to pay much attention to the chair-bound boy besides the feeding, washing, wiping, and changing of him. So the hours spent with Petey allowed Layla to practice sign language by teaching her eager pupil what she learned, further deepening their wordless kinship.

The five-year-old looked into Petey's eyes and saw that he had a world of thoughts and feelings inside that he wished he could say and no way to say them. Layla didn't know how, but she felt she understood Petey the way some people can understand a foreign language or figure out secret codes.

One day, when Mrs. Yeagley had Layla putting her hands on Petey – on his lolling head, his twig-like legs and in-turned feet, his bony arms and hands, fists bent tight against his chest when they weren't jabbing out uncontrollably, sparring like a champ at a ceaseless foe – an idea popped into the little girl's head.

She decided to teach Petey the word *mama*. Even though she didn't need the word the way most kids did – *please, Mama; thank you, Mama; I'm sorry, Mama; look, Mama* – Layla saw what a stir it made when Micah and Jake first said *mama* to Ida Mae. Patiently, Layla made the sign over and over, gesturing to Ida Mae. After Petey practiced for several days, the excited child summoned Mrs. Yeagley. She pointed to Petey, rapidly opening and closing her hand by her mouth.

"You want me to talk to Petey?" Mrs. Yeagley asked.

Layla shook her head, pointing from Petey to her.

"Petey's gonna talk to me?" Mrs. Yeagley asked.

Brimming with joy for Petey, Layla nodded.

Mrs. Yeagley knelt down in arthritic kinks and halts in front of Petey, her eyes wide with anticipation, ready for another miracle. Rachel healed. Samson risen. And now words from the needy son God saw fit to give her.

"Talk to me Petey. Go ahead and talk to Mama."

Layla nodded to Petey and reminded him of the sign. Petey, fiercely attempting to control his waving arms, hands fluttering like moths, finally got his thumb to touch his chin, fingers spread open. He made his happy sound, and then nearly poked himself in the eye because he couldn't control his jerking hand.

"Come on, Petey. Mama's waitin'. Go ahead an' talk."

Layla wanted to shout, "He did! He did! He said *mama*!"

Layla made the sign for *Look*. Mrs. Yeagley knew her mute charge was learning sign language at school and the family already had developed their own signals for communicating the basics after Layla's injury.

Look, Layla repeated.

"I'm lookin' an' I'm listenin'," Mrs. Yeagley said.

Mama, Layla gestured, demonstrating so Ida Mae knew what to look for. Layla pointed to Petey.

With Herculean effort Petey struggled again to make his hand perform the *mama* sign. Finally, he did. But as soon as his thumb met his chin, his hand flung away like a trapped bird let loose.

Petey shrieked with joy. Layla grinned ear to ear.

Mrs. Yeagley rose with difficulty and brushed off her housedress. "I don't know what kind of foolery you're up to, Layla Grace Tompkin," she said. "But it don't set well with me. If you're not goin' to be workin' on healin' Petey, make yourself useful in the garden pickin' beans with Rachel. Go on now. Do one or the other. But don't you be wastin' my time again."

Vexation and tears boiled up inside the frustrated child. When she didn't feel she was doing much but comforting people with her hands, Ida Mae praised her. But when she taught Petey a word, an actual word that he communicated, his own mother dismissed it as nothing.

As disappointed as Layla felt about Ida Mae not recognizing the *mama* sign, she felt worse for Petey. Wiping her eyes, she thought, "not one of us has to work as hard at a thing as Petey."

Petey lay slumped in his chair, drool running down his face. Layla wiped it off with the rag and sat there patting his leg. Patting and patting.

I know you said "mama," Petey. I know you can say other things too. The words were so strong in her mind she was hoping Petey could hear them.

Petey started to moan. Not like he was hurting – more of a lonely sound like the coo of a mourning dove or the forlorn whistle of a distant train. Something about Petey's moaning soothed the dejected child, although she didn't know why. She guessed that with her patting and his sounds they were a comfort to each other.

When Ed came to pick up Layla that evening, Mrs. Yeagley gave him an earful about how disobedient Layla was, not doing what she was told to do. Ida Mae failed to say anything about the situation that caused her ire and Layla had no way to explain. Ed thanked the out-of-joint mother.

After returning home, Ed sat his daughter down and talked about it. He wondered if Ida Mae's pique had something to do with pressuring Layla to use the "gift" that the fervent mother insisted his daughter possessed. Maybe Layla had refused.

"Did Mrs. Yeagley make you do anything you didn't want to?"

Layla, still smoldering over the way Petey's own mama dismissed his extraordinary accomplishment, shook her head. She was frustrated to tears that she couldn't explain what had happened.

Most of the time when Ida Mae complained about his daughter's behavior, Ed told Layla not to let it happen again. Then he'd hug her. But if the misconduct sounded serious, like today, Ed would say, "Now what would your mama think about your behavin' like that, Layla Grace Tompkin?"

Ed only called his daughter by her entire given name when he was upset by her conduct, or worried, or when he was weary of telling her a thing for the third or fourth time. But none of that was too often.

When her father talked about her mother being disappointed by her behavior, Layla thought, "I'd rather have a hundred paddlings by Mrs. Yeagley, instead."

CHAPTER TWELVE

WHEN Mrs. Phoebe saw that the five-year-old already knew her alphabet, she immediately moved on to phonetics.

"Sound out the letters in your head, Layla, and put them together. *C-a-t. R-a-t. S-a-t.*"

Soon after, her teacher had Layla writing *the fat cat sat on the mat.* "I've never seen such a fast learner," said Mrs. Phoebe.

On the weekends, Mrs. Phoebe gave the enthusiastic child second-grade workbooks to take home. She made Layla a necklace out of yarn and, with a clothespin, clipped a piece of paper to it. That way, whenever Layla heard a new word, she could write it down. Or if she wanted to say something, she could try to spell it out.

Ultimately, sign language turned out to be limiting because nobody remembered many gestures except Mrs. Phoebe. Head nods sufficed for most communication.

As Layla went through the grades from kindergarten on up, she loved learning. Every bit of it. The hole left from losing her mother, losing speech, losing taste and chewed food, filled with the rapture of words and ideas. Layla was astonished by how the world was full of so many different people and places, and how scientists invented rocket ships that traveled to the moon but couldn't discover the secret of how honeybees found the way back to their hive.

But despite Layla's love of learning, school was also a torment. Lon Randall and the other bullyboys played their part. So was being shunned by some because she couldn't talk. Even friends like Sarah Jane and Lizzie embarrassed her by running over to get "healing" when they got hurt on the playground. Wide-eyed, students circled around Layla, looking for a reason to be touched by the tongueless healer.

"Can you make this cut go away, Layla?"

"Make me quit biting my nails."

"Please take away my sty."

But other kids jeered. "*Ssssssnake* girl. *Sssssnake* girl. Watch out she doesn't bite." Some even called her "witch," a term some parents used for the girl with the so-called magical powers.

Yet overshadowing everything else was the dreaded hiss that permeated each day. S*erpent sounds*.

All those sounds from that terrible night – hissing combined with the slurry of her desperate gasps – were linked together with pain, fear, and a trauma buried so far down in her body, Layla couldn't figure how to root it out. Unfortunately, the number of everyday sounds that shimmied with sibilance was past imagining; a teacher shushing a student, teakettles, bicycle pumps, the air brakes of a truck.

About a year after she lost her tongue, Ed said to his daughter, "I don't know how you heard that coon diggin' in the compost pile. You have the ears of a dog or a bobcat. Sometimes I think you hear the telephone before it rings."

Saying his daughter had keen ears was saying a lot because the sensibilities of most mountain folk were as fine-tuned as a fiddler's strings.

Every person above toddling age could recognize the song of spring's first robin. Or could name the month, almost to the day, by when the sound of tree frogs began, or the start of cicada whirr.

Most knew ripeness in their thumb, rain in their bones,

and the loom of snow in their nose. And even though some mountain folk never went past eighth grade, it was hard to pull the wool over someone's eyes who'd been through the lambing, shearing, and knitting of that wool.

Ed finally asked Doc Fredericks why certain sounds made his daughter so jumpy. Doc said it was fairly common for one sense to get stronger when another is lost. "A deaf person sees more acutely than a hearing person," he said. "And a person lacking sight can sometimes tell the difference between a pinch of sugar and a pinch of salt just by the feel of it."

For Layla too touch was proving to be a powerful tool – more direct than voice and just as varied – swift, lingering, shallow, deep. To get someone's attention, she tapped on an arm, a shoulder or a back. Whenever she perceived pain or strife, she comforted with a consoling hand.

However, the once talkative child's enormous loss of speech wasn't nearly as crippling as her fear of sibilant sounds. At home, she jammed wads of toilet paper into her ears to muffle the sound of fatback sizzling in a skillet, or the whistle of wind as it gushed through window cracks. But Layla could hardly go around looking like an outhouse at school. So when kids called her *SSSssnake girl*, there was nothing to muffle the hiss. *Fraidy-cat, fraidy-cat*, some taunted if she exhibited the least bit of fear.

Though Mrs. Phoebe didn't fully understand the cause of Layla's distress, attributing it, as Ed did, more to the frustrations of communicating, she allowed her star pupil to spend time in the school's library as soon as she learned to read. In the solitude of the library's safe haven, no bigger than a small bedroom, books became Layla's escape.

In hopes it might help the child to have a way to express her feelings and fears, Mrs. Phoebe gave the precocious little girl a notebook. "Layla," she said. "This is a journal. You can draw pictures in it, or write down all the things you'd talk about with a special friend – what pleases or displeases you. Questions. Even secrets."

At first Layla only journaled when something special happened. But soon she was making daily entries. Layla showed a few of her pages to her teacher, who beamed with satisfaction. After that, every year on Layla's birthday, Mrs. Phoebe gave her a beautifully wrapped brand-new journal, just as she continued to guide this special child through the years,

Journaling helped the mute girl hash out what back-and-forth conversation or having a heart-to-heart achieved for others. But writing about her phobia of *hiss* didn't help. In fact, year by year, her fears intensified. Sometimes Layla wished she'd lost her hearing instead. But ultimately, it was a waste of time.

She was never offered the choice.

CHAPTER THIRTEEN

EVER since Layla's birth, Ed and his daughter drove to Shady Grove for Thanksgiving and Christmas. In the Lovell home, stuffed fuller than a holiday turkey with merry chaos and mouthwatering aromas, the kids tumbled and bickered, shouted and laughed. But this November was the first time since Layla lost her tongue five months earlier that the whole family was together.

Of course, Auntie Avis had hands-on experience with her niece's speech and eating difficulties. Abbey too. After Avis returned home from caring for Layla, she suggested that, since it was summer, ten-year-old Abbey go to Fox Hollow to keep her cousin company and help out during the little girl's pain-filled weeks of recuperation. Abbey read stories to Layla, brought her soup and milkshakes, and tended the five-year-old's wound.

Wolfy and little Frank, however, hadn't seen Layla since her injury and were unsure about how to respond to their mute cousin.

"She's still the same sweet Layla, inside," Avis said. "Just treat her like you always do."

"Pretend you're playing a guessing game," Abbey told her brothers. "Keep asking questions till you say the words she's trying to say."

Yet after Ed and Layla arrived, stomped the newly fallen snow from their shoes, and exchanged hugs, the boys swapped nervous glances.

Instead of Layla's usual "Wolfy, Wolfy, swing me around," or "Frankie, look how high I can jump," their cousin uttered a single word: "Hi."

"Here, let me take your bags," said Uncle Frank. "You two go on and sit by the fire and warm up." Avis bustled toward the kitchen. "Hot cider's coming up."

"Want Wolfy to ride you piggyback?" Abbey asked. Layla's eyes lit up. Abbey raised her eyebrows in her brother's direction and gave him a penetrating look. "Sure," Wolfy said, and knelt down. "Hop up, Layla." He rose carefully. "Hold on tight," Wolfy cautioned, concerned by how fragile his cousin looked.

Ed was already settled in an easy chair in front of the

fireplace. "There's a box in my suitcase for you kids if you want to go get it."

Frankie, who Avis swore was part rubber ball, bounced over to Ed and hugged him. "Thanks, Uncle Ed." Then the seven-year-old raced toward the sewing room that doubled as the guest bedroom where Ed slept. Layla bunked with her cousin Abbey just the way Abbey shared Layla's bed when the Lovell brood visited the Tompkin house. But, at the Tompkins', Wolfy and little Frank also slept in Layla's room on a cot that Ed set up at the foot of Layla's bed. At night, the girls attempted to doze off but were thwarted by the boys, who whispered and argued about hogging the bed and snickered in the dark as they dove under the covers to smell each other's cabbagey farts until Abbey ordered them to "Stop it!!"

Sometimes, when the weather was good, the boys camped out in a pup tent in the front of the Tompkin home. But by morning, they both were back inside, spooked by a an screeching owl or a possum rustling around in the brush.

"It's darker than a stack of black cats out there," said Wolfy, who was accustomed to the brightly-lit streets of Shady Grove.

As the cousins crowded into Avis's sewing room where the daybed, usually piled high with mending projects, was made up for their uncle, Abbey said, "Let *me* open Uncle Ed's suitcase." Ever the arbiter of how things should be done, Abbey shoved Frankie to the side. "You'll just mess up everything."

Being the oldest, it was Abbey's job to look out for her brothers and cousin – authority she used to lord over her younger charges. But Abbey came by her clout naturally too, as there was a good bit of majordomo in her. Certainly, Layla could be mulish. But Abbey went right past obstinacy to getting her own way, even when she wasn't at home.

When Layla's three cousins came to visit her in Fox Hollow, the cousins made mayhem while Avis scrubbed floors, washed curtains, and linseed-oiled the furniture in the five-room log house. While Avis spiffed up hearth and home, buoyed by the feeling that she was providing earthly hands for her sister, there were stretches of time when the children did chores. They shelled peas, swept, and hoed weeds till they got blisters. Other times they ran around playing any game they could conjure up.

Fox and dog was a favorite, aside from the fact that Abbey always got to be the fox. Whenever the cousins played the game, Abbey piped up before anyone else could get a word in edgewise, "Oldest gets to choose first." The only exception was that you got first dibs if it was your birthday. "You're the dogs," Abbey would say, no surprise to the others. The dogs had to run around gathering up worm-coddled apples from the trees so that fox-Abbey could drop them into a trail of clues. Then Wolfy, little Frank, and Layla would try to track the fox to its hidey-hole.

Once, before Layla lost her tongue, the "dog pack" was so engrossed in sniffing out the fox, they rounded a bend without proper attention to their surroundings and found themselves between a very upset and very real mama bear on one side of the lane and her two cubs on the other side.

"Be still," little Layla whispered. Wolfy and Frankie screamed so loud that Abbey, who wasn't far, came running from the opposite direction.

"Shush! Don't move!" Abbey said. "Now back away *real slow*!" To distract the growling mass of brown fur, Abbey, who was nine at the time, gently rolled one of the runty little apples from her pocket toward the bear. While the mother of the cubs kept an eye on Abbey, who was as equally frightened and determined, the bear sniffed in the direction of the apple that landed a few feet away. Abbey rolled another fruit. When she saw that her brothers and cousin were out of sight, she warily began to retreat. By the time Abbey was almost to the mailbox at the bottom of the lane, she heard her frantic mother and uncle calling and saw Ed, shotgun in hand, racing toward her.

When they got back to the house where Layla, Wolfy, and little Frank had been ordered to stay put, Ed was uncharacteristically angry and told the kids, "Keep in seein' distance till you get growed up and get more sense!"

Abbey's quick thinking and courage in the face of danger earned her the name of "Mama Bear." And everyone knew you didn't mess with a mama bear.

In her mother's sewing room, Abbey unlatched her uncle's suitcase, lifted out the box, and handed it to Frankie. He shook the box. "Another puzzle!" the seven-year-old said. Puzzles were a holiday tradition that Ed started years ago when he mounted a poster – usually a nature scene – onto Masonite and jigsawed it into shapes. Over the seasons, the pieces grew smaller and smaller to challenge the children's agile hands and wily brains.

"What's it a picture of this time, Layla?" Frankie asked.

A hush descended over the sewing room until Abbey broke in. "Does it have mountains?" Layla nodded. "Animals?" Wolfy asked. Layla nodded again.

Frankie chimed in. "Are there any dogs?" Layla shook her head.

"We'll find out when we put it together," Abbey said.

"Let's go spread out the pieces on the table."

With Layla still hanging onto Wolfy, the cousins trotted into the living room to the card table Avis always set up in the corner so the youngsters could detour from their play and fit another piece into the picture.

Layla, watching from her elevated vantage point, slid off Wolfy's back and plucked a corner piece out of the pile.

"Look! Here's another corner," said Abbey. Before long the children were fitting together the outer edges even though they didn't have a clue of what went where. Through trial and error, a landscape slowly began to take shape.

By suppertime, Layla's curtailed speech didn't seem so odd, though the normal decibel level of the cousins was considerably subdued. Following grace, the cousins – except for Layla – competed for the prize of gnawing a turkey leg after the meat was cut off, and getting a piece of crispy skin from the turkey breast by shouting, "my turn!"

Layla sat silently and sipped soup while her cousins all clamored for the tastes she longed for: turkey, green-bean casserole with fried onions, candied yams, and mincemeat pie. But after the meal, Frankie, Wolfy, and Abbey, as if by prearrangement, made sure that Layla ended up with the wishbone. Layla tucked the splintered bone into her pocket and fingered it, hoping for her wish to come true. And that night, when she crawled into bed, she slipped the broken *Y* under her pillow. But in the morning, the remnant of her tongue hadn't grown longer. And it worked no better than it had the day before.

CHAPTER FOURTEEN

LAYLA was almost seven. She squatted on the front porch, placing her hands over old Mr. Jackson's right sock that smelled like mushrooms gone slimy. "Gout's got me good, this time," he said. "Over more to the big toe, honey. That's the ticket. Yes...you're right there on it. Yes, indeed."

The hair above his sock was coarse and springy as a Brillo pad. Not at all like the silky leg hair of the mill boss's wife, Nancy Addison. When Layla put her hands Mrs. Addison's sprained ankle, swollen double and the color of an eggplant, the child felt a strange intimacy, like they were whispering secrets to each other. A sweet cloud of perfume engulfed Layla as she worked on Nancy Addison, unlike the body odor that lurked like bagpipe drone beneath Mr. Jackson's clothes.

While Layla was laying her hands on Mr. Jackson, Ed kept a careful eye out through the kitchen window while he cleaned up breakfast dishes and processed batches of Layla's blender soups.

Ed was still trying to sort out the snake story and Layla's knack for healing, whatever the cause. If it was a Godly gift – how else could it be explained? – it wouldn't be right to forbid Layla to use those gifts as long as she seemed to want to. And it wouldn't be right to take money. So the ailing brought offerings in exchange for the healings of his mute daughter. Preserves, a chicken, bartered services.

Time and again, Ed asked his daughter if she'd rather be doing something else. But Layla insisted that most of the time she *liked* helping people. When it made them feel better, she felt better too.

Doc Fredericks, however, continued to be skeptical about the healing. In fact, at Layla's recent checkup, he said, only partly in jest, "Don't know why I studied all those years in medical school when people flock to a child for healing."

But for Ed, his daughter's power to heal was born out by too many examples to ignore, and people stood in line to have the hands of his little girl placed on their ailments. Not surprisingly, congregants of the Holiness church sought out Layla. But so did a number of town folk, members from other churches, and even some of Ed's fellow workers at the mill.

Layla didn't understand her healing gift any better than her father did. She was still trying to figure out what she was supposed to do for the people who came to her pleading, "Lay your healin' on my *arthur-i-tis*, Layla." "Knit back my splintered foot bones." "Take the cares off my heart." Obediently, the child placed her hands where folks said they hurt.

Layla knew it was selfish thinking, but there were times she wished she could be running around instead of sitting with her hands on one person after another.

While most children Layla's age played and involved themselves with everyday doings, the young healer was gradually learning anatomy and physiology through her hands. She learned to pay attention to bone structure, muscle tone, temperature, and pulses.

For the most part, any doctor could make similar observations. But there was something else. Something so strange, so out of the ordinary it put Layla in mind of the freak show she'd heard about.

The year before, when Layla was six, Ed took her to a circus that came through Wayland. Along with the spot-lighted performers – the tutu-clad poodle mincing on its hind legs as it pushed a baby carriage, the droopy-eyed, flop-footed clown in polka dots, and tumbling acrobats that stacked up on top of each other like a fancy wedding cake – there was a separate tent off to the side accessible to those willing to ante up a quarter to gawk.

"Inside that tent are folks who are different," Ed said. "They might be real tall. Or shorter than you. Hairy all over like a bear. Or odd-shaped.

"Mind you, they get hungry and tired just like everyone else. The men put on their pants one leg at a time and the women like what they like and don't like what they don't, just like you and me, Ducky."

When Layla realized nature's oopsies were quarantined just like people who had tuberculosis, she feared she might be looked at the same way if she revealed the weird sensations she experienced during her healing sessions.

When whomever she was working on started to breathe in unison with her own slow breath – a telling sign that God energy was coming through her hands – Layla noticed that when she touched a person, fully clothed as they always were, somehow emotions vibrated through her fingers. Colors too.

With her hands on someone's cough-wracked chest, she sometimes felt bilious green clogging her own heart. Cupping around the neck and under the chin of a ravaged throat, she saw undisgorged black. And splaying her fingers like a sunflower over a cramped belly, she'd sometimes shudder with red-hot rage.

Layla quickly learned to let the feelings of another pass through her the way a stream takes up bits and pieces of all it flows over – rocks and weedy green, tadpoles and trout – and continues to move on. Though it never occurred to Layla to lay healing on herself, she tried, when she remembered, to let pain flow away. And she kept her odd ability to see color and feel someone else's emotion as secret as her dread of hiss.

Just as Ed was packing boiled potatoes and steamed spinach into the blender to liquefy into Layla's soup, the phone rang – Avis's Saturday call.

"Ed, I'm at a loss," Avis said. "Between Camp Fire Girls, Boy Scouts, Little League, PTA, choir practice, and everything else, my brain is a pretzel trying to squeeze an hour out of the day, much less a day in the month to come."

Avis continued to fret. "Because of Frankie's baseball tournament, we can't even make it for little Layla's birthday this year. But we're sending her seven presents – like birthday candles – one for each year."

"We'll miss you. 'Specially Layla," Ed replied.

The overtaxed father didn't let on how much *he* depended on Avis's coming, as well, especially since he felt that just below the surface, his capabilities as a parent were always inadequate.

When she visited, his sister-in-law dealt with tasks Ed had no time for, or that were as foreign to him as Borneo or the Cameroons. By the time Avis left from her quarterly whirlwind visits and headed back on the hundred-mile trek to Shady Grove, father, daughter, and the house glowed with deep-down attention.

Now that his sister-in-law wasn't coming, Ed figured he'd better tackle the refrigerator, long overdue for a defrosting. The freezer section was such an igloo of ice he could hardly wedge in the cartons of ice cream that made up a sizable part of Layla's diet, especially in her fortified milkshakes.

Forty minutes later, the phone rang.

"Hi Ed. Avis again."

"Everything all right?"

"Oh yes. Except letting our times together start to slide by didn't sit right with us. And this idea started brewing. Actually, Abbey suggested it. So I wanted to run it by you."

"Go ahead, Avis. Only walk, don't run, so I have time to give it a look as it goes by."

Since the phone cord had enough stretch, while he talked to Avis, Ed continued to exchange pans of hot water with drip trays of melted ice.

"Remember after Layla's accident when I had to leave and Layla was so low and hurting?"

"I do," Ed replied, wishing he wasn't gripped by a knot of fear every time Layla cried since then.

"And, it being summer, how Abbey came down to visit Layla on the Greyhound all those times?"

"I do. Regular little nurse she was, doin' all the things the doctor said to do."

"Abbey was ten that summer. Now I know that seven years old is quite a bit younger. But we could do the same thing we did with Abbey. You put Layla on the bus in Wayland. Sit her right up near the driver where he can keep an eye on her like we did with Abbey. And we'll meet her at the station in Shady Grove. Think of the load of things she could do, especially during the summer, while you're at the mill. Be a nice change from her usual. Swimming at the pool, picnics, the library, bowling, sidewalks to roller-skate and ride bikes on. And you know we'd just love her to pieces."

"Somethin' to think about, Avis. Somethin' to think about," Ed said, with the same caution he was exercising to carry an almost-to-the brim bread pan of hot water over to the refrigerator.

Though Layla didn't make a big deal out of it, in his heart, Ed knew his daughter's summer bore little resemblance to what Avis proposed. He didn't have to be at the Yeagleys' to figure out what was going on. Word got around. Hearing the number of reports about "who" got helped with "what" by his daughter's hands, Ed knew Ida Mae had Layla doing more healing than playing.

Added to the ever-growing reputation of Layla's healing power was the fact that she was such an enchanting child. Ed was conflicted and didn't know whether he should insist that his little girl be treated like the Yeagley children or any other seven-year-old, or let Layla use her God-given gifts to help others. It was a hard call. So was his answer to Avis about letting his daughter taste the delights of everything her aunt could provide for her that he couldn't.

"Course, Avis," Ed was quick to add, "even if it sits right with us, it's Layla who'll have the final weigh-in on how she feels. But I'm guessin' she'll go for it faster than I can get the words out of my mouth."

"Oh, I hope so," Avis said.

"Tell you what. Let me give it a think through, run it by Layla, and give you a call back later."

"All righty then," Avis said. "Talk to you later. Hugs to everybody."

"You too." Ed held the phone between his ear and shoulder until he finished balancing a pan of ice melt, on the brink of spilling, back to the sink.

Harder to steady was his gut reaction to the thought of letting Layla out of earshot, out of easy reach. And the secret fear that she might prefer life with her aunt's family.

Before becoming a parent, Ed never understood how much could be at stake with the decisions he made," even a commonplace choice like leaving a window open on a warm night.

CHAPTER FIFTEEN

"JUST so you have them," Ed said, as he printed out the names, telephone numbers, and addresses for both ends of his daughter's journey before she climbed on the Greyhound to visit her aunt, uncle, and cousins. For most of her trip, Layla was no more concerned about something going awry than she was about her pigtails that hadn't turned out right that morning – one fat, one skinny.

But as the bus passed Shady Grove's municipal park, the Jefferson Hotel with its green awning and mammoth planter of pink begonias and ornamental grass out front, and the big plate-glass window of the Wells Fargo Bank, the seven-year-old's eyes widened and her breath came in little spurts at one possibility suggested by the cardboard square that hung on a string around her neck. "What if they aren't there?"

"There's the bus!" yelled little Frank, bouncing with spring-loaded exuberance. The sports-crazy nine-year-old was pencil-thin. "Not enough thickness to make a shadow," his father said.

Ten-year-old Wolfy and soon-to-be teenage Abbey were too old for such juvenile displays, but that didn't stop them from waving so energetically they looked like they were trying to erase the blue from the sky.

As the bus swung into the station, Layla, nose pressed to the window, strained to see if anyone was waiting. When she caught sight of her uncle and cousins, her clutch on the neck-dangled card relaxed and she waved back.

"Here's our little Layla," Uncle Frank said, as he lifted the little girl down from the top step of the bus and swung her around in the luscious July air. Uncle Frank's upper lip bore the scar from a repaired cleft palate when he was a baby. His mouth was slightly off center, as well. But his voice was as warm and even as his personality.

"Brass tacks," Ed once said about Frank Lovell. "Gets the job done, but with class."

The bus driver handed down Layla's brown Samsonite suitcase. Even though the luggage was nearly empty, it weighed almost as much as the little girl.

Avis suggested that her niece bring something that would accommodate Abbey's latest hand-me-downs and the jars of watermelon pickles, blackberry preserves, stewed tomatoes, and such that her aunt always brought when she visited Ed and Layla.

"Trip good?" Uncle Frank asked.

Layla nodded happily.

"Did you get numb bum?" Wolfy asked. "That's what I get when we drive a long way."

"Gotta make a quick call before we leave," Uncle Frank said. "Your dad is on pins and needles till he knows you're here safe and sound. And your aunt is home about to bust a gusset waiting for you. Need to use the restroom, honey? Two hours is a long stretch." Layla shook her head.

"Everyone in the car, then," Frank said.

The kids played rock, paper, scissors on the car ride home until Frankie started with the knock-knock jokes.

"Wait!" said Abbey. "Let Layla do the *knock knock*. Like this." Abbey rapped her knuckles against the car frame.

As Uncle Frank stopped at a red light minutes from Oak Street where the Lovells lived, Layla knocked against the car door. "Who's there?" Wolfy and Abbey chimed in unison.

"Pencil!" replied Frankie.

"Not that one again," Abbey groaned.

"Pencil who?" asked Wolfy.

"Pencil fall down if you don't have a belt!" Frankie laughed so hard he hiccoughed.

Little Layla was happy through-and-through. At the Yeagleys', she never felt like she belonged the way she did at home or with Auntie Avis, Uncle Frank, and her cousins.

"How come," Frankie said, scratching a mosquito bite, "when people bite you the bite goes *in* but when bugs bite it pops *out*?"

"Poison," Wolfy said.

Layla wished she could tell her cousins about the swallowtail butterfly she found on a log, its striped wings barely fluttering. When she bent closer, she saw an assassin bug injecting poison and sucking out the butterfly's liquefied insides. That's what her father said when she showed him her journal with a picture of it.

That's so cruel, Layla wrote when he explained what was happening.

"Dying is as natural as bein' born, Ducky," Ed said. "There are slow ways to die and fast. Can't do much about either one." But his heavy sigh afterward made Layla think her father wasn't entirely satisfied with that explanation.

When the Studebaker pulled into the driveway of the Lovells' yellowy-beige house, expectation and thrill washed through Layla the way it did when she read *The Wizard of Oz*.

Hopeful. That's how the story of Oz made her feel. Just keep trying and everything that feels like a big hole in your life will get filled up. It seemed that yellow brick roads and yellow brick houses led Layla to all that was wonderful.

As soon as Uncle Frank stopped the car in the driveway, Frankie jetted out before anyone else. "Last one in is a rotten egg," he called. "Ida Mae Yeagley would never have brooked such disorderly nonsense," thought Layla, as she and Abbey waited politely for Uncle Frank to unload her suitcase from the trunk.

When Layla entered Auntie Avis's sewing room, there was a gift-wrapped box in the center of the daybed.

"Open it, open it," everyone kept repeating.

Excited as she was, Layla eased the cellophane-taped ends apart so as not to tear the wrapping paper.

"Go ahead and have at it," said Uncle Frank.

Layla tugged it open, dug down inside the wads of newspaper and pulled out a metal skate.

"Awhhh," she exclaimed, and immediately pulled out the mate.

"Try 'em on," said Abbey.

After tightening the sliding metal plates into place with the key and cinching the straps, Abbey gave Layla a little shove so that she rolled across the small room. The kids took turns catching her on the other side.

"Everybody come get some lemonade," Avis said. "Then go outside and play."

Layla coasted from dresser to door. From hallway to the kitchen table and then, hanging on to the porch handrail, clonked down the porch steps to the sidewalk.

Inside the phone rang. Avis pulled herself away from the living-room window where she was watching Abbey teach Layla the basics of start and stop.

"Ed. What a surprise? Didn't Frank call to tell you Layla got in just fine?"

"He did, Avis. I'm calling for another reason. Wish I didn't have to, but Mrs. Yeagley just phoned. It's about Petey – her son with palsy. He got sick a week ago and now he's taken a turn for the worse. Ida Mae is distraught as can be. She's asking for Layla to come back and treat him."

"Oh Ed," Avis said. "Sad as it is for that poor boy, they have Layla all the time. Don't pull her back early. She's having so much fun here, just being a little girl with no other responsibilities on her."

"I know, Avis. But Layla and Petey, well, they're awfully close. I figured it should be her decision too."

"Ed, I think that's an awfully big burden to put on her. She's outside roller-skating right now, you should see her!"

"Well, where Petey is concerned, I'm not sure Layla would see it that way."

"Can't Doc Fredericks help him?"

"Evidently Doc was up there yesterday. Gave him a penicillin shot. But he warned that bronchitis is often too much for kids like Petey. That's why Ida Mae thinks that God-healing is the only thing can save him."

"Can we sit tight, Ed? Just for today? See how he's doing tomorrow?"

"I suppose so, Avis. I'll let Ida Mae know we're gonna wait a bit."

Outside, after twenty minutes of scoot and glide, Layla got the hang of skating. She was starting to go faster when she heard her aunt calling her from the front door. Avis looked so perturbed, Layla wondered if she had done something wrong. "Your daddy's on the phone, sweetheart. Wants to talk to you." She handed Layla the phone.

"Hi Ducky. Havin' a good time?"

"Ahhuh!" Layla said, out of breath from coming in so fast.

"You know how we always talk things over?" Layla knew something serious must be at stake and pressed the phone closer to her ear.

"Well, Petey is having a bad time of it. Coughing pretty bad. Mrs. Yeagley called to see if you could come back and help him. I hoped we could wait till tomorrow to see how he was doing, but she's not easy with that. You know it'd be fine in my book if you wanted to stay there and see how things go. But it's your decision, Ducky. Want to think about it and call back?"

"Oooh," Layla said, nodding her head, emphatically.

"Okay, then, Ducky. I'll be there to meet your bus in Wayland. Put Avis on, again." Layla handed the phone back to her troubled aunt.

"Just a second, Ed," Avis said. "Layla, honey. Go get your things together."

"A real shame all the way around." Layla heard Avis say.

When Ed and Layla showed up at the Yeagleys' that evening, Ida Mae led them into the living room, where Petey was propped up on the sheet-covered sofa, away from the hubbub of the rest of the household.

"Penicillin's kicked in and his fever's broken," the worried mother said, briefly touching the back of her hand to her son's lolling forehead. "He's a good deal less phlegmmy too."

Ed watched his daughter yawn from a long day, then kneel down beside Petey. She cooed to his slumped body. Petey responded with a wheezy moan, punctuated by several weak coughs in rapid succession. Back and forth the two went, cooing and moaning, sounding like they were speaking some private language. Then Layla placed her hands on the thirteen-year-old's birdcage chest. Only the crying of a child from another room and the muffled voice of someone talking interrupted the heavy quiet that settled over the living room.

Ed watched, quarreling with himself. Petey, frail though he was, didn't seem all that sick. One part of Ed wanted to shake the substantial body of Ida Mae Yeagley and give her a piece of his mind. Ed felt even guiltier about bringing Layla back from Shady Grove, especially since he'd overridden his sister-in-law's advice. Also, he never felt easy about exposing his daughter, with her own vulnerabilities, to ailments that were contagious. When it came to weighing his daughter's welfare against the needs of others, Ed wasn't always sure how or where to draw the line. Having a daughter with special needs and special gifts was a balancing act he was still trying to figure out. "Should've listened to Avis," he thought.

A half an hour later, as Ed drove his dozing daughter home and tucked her into bed, the nauseous feeling in his stomach was less about missing supper than what a disappointing father he was. Still, if he kept Petey's illness secret and Layla found out about it, he would be guilty of lying – a cardinal sin, worse than anything else, in their household. In fact, whenever Ed saw Layla beating around the bush about something that happened, he reminded her, "We know we can trust each other if we always tell the truth." Could he do less?

Avis and Ed agreed that Layla should return to Shady Grove as soon as the Yeagley boy was out of the woods, and Layla, as much as she loved Petey, was relieved she wasn't going to lose out on her entire vacation. So, the next day when she went to the Yeagleys' to treat Petey, she was further relieved he had perked up, stopped wheezing, and his cough was down to nil. It being Sunday, one of the few that the Yeagley family missed church because of illness, Ed said he would come back for Layla in an hour, hoping to get his daughter on the afternoon bus to Shady Grove. But when he returned, Layla was in the kitchen treating Mr. Harpster's cataracts. There were four other people standing in line.

Ed was extremely put out with Ida Mae. "Finish up what you're doing, Layla. We've got to get going."

With a squirming four-year-old in tow, a young mother entreated, "Can't she stay a while? I need help something desperate." The flowers on the woman's dress were as faded looking as she was. "A lump," she whispered, gesturing modestly to her left breast. "Think I've got the cancer."

"I'll get my father to drive Layla home, later," suggested Rebekah Yeagley, who was shepherding people in and out.

Ed looked at Layla. "*Time to go.*"

Layla looked at the frantic woman and the distress of those who waited. She knew how she would have felt if anyone refused relief to her after her tongue was taken. *No*, Layla shook her head.

"All right then," Ed said, dreading another call to Avis. "I'll be home if you need me."

The small boy was now gyrating and holding his crotch.

"Caleb," Rebekah said, pointing. "The bathroom is right down that hall. Rachel'll take you."

Mr. Harpster squinched his eyes shut and blinked them open several times after Layla lifted her hands. "Clearer," he said, smiling. "Long as I don't shoot my dog, I'm good to go hunting."

Caleb's mother was next in line. Layla was fearful because she knew people died from cancer. The woman sat down and Layla started to position her hands, self-conscious because of the location she needed to touch. Just then, the little boy hobbled back, his pants around his legs, screaming.

Ida Mae poked her head into the kitchen and demanded, "What in the name of Sam Hill is goin' on?"

"I don't know, Mama," Rachel said. "Truly I don't. I flushed the toilet after he finished his business and he ran off before I could get his trousers up."

"Whirlypool! There's a whirlypool in there," Caleb

sobbed. "You told me don't go near 'cuz they suck you down."

"That's a different kind of a toilet is all," the red-faced woman said, pulling up her son's underwear.

"Awfully sorry for the disturbance, Mrs. Yeagley. Outhouse is all he's used to."

To avoid further embarrassment for the boy and his mother, people suppressed their amusement and turned the conversation to the size of the corn crop this season and the number of Japanese beetles.

Layla placed her hands lightly over the woman's chest area, grateful that everyone's attention seemed elsewhere. She was relieved that the sense she picked up was water. Water lumps made her hands feel *fizzy*. Scar lumps felt dead as the poor swallowtail butterfly, sucked dry of life. And cancer lumps sent sharp lightning bolts into her palms.

The young healer treated another woman for dizziness and a man with a swollen elbow. She thought she was finished when someone else showed up. "Keep blowin' and blowin' but my sinuses fill right back up. Aches somethin' awful right here under my eyes."

It was almost suppertime when Layla heard the phone ring. "Your father wants you home now," Rebekah said. "Says he's comin' to get you, no two ways about it."

❧

The next morning, Ed put Layla on the early bus before he went to work. Layla was thrilled when she arrived in time to visit a veterinary clinic along with the twelve-year-olds in Abbey's Camp Fire Girls troop.

That night the cousins used stuffed animals and Abbey's doctor's kit to play animal hospital.

"What's wrong with your patient, Layla?"

Layla pointed to the bear's stomach.

"Oh, a stomachache," Abbey said.

Layla shook her head and fumbled in her skirt pocket for a pencil and notepaper. All her clothes had pockets, and if they didn't, Aunt Avis sewed one in.

A bee, Layla wrote.

"A bee?" asked Abbey, doubtfully. She was busy examining the floppy ears of a rabbit.

From the honey he ate.

"That could be serious. We might have to operate."

Layla nodded, enthusiastically.

"Be right back."

Abbey trotted into the sewing room where Layla was staying even though, more often than not, Layla snuck into Abbey's room, crawled into bed for an extra bedtime story, and the two cousins ended up falling asleep together the way they usually did when Ed was there too.

Abbey returned from the sewing room with a sharp

scissors, a spool of brown thread, and a needle. Layla watched aghast as Abbey jabbed the scissor points into the bear's belly.

Abbey cut open the bear's abdomen and rummaged around in the lumpy stuffing before plucking out an invisible bee with a tweezers.

As Layla watched, mesmerized, she wished there were a way to go inside her own body and yank out her secret terror of hiss. But the problem was that Layla had no idea where her fear was hiding. She wouldn't know the place to begin looking any more than she knew where the "soul" was that Ida Mae talked about saving and keeping pure.

Sometimes Layla felt the fear of hiss in her brain. Other times, at the back of her throat where the air went down or in the muscles that gripped the sides of her neck all the way to her shoulders. Or clamped around her ribs and inside of her stomach. Or in her kneecaps that clenched so tightly, they hurt. When that happened, Layla felt like she would snap in two, like Ray Runkle's guitar string the time in church when he turned the tuning peg too far.

Abbey closed the bear up with neat little stitches. When the bandages were in place, Layla gave the bear's stomach, now lopsided from uneven stuffing, a moment of healing touch. Abbey watched Layla and then put her hands next to her cousin's until they were touching.

"How do you make your hands hot like that?" Abbey

asked. Layla shrugged. "Do you *think* something to make them that way?"

Layla shook her head, realizing that when she was in the midst of healing she didn't think about anything except the other person. Like hiding in a coat closet or being underwater, everything seemed different from normal. Slower. Calmer. More silent.

"Come on," Abbey said, hearing the television go on in the living room. "*Ozzie and Harriet* is on." They crowded onto the couch with the rest of the family.

By the end of her visit, Layla was roller-skating with ease. She'd seen *The Music Man* at the drive-in movie. Watched performers on the Ed Sullivan show and afterwards, the four cousins tap-danced on the driveway, clickity-clacking noisily because of the Coke-bottle caps they'd pressed into the bottom of their sneakers.

With her blond hair tinged green from swimming-pool chlorine and scabs on her knees from a skating fall, Layla rode the bus home, her mind full of dreamy memories from her two-week stay, and her suitcase full of clothes, homemade jam, and books from Abbey.

Layla was excited to see her father. And excited, if he agreed, to let her make the journey back to see her cousins in August.

On the bus, with a skate key around her neck, the seven-year-old felt bigger. Her heart felt bigger. Her world felt bigger.

Layla returned to Ida Mae's strict regime of chores and *thou shalts* and long hours of laying hands on one person after another. When the eagle-eyed matron demanded, "What's got into you, Layla Tompkin? Mopin' around like a sad sack," the little girl just shrugged.

"Then put a smile on your face and gratitude in your heart. You know," Ida Mae said, lifting the child's lowered chin, "you can always tell your troubles to Jesus?"

Layla nodded. She was grateful that Petey recovered. And grateful too that she didn't have to touch Zeb. It was a giant relief to Layla when the eighteen-year-old troublemaker ran off, though it knocked the starch out of poor Ida Mae for the longest while.

After work, when Ed came to pick up Layla, he noted the difference too and decided that Shady Grove was a good place for Layla to spend some vacation time every summer.

Over the ensuing years, Layla came back a little altered after each visit. Painted fingernails. Knowing how to make meringue – *mer-in-goo*, Auntie Avis called it, laughingly. How to French braid her hair. And what to do when her *time* came.

When Abbey learned to jitterbug or do the twist, Layla learned. As a popular city-girl teenager, Abbey introduced her country cousin to rock 'n' roll and the Beatles – the devil's music, according to Ida Mae Yeagley.

And every year, her reputation as a healer grew.

CHAPTER SIXTEEN

SCHOOL ended earlier in Fox Hollow than it did in the city, so Aunt Avis invited Layla to come to Shady Grove a week before Abbey's graduation from high school. "That way, Ed can join us for the ceremony and afterwards we'll have us a *double* celebration," Avis said. "*Two big milestones!* Abbey a high school graduate! And our Layla turning thirteen!"

One of Abbey's classmates was having a dance during the week and Avis urged her niece to go. Layla balked. It wasn't that she couldn't dance. Her cousins taught her to "cut a rug" in their Shady Grove living room. Wolfy once swung Layla around and dipped her so far back she choked on her own spit. But being a force of nature, Auntie Avis prevailed. As stand-in mother bird, she was trying to find ways to push her fledgling niece out of her woodland nest into a wider social world, a world where she'd have more choice, more opportunity.

"There, look at you! So grown-up," Avis said, as she brushed her niece's long blond hair, swept it up into a chignon, and pinned the new do in place.

At home, Layla was more familiar with cotter pins than hair pins. With her hair straight and loose, rubber-banded into a ponytail, or in one long pigtail in the back, the newly turned teen cared little for fuss and muss.

"Honeybunch, hold your mouth like this," Auntie Avis said. She dabbed soft, rosy gloss onto her niece's lips. "Turn around and look," Avis said, swiveling Layla around to face the bathroom mirror. "Now don't you look *extra* pretty!" Avis's voice had a catch in it when she saw the spitting image of her dear, gone-too-soon sister reflected in the mirror.

At the party, when she wasn't dancing, Abbey stuck by Layla and whispered in her ear, "That's Chip. He's Mr. Popular and, boy, does he know it. Over there, the groovy-looking girl with the Twiggy hair, that's Charlotte. She's super-nice but she scandalized the school when she showed up in hip-huggers. When Mama told Gramma Lovell what happened, you know what she said?"

Layla shook her head.

"This is so funny." Abbey bent closer to her cousin's ear. "'Now-a-days,' Gramma said, all proper sounding, 'with the boys and their long hair and the girls parading around in pants, you have to turn 'em upside down and shake 'em to see if they're male or female.'"

They both giggled. But Layla knew most folks she came in contact with would agree with Grandma Lovell.

"See that girl in the chartreuse dress over by the punch bowl?"

Layla nodded.

"We call her Sox." Seeing her cousin's puzzled look, Abbey explained. "Because she stuffs her bra so she'll look bigger."

Layla was mystified. The hundred miles between the cousins was, in many ways, the distance between two worlds. By the end of the evening, Layla's cheeks ached from smiling so much, and she was weary from nodding at all the silly chitchat. Despite Avis's valiant attempt, Layla's preference for staying home to play gin rummy with Frankie or read a book was as stubbornly fixed as ever.

Abbey was already excited about starting nursing school in Petersburg come September, eager for her life to be full of changing places and faces.

I don't want to lose you, Abbey, Layla wrote before she left. *You're my best friend.*

"We'll be together on holidays," Abbey said. "And we

can write letters to each other all the time. Don't worry, Layla. Nothing in the world could ever separate us."

Back in Fox Hollow, shortly after returning from her cousin's graduation, Layla and Ed were in the Piggly Wiggly doing their big monthly shopping.

Before Layla lost her tongue, their shopping trip also included going to the Wayland Hi-Boy and ordering the blue-plate special. After their meal, she and her father would split a piece of the pie of the day. But pie and blue-plate specials were now just savored memories.

Rounding the corner of the beverages aisle, they bumped into Mrs. Markham, one of Layla's teachers.

"Ed, Layla," Mrs. Markham said. "Look!" She reached up to a high shelf and pulled down a box of Lipton tea bags.

"For months my tendonitis was so bad I couldn't even raise my arm to write at the top of the chalkboard. Layla gave me treatments at lunchtime."

Layla looked down at her feet. She liked her teacher and was glad to help, but it made her look like such a brown-nose to the other kids who either thought she was a celebrity or a freak.

"It's unbelievable. Just unbelievable!" Mrs. Markham said. "I've been so busy with end-of-school tasks, I haven't had a chance, but next week, I'm bringing something special over to show my appreciation."

"No need," Ed said. "Glad you're on the mend." He was pleased that Layla got on well with her teachers and was an *A* student, though he wished she had more friends her own age.

Mrs. Markham squeezed Layla's wrist gratefully and continued down the aisle.

Loading a can of Folgers coffee into their shopping basket, Ed said, "Ducky, why don't you go get your ice cream."

The indignant adolescent, reminding her father for the nth time, scribbled a note and thrust it in front of his face. *That's not a proper name for a grown girl!*

"I'll try and remember from now on," Ed replied, chucking his daughter under her fine-boned chin.

Most of the time, when her father slipped up and called her Ducky, Layla let it slide. She knew that if she glared at him, he would launch into a retelling of the day she was born.

He always began the same way. "Before nurse Lacey laid you in your mama's arms, she toweled off the wet and your hair was downy as a ducklin'. So from then on, I called you Ducky."

Ducky sounded fine when she was little, but downright silly now that she was a teenager. Especially since her duckling hair came halfway down her back and she was almost the same height as her father – five inches shy of the six-foot cellar door where, every birthday Ed measured with a yardstick to see how tall she grew that year. "If you get much bigger we'll have to get a new door," Ed said, making a mark with his thick-leaded carpenter's pencil.

At the end of August, before school started up again, Layla complained about going to the Yeagleys' after school.

I'm old enough to stay by myself, she wrote to her father in no uncertain terms.

Summer had been interminable, always at Ida Mae's beck and call, unable to go outside because she had to heal whoever in the family was ailing as well as the problems of others who dropped by. And Layla's annual summer vacation with her relatives in Shady Grove only reinforced her independent bristle.

When Layla first broached the idea of not going to the Yeagleys' after school, Ed countered: "Don't see any good reason to leave you alone in a house all by yourself."

Layla huffed off to her room. After half an hour she marched back to her father, who was flat on his back under the kitchen sink trying to fix a leak. She plopped a sheet of paper on his stomach.

Ed finished working on the drainpipe, sat up, wiped off his hands and, remaining on the floor, read the list.

You always say to make a Benjamin Franklin list when you have a big decision. So here it is.

Reasons Not to Stay by Myself

1. *Safety.*

Reasons to Stay Home by Myself

1. *The operator knows my emergency code if I need help.*
2. *I need more time to do homework.*
3. *I want more time to read.*
4. *I can't do what I need to if I'm doing chores and busy healing at the Yeagleys'.*
5. *I could get an earlier start on supper.*
6. *I could use the extra time to do more chores at home.*
7. *I've been riding a bus to Shady Grove by myself since I was seven.*
8. *I get tired of being around people all day.*
9. *I can keep the door locked.*
10. *Frankie showed me how to kick someone in the nads.*

Positive reasons to stay home = 10
Negative reasons = 1
Positive side wins fair and square!

When Ed ran the idea by Avis, she didn't see any harm in trying it. But Ida Mae Yeagley warned Ed against it, saying, "Calamity and sin are always vying for the upper hand, and leavin' a child alone is invitin' trouble."

When Ed decided to allow a trial period, Ida Mae said, "If it don't work out, Layla's free to come back. You know she is. And I was wonderin' if she might come a time or two a week and use her gift on us?"

"I'm sure she'll come by if you need her," Ed replied, taking note of whose welfare was foremost in Ida Mae's mind.

So, after several more weeks of arguing back and forth, the teenager won the right to stay at home by herself.

CHAPTER SEVENTEEN

AFTER school, on a blustery March day, Layla waved good-bye to Sarah Jane and hopped off the school bus. As soon as she disembarked, the first thing Layla did was to check the mailbox before walking up the lane to the house.

Ahhee! she shouted. A letter from Abbey! Now that she was newly alone with no one in earshot to question or judge what came out, Layla took pleasure in trying to vocalize more frequently. She sang songs and tried articulating in different ways, but her sounds bore little resemblance to the words that burned so clearly in her mind.

Ahhee, Layla shouted again. No matter what had

happened at school during the day, her insides did cartwheels whenever she saw mail from her older cousin.

After Abbey left Shady Grove to go to nursing school in Petersburg, their letters took on a deeper intimacy. Abbey focused less on the shenanigans of Wolfy, Frankie, and the family in general, instead sharing the details of her exciting new chapter of life.

Layla felt pride in the new direction it gave their relationship. Yes, *pride*. There was no other word for it. The fact that Abbey treated her cousin like a peer despite their age difference gave Layla a sense of self-importance – a character flaw that would have compelled Ida Mae Yeagley to peg her down a notch or three if she knew. Though Layla never could have added it to her Ben Franklin list, Ida Mae's constant criticism was another reason the growing girl was glad to be on her own after school. Clutching the mail in her hand, Layla trotted to the house.

On a mild day, the teen would have gone to her "thinking" rock to relish Abbey's letter. The flat-topped, massive granite boulder jutted out over the edge of the creek that bordered the Tompkin property and, as far as Layla knew, not a living soul ever went there except for the forest creatures. In the solitude of nature, the rock was her special place to read, write, or to let her thoughts flow with the stream's current. Sometimes she sat there so long she felt she was part of the rock, embedded beside the creek for more years than Moses and Methuselah put together. But it was chilly today and much too windy.

Once inside, Layla bolted the door, shouldered off her book bag, hung up her jacket, and bounced into the living room. Usually, the newly turned teen made a practice of doing an *extra* chore first thing, so she wouldn't forget. Something quick like dusting or wiping down the stove to prove to her father how responsible she was. But today she sprawled on the sofa and tore open Abbey's latest letter.

March 9, 1968

Dear Cuz,
Boy oh boy, more than halfway through my first year of nursing school and it still seems more like housekeeping than healing. Making beds, giving sponge baths, changing bandages, washing out bedpans. Still, I love it. I don't know if it's because I helped with my two little brothers or when I helped you after you lost your tongue, but it all seems pretty routine.

We're learning to draw blood and give shots. I keep thinking how great it would be if nurses could take away pain by laying their hands on a patient like you do instead of stabbing them with needles. I've always wondered how do you do that anyway. I know you've tried to explain it to me before, but I still don't understand what actually happens. Why do you think it works?

The head nurse says I'm good with people and have an eye for the kind of details doctors may not notice because they're so busy. The small changes that show whether a patient is on the way up or down. But she also says I have a mouth on me (surprise, surprise!) that's going to get me into trouble if I don't get it under control. Talking too much and saying exactly what's on my mind.

I wanted to tell her, "Too bad we can't all be perfect like you, Nurse Ty-D-Bol." But I kept my mouth shut. See how much I'm learning?

Guess what? I'm going to have my picture in the paper. Since our class is the biggest ever in the history of the nursing school, a reporter for the Daily Mirror is doing an article about us. He said the story would be about the urgent need for nurses with all the injured soldiers coming back from Vietnam. The reporter wanted to know if he could ask me a few questions to get a student's point of view. Hope I remember to "watch my mouth."

What's shakin' with you, Cuz? Any cute guys in eighth grade? Oh! And congratulations on getting your period! Ain't being a woman fun! Seriously, though, I think if all that hassle means I can have a baby, it's okay by me.

Write! Write! Write!

Can't wait to see you at Easter.

Tons of love,
Your Abbey

Layla had homework, chores, and then getting supper cooking, but she was so excited to get Abbey's letter she couldn't help answering her right away. In the kitchen, before she got paper and pencil from the counter, she took the dishrag and gave the stove a quick once-over, swiping under the grates of the gas burners to get rid of any lingering grease splatters. She wiped her hands and raced back to the living room to write.

March 16, 1968

Dear Abbey,
Abbey Lovell, Student Nurse! Just like all those Cherry Ames books.

In answer to your question, NO, there aren't any cute boys in my class. And if there were any good-looking ones, none of them would give me a second glance. Most kids think that because I don't talk I'm an idiot or a freak. Or both. Even though they know I make good grades. And even if I get their warts to fall off.

In your last letter you asked how I take away someone's pain. I wish I knew. Mrs. Yeagley keeps calling it a gift. But gifts, when you open them, have something inside. Maybe not like a pair of skates or a book, but something you could hang your hat on. Really, I don't think I'm doing anything but giving folks the comfort of touch, the way a daddy or a mama soothes you when you get hurt or sick. It seems to me some people are so hungry for the feel of a caring hand that if the Yeagleys' dog, Samson, put his paw on them, they'd feel better. But I'll try to describe what happens as close as I can.

When I lay my hands on a body, I feel things. Not feel-feel like if something is rough or smooth. It's more like a kind of knowing. I just know things and I don't know how I know them. But I bet that's happened to you too. Haven't you ever felt like someone was staring at you behind your back and you turned around and they were? Well, it's that kind of knowing.

Sometimes, when I put my hands on a person, I feel my heart wrench open till it brings me to tears. But whatever sense of ache or feeling I get,

I let it pass through me like the wind coming through one window and passing out another. All the while, I'm just letting go of my own self and letting God be the wind blowing away pain and affliction and me be the window.

I bet you could do it, Abbey. I really do. You should try it sometime. Everybody has some secret power. It's your own special voice.

Please, please, please send me a copy of the picture and newspaper article you are in. I hope you didn't say anything about Nurse Ty-D-Bol. She could flush your straight A's right down the commode.

Won't be long until we come for Easter. Daddy said it's kind of sad that all us kids are too big for Easter egg hunts, now. Wouldn't it be fun to color eggs and hide them for all the grown-ups? I guess maybe now that you're away at school, you're almost one of the grown-ups too. I hope we

Layla's pencil froze midair.

She rolled off the couch to the floor and silently crept to the kitchen window, stooping so low she was practically crawling. Branches snapped and there were distinct rustling sounds as something retreated from the laurel bushes.

A marauding bear? Lyman Jeeter? Some stranger?

Months after Layla's tongue was taken, the sheriff finally located the Jeeter brothers back at home.

"Trapping beaver," they told him. "Make us money selling the fur. Smoke the meat for winter."

"Takes a sharp knife for skinning," Sheriff Dones said, wrangling offhanded interest.

"Yup!" Lyman said, with a perfunctory nod.

"Hard to keep an edge on it?" asked the sheriff.

"Got me a good flint," Joab, the younger brother said, reaching into the pocket of his filthy dungarees.

"Never could get the hang of a flint," the sheriff said.

Joab's face, grimy as a coal miner, lit up. Though the brothers, both somewhere in their twenties, were no doubt resourceful, living alone with no nearby kin, surviving by the skin of their teeth, Joab bit the sheriff's bait unwitting as a first-season trout. He entered the dark interior of their one-room hovel and returned, knife in hand. The five-inch blade was well equipped, in experienced hands, to swiftly sever, slice, gut or surgically remove one body part from another. Holding the flint in one hand and the skinning knife in the other, Joab summoned a sizable hawker, spat on the stone, and proudly demonstrated how to angle the blade for the sharpest edge. The sheriff's subsequent questions, however, relating to the night of Layla's tragic loss were unproductive. With a trapping trip as an alibi and no witnesses or evidence to prove otherwise, Sheriff Dones left, handcuffs still jangling from his belt loop.

Since Layla no longer heard sounds in the bushes outside, she rose from her semi-crawl and peeked out the window of the kitchen door. Cautiously, she unfastened the bolt and eased the door open a crack, ready to slam it shut. Even though she promised her father she'd stay inside with the door locked, she unlatched the screen and took a tentative step onto the porch. She sniffed for bear. Listened and looked for movement – a futile effort with the gusting wind lashing leaves and branches. But she was certain she heard something out of the ordinary. She stood on the front porch for a while, then went back in, re-bolted the door, and finished her letter.

There was a commotion outside near the laurel bushes. I've been hearing it for a few weeks now but I can't tell Daddy because he'll say it's too dangerous for me to stay by myself. I didn't find anything, but I'll keep you posted. See you in twenty-nine more days.

Mountains of love and a bushel of hugs and kisses,

Layla

Hurriedly, Layla folded and sealed the envelope so her

father couldn't see the part about unexplained noises. If her father knew, he'd insist she stay with the Yeagleys after school and Ida Mae would have her busy every minute. Being on her own, Layla felt positively liberated. Time to be herself. Time for other things besides healing, healing, healing. *Happy as a tick on a fat dog*, her aunt would say.

She just had to be extra-careful from now on.

CHAPTER EIGHTEEN

WITH her long, fifteen-year-old legs, Layla jumped off the school bus, just missing an icy patch. When she tried to open the mailbox and her fingers fumbled inside her thick mittens, she overreacted with pent-up fury.

During study period, she'd been so deeply engrossed, reading about Jacques Cousteau's underwater explorations, she was caught by surprise when the schoolroom radiator hissed into superdrive. In the relative quiet of the classroom, Layla's gasp, accompanied by the sudden jolt of her traitorous body, drew all eyes as well as a few knowing snickers. Inside the teen, her heart banged against her breastbone while, outside, she feigned composure.

With ten years of practice, Layla knew to camouflage her features until they were as smooth as a Sunday tablecloth. She lowered her eyelids over her over-widened eyes. Relaxed her squeezed-together lips. Softened the muscles of her face. And burned in shame at the public nakedness of her fear.

Still smarting from the humiliation of today's incident, Layla wished there was a way to worm out of tonight's Valentine's dance at Cumberland High. Maybe she could come down with the flu, break an ankle, get abducted by aliens. Maybe horrible weather would blow through and cause another cancellation the way it did the week before when the dance was called off because of an ice storm that turned most of the roads within a fifty-mile radius of Fox Hollow into skating rinks. Power lines went down right and left and every twig, branch, and pine needle was encased in crystal.

Layla didn't have a date for the dance. Still, she was obligated to go and go *early* because she was on the decorating committee – finagled into helping on account of her artistic skills.

But all of Layla's frustrations evaporated when she pulled a letter from Abbey out of the mailbox. She whooped her way up the lane to the house when she stopped short.

An unfamiliar car, motor running, was parked near the front porch. Her mind raced. Head back to the main road? Take off into the woods through the snowdrifts? Risk finding out who was in the car? Suddenly, the motor went silent, the door opened, and out stepped Joella Bates carrying her cumbersome two-year-old grandson.

"I'm sorry not to wait till your father gets home," Joella called out, as Layla came near. "I know you don't see folks 'cept when he's here but I hoped you would lay healing on little Willie."

Layla, flustered and perturbed, indicated with an apologetic shrug that she wasn't allowed.

"I know your father's rule, honey. But look at little Willie's face. He's so swollen with the pox, you wouldn't know if his eyes are brown or blue."

Joella had tied socks over her grandson's relentless little fingers to keep him from clawing the flesh off his arms and cheeks.

Too cold to settle the matter outside, Layla unlocked the door and motioned them inside.

Before she took off her coat, Layla grabbed paper and pencil. *Can't Doc Fredericks help him?*

"Doc says, nothin' to do but let the pox run its course."

Layla was in a quandary. Even though when she laid her hands on people, she had sensations – heat, tingle, color and emotions – deep in her heart she felt most of what she did was give comfort. She wished she had some confirmation otherwise, but just last week, Mr. Leos, who she'd been treating for a while, died from heart failure.

And though many claimed she eased their pain, Layla could see that the bulk of ailments would, left to their own devices, run their course with or without treatment, just like Doc said.

"How could she turn them back?" Layla thought. Surely her father would understand. And the faster she got to it, the quicker she could read Abbey's letter.

Grandmother Bates plunked little Willie onto the living-room sofa and spread out the quilt that was bundled around him onto the seat cushions. Meanwhile, Layla smacked her cold hands together, vigorously rubbing them to spark circulation. Cupping her hands over Willie's head, over the stiff clumps of pinkish brown, matted with calamine lotion, Layla worked her way down the boy's oozing pustules from face to feet.

"I have another grandson, grown now," Joella rattled on as Layla worked on Willie. "He's a gem. Real intelligent. Asks more questions than a Philadelphia lawyer. He didn't get that from licking the wallpaper, I can tell you. His mother's smarter than a tree full of owls. He became a preacher, he did. Not a man-made preacher. He was God-called. Next time he comes to visit, I want you two to meet."

"*Ucchh!*" Joella winced, massaging her fingers. "I have arthritis in this hand so bad. Maybe you could give me some help after you're done with Willie."

Layla, eyes closed, nodded.

"This is a fused finger," Joella said, rubbing her pinky. "Didn't I go to the basement and fracture it. Last year I had what you could call a pimple that kept bursting open and Doc Fredericks said, 'Joella, we better take care of it. Infection could get in there and go to your knees.'"

Fidgety Willie relaxed and settled down. His eyelids fluttered closed. While little Willie snoozed peaceably on the living-room couch, Layla tended to his grandmother's painful hands.

At the end of the treatment, Joella tried to put a folded bill into Layla's pocket. "I know you and your father favor my plum butter. But I couldn't carry over a jar and carry Willie too." Layla, who never accepted money, refused.

As soon as grandmother and grandson were out the door, Layla washed her hands of calamine and pox crud and ripped open Abbey's letter.

February 15, 1970

Dear Cuz,
News flash! I'M ENGAGED!

Who would have thought that two years after that quiet fella came to our nursing class to take pictures and write an article, he'd be asking me to marry him. On Valentine's Day, too! We had a date to go out for supper but I was late getting off my shift at the hospital and totally beat. When I got back to my apartment Roy was waiting, half-frozen because the heater in his Plymouth is on the fritz.

I got ready to go for the steak supper he promised and he said, "Abs, would you mind proofing this article I have to get in before my deadline tonight?"

I was tired. I was hungry. So you can imagine how friendly I was. I groaned and took the copy, plopped down on couch and started to read.

February 14, 1970

If all goes well, twenty-three-year-old newsman for the Petersburg Daily Mirror, Roy Brooks will soon be reporting from a new location.

When I read that first line, Layla, I turned the color of a hospital bedsheet. "Keep reading," Roy said.

He will be moving to an unknown address in order to undertake additional assignments. But this can only be accomplished if Abbey Lovell, the woman with whom he wants to spend the rest of his life, will agree to marry him. Why a knock-out of a girl, smart, funny, full of life would go for an underpaid, nearsighted journalist like Brooks is a mystery. But life is a gamble and he can't imagine existing without her.

When I looked up, Roy was kneeling on the floor holding a ring in his hand. I'm sure you don't have to guess what I said. Even though it's soon, we're thinking of getting married at the end of July when everyone has vacation time.

So here's the big question. Will you be my maid of honor? You just have to say yes.

It's past midnight now, but I had to write to you. I know we'll be together for your fifteenth birthday in June but I'm hoping we can get together before that because Roy wonked his ankle up pretty bad. It's been swollen and painful for three months ever since he tripped over a curb trying to get a photo. The doctors want to put a cast on it and he hates that idea. Don't want him limping down the aisle. Do you think you could come to Petersburg? Soon?

A heartful of love,
Your Abbey

Layla felt she was about to burst open, unable to contain all the excitement and joy that was brimming inside. Roy's proposal, Abbey's wedding, asked to be maid of honor, getting to see her cousin soon – it all came together like one of those final chords in a hymn where everything sounds so full of harmony and upliftment, so full of "now and ever shall be," you just soar right out of your skin.

She took out a pencil and paper to write back, but all she could think to say was, *Yes!*

Yes! Yes! Yes!

CHAPTER NINETEEN

GARLANDS of hearts cut out of glossy paper hung from the gymnasium's basketball hoops. Streamers festooned the ceiling and bleachers, each end tied with a cluster of red crepe-paper roses. A giant collage poster with cutouts of celebrity heartthrobs was taped up in back of the cafeteria table where the social studies teacher, Mr. Boyce, sat changing records and trying his best to keep the party lively, but in control.

Her decorating job complete, Layla put her nylon footies and white pumps back on. Her shoes were far too slippy to wear while standing on ladder tops and climbing up and down the bleacher steps. Since Layla had been Ed's helper from the time she was little, and was no stranger to ladders and hammers, she was elected to put up the ceiling swags and posters while the other girls arranged cookie platters around the punch bowl and positioned the dishes filled with pastel Necco candy hearts embossed with *Be Mine*, *Love Bug*, *Class Act*, *Sweet Talk* – all the catch phrases Layla couldn't say and nobody ever said to her.

From the sidelines, Layla watched couples on the gym floor dancing cheek-to-cheek to the blaring PA system. Hovering by the refreshment table, Layla saw giggly females flounce their skirts, preen their hair, and sip cups of red Hawaiian Punch spiked with ginger ale. She noticed how they eye-flirted with the strutting males who snarfed down brownies and laughed too loud. "Hens and roosters," she thought, "showing off for each other."

Though Layla wasn't fooled by the blatant mating display, her curiosity was, nevertheless, piqued by the girls in her class who dished about every detail of every boy they made out with. With all the twittery folderol over boys, Layla had a potent desire to discover what the fuss was about, however unlikely her prospects.

That's why after Mr. Boyce announced, "All right, everybody switch partners," Layla was not only vulnerable but receptive when Rance Avery, one of the finer-looking specimens in the tenth grade, walked over and ask her to dance.

As they slow-danced to the Carpenters "Close to You", Rance slid both arms around Layla's willowy waist. Anchorless, Layla placed her hands, embarrassed at how sweaty they were, on Rance's shoulders. By the time Karen crooned, *so they sprinkled moon dust in your hair of gold, and starlight in your eyes of blue,* Rance was gazing into Layla's extremely blue eyes.

Layla didn't know whether to look into Rance's eyes or put her head on his shoulder the way the other girls did. While most of the couples swayed, stepping from side to side, barely moving, their bodies getting closer and closer, their mouths meeting in closed-eye kisses, Layla was too nonplussed to do anything but smile bashfully and lower her eyes. But by the end of the song, the repeated refrain, *close to you* reached deeper and deeper inside Layla and, as the music swelled, so did indescribable urgencies. Rance, gripped by a similar surge of hormones, lowered his face to Layla's and pressed his lips against her lips. Layla felt a warm, thrilling rush spread through her body. But when Rance thrust his tongue inside her mouth and probed its strangely cavernous inside, the spell was broken. Although Layla was intrigued by the sensations of Rance's tongue against her teeth and inside her cheeks, with nothing but a stub, she was at a loss about what to do in return. Seconds later, the kiss, her *first*, was over.

"Thanks for the dance," Rance said. He gave her

shoulder a perfunctory squeeze and headed over to the punch table.

Abandoned mid-floor, Layla felt so many eyes staring at her, she beelined to the girls' restroom, closed herself in one of the stalls and sat there trying to process what had just happened.

After the dance, other kids teased Rance for trying to French a girl with no tongue. Called Stumpy behind her back, Layla knew the improbability of ever getting kissed again.

Like Doc Fredericks, who doctored almost every man, woman, child on the mountain and, on occasion, even doctored a mare having a difficult birth when the vet was on an all-nighter, Layla was asked to lay hands on most folks for one thing or another. On top of being called Stumpy, Layla could feel any notion of romance drain away once she touched a boy for an ailment.

Over the years, she cleared warts as big as raisins from Buddy Martin and his brother, Cam. Normally, warts fell off a day or two after she put her hands on them. Folks tried the usual remedies – castor oil, banana skin, raw bacon – but, if the warts persisted, they came to Layla. Rodney Foster's mama brought him in for toothache almost as many times as he had teeth in his head. But accident-prone Bucky Bates took the prize when it came to the number of times she'd ever healed a boy. Bucky's mother constantly hauled him over for sprains and strains and begged Layla to help him so he'd stop grousing and quit shirking his chores.

Infected wounds, acne, bellyaches, ear complaints – Layla touched more boys in her high school years than Lanie Oakes, who was what Auntie Avis called *fast and loose.* Lanie slowed down considerably when she got herself a bun in the oven shortly after her father found Dill Martin on top of her in the barn. Holding a shotgun on the two, Luther Oakes ordered, "get hitched or *else.*"

Layla realized she had more chance of "getting hitched" to a team of horses than to a marrying man.

During the remainder of high school, Layla wasn't much for parties and dating.

Tagging along to that awkward party with Abbey, and the Valentine's-party kiss, did nothing to dispel Layla's opinion of boys. Neither had the skeezy advances from the oldest Yeagley boy, Zeb, before he ran off.

So from tenth grade on, the teenager's social life consisted of school, visiting Abbey at nursing school in Petersburg, spending time at her aunt and uncle's in Shady Grove, and going places with her father or Mrs. Phoebe. Along with homework, healing, cooking and chores, not much time was left for thinking about the inane ditties her classmates wrote in each other's autograph books:

I wish you luck. I wish you joy. But first of all a baby boy. And when his hair begins to curl, I wish you then a baby girl.

Or

Two in a car, two little kisses. Three days later, Mr. and Mrs.

And then there was the singsong rhyme other girls teased each other about with each new boyfriend:

First comes love. Then comes marriage. Then comes blank-blank with a baby carriage.

By graduation, all the girls had their name filled into "blank-blank" at least once.

All except Layla.

PART III

TESTED

CHAPTER TWENTY

IN 1972, Layla was in her last year of high school. Abbey had been married for nearly two years. And Vietnam landed on Doc Fredericks' front porch bearing his legless son, Brian.

Brian had planned to join his father's medical practice in a few years. Or, if he married the sweetheart he left in North Carolina, maybe open his own office in Durham.

But two years before, after graduating from medical school and in his second year of internship at Duke University Hospital, the patriotic twenty-nine-year-old enlisted as a medic.

Brian's mother, Eileen, distraught by the news, tried

to dissuade her son. "Why get into that terrible mess when you're exempt from service?"

"I can't stand by and watch so many shot-up, hacked-off men coming back from 'Nam and do nothing."

For three interminable months after the land mine blew off Brian's legs, Doc attempted to alleviate his son's agony. He tried every pill, shot, and combination of pharmaceuticals – narcotics, anticonvulsants, antidepressants, and local anesthetics. Doc consulted with Walter Reed Army Medical Center. He phoned experts around the country who were dealing with a steady stream of amputees returning from Vietnam.

But time after time he heard the same thing. "Finding a treatment for phantom pain is challenging. We don't know the cause. And for difficult cases, we haven't found a cure."

The physician heeded every shred of advice. Medications were administered, along with a good measure of optimism. A physical therapist was engaged to stretch, strengthen, and put Brian's stumps through range of motion. Once a week, Eileen Fredericks drove her son to a psychiatrist in Petersburg, banging her own legs black-and-blue as she loaded and unloaded the cumbersome metal chair from the trunk of their Buick. But nothing curbed Brian's excruciating pain.

"Not good," Brian would say after another night of

agony, growing more and more laconic with pain and hopelessness.

Doc was at a loss. A physician, who couldn't help his own flesh and blood. A husband, unable to ease his wife's anguish as she put on a prosthetic smile each morning and went to bed sobbing, the bags under her eyes permanently swollen with tears.

Finally out of options, Doc found himself grasping at straws. Desperate straws. As a man of science, his mind balked. But as a father, he felt duty-bound to explore every possibility. One by one, Doc and Eileen considered the alternatives.

"We could fly to Lourdes," Eileen said, too distressed to fully consider the hazards of crossing continents to bathe Brian in the grotto springs. Doc shook his head. "Awfully risky trip for a long shot, Eileen."

Needing to try something, anything, Eileen said, "My cousin says there's a Native American healer in the Dakotas who does wonders...cancer, mental illness, all manner of maladies."

"Again, with no guarantees, it's a risky trip for Brian in his condition. Why don't we look for something closer." Doc gave his wife a consoling pat, hardly able to bear her look of despair.

"What about Layla Tompkin?" Eileen suggested, unwilling to give up.

"I suppose it's worth a try," Doc said.

So the doctor called on the much-praised local healer, seventeen at the time – the little girl he knew and cared for since two weeks after her birth, when her distraught father brought her in for what turned out to be the colic. During those seventeen years, Doc Fredericks saw Layla through the croup, the chicken pox, a bad bout of tonsillitis and, most notably, the trauma of losing her tongue when she was five.

Though most people would say a serpent bit off the little girl's tongue, the doctor never, not even for a minute, believed such malarkey. "Might as well believe in the tooth fairy," he thought, frustrated that the sheriff's investigation came up empty-handed and that the truth never surfaced.

Before his son's return from the war, when Doc Fredericks thought about faith healing, one word came to mind: *placebo*. Doc was incredulous and mildly perturbed that so many of his patients chose to go to Layla.

When Layla arrived at the Fredericks' Doc introduced her to Brian – a more chiseled version of his father, but with a forbidding countenance and haunted eyes.

When Brian saw the young healer hesitate, a smile softened his features. "Thanks for coming. Appreciate it," he said.

Layla stooped down in front of the injured soldier's wheelchair and glanced up at Brian.

He nodded. "Go ahead. Whatever happens will be fine."

Even though Layla was well-acquainted with the power of the unseen, the first time she worked her hands down Brian's thighs to where his legs used to be, that limbless space sent so strong a shock wave through her she would've been knocked down if she wasn't already kneeling.

There was no way to explain why the searing throb of Brian's missing limbs subsided when the mute teen placed her hands on the space where, once, his size 34 long trousers and 11½ shoes had been. But it did.

"Unbelievable. I can barely feel anything!" Brian's voice was flooded with emotion.

When Layla's first session brought Brian relief, uncertainty began to worm deep into Doc's core. His concept of hooey turned into the smallest flicker of hope. Guarded to be sure, but nonetheless, *hope.* From then on, Layla treated Brian on a regular basis.

The sixty-year-old physician researched everything he could find about spontaneous healing. If Doc wasn't summoned on an emergency house call, after office hours and before weariness dragged him to bed, he poured over his medical journals until he fell asleep in his reading chair. Silently, he sat and observed firsthand how his son's intractable pain vanished during Layla's prayerful ministrations. For days afterward, as well. Yet Doc couldn't determine whether the relief Layla provided was medical mystery or miracle.

Miracle was a word that stuck in the doctor's skeptical gullet, no more swallowable than snake oil – stuck in Doc's spiritual craw as well, as he cared for his maimed son.

Though Doc adhered to scrupulous methodology himself, he recognized that the practice of medicine was as much art as science, especially in a country setting where old fashioned "can-do" sometimes had to substitute for the care options at Mercy Hospital, eighty-five miles away.

There were no procedures in the medical tomes that addressed some of the unusual situations a rural doctor faced. Like the time Velda Uddie went into early labor during a blizzard. The storm dumped three feet of snow on Wayland and blanketed the entire Tennessee region of the Great Smoky Mountains. Doc plowed his way to the outskirts of town on his neighbor's tractor and delivered a baby so premature it was still covered with silky lanugo.

Holding the newborn, hairy as a little monkey, in the palm of his hand, Doc asked, "Think you can find a small, sturdy container?"

Len Uddie quickly emptied a cigar box that held the proud-papa tokens he wasn't expecting to pass out for several more months. Doc padded the box with a diaper, worn soft by copious washings from five previous Uddie babies, and put little Georgie into the warming oven of the woodstove until the roads cleared enough for an ambulance to get through.

Sixteen years later, in his office that occupied a wing on the first floor of the Fredericks' home, the doctor, stethoscope looping out of the pocket of his white coat, held open the waiting-room door.

"Come on in, George," Doc said, his moon face widening with a benign smile. Beneath his wire-rims, the doctor's keen eyes were already assessing the problem.

As the teenager limped from the waiting area into the examination room, stoically masking the pain of a high school football injury, Doc chuckled to himself. Every time he saw George, growing more good-looking and husky by the year, he couldn't help remembering the boy's precarious entrance into the world.

Yes, Doc knew that a dose of encouragement, even if it was nothing more than a warm cigar box, could be as potent as a shot of penicillin. Yet, when it came to faith healing, his logical brain mutinied at the lack of demonstrable data.

For a great many, however, no logical explanation was needed. *They believed!* And a good deal of their belief was confirmed by the power that flowed from the hands of Layla Tompkin.

On the night when Eileen Fredericks sponge-bathed five-year-old Layla's red-stained body, back when Vietnam was a faraway country of lithe, tea-colored people in lampshade hats, with rice paddies not yet soaked by American blood, it was unfathomable that, twelve years later, she would be washing her grown son's remaining limbs. And that the little girl whom she buttoned into Brian's pajama tops would be relieving his suffering.

No words were adequate for Brian's respite from pain. But underneath each reprieve there was a fierce arm-wrestle of emotions. A slam to one side was the possibility of cure. To the other, fear that over time the benefits of Layla's healing would diminish or fail completely.

The stakes were too mind-bending to comprehend.

CHAPTER TWENTY-ONE

FOR months, Layla went to the Fredericks' to treat Brian's phantom legs. During their time together, Layla, now eighteen, and thirty-year-old Brian grew increasingly close. On several occasions, Brian caressed Layla's hair as she worked on him.

"Sorry," he'd say, and quickly pull his hands away.

Layla kept her focus. But not always. At times, Layla was drawn away from that place she disappeared into during a healing session, acutely aware of the feel of Brian's hands. How capable they felt. How tender. So unlike the pawings of Zeb or the fumbling teenage boys.

Brian's desire moved her in ways she couldn't explain and aroused in her a strange longing.

Because Layla cared so deeply about Brian, she was discouraged that there would always be a temporary lull in his pain but no lasting improvement. She often brooded as she rode the bus from Wayland back up the mountain, wondering if she made the right decision to devote her life to being a healer.

After graduating from Cumberland High, Layla struggled with a fork-in-the-road choice. Go to college, or heal full-time.

Her family and teachers urged college.

"Your mama dreamed you'd go to college," said Ed. "We talked about it before you were born."

"A librarian," Auntie Avis suggested. "You'd be a wonderful librarian, loving books the way you do."

"Think of all the people you'd never meet otherwise," Abbey said. "Maybe, even your future husband, like me."

Mrs. Phoebe secured two scholarships so that Layla could attend college in Petersburg. Layla even had a place to stay.

"You can live with us," Abbey said. "Roy says we can fix up the study for you. Nobody uses it now that he's been promoted to assistant editor and I'm full-time at the hospital. Just an empty room gathering dust."

But contrary opinions ignited like brushfire throughout the area.

"It'd be a mighty loss," was a phrase on the tongue of many. "A sin to receive gifts from God and not use them."

Ida Mae had drummed the "gifts" lesson home with a steady beat. As a young child, whenever Layla looked woebegone about staying inside to lay hands on someone's ailment, the zealous matron quoted scripture about responsibility.

"We all have different gifts, according to the grace given to us, Layla. *If a man's gift is serving, let him serve; if it is teaching, let him teach; if it is contributing to the needs of others, let him give generously; if it is showing mercy, let him do it cheerfully.* It's right there in the Bible, Layla.

"My gift is to teach you, like I do with all my children. And to serve my husband and my family. That's my job from God. And yours is to help others. Now go use your gifts *cheerfully*."

Layla dithered back and forth. One day she was inclined to continue with her education, the next day, she was not.

"Let's go to Petersburg and visit the college," Mrs. Phoebe said, "just you and me. We'll walk around the campus, get a Coke in the student union, meet with a freshman advisor. Maybe even take in a movie afterwards."

Layla went through the college catalog, savoring the courses in her mind as if she were reading the menu of a gourmet restaurant. She hungered for learning.

Still, she felt responsible to those she treated. It was a good feeling too, thinking she was helping people.

❧

When Mrs. Phoebe picked up Layla to go to Petersburg it was beastly hot – the kind of heat that slapped you in the face when you walked outside and sucked the energy out of you like a soda straw. Though Layla had many other teachers, Mrs. Phoebe kept in touch with her star pupil, sometimes inviting her to special performances or movies in the city.

"After Tom died in Vietnam, I never got to have children of my own," Mrs. Phoebe said. "Tom and I were hoping to start a family after he came back from the war. That dream died when he did. So now my students are my children."

Layla followed Mrs. Phoebe across the quadrangle to the advising office. In all her eighteen years, she'd never seen such an imposing accumulation of bricks and mortar. Such great expanses of mown lawn.

The advisor, Mr. Gregory, in a white short-sleeved shirt and a clip-on bow tie, gave them a cordial greeting. He talked enthusiastically as he flipped the colorful pages of a brochure to illustrate the merits of the college, the faculty, the students, and the campus.

"Any questions so far?" he asked, addressing his query to Mrs. Phoebe.

No. Layla shook her head, pencil and paper in her lap.

"Let's take a look at your high school transcript," Mr. Gregory said, shuffling through Layla's file. "Impressive. Very impressive. Just the kind of academic achiever we welcome. Not quite the level of math we'd like to see under your belt. But we can double up on your courses the first year to catch you up to speed. And you'll need to fulfill a language requirement."

Layla looked at Mrs. Phoebe, petrified.

"Twelve credits of either Spanish, French, German or Latin. This year, we also started offering Russian," Mr. Gregory said.

Layla couldn't understand the benefit of learning another language when she couldn't even speak her own.

Couldn't I take something else instead? Layla slid her note over to Mrs. Phoebe, who posed the question to Mr. Gregory.

"I understand your reluctance, especially in your situation, Layla. But core courses are designed to give our students a well-rounded education. By the time you are a junior you'll have more freedom to pick and choose your courses."

Layla and Mrs. Phoebe shook hands with the advisor and, in the extreme heat, toured the campus with a student guide who chatted nonstop. Layla nodded as she tagged along, feeling like a bobblehead. By the time she and Mrs. Phoebe headed back to the parking lot, Layla's idea of what college would be like was as overcooked as she was. Juicy anticipation had boiled down to dry realities.

Afterwards, as the two made their way across town to the Center Cinema, the constant weave of pedestrians made Layla feel woozy. The passing cars and whining traffic chafed, a constant reminder to go, go, go, nagging that things needed doing. No time to slow down or be still even for the peace and pleasure of it. Life on the hurry-up.

"Air-conditioning! What a relief," said Mrs. Phoebe. She flapped open her red cushioned seat and sank down. Mrs. Phoebe undid the clasp of her handbag and fished out a hankie edged with frill as delicate as Queen Anne's lace. She dabbed the damp from her forehead, her upper lip, and the nape of her neck.

Later, Layla wrote in her journal. *The movie,* THE TEN COMMANDMENTS, *was an old rerun but one that Mrs. Phoebe thought we might enjoy. It showed Bible Moses big as you please up there on the movie screen witnessing miracles. Not everyday miracles like a lowly crawling worm transforming into butterfly. Or a tiny black seed growing into apples and more trees.*

No, the Moses miracles were miracles with a capital

M. *Flaming bushes that didn't burn up. A walking stick turned serpent. Seas opening up to dry land.*

After the movie, Layla treated Mrs. Phoebe to ice cream at Woolworth's. They sat down at the counter on revolving stools. After they ordered their sundaes, one strawberry, the other chocolate, Layla couldn't resist a spin.

While they waited Mrs. Phoebe asked, "Did you like the movie, Layla?"

The wide-eyed teen nodded, impressed. It was thrilling to see history fleshed out on the huge movie screen in front of her eyes. To see how things looked and sounded and happened way back when. But despite the tribulation and triumph of the story, something disturbed Layla.

She dug for her notepad and wrote, *I know God needed to make Pharaoh let the people of Israel go free, but why did God let little Egyptian children die?*

The soda jerk brought their cherry-topped sundaes mounded with whipped cream. Layla plucked her cherry by the stem and nestled it in Mrs. Phoebe's sundae.

Lifting one of her maraschinos, Mrs. Phoebe pondered her answer. Her brown eyes were the clear color of root beer that once had fizz, but ever since her husband was killed in Vietnam, they looked like a curtain had shut out the light.

"I guess there's different ways to think about the words in the Bible, just like there are different ways to show your faith in God." Mrs. Phoebe nibbled the cherry.

Placing the stem on her paper napkin, Mrs. Phoebe asked, "What did people in the church you went to with the Yeagleys think about Moses?"

One thing, Layla wrote, *is that the movie-Moses didn't look near as happy about obeying God as the people in the Praise and Glory Holiness Church. Moses didn't look any holier to have God in his life, either. Maybe the real Moses did, but Mr. Charlton Heston looked like he had more grumble than praise in that tight jaw of his.*

Mrs. Phoebe laughed as she read.

But I guess, Layla continued, *there's a difference between how some folks feel about God. Some get stiff knees praying while others feel a God-joy that makes them dance.*

Mrs. Phoebe tunneled her spoon down the side of her glass tulip dish, trying to get at some of the strawberry syrup that had run down. "How do you feel about having the gift of healing?"

I don't have the foggiest notion of God's ways, Layla wrote. She reached for her napkin and blotted a string of drool that was leaking from the side of her mouth.

Wishing she could write faster, she jotted, *There are times I can't begin to figure out why something happens or doesn't happen. I know I'll never understand so I just have to believe God has his reasons.*

"Did you know, Layla," Mrs. Phoebe said, her mouth not working so well because it was cold, "when I went to the university in Asheville before I came here to teach, I had a course where we studied about different religions. Why there are as many ways to believe in God as there are leaves on that oak tree out there by the curb. For instance, in Turkey. Remember Turkey from geography class?"

Sort of, Layla shrugged.

"Well, there are religious people called dervishes who whirl their way to God just like you say sometimes happened in the Holiness Church. And there's shaking and quaking and states of mystic trance the world over." Mrs. Phoebe spooned up some ice cream and sauce and let it melt in her mouth before she swallowed.

"There are folks who don't believe in medicine of any kind except the healing power of God, and some who believe God has called them to become doctors or surgeons.

"Some give up all their earthly possessions as a sign of faith," Mrs. Phoebe said, swirling her spoon in the softening pink. "And some praise God by filling up their churches with gold and silver and precious jewels. Some won't kill a fly because it's a creature of God and some kill thousands of people because they think it's the will of God. What strikes me peculiar, Layla, is that whether there's sameness or difference, everyone thinks their way is *right*.

"I suppose," Mrs. Phoebe continued, "that every soul on earth has a different way of hearing and seeing things."

Confusing, Layla wrote, getting a drip of chocolate sauce on the paper.

"I agree," Mrs. Phoebe said. "The questions drive me crazy. But so do the answers. Especially when I wonder why my dear Tom was killed by someone who didn't even know him. If they had, I'm sure they would have befriended him instead of throwing a grenade. I just keep trying to find a way to make some *goodness* come from all the sorrow."

Layla reached over and touched the hand of her friend. Heartache and uncertainty surged into Layla's fingers as if Mrs. Phoebe were Moses asking God how she'd be able to get through her sea of sadness into the land of milk and honey.

Layla knew that every soul in the world had something that wracked their heart or body at one time or another. It was humbling to touch on that kinship. After all that Mrs. Phoebe had done for her, Layla hoped she could offer back a bit of comfort.

Once she was home, Layla pondered her visit to the college. She knew she could learn about most things through books without the dilemmas of core requirements and loquacious classmates trying to exchange the usual pleasantries. The speechless teen couldn't imagine how she'd fit in.

And ultimately, Layla couldn't imagine living in a city full of car exhaust and teeming with people. Time in the city was unrelenting. No way to go fast enough to keep up, or slow enough to take it all in. She couldn't imagine being away from the pungent evergreens and quietness of the woods. Quiet so heavy its weight held you to the moment. She couldn't fathom living apart from her father.

I'm never lonely in the woods, she wrote in her journal. *There's a companionable ease among the trees and critters just going about the day with the plain truth of being. Foraging. Eating. Fighting for a patch or perch. Making shelter. Going about the business of begetting. Raising a family. And when the time comes, letting go without fuss or regret. People are a different animal.*

The good thing about having her days to herself was that the self-avowed bookworm had time to read.

The not-so-good thing about being at home all day was that some folks showed up at the door unannounced.

Healer, Layla finally decided. No looking back. No second-guessing.

Yet, soon after her decision, doubt began to seep into her heart and mind like dark water. Into her hands too, she suspected, because the ability to heal weighed on her more and more. Sometimes her "gift" felt more like a burden than a blessing, especially when she couldn't bring Brian permanent relief or when, despite her ministrations, someone died.

She began to feel she was slipping. After all, she reasoned, she once raised a dog from the dead. Was it because she wasn't going to church? When she was thirteen, staying at home by herself after school, trying to distance herself from Ida Mae, her attendance at the Praise and Glory Holiness Church had all but stopped.

To address her qualms about being a healer, one remedy that came to mind was to start attending church again. Attempt to get her ear closer to God's message for her. Because Layla's parents were Baptist, it seemed logical for the eighteen-year-old to start going to the Smoky Mountain Clear Springs of God Baptist Church. Ed went with her once, but afterwards said, "I've gotten out of the habit of dressin' up for the Lord who saw fit to bring me into the world without a stitch on. And," he added, "I feel more praiseful kneelin' in a row of peas than a row of people."

Layla knew her father depended on his weekends to undertake chores he couldn't get to on weekdays, so she hated having to borrow their only vehicle to drive to church. Ed needed the truck to haul brush, tinker with the engine, or change the oil.

Now a well-known healer, Layla already knew many of the folks in the Baptist congregation because they came to her for help, but none lived close enough to presume upon for a ride.

When the Yeagleys heard that Layla was attending church again, they drew her in like a bear to a beehive. They stopped by on their way to Praise and Glory Holiness

Church, pressing her to join them. It was hard to resist the cajoling of her childhood playmates. Jake and Micah, who were fourteen and sixteen, still lived at home. "God is merciful," Ida Mae proclaimed, knowing her youngest sons were not old enough for the war.

Sarah Jane, who graduated high school in the same class as Layla, lived at home as well, though the glint of her engagement ring presaged a change of address as soon as she and Bucky Bates tied the knot – assuming of course that, with Bucky's tendency toward accidents, he didn't trip and break his neck going down the aisle. But Sarah Jane was no stranger to mishap either, having almost drowned when she was five. One more reminder to celebrate life's happy moments at every opportunity.

Rebekah, Rachel, and Elizabeth had families of their own, now. Lizzie, two years older than Layla, was married and expecting. And no one knew the whereabouts of Zeb – or if they did, they didn't say, because the law was usually after him.

Still, it was poor Petey who always persuaded Layla to join them. From his wheelchair in the back of the hay wagon, Petey would struggle to sign *I love you.* It wasn't hard for Layla to interpret, since she was the one who taught him.

Petey was twenty-four even though he looked more like a scrawny kid of twelve. Doc Fredericks, by way of preparing Mr. and Mrs. Yeagley for the future, told them when their son was very young, "When a person has all the ailments that come with a severe palsy like Petey's, many don't make it past their teens."

Mrs. Yeagley was always reminding Layla, "God brought you to our family to keep Petey alive."

That was the part Layla didn't like about being given gifts of the Spirit – feeling that if Petey or Brian or someone else languished or failed, she was partly responsible. That maybe she wasn't trying hard enough, or that she was letting herself become so clogged up with selfish thinking and useless wishes that God's spirit couldn't get through.

Images from the movie kept playing and replaying in Layla's mind. She remembered how God turned the walking staff of Moses – a man who had trouble with speech the same as she did – into a serpent. And as further proof of His power, when God told Moses to *put out your hand and take it by the tail*, the serpent turned back into a walking staff.

Maybe, Layla thought, the serpent was a *sign* for her too. A sign of the direction that she needed to go.

A test to lead her out of uncertainty.

CHAPTER TWENTY-TWO

AFTER seeing *The Ten Commandments*, Layla's father said, "Ducky, you're grown now with a mind of your own. I wish you'd gone on to college, but you decided against it. Now I'm gonna voice another wish, and you can do as you please with it. You know I try not to judge what others believe or how they pray. But, since you're goin' back to the Holiness Church, I'm sincerely hopin' that you don't go handlin' vipers."

When her father said that, Layla got the distinct feeling that he and Mrs. Phoebe had talked privately and that both were worried.

"It's one thing," Ed said, "to lay healin' on Pastor

Simpson when the rattler got him. Or Elmer Stiles when the copper struck his hand. But you an' the Holy Spirit already wrassled with the serpent part of faith. You don't have a thing to prove to God about bein' true to His word. So let that alone, Ducky. You hear?"

Layla nodded.

Yet the very next Sunday, as steam rose from the asphalt after a drenching thunderstorm, the eighteen-year-old entered Praise and Glory's sagging wooden church and Jesus took hold of her spirit, once again. When that happened, no earthly promise to her father or herself was binding.

Ellie Mae Runkle welcomed Layla with a holy kiss on her lips. "Hello, sister." The members of the Holiness church, some twenty-five in number, greeted by laying the holy kiss of Jesus on one another, man to man and woman to woman.

Layla was wearing a blue dress. She loved sky blue because it was the shade of her mother's eyes. And her own. Fortunately, she hadn't cut her hair like some in her high school. The Holiness church followed strict dress codes. Long hair for women, short for men. Mostly long dresses for women. And no makeup or jewelry was allowed so Layla kept her gold locket from Auntie Avis hidden beneath her dress. The men wore shirts and slacks. A few came in their bib overalls since ties weren't required, which was a boon when the service became fevered.

Sissy Parsons shook her tambourine so vigorously it blotted out the dry rattle coming from one of the wooden boxes that contained a riled-up rattlesnake. Overhead, the whump of the ceiling fan added to the beat of the music.

Pastor Simpson spoke into the microphone and began his sermon.

"What does it take to be *faithful*?" He waited for the congregation to quiet down.

"The Bible says 'Be joyful in hope, patient in affliction, faithful in prayer.' Brothers and sisters, know that the testing of your faith develops perseverance. And perseverance must finish its work so that you may be mature and complete, not lacking anything." The preacher's sermon was followed by the familiar words in Mark: 16.

"In my name shall they cast out devils; they shall speak with new tongues."

"Hallelujah," the congregants sang out. "Sweet Jeezus."

"They shall take up serpents; and if they drink any deadly thing, it shall not hurt them; they shall lay hands on the sick, and they shall recover."

"Praise Jeezus!" everyone shouted.

Dolly started playing "I Saw the Light". Ray sang, his fingers chording up and down his electric guitar. To Layla, it felt like he was strumming on the ligaments that held her body together.

The worshippers began clapping to the beat.

No more darkness, No more night.

People jumped up and down in place and skipped along the aisle.

Now I'm so happy, no sorrow in sight. Praise the Lord, I saw the light.

Ned Cole started whirling. Whirling in circles round and round like he was caught up in a tornado of Spirit.

The air sparked like after an electric storm and Layla felt the Holy Spirit of God enter the room. There were shouts. *"Glory! Glory to God! Come into my heart, Sweet Jesus!"* Sobs of joy erupted. People prayed in tongues.

Melly Nibbs fell to the floor convulsing and speaking in tongues. *"Ladadadahdahda dahheeniosa..."*

"Hallelujah! She's got the spirit," Sissy Parsons shouted, shaking her tambourine.

Viola Flemming turned to Layla and cried, "Lord, lay your healin' on me. Drive the canker from m'bones."

Brother Fergus came over and anointed Viola with oil from a small vial and Layla felt the Holy Spirit start to pulse and tingle through her body. She laid her hands on Viola as did others who were nearby, all of them praying.

There was an ecstasy in that room and in Layla like no other. Peace and pleasure she couldn't describe. Unabashed wildness. Buoyant serenity. Pain and joy meshed together until you couldn't tell one from the other.

Kerosene mixed in water was passed around in a mason jar for drinking by those in the thrall of the Holy Spirit. Pastor Simpson and Treach Eckles got that tranced look of being anointed.

"Are you sanctified?" the preacher asked the congregation. "Sanctified to follow and obey the last words of Jesus?"

"In the name of Jesus," Pastor Simpson shouted. "In the name of Jeezus," the congregation cried out.

As the music intensified, Pastor Simpson reached into a wooden box near the pulpit and pulled out the fat, dark, muscular body of a five-foot timber rattler by its middle and held it aloft to God. The rattler was so thick around, the preacher's hand couldn't circle the serpent's body. The black-and-beige patterns of the rattler and the brown-checked shirt the pastor was wearing paired them together like one, united in the Holy Spirit.

The serpent waved to and fro, sniffing the air as Pastor Simpson danced from one foot to the other singing and praising and letting the serpent twine around his neck, slither over his head, and circle up his arm.

Treach Eckles, a whip-thin member of the congregation who frequently felt the call of the Holy Spirit to handle, reached into another box and pulled out a glistening jumble of snakes curled and coiled together – a cottonmouth and two copperheads – writhing in his hand like a tentacled sea creature. He held the knot of serpents up in the air in the palm of his hand like he was exhibiting a prize pie at the county fair. Treach lowered the twisting bundle and cradled it to his chest like a baby. Then he held the serpents out to the side in his hand and danced with jerks and hitches like the Lord was kinking his body with spasms of Spirit. The serpents were passed on. Layla reached out to take one. But, at the last minute, withdrew.

Buddy Wells took the copperhead, gently lifting it by the neck. He held the snake's long body up in the air and gazed at it, turning it this way and that like he was choosing a new necktie. Then he smoothed the dangling body of that copperhead from neck to tail, fingering it like silk.

Though the serpents seemed calmed by the surging music and the passionate praying, Layla, with her keen ears, sometimes heard hissing. That dread sound that usually stopped her blood cold was countered by such a feeling of rapture, she was freed from fleshly blight. Fear drained out and in its absence she was filled with pure peace.

Sometimes, when Layla thought of her mother or had a hunger for something she couldn't name and that nothing seemed to satisfy, she felt a powerful God-yearning. Those times, she was glad she had no tongue to plead for one thing and beg for another.

But then there were times she felt so full of God she was a creek flooding its banks. A tongue was useless because there were no words of praise big enough for all the glory she felt. Times when she felt God's presence everywhere: in the sun, the rain, in every breath of air. In her heart that pumped God from her head to toes.

Layla wished there was a way to hold onto that feeling in the fracas of daily life instead of getting sidetracked by so many no-count worries. But no matter how hard she tried to hang on to that feeling of bliss, when troubles came, she was, as her father often said, "full of wrath and cabbage."

Tossing back a veil of blond that enshrouded her face during her ministrations to Viola, Layla felt she fell short because she was blocking God's full anointing. Not allowing herself to follow *all* of the signs.

"I'll pray for God to tender my spirit," she thought.

"Even though it's the one thing Daddy warned me against."

CHAPTER TWENTY-THREE

ON the days when she treated Brian and anyone else who couldn't easily travel to her, Layla hitched a ride with her father as far as Wayland, a mile before he got to the mill. The stove was off. Windows closed in case an unpredictable October thunder-bumper. Her thermos was in her tote that already contained a hairbrush, tissues, lip balm, a nail file, an extra Kotex in case she got her "friend," a toothbrush to freshen up the scumlike film on her teeth that a tongue usually swiped clean, and emergency information that someone could read in case she got in a bind.

When Layla slammed the door of the truck and settled

into the seat it seemed like she covered every eventuality, but, over and over, experience taught her that life was dicey and full of the unforeseen. On their way into town, their truck could have a blowout. A rock could tumble from the mountain and kill them. Or the lottery ticket that Ed went in on with five men from the mill could win them a heap of easy living.

Ed wasn't enthusiastic about buying in on the lottery. "I've got my daughter," he said. "A house, a job, joints that bend without too much twinge, and a porch swing. What more riches can a man ask for?"

He left out the part about having a chronic cough from the built-up sawdust in his lungs. After a bad bout of coughing he'd sometimes say, "One of these days, I'm gonna cough up enough lumber to re-side the barn." But despite his thriftiness, Ed's fellow workers cajoled him into throwing a dollar into the lottery pot.

Layla knew a good part of her father's economies had to do with making sure she didn't have to work now or ever. Layla would have felt more sting in that knowledge except she did provide bartered benefits from her healing. The Tompkins' had a well-stocked larder and a variety of in-kind help, including free medical care from Doc Fredericks.

Layla pressed her father to take advantage of Doc's offer. Otherwise, Ed never would've gone for x-rays and prescriptions for his nagging bronchitis. When Ed stopped taking his medication because it made him dopey, Doc told him he should wear a mask to protect his lungs from further damage.

"Healthy is just a slower way to die," Ed replied, with a stubborn smile.

Just as Ed was resistant to pharmaceuticals, Doc hadn't put much, if any, stock in faith healing. Not until Layla relieved the pain in Brian's legs, even though they were rotting in pieces in some Vietnamese jungle. But Doc allowed that there were plenty of exceptions to the medical books.

"Layla," Doc said. "There's an ocean of things modern medicine doesn't have a clue about. I'd be hard put to say we held as much as one drop of knowledge from that ocean. I've seen people eaten through with cancer find relief from a sugar pill. And people languish and die from a broken heart. Shakespeare had more rhyme and reason in what he wrote than we doctors sometimes do. But whatever you do that's bringing relief to Brian, we couldn't be more grateful.

"And," the doctor added, "I'm sure the fact that you're an extremely pretty young woman touching him with gentle love helps his spirits as much as any medicine."

Layla blushed at the doctor's remark. Especially when she remembered times when she worked up Brian's thighs from their amputation above the knees and felt another stump straining against the material of his khakis.

Disembarking from the bus on her return home from treating Brian, Layla was caught in an undertow of leave-takings. Autumnal migrations. The slow leach of pliant green. The smell of ferment. Understructures blown bare.

She checked the mailbox. There was a water bill and a letter from Abbey. She slid the bill in her tote bag, perched on a nearby fallen log and ripped open her cousin's letter, eager for news and hoping to dispel the sad ache she felt.

October 18, 1973

Dear Cuz,
Some may remember 1973 because we are now officially out of Vietnam. If only people could see some of the cases that end up at Mercy they might wonder like I do – and I know you do too – how blowing out somebody's guts does any good in the long run.

Others may remember this as the year of the big Watergate scandal. But for me, it will always be the year somebody came into our lives that we don't get to meet until next May.

I'm sure you've guessed by now. I'm pregnant!

I was waiting to see if I skipped my period for a second month. Why they call it morning sickness is a complete mystery. For me it's all day long. Good thing there are handy little pans for such things where I work. I've eaten so many Saltines you could box me up and stamp Nabisco on my forehead.

The day after I got the test results and told Roy, I was lying on the couch after work. He told me to close my eyes. I heard a bag crinkle and Roy said, "You can open your eyes now."

He had the tiniest little shoes you ever saw on his pointer fingers and was making them dance on my belly. I could have just cried I was so happy.

I sure wouldn't want to go through this without him. Or without you. I'm counting on you to be there to help when the baby comes. And then to visit all the time. So mark your calendar now.

Got to make this a short letter and get to bed. I'm so tired all the time I nearly crawled into a patient's bed that I was making up while she was in x-ray.

Make sure you tell Uncle Ed for me. I made Mama promise not to tell anyone else until I told you.

Can't wait to see you at Thanksgiving.

Oodles of hugs and kisses,

Your Abbey (and baby)

Airborne as a whirling leaf, Layla floated home, hoping to squeeze in a letter to Abbey before folks showed up for their afternoon appointments.

October 25, 1973

Dear Abbey,
I can hardly believe you're going to have a child. How can something that occurs every day, everywhere, seem like a singular miracle when it happens to someone you love?

Of course I'll be there to help any way I can.

Have you tried red raspberry leaf tea or nettle tea for your morning sickness? Women around here swear by both of them. Hope you're over the worst of it by Thanksgiving. Smelling all that cooking food when you're nauseous is a torture. It drives me half out of my mind for the opposite reason.

Last week, when it looked like we might have our first frost, I picked all the unripe tomatoes and put up green tomato mincemeat for Thanksgiving pies. Daddy says, "If you could take a bite of autumn, it'd taste like what's in those jars."

Daddy was thrilled to hear about the baby

and said that Auntie Avis sounded like she was in seventh heaven.

Wolfy must be pleased as punch to be an uncle. Now that he's dating that secretary he met at the insurance company, he might not be too far behind. But I'd watch out for Frankie. Hand him his bundled-up niece or nephew and he'd just as soon play ball with the baby as burp it. By the way, tell Frankie congratulations for me on getting chosen for the Appalachian rookie league. Who'd have thought he might someday have a baseball card with his picture on it.

Me, graduated. You, having a baby. It's hard to imagine us all going off to our own lives. I can't grasp Auntie Avis being old enough to be a grandma. I know we've gotten older. But it takes me aback to think they did too.

Nothing much going on here. Just the usual. I'm going to the Yeagleys' church more and more these days. I know you asked why. I'd tell you the reasons but it's hard to explain. I'm so full of doubts. Does my healing really work? Is being a healer what I'm supposed to do? And now another confusion – last week a famous tent-preacher phoned, named Reverend Harry or Gary, wanting to know if I'd travel with him and offer healing during the revival services. I heard Daddy on the phone say, "Thank you for the offer, but that won't be possible." And then he said "no" four other ways. And finally he said, "That's my final word, Reverend." Afterwards, Daddy said, "You're of age now, Layla. It's your decision. But travelin' around like that, sleepin' here, there, and everywhere, is a rootless life. If your mama were alive, I'm sure she'd agree that you belong here with your family."

Oh Abbey, there's so much to figure out, it feels too big for my brain. When I'm in church, though, I feel more God-guided.

Can't wait to see you in a month. Until then, I'm reaching my hands across the miles to make the collywobbles in your tummy go away. Hope it works.

Mountains of love,
Layla

Layla was in the midst of addressing the envelope when there was a knock at the door. Surprised she'd lost track of the time, the excited eighteen-year-old unbolted the lock and greeted Mrs. Ludlow for her weekly appointment. The elderly woman entered the kitchen, her spine so hunched with rheumatism she perpetually viewed the world through the upper latitude of her eyes.

"Hope those pretty hands of yours can work some help on these old bones," Mrs. Ludlow said, straining to raise her face to Layla.

Layla smiled, nodding her hope in return as she helped this former seamstress at the bridal shop in town struggle out of her coat.

With all the effort some people made to seek healing, Layla wished she had some indication that it worked – an alteration as obvious as one of Mrs. Ludlow's shortened hems, added tucks, or let-out seams.

Once Mrs. Ludlow made herself as comfortable as possible on a chair, Layla placed her hands on the woman's crippled back. The mute healer could feel her palms and fingers heat up, full of prickly tingle that flowed into Mrs. Ludlow's tight muscles and sore bones. Questions, doubts – all Layla's uncertainties – seeped into the background. But there was no uncertainty in her heart. With every beat it sang a clear song of pure joy, over and over. *A baby. A baby. Abbey's having baby.*

CHAPTER TWENTY-FOUR

NEARLY a year had flown by since Layla's high school graduation. Even though she was active in church and being called on by more and more people for healing, she was still trying to break through her hard shell of doubt. Brian still struggled. And a number of those who came for healing, though they said they felt better, were in a holding pattern, neither better nor worse.

Cherry trees and dogwoods were turning the April sky into a pink-and-white flower garden.

In her journal, Layla wrote: *Being at home while Daddy works never grows tiresome. Every day, there's something new to behold. And there are always healing sessions and plenty of chores, interspersed with reading, to keep me busy. Through books, my world is as wide and full as a star-filled night sky. But just like thinking about eating an apple and biting into its crisp tanginess is not the same thing, I know that reading about something and living it is different too. Experience always teaches me the distinction between imagining and doing. No matter how many ways my mind imagines something, reality is always different. Sometimes better. Sometimes worse. But always different.*

Suddenly, Layla heard a motorcycle sputter on Fox Hollow Road. There wasn't much local traffic and the only motorcycle Layla was familiar with belonged to Zeb Yeagley.

Recently, after her weekly session with Brian, as she was getting ready to board the bus in Wayland to return home, Layla caught sight of Zeb. He was shambling along the sidewalk holding a paper bag suspiciously shaped like a bottle. Though they hadn't seen each other for several years, the unkempt troublemaker pointed a shaky finger at her. "I'm comin' to get you..." Layla didn't hear the rest of what he said, because she hurried onto the bus.

Ed always said, "Keep away from trouble and trouble will keep away from you." But that wasn't so easy when trouble came looking for you.

Now, day and night, Layla was alert for the sound of Zeb's cycle. Not so she could greet him, but to make herself scarce. Almost thirty, Zeb was still rattlesnake-mean as ever. He'd landed himself in jail. Landed in the hospital. Landed out of every job he ever had. And, as far anyone knew, out of the good graces of his family until he promised to stop his drinking and devilment. Drinking was a particular sore point, since alcohol, along with tobacco, was prohibited by their religion. The motor on this cycle, however, sounded lower, more beefed-up than the motor on Zeb's. Finally it stopped.

Layla waited for the sound of the engine to restart, wondering if it might be Zeb, after all.

To listen more closely, Layla stopped pinging peas into the metal bowl and turning pages in *To Kill a Mockingbird*, a story she was so deep into she could hardly get the chores done. As she looked down the lane she made out a speck of black and a speckle of shine. Contrary to her usual reaction, she remained in her chair.

Layla focused on the moving dot, mesmerized. Her head told her feet to get going. Her feet told her head to do the same. Neither budged, however, as the young woman rose from the porch chair, staring.

Before long, Layla could make out a man and a motorcycle. The motorcycle was bigger than Zeb's; the man differently shaped. Though Layla couldn't yet tell how tall, this man was more compact, muscled like a workhorse. Zeb was scraggled and stringy.

An apparition in black, the booted male advanced, dark hair tied back in a ponytail. Around the mountains, a man with long hair wasn't looked on too kindly. His leather pants were black. His black vest had shiny chrome snaps and, underneath it, he wore no shirt.

Layla felt a buzz the way she did when she passed by the transformer station in Wayland. As the man got closer, she could see that he was heavily tattooed – words, pictures – more ink than the *Smoky Mountain Gazette*. He was so marked up that one of the tattoos didn't register until he was a few feet away. When the picture came clear, the hairs on Layla's arms and neck quilled.

Starting at his collarbone, the tail of a serpent wound around the man's considerable neck. The body of the serpent continued up over his jawbone with the snake's scaled head depicted on his wind-burned cheek. The serpent's open jaw and jutting fangs protruded just over the side of the man's chapped top lip. And the serpent's lower jaw curved under his bottom lip.

Snake-man threw the kickstand of his cycle down, strode to the bottom of the steps, and thrust out his hand.

"Hi, I'm Damian." He smiled. When his mouth widened, the head of the serpent at the side of his lips drew back as if readying to strike.

Layla stood transfixed. Finally, she returned the greeting by shaking his outstretched hand. When her fingers touched his, she felt an electric jolt – like touching metal on a dry winter day.

"Sorry to disturb you, but my bike broke down. I was

visiting a buddy of mine in Wayland and swerved to miss a mongrel. Hit a rock and cracked the fork.

"Seems like I've come nearly ten miles from town, is that about right?"

Layla nodded.

"Didn't know if I should go back or if maybe there was a repair shop nearby. When I saw your path, I thought I'd try my luck. Find a phone. Maybe even a welding torch. You wouldn't happen to have either, would you?"

Layla stood, speechless.

"I really apologize for barging in on you like this," Damian said, retreating a step.

He hesitated. "Have we met before? Seems like I know you from somewhere."

Layla managed to shake her head.

"What's your name?"

Layla's gaze remained riveted on the reptilian tattoo.

"Fan si pan...Asian viper," Damian said, familiar with people's stares.

Embarrassed, Layla raised her gaze from the snake to the man's dark eyes. Though Damian appeared somewhere in his early twenties, his eyes had the look of old people who've seen the world go round so many times nothing much surprises them.

Damian's eyes had no sign of serpent in them.

"No name, hunh?"

A flying saucer could have set down on the driveway.

A deerskin-clad Cherokee could have escaped from a diorama in the Petersburg Natural History Museum and wandered onto her doorstep. Neither would have been less startling.

"Even if you could bring me a phone book, that'd be a big help," Damian said. "Find where the nearest auto shop is."

With no reply, Damian looked down at the ground, prodding a stone with the toe of his boot. "Hey. Sorry to have bothered you." He started to turn away.

Layla made a little sound to stop him, reached into her skirt pocket, took out a notepad and wrote her name.

"Layla..." Damian said, as she held out the pad for him to read.

She smiled.

"So you like to write?"

Layla nodded.

"You like to read too, huh?" Damian asked, gesturing to the book on the porch.

Layla's head bobbed, shyly.

"I like to too. But I can only fit a couple books in my saddlebag. Mostly, I write."

Curious, the captivated young woman raised her eyebrows.

"Rants, poetry, existential scribblings, stuff like that."

Damian walked to the front of his cycle and ran his hand over the fractured metal. "Better get this up and running. Do you have a phone I could use?"

Raising her hand, Layla shook her head.

"No phone. Well, I better keep walking while I've got light. About how far to the nearest town?"

Layla grew flustered. She didn't mean to say they had no phone. Just that she thought there was a welder in the barn for truck and tractor repairs.

Damian mistook her agitation.

"Hey, I didn't mean to trouble you." Jabbing with his black boot, Damian knocked up the kickstand of his cycle and turned the heavy machine in the direction of the road.

Layla started to dash down some words but they jumbled into her mind so fast she didn't know what to write first. Without thinking, she ran down the steps to catch him. Damian stopped and engaged the kickstand. Layla didn't know what possessed her. Maybe the serpent on his cheek stunned the sense out of her. But she opened her mouth so he could see her tongue stump.

Instead of looking away or being repelled, Damian inspected closely, nodding. With his pointer finger under her chin, he nudged her mouth shut, gently as if he were letting a ladybird take wing and fly off.

Damian's arm was inked with words in no apparent order. Some Layla knew, some foreign. *Phuong Quy unburied Han...* dozens of words circled the front and back of the brawny arm raised to her jaw.

On Damian's other arm, familiar names - Fred,

Melvin, Colby - too many to read. Each name had a little cross or star in front of it.

"Know what?"

Layla shook her head.

"People talk too much." Damian looked down.

"Besides, what good is talking when ..." his jaw tightened. "Anyway, who listens?"

Layla motioned Damian to follow.

She pointed to his cracked cycle, then the barn.

"You have a welder?"

I think so, she conveyed with a simultaneous nod and shrug.

"That'd be a lifesaver."

Damian followed Layla. Layla in motion – swaying hair, tall grace like flowing water. Followed her to the barn where she pointed out a line of tools shelved next to cans of grease and oil.

Clevis, one of Buttermilk's grown kittens, wandered in and started clawing on Damian's leather pants.

"Stop that!" Damian snapped. He leaned down and lifted the cat high in the air. Then he draped the cat around his substantial neck. Layla wanted to warn Damian. Caution him that Clevis had a mind of his own, a hunter's heart and eighteen piercing nails that could make you regret mistaking him for a house pet instead of a barn cat.

As Damian surveyed the cluttered shelves in the barn that smelled of hay and dung, Layla moved closer to alert him, maybe even make a grab for the temperamental feline. But before she could shape her hand into cat claw and snarl to communicate imminent danger, Clevis settled himself limp as a fur stole around Damian's shoulders. The cat, a patchy jigsaw of ginger and white, laid his head down, closed his eyes, and purred.

"Well, I'll be," Damian said, hoisting a welder off the wood plank and brushing off the cobwebs. He pivoted around, bumping into Layla.

"Sorry," he said, grabbing her shoulder to steady her, then quickly stepping back. Discombobulated, they stood embarrassed in the dusty light.

After a long moment, Damian asked, "Mind if I bring my bike over and fire this up?"

Layla shook her head.

As Damian edged past her and through the barn door, Layla felt a strong pull – like the Scotty dog magnets she played with as a child that glommed together when they got too close to each other.

She thought she'd better go back to the house and get cotton balls and peroxide for the imminent cat attack. But Clevis continued to sprawl comfortably, as much a part of Damian's neck as the coiled tail of the inky serpent. Layla's blue eyes were wide with astonishment, brows arched, mouth gaping in disbelief.

"Animals know," Damian said. "They can tell I don't have an ounce of fight left in me. No more killing."

A spike of fear shot up at his words. But Damian sounded so sad, Layla couldn't be scared. Besides, Clevis, one ear partly chewed off, might be ornery but he was no fool.

When Damian knelt down to fire up the welding torch, Clevis, roused, jumped down to watch from the sidelines. In less than an hour, the motorcycle was repaired.

"I'd like to repay your kindness and the use of your tools." Damian stood and brushed himself off. "Whatever would be useful? Mucking out the barn. Wood chopping..."

Those bundled muscles and the power of an axe in the hand of a man who admitted to violence gave Layla pause. Why would a person with a fanged serpent speaking right alongside the words he spoke be someone to trust with an implement of severing? But that was her head talking. Her instincts told her otherwise.

Hearing a low grumble, it took Layla a minute to realize it was her own stomach twisting with hunger and strangeness. Past noon, she hadn't yet eaten.

Pointing to Damian, she mimed with fluid, well-practiced movements.

"Are you are asking if I'd like to eat?"

She nodded.

"If it wouldn't put you out, you can't imagine how welcome that'd be from my usual grub." Damian looked at the woodpile to the side of the porch under the red maple.

"How about I split some wood while you get lunch?"

Damian headed toward the red maple, just beginning to leaf out in thready red-gold.

"Layla," he called.

She turned.

He moved toward her.

"I hate to bother. But I don't eat anything animal. Not anymore."

Seeing her bewilderment, he said, "A peanut butter sandwich. Greens. No faces."

Over the years, the time Layla would have spent talking, she looked and listened, instead. Not only did she gain understanding from her hands when she touched on someone's body, but she learned to hear to what was underneath their words. Hear what *wasn't* said.

It was the sort of listening that started long ago, sitting on the porch with her father and aunt the evening they wrote the *Important Things to Remember* list. Since then, Layla's ears had widened to a multitude of knowing. She heard loneliness roll out of people like the mist over the mountains and hang there in mournful silence – loneliness that spoke to her in a silent tongue. She heard weeping and sighs locked inside people's hearts. She heard their woe bearing down with such weight she could hardly breathe. Their loss, their hard hate and pure despair – all walling them away from their own selves, from others, and from God. But she never heard anything like the profound sorrow and hurt that poured from Damian.

Tears rolled down her cheeks.

When Damian saw he'd upset Layla, he charged over to a big boulder by the side of the house and laid his fist into it with a fierce roar.

The shaken girl started toward him.

"Keep away!" he yelled, holding his bloody hand. Stone-faced, Damian strode to his bike, swung onto it, released the stand, and revved the motor.

Layla rushed over and stood in front of his bike, clutching the handlebars.

Head bowed, hunched over, Damian's breath came in ragged intakes under the motor's roar.

No, she shook her head. *No. It's not my pain you see. That's not why I'm crying. It's your pain coming through me.* She didn't know if Damian understood.

Provoked by unknown boldness, Layla reached up and laid her fingers on his cheek right over the demon-eyed reptile. Messages ran through her hand, into her blood and heart. Vibrations of kinship. They were both serpent-bit in different ways. Layla had her tongue taken: Damian, his soul. Some of his mind too, it seemed.

After a minute, Damian's cycle went quiet.

Her hand still on his serpent-inked cheek, Layla could feel Damian's struggle as he mumbled, "Make the dream bigger than the night."

Layla shook her head, not comprehending.

"That's what the chaplain in 'Nam said. Said it was a Jewish saying to get through the unthinkable."

Damian clenched and unclenched his jaw, making the inked serpent under Layla's fingers feel alive.

"Didn't work." Damian's voice was as raw as the bleeding knuckles of his hand.

Layla continued to channel healing, distracted by a sweet ache low in her pelvis.

"Then, for a minute… Shit."

Pointing to his banged-up knuckles and to the house, Layla mimed washing.

Damian sat stock-still, as if contact with the boulder had Midas-changed him to stone.

Out of nowhere, Clevis jumped onto the Harley in front of Damian, put his big, filthy paws on Damian's hand and started licking.

"Well, I'll be damned." Damian lifted Clevis away from his hand and lowered him gently to the ground. "See that, Layla? The wrong beasts got dominion over the earth."

Her eyes widened.

"Hey, forget it. I'm going to split wood and get going." He dismounted from his bike and headed toward the woodpile, cautiously flexing his bloodied hand.

Layla beelined to the kitchen and started to cook. Collard greens without bacon. Eggs scrambled up with onions and mushrooms, fried potatoes, and leftover apple cobbler from the night before.

Nothing she used had a face except the field mushrooms that, when sliced in half, looked like two barn owls. In the midst of her kitchen dance, hastening to and fro, pivoting, hands and feet in constant motion, Layla kept glancing out the window at the steady fury of Damian's log splitting. She knew he meant to keep to the exchange of work, but had an inkling he'd head off on his Harley soon as he chopped a hefty pile.

Damian's behavior wasn't all that erratic compared to other veterans Layla encountered. For years now, the mountain communities lost their men to Vietnam. Not a family didn't have kith or kin who wasn't killed, missing limbs, shattered or shell-shocked. Brian. Mrs. Phoebe's husband, who had died a hero's death near Saigon. Mr. Vittie, who, before he was drafted, worked at the mill with her dad. When Mr. Vittie came back, nerves shot and so jiggy Mr. Addison had to lay him off, Ed said, "Poor Mack Vittie is wanderin' somewhere in these mountains full of whiskey and regret."

Zeb was the only Yeagley old enough to be drafted. Fortunately, Mrs. Yeagley's prayers for the safety of her son were answered. After a few months, Zeb was discharged.

Even though Vietnam was on the other side of the world, Layla couldn't help but wonder whether there were as many a'grieved hearts in that country on account of the war as there were in the Smoky Mountains.

Damian rammed into log after log as if he were trying to split one self from another. Or at least hack out the demons lodged inside.

Layla's insides were as scrambled as the eggs she beat together. Her heart was in her throat, her mind was in her fingers, and her stomach was jumping up and down in the empty space her heart left. She fried onions and potatoes in separate skillets, set the table and put out food, all the while keeping tabs on the fear-inspiring movements of the serpent-painted man.

Layla kept thinking of things to add to the meal, from yesterday's bread to a jar of chokecherry jam from the pantry. On the same shelf, three blue mason jars of relish remained from her mama that were too old to eat for fear of food poisoning. Auntie Avis never did pitch them, Ed was too busy, and Layla couldn't bear to. Not with her mother's lettering on the jars eight months before she was born. *Chow Chow Sept. '54.*

She could picture her mama sitting at the kitchen table, dicing sweet peppers and onions, chopping up green tomatoes and shredding heads of cabbage with the double-bladed cutter into the big wooden bowl, baby Layla no bigger than a radish seed in her womb. Maybe her mama was wearing her blue-flowered dress before it got cut up for quilting pieces.

As she continued to cook, Layla's mind stitched together a patchwork of its own out of pictures and feelings, old and new, fitting them together every which way.

A quick look out the window showed Damian was splitting wood as hard and steady as when he began forty minutes prior. The meal was ready except for the eggs, and Layla didn't plan to cook them until Damian was washing up.

Wiping her hands, the keyed-up cook headed outside. The screech of the screen door made Damian glance up just as he was putting another log onto the chopping stump. Layla motioned for him to come inside to eat.

Without missing a beat, Damian continued to lift up the axe and bury it into wood.

Wispy Layla, shy by four inches of Damian's near six feet, didn't know where she got the gumption but she walked right up and put her hands on the axe handle. She looked the sweat-sheened man directly in the eyes, staring into their brute power until she melted open his hands, took away the axe, and set it down. Then she grasped the top of Damian's arm, though it gave her pause to feel the steel of it, and guided him to the house ala Mrs. Bartram, her fourth grade teacher, who used to march disobedient students up to the front of the class. The heels of Mrs. Bartram's sensible shoes clicked briskly against the floorboards as she hauled the unlucky pupil – usually Lon Randall for throwing spitballs – to the front, drew a chalk circle on the blackboard, and made him put his nose in the circle and keep it there until she said otherwise.

Inside, Layla handed Damian a towel from the linen closet and showed him to the bathroom. Meanwhile, she scrambled the eggs and wondered which response her father would have if he came in unexpectedly and saw this bloody-knuckled, inked-up stranger in their bathroom. Grab his shotgun? Or call the sheriff?

The eggs were done and Layla was putting bowls of potatoes and greens on the table when Damian entered the kitchen remarkably scrubbed up and gentled down. Layla piled his plate with food and nodded her head to indicate where he should sit. She'd already served her own thick soup.

Damian had his napkin open and fork in hand by the time she sat down and bowed her head in silent grace. When Layla looked up, Damian's fork was on the table and his eyes were staring a million miles away.

"Apologies." Damian said, quietly. "I'm as much out of the habit of social graces as God's graces."

Layla nodded for him to start eating. Damian lit into the vittles with the speed of hunger but with an exactitude that put Layla in mind of Doc Fredericks. Every forkful was sized with intention and studied before he popped it into his mouth. He chewed with deep satisfaction.

Layla's mouth started watering at the memory of

collards and bacon; funny because she didn't put meat in the pot, not a smidgen.

Curious, she thought, how things get linked in the mind. Like collards and bacon. Smelling sawdust and thinking about her father. Hiss and terror.

When Layla opened her lips to sip soup, a stream of saliva ran down the corner of her mouth. Mortified, she grabbed her napkin and wadded it to her mouth.

Damian looked up from a forkful of collards.

As a hot flush of red rose up her neck into her face, Layla's eyes teared. She was just about to bolt from the table when Damian reached over the water pitcher and placed his hand on her wrist. Leaning forward, close enough for Layla to feel his body heat, he slowly pulled down her napkin.

"Don't hide, Layla," he said. "The world is full of shameful things. But a dribble from your mouth isn't one of them." Before sitting back in his chair, he gently blotted a tear beading down her cheek.

"It's been a long time, Layla. A long time since food tasted like anything but ash. A long time since I have been right with the world or the world's been right with me." Damian picked up his fork, but instead of resuming his meal, he sat there staring at the tines. "If you'll work at not hiding, I'll work at believing some small piece of life might make sense again."

When Damian looked back up into her eyes, she felt

he was looking to a part that not even her closest family saw. A secret part, hidden even to herself.

"Bargain?" Damian asked. He held out his hand.

Layla extended her hand to shake on it. With both hands, Damian took her slender one and held it for a moment. In turn, Layla took her other hand and covered his gouged knuckles, swollen red and blue. Damian's eyes closed. He exhaled, almost a sigh, and then let go.

With a look akin to ecstasy, he resumed eating. Layla pushed a jar of pickled beets over and sawed off a thick slice of bread. "I can't remember anything ever tasting this good," Damian said, swallowing a bite of the bread.

"Reminds me of when I was in high school in Chicago. I used to work summers as a caddy. Ever play golf?"

Layla shook her head.

"Well one of my classmates, Gene, was a hardscrabble kid from the other side of the tracks. Each of us carried a paper-sack lunch rolled up under our belt so we could eat during breaks. One time, during a tournament, Gene was caddying for a pro golfer who asked what was in the bag.

"'A sandwich,' Gene said.

"'What kind?' asked the pro.

"'Peanut butter and jelly.'

"'Can I have half?'

"'Sure,' Gene answered, unrolling his bag.

"After the pro took a bite or two of the sandwich, he asked Gene, 'Do you always have the same kind?'"

"'"Sometimes it's bologna.'

"'"But it's always on homemade bread like this?' the pro asked.

"'"Sure,' Gene replied. There was no way his family could afford store-bought bread on the salary his father earned in the slaughterhouse.

"'"How about I make you a deal?' asked the pro. 'You bring me two of these sandwiches every day and come lunchtime, you can order anything you want from the clubhouse restaurant.'

"Gene, who had never tasted a roast beef sandwich or a turkey club, said he'd remember those few days for the rest of his life.

"Who knows? Maybe the pro had memories like that too."

Layla smiled and sipped soup. They ate, quietly. The only sounds were the clink of silverware, a fly zigzagging around the jam jar, the glug of water as it poured from the stoneware pitcher, birds, and an occasional squabble from the barnyard.

Damian ate with the same steady concentration that he chopped wood. What might have been strained, two improbable strangers sharing a meal, seemed natural. Even the fierce serpent on Damian's face and the tattoos on his arms faded into background.

"Those your husband's?" Damian asked, glancing at Ed's barn boots by the door.

Layla shook her head.

She couldn't think of a way to mime explanation, so she wrote – *my father's* – on her notepad.

"Oh," Damian said. "My folks still live in Chicago where I grew up."

Neatly halving a beet, Damian continued. "Illinois... land of Lincoln, Sandburg. You know Carl Sandburg, Layla?"

Remembering a poem about fog and cat feet from high school, the enchanted young woman gestured, thumb and forefinger an inch apart – *a little.*

Damian rested his fork on the edge of his plate, tipped the wooden chair back on two legs – Ida Mae would've scolded – his hands folded across his stomach. Looking up at the ceiling, he said, "Smash down the cities." His low voice rumbled like a storm coming in over the mountains.

> *"Knock the walls to pieces.*
> *Break the factories and cathedrals, ware-*
> *houses and homes*
> *Into loose piles of stone and lumber and*
> *black burnt wood:*
> *You are the soldiers and we command*
> *you.*

"That's from Sandburg's poem 'And They Obey'. Insane, huh?"

Layla nodded, swallowing hard.

Damian tore off a hunk of his bread and sopped up the collard's greenish liquor. "No mention of human atrocities." He looked up as he put the bread in his mouth and saw the shocked expression on Layla's face.

Seeing the distress he caused, Damian slammed his napkin on the table and started to get up.

Jackrabbit-quick, Layla was at his side, pushing him down.

Layla brought over the pan of apple cobbler, dished up a big bowlful, and sat back down to finish her soup, swallowing ever so slowly, praying she didn't choke.

"My parents," Damian said, starting to calm down and savor the cinnamon chunks, "have an apple tree in their backyard. When I was a boy, I used to climb the tree at night thinking I could get high enough to pull a star from the sky."

Layla smiled.

"Ever imagine crazy possibilities when you were a kid?"

Yes, she nodded.

"Like what?"

She pointed up.

"You tried to reach a star too?"

Damian seemed so hopeful she hated to say no.

Heaven, she wrote. *On my rope swing. To see Mama.*

"How long ago did your mama die?"

Almost nineteen years ago come June, she jotted. *Birthing me.*

Damian ran his spoon around the bowl to get the last of the syrupy juice. "So much loss," he said, studying her intently. "You'd never know."

Layla scooped more cobbler into his bowl.

"Know what I usually eat?"

She shook her head.

"Peanut butter. Crackers. Boiled rice. Convenience-store crap. Doesn't make much difference."

Imagining someone who could taste but didn't care made Layla think about sick people who lost interest in food when they were about to die. She got the sense that Damian was set on dying. But something underneath, something tenacious as quack grass was struggling to live.

Damian spooned every last bit from the bottom of his bowl. But he held up his hand when she tried to serve more.

"Can't. Not another bite. That meal was the closest thing to religion I've felt in a long time." Damian wiped his mouth. He got up and put out his hand.

"No way to thank you enough, Layla." Damian took her hand and pressed it with the both of his. Flustered that he was about to disappear forever, Layla motioned him into the living room.

"Can't, Layla. I'm not decent company."

Layla wanted to say, *don't go*. She wanted to say that she liked the spark of his mind and the heat coming off his body. Even the ache of his soul.

Not having speech, Layla usually took one of two paths. If a matter was not worth talking about, she let it slide because, in all likelihood, it wasn't worth acting on either. But if it was important, she skipped over *verbalizing* into *doing*.

Layla could feel Damian's loneliness, but she knew it would be unspeakably bold to kiss him.

Damian, eyes full of conflict, reached to caress the flaxen hair at the side of Layla's face.

Hoping her mama or Auntie Avis would send her a message about what to do next, Layla twisted the gold heart around her neck when, abruptly, Damian turned on his heels and hurried out of the kitchen.

The screen screeched open and smacked shut. Damian's boots pounded down the front steps. Racing over, the stunned girl watched from behind the metal screen as a blur of black leather swung onto the cycle and revved the motor. Layla wanted to run out and stop Damian like she did earlier, but she hesitated.

Maybe Damian found it too difficult to be with a person who couldn't keep up a conversation. A familiar story. One whose ending she could predict.

From behind the screen's mesh that hid her grief like

a widow's veil, Layla waved a meager good-bye.

For the briefest moment, Damian lifted his head toward the house. Layla flung open the door and ran out. But Damian was already turning to head away.

Layla yelled his name. *"Aameee...Aaameee..."* But she could hardly hear her own voice over the accelerating motor. Flying down the porch steps, Layla ran after Damian, hoping, once again, to catch him before he left. After a hundred yards, winded and coughing from the dust kicked up by Damian's Harley, Layla slowed and came to a heart-thudding stop.

She watched Damian disappear, fleeting as a dream upon waking. She listened as the sound of his motorcycle receded, siphoning her emotions along with it, leaving her as hollow and as full of echo as an empty well.

Layla dragged back to the house and sank down on the front steps. Knowing she'd never see him again, tears flooded down her cheeks. She felt like crying until her heart dissolved into salty slosh so it wouldn't ache so much.

Inside the kitchen, there was evidence that she hadn't conjured up Damian. There was two of everything except for the fork, knife, and plate that she didn't need. All signs of another person that would concern her father.

What if her father had walked in on them in the kitchen eating together? What if he caught Damian dabbing his daughter's mouth or caressing her hair?

Layla knew she must put the kitchen back in order before her father returned from the mill. Otherwise, she'd have much more to explain than her roiling emotions and racing heart had words for. She wiped her drenched cheeks, stood up and brushed off.

"Might as well cry when I have a dish towel in my hand," she thought, and went back inside to do the dishes.

CHAPTER TWENTY-FIVE

"HOW'D all those logs get split?" Ed asked, motioning to the pile of neatly stacked wood.

He'd just entered the kitchen after brushing the sawdust off of his shirt and pants, and stomping his feet on the doormat as the porch responded with dull, hollow thuds.

Layla, barely finished with the dirty dishes from lunch before rushing into supper preparations, hadn't thought about *what* or *how* she would tell her father.

Physically and emotionally breathless, she held up her "just-a-minute" finger with a sheepish smile. While Ed shook out his lunch box and rinsed his thermos, his daughter knew it would take more than the notepad in her pocket to explain. She went to the counter – the one her mother declared, "Finer than bee's knees" after Ed installed the harvest-gold Formica in their newly-built kitchen before Layla was even born – and slowly retrieved the tablet they kept on top of the skinny Cumberland County phone directory.

Ed poured himself a glass of iced tea and settled down at the kitchen table opposite his daughter. Gathering her thoughts, Layla engaged in an overly methodical easing of a tablet page from the spiral binding so that the top ripped evenly. She stalled some more as she smoothed down the resulting fringe, then wrote quickly and slid the paper across the table to her father.

A fella's motorbike broke down.

Her mind raced for a way to gussy up the truth without telling a lie. She felt like the time she tagged along to Abbey's dance when she was thirteen and Auntie Avis spent so much energy giving her a fancy updo and applying lip gloss. But it never took long for the unadorned truth of her missing tongue to surface.

Still, how could Layla describe all that took place with Damian when she, herself, didn't have a full grasp of what happened?

Said he'd been visiting a buddy in Wayland, Layla wrote. Certainly a more palatable detail than ponytail, bizarre tattoos, and a bloody fist.

"Why'd he do it?"

He used some of your tools to fix his cycle so he wanted to repay you.

Ed nodded approval. "Mighty decent."

He sat quietly. Sometimes he could coax more from his daughter by being silent than with a string of questions. And Ed knew Layla well enough to know there was more to the story than she was letting on. Though her impassive face might fool others, Ed saw the way her thumbnail scraped at a dried speck of food on the table and the way she kept repositioning herself in her chair, knowing that something didn't sit right.

"Did he say what his name was?"

Damian. Unwittingly, Layla's cheeks colored up. Bending down quickly to avert her face she wrote, *He was in Vietnam.*

"Hmmph..." Ed, said, contemplating his tea glass. He took several swallows all in a row.

Initially, when he saw the big pile of hewn firewood, Ed couldn't help but be pleased. Still, he was concerned that a stranger came up the lane and that his very attractive daughter let him stay without knowing zip-a-dee doodah about him.

Layla didn't lie about Damian, but she didn't go into the specifics of her visitor's inked skin and explosive behavior. It would make the worry lines on her father's forehead deepen from furrow to gully. And besides, her father brought her up to trust in her animal instincts more than societal shoulds and shouldn'ts.

Ed followed his own good advice, as well. So when the weatherman said a storm would miss the area but the nattering birds turned manic, Ed didn't bother taking the tractor out of the barn. And sure enough, when the rain swept in, there wasn't the waste of time or gas to head back from the field. No wet clothes to peel off.

"Trust your gut and your good senses, Ducky. Don't be one of those fools who has to pee on an electric fence to figure out if somethin's true or not."

Layla's gut told her that Damian wasn't a danger to anyone but himself, so she was adhering to her father's advice about that part.

Layla twiddled the pencil between her thumb and forefinger, wary about divulging one word more than necessary. And Ed tried to remember his sister-in-law's frequent admonishments.

"You've got to let her grow up," Avis said, when Ed protested that his sister-in-law let sixteen-year-old Layla take the Lovells' Studebaker out for a spin on city streets. "You've raised Layla to have a good head on her shoulders, so now, let her use it."

"I'm vigilant, is all," Ed replied.

"Ed, I know it's hard. Lord knows I was always trying to slow Abbey down. And then, the boys! Whoooeee! They're a different breed altogether. And neither one like the other. Parents and kids, we're all growing up together – figuring it out at the same time. And all of us pretending like we know what we're doing."

They both laughed. Avis sighed, "Most days, by the end, I think, if I knew yesterday what I learned today, I never would have behaved the way I did. That means tomorrow, I'll just be in a new pickle. Only thing I know for sure is to love 'em. Especially when they're the least lovable."

Ed felt confident he was carrying out that part of Avis's advice – to love his daughter no matter what. And yes, maybe, he reasoned, he was too protective. But what parent, even the most natural born, didn't occasionally snag their offspring on a sharp tooth as they ferried them to safety?

Looking at his daughter over the rim of his iced-tea glass, Ed balanced the echo of Avis's words with his own common sense. All in all, Layla didn't look any worse for the wear. Nothing to indicate that the encounter his daughter was so clammed up about brutalized her in any way.

Like parents and children everywhere, father and daughter engaged in the complex process of sizing each other up, reading between the lines, and assessing the variables of the moment to figure out the most fruitful course to get what they wanted. ...Or in Layla's case, to head off what she didn't want.

"Funny," Avis once voiced to Ed, "how you want to know everything so you can keep your kids safe. But when you find out, you wonder if there are some things you'd be better off not knowing."

"Well..." Ed said, deciding to let the Damian matter rest for the time being. "I'd better go to the barn and close things up for the night while you're fixin' supper. See you later, Ducky."

Layla nodded assent, hastened over to the stove so her father couldn't see the look of relief on her face, and began cooking up collards for the second time that day.

This time with bacon.

CHAPTER TWENTY-SIX

THE day after Damian left, the serpent-faced stranger consumed Layla's thoughts. She was bleary from lack of sleep and muddled from strange dreams. She couldn't tell if her dreams were predictors of things to come, past dregs, or a bit of everything stirred together.

She was heartsick, as well.

She'd all but given up on the idea of having a boyfriend, getting married or having kids. Like apples high in a tree, so many of an ordinary young woman's expectations were out of Layla's reach. But the way Damian looked at her, the way he touched her hand and stroked her hair, stirred her emotions until they raced around like wood mice.

After packing a lunch for Ed, Layla filled a large thermos with her fortified drink, since she'd be home later than usual. On Tuesdays, she rode to work with Ed so she could give Brian Fredericks his weekly treatment. And today, she also had to stop at the Crest View nursing home because one of her regulars, seventy-three-year-old Thelma Vincent, was spending time there while her hip mended. A few days ago, Thelma phoned Layla.

"Don't want to bother ya' none, Layla. But if you could make it over to the home I'd be ever so grateful. Tripped over the cat and broke my pelvic. Furry thing thinks he's a throw rug. But with that bad shoulder of mine, you know, I'm strugglin' with the walker. So I was hopin' you could lay some of your healin' on me."

"Uhhuh," Layla replied, her sympathetic utterance laden with all the words she couldn't say.

"Oh, you're a saint, for sure. Be gettin' another star in your crown, you will. You don't know how much I appreciate it. Can't wait to get outta this place. Smells like piss! They use a spray. 'Fresh air' sumpthin' or other. But it don't fool nobody. Nothin' but old folks here, either. I don't like old people!"

Layla smiled. That was Thelma Vincent. Crusty as fried chicken on the outside but tender to the bone on the inside.

TODAY, Brian was in his room when Layla got to the Fredericks' home. In the red-brick Colonial, which accommodated the stride of each day as reliably as a pair of Buster Browns, Brian wasn't in his old bedroom on the second floor, but the first-floor parlor that was specially equipped with a hospital bed that raised and lowered, and a trapeze contraption above the bed so he could pull himself up.

Beside the bed was an oversized nightstand. Carefully arranged on top of the finely crafted cherrywood, there was a stack of books, a pile of magazines, a telephone, a no-nonsense, wooden-handled brass bell any schoolmarm would have prized, a pitcher, a glass, and a box of tissues. But inside the cabinet door, it was all business. Toilet paper, bedpan, urinal, emesis basin, wipes, enema kit, prescriptions, emergency towels, vials, and syringes.

Next to the cabinet was a bedside commode and wastebasket. Opposite the bed was a television set with framed family photographs on top, an easy chair, and a corner desk that could accommodate a wheelchair. An armoire served as a closet. The swirled wood of the armoire had a full-length mirror on the door until Brian insisted that it be removed. Instead he had taped up a handwritten sign. *One Should Love Some Things More Than Life And Fear Some Things More Than Death.*

Most days, Brian tried to spend time outside on the front porch, greeting patients as they came in, reading in the fresh air, or easing his wheelchair down the ramp that was added beside the porch steps so he could take a spin around the neighborhood or go downtown. But there was no way to get into the swing of a routine. His pain came for hours, sometimes days, at a time. Stabbing pain. Pain that bored through his phantom heel bone and burned like a fuse of dynamite through his missing tibia. Closed off in his room, Brian swallowed pills or injected himself with a hefty dose of opiates and tried to gut it through.

Doc hoped that, down the line, his paraplegic son would somehow be able to fulfill the remaining year of requirements for his medical degree so that Brian could join him as a partner. Or, at least, assist with the practice. He plied Brian with the latest medical journals.

"Relying on you, son, to keep me up-to-date about what's new on the horizon." Doc prayed that motivation and the prosthetics that Brian would eventually be fitted for – if his pain could be brought under control – would give his son a forward goal. But after two years of medication, therapies, and healing sessions, hope was dwindling.

"Come in," Brian called when he heard the soft tapping. His voice sounded like backed-up sewer sludge.

"Hi Layla." Brian stared off into space as the pretty young girl slid open one of the parlor's double doors.

Layla knew as soon as she heard his voice on the other

side of the door that he was in one of his black moods. She set her tote bag on the upholstered easy chair in the corner. Like the tenor of Brian's voice, Layla's quilted carry-all took the shape of what it held inside. Sometimes, it was jammed full of groceries, reading material, her journal, and a jar or bundle from one of her clients. Other times, it was slack with the barest necessities.

The burgundy Windsor chair and the floor lamp with its Tiffany shade were part of the former parlor decor, but the Oriental rug had been rolled up and put into storage to allow for easier movement of Brian's wheelchair on the hardwood floor.

The hospital equipment and the antiseptic smell that masked the odors from the bedside commode seemed like an insult alongside the elegant vestiges of propriety where, once, the formalities of china teacups and delicately spooned-out sugar took place.

Layla stooped down until she was eye level with Brian, visually asking permission to begin touching him.

"Go ahead," Brian snapped.

"In 'Nam, we treated only the wounded who could make it. Play God. Decide who could survive and who couldn't. What does that mean, *survive?*"

Layla shrugged.

"Keep what's left from leaking out? Keep the motor running at all costs even if the car is totaled?"

Foregoing her usual healing points on Brian's stumps,

thighs, and lower spine, Layla stood and placed her hands on the crown of the troubled vet's head. She cupped her palms and slender fingers like a cap over the top of his skull – the first spot in most babies – though Layla wasn't one of them – to be introduced to light and air, and to experience vagaries outside the womb. Soft and yielding, that spot, even when the skull grew together, remembered its vulnerability, its bond to realms beyond the boundaries of flesh and bone. So, when someone was deep within themselves, disconnected from their surroundings, it was the most reliable place to begin healing.

"Survive for a bag of breath?" Brian said.

Closing his eyes, Brian mumbled more to himself than Layla. "Gotta stay strong..."

Layla kept separating what her ears heard from the work of keeping her hands as clear and free as she could for the healing to come. Having been through Brian's depressions before, she tried not to allow herself to be drawn in because, like a spruce tree's pungent sap, if you touched its stickiness it fused your fingers together.

Her hands slid down to the base of Brian's skull, the bumpy ridge just above the neck. A wild creature lurked inside that dark cave, ready to pounce with bared claws or primed to flee or fight to the last gasp.

Slowly, Layla felt Brian's body begin to relax a little. Through gritted teeth, he began to sob noiselessly. After a minute, Brian took a deep breath.

"Shit, Layla. I'm sorry. Old wounds... One of the men in our platoon, a buddy of mine on reconnaissance, was ambushed. Got shot...couldn't tell how many times. Suddenly the air was exploding all around us – bullets, grenades, machine guns. Our sergeant, a kid drafted right out of college, told me to stay put but my buddy was less than fifty feet away, lying in the undergrowth. So my brain says, *That's my friend out there.* And at the same time, it said, *This sarge doesn't have a clue that in school, I was a halfback nicknamed Grease. No one could catch me.* Then, boom – I scramble out of the foxhole and make a dash for it."

Layla let one hand float down from the back of Brian's head and rest on his throat to unclog all the words still stuck inside. Ever since she began treating him, Layla wondered how Brian lost his legs, but he never offered an explanation.

"One minute I was running; the next, I wasn't. Sarge was the one who dragged me off the field and saved my life. Sometimes I hate him for it. Sarge took it hard – felt responsible when any of his men got hurt or killed – like it was his fault. He's kept in touch ever since, and I know he keeps in touch with some of the others too. Two years we've been writing back and forth. He even came to see how I was doing, for God's sake – showed up yesterday out of nowhere but he wouldn't stay the night. Wouldn't even stay for lunch. I wish he had. It's good to be with someone who's crazy the same way you are. Nobody really understands what 'Nam was like, Layla. You had to be there, holed up in mud, stinking to high heaven and wondering if you're the next one to go.

"*'Chance,'* Sarge said. Told me it was the one thing that still made sense from his courses in college. Said the rest of those philosophical arguments about truth and justice got blown to bits. We talked all morning. The good, the bad, and the ugly. Then he zoomed off on his Harley."

Layla's hands froze.

"Jeez, Layla. Your hands have gone ice cold."

Layla reached in her pocket for paper.

Damian?

"Yeah, Damian. How the heck do you know? My folks tell you?"

Layla shook her head.

His bike broke down near our house. He used some of Daddy's tools to fix it.

"That bum! Leave it to Damian to find the prettiest girl in the county. Did he wow you with his long hair and black leather?"

Cheeks suddenly scarlet, Layla lowered her eyes.

"Oh my God, he did, didn't he?"

Layla continued to look down.

"Did something happen, Layla?"

The almost nineteen-year-old, face hot enough to make toast, shook her head.

"You could tell me if it did. You know that, don't you? Same as you know things about me that nobody else knows."

Head bowed, Layla nodded.

"Don't worry. Your secret's safe with me."

Layla knelt down and began to work on Brian's absent legs – the aborted muscles and tendons, the emptiness in his pinned-up trouser legs from missing bones that once earned him the name of Grease. One impulsive instant, no more than a second, he made a decision that left him second-guessing everything else.

With little more said, Layla finished her session with Brian. As usual, they embraced before she left – a habit that began early on when a grateful Brian, relieved after a stint of unendurable pain, asked if she would mind.

And even though they kept their feelings for each other at the level of brother and sister, partly because of their twelve-year age difference and partly because of the inappropriate circumstances of their relationship, today Brian's hug lasted a bit longer and held more unspoken words than usual.

CHAPTER TWENTY-SEVEN

ON the way to the nursing home, Layla passed Memorial Park, though *parklet* would be a more accurate description. Next to the Wayland post office, the small grassy square, rimmed with a waist-high hedge of boxwood, was shaded by sassafras trees and spreading maples. Flanked by a bench on either side, a bronze plaque commemorated hometown soldiers who had fallen during World War II.

At first, Layla walked past the green oasis, but then backtracked and sank down on a bench. She felt such anonymity in the city. There she was, near enough to touch all those bronze names, each one a person with secrets and pastimes, dashed dreams and fierce desires just like hers.

How could all the miracle and mundane inside a person just stop? In the midst of joy or terror, in the midst of sleep or swatting a fly, suddenly be cut off at the pass. Or like Brian, at the knees.

Layla unscrewed the top of her thermos and sipped the tasteless liquid inside as she tried to process the hodge-podge that scudded through her mind as shapeshifting as the gusting clouds above.

The overwrought healer felt she was going as crazy as everyone around her. Maybe it was fatigue from a night of wakeful dreaming and flittery wisps of sleep that did nothing to give her a fresh start on her day. Whatever the reason, the phrase, "April showers bring May flowers", kept going through her mind. Even though it *was* April and daffodils and forsythia as yellow as sunshine already braved the erratic spurts of warmth and overnight temperature drops, why did the words of an inane rhyme stick like a broken record in her head when it was Damian who was foremost in her thoughts?

Was it a *sign*?

A sign that maybe her dreams would blossom? Or a sign that she should have brought an umbrella?

After gathering her wits as best as she could, Layla walked on to the nursing home. Thelma was right about the smell. An undertone of urine greeted Layla as she opened Crest View's front door. Not even the entryway pedestal that held an outsized urn of mums and roses amidst glitter-flocked ferns masked the odor.

The softly contoured receptionist ran her finger down a list. "Eighty-three. Down the hall to the right."

Layla walked behind a stooped old lady shuffling down the hall, intermittently muttering and flatulating in mantra-like repetition. "I don't know where to go. I don't know what to do." *Zzzttzzzpttthhhh.* The noisy discharge was followed by a relieved "ahhhhh...."

"I don't know where to go..." *Zzzzzzstttsss....* "I don't know what to do."

Maybe Wolfy and little Frank got it right when they reveled in their toilet-brained humor under the cot covers, seeing who could fart the most and smell the worst.

Polite girls were taught to squinch their butt checks closed, practice the surreptitious one-cheek raise as they sat to allow for a measured, hopefully silent, release. And all for what? A lifetime of propriety that ends with so many losses, including your sphincter.

After the slow walk down the worn carpet of the hallway, Layla tapped on Thelma Vincent's door. When no one answered, Layla eased the door open and peeked in. Empty. Even when Layla ooo-hooed, her version of yoohoo, no one answered.

Layla began to wonder if Thelma took a turn for the worse. Common knowledge had it that just as "pneumonia was an old man's friend," a broken hip spelled the end of a good many women.

Overuse – that's what it was, Layla thought. The strain of carrying around pre-birth babies, muscle-tethered to the side posts of the pelvis. And, once born, making a lap for feeding, sleep, and comfort. Hauling a child around on a hip tipped up at an angle to prevent slippage, leaving a free arm for needful chores. Hip-bumping doors open when the hands were full. Bending over and stooping down to pick up and clean too many times a day to count. And at the end of the day, bearing the weight and joining in the reciprocal swivel and thrust that carried their husbands off to sleep.

No wonder hip bones are the shape of butterfly wings, thought Layla. They cradle metamorphosis and run themselves ragged, day after day, until they finally give out.

An aide, pushing a resident in his wheelchair, passed by and noticed the flummoxed girl standing in the open doorway.

"They're in the dining room, honey. Take the corridor all the way down and hang a left."

Of course, Layla thought, chiding herself for not planning more carefully. It was noon.

Layla spotted Mrs. Vincent, her walker parked beside her chair, sitting near the end of a long institutional table.

"Was expectin' you earlier," Thelma said, wrapping her hands around Layla's in greeting.

"Magic hands," Thelma announced loudly to the residents around her. "Truly magic! Heal the warts right off a toad." Layla looked down and blushed.

"Should I come down to the room right now?" Thelma asked, starting to reach for her walker.

Layla shook her head.

"Well, then grab a chair and sit yourself down. I'm sure they'll bring you a soup or something. Usually someone or other doesn't show up for a meal and they have extra. You can eat soup, can't you?"

Layla nodded yes but politely refused, pulling her thermos out of her tote bag.

A woman across the table, a cottony white cloud of hair framing her frail features, asked her tablemate, "Harold, would you please hand me a spoon?"

"Sure," he said. He reached over and spread his fluttering hand over her unused place setting.

"Is this it?" he asked, touching his fingertip to the knife.

"No. The one next to it," said the shawl-wrapped woman whose eyesight was adequate, but who couldn't extend her paralyzed arm that far.

"Is this it?" he asked, once again. His hand that traced around the edge of a teaspoon was a map of blue-veined tributaries.

"The next one," guided the slow, deliberate voice of the stroke-compromised woman.

"Ah, here it is," Harold said, with a faint smile of satisfaction.

When it came to old people, Layla had noticed over the years that *faint* didn't mean halfhearted, just the economy of the very elderly or extremely ill who learn to mete out their energy with thrifty foresight. Their frugality was evident in the half-raised hand to signal farewell; in tears shed, one by one, so as not to completely desiccate the body in a single outburst.

"Can you open these crackers for me, dear?" Mrs. Vincent asked Layla, after struggling to tear the cellophane. Layla took the packet and opened them up in a swift gesture.

"How'd you do that?" Thelma asked.

"Because my hands and fingers still work," Layla thought, as she gave back the crackers, feeling strangely guilty just for being young.

Layla surveyed the table full of soup-eaters. Among them, at the far end, was a gaunt man with a string of snot that rolled up and down like a yo-yo as he exhaled and inhaled. Across from Layla, Mrs. Cloud-hair raised her spoon to her mouth with her excruciatingly slow, clumsy left hand, spilling all but a few drops of soup by the time it got to her lips.

The scene reminded Layla of the coloring books she had as a child where a recognizable shape formed – a rabbit, a boat, a house – when you connected a page full of dots. Linking together all the moles, brown spots, warts, and flesh tags of the people around her, a picture emerged: life in decline.

Even after Layla finished treating Mrs. Vincent and was on the bus back home from Wayland, she couldn't shake the cloying smell of the nursing home. It *was* full of old people, just like Thelma said. Full of diminishments where choice had dwindled to white toast or wheat? Bingo or television? Jell-O or applesauce? It seemed like lots of folks were waiting around killing time until time killed them, and not just at the nursing home, either.

As the bus neared her house, Layla stood up to remind the driver that she wanted to get off. Though, technically, the bus didn't make local stops, the accommodating driver always let off a resident along the route to the next township.

The lane that led to the Tompkin home was tree-lined with feathery hemlocks and tall pines. In the slightly overcast afternoon, Layla dismounted, walked a hundred feet up the gravel path until no one from the road could see her, and stopped. Squinting, she peered toward the house, craning her neck, hoping against hope that Damian's Harley was there.

It wasn't.

She also confirmed that Zeb's motorcycle or the Jeeter brothers' bicycle wasn't out front. There was no way she'd let herself get caught alone with Zeb, especially since she knew he was back in the area after her recent encounter with him at the bus stop in Wayland. And Lyman Jeeter gave her the heebie-jeebies when he rode over to use the phone and pressed his face, grimy as a coal miner, to the window.

With the coast clear, Layla clutched her tote bag to her chest and ran.

Ran like a little kid.

Ran because she could.

Ran as if she could magically catch up with Damian.

CHAPTER TWENTY-EIGHT

LAYLA sat on the porch humming songs and cutting up the last of the winter squash from the root cellar. It was the kind of flawless blue day when she could feel herself and the trees exchanging breaths like lovers.

She was ready to leave as soon as Abbey went into labor. All her essentials were packed: clothes, toiletries, protein powder and, most importantly, the surprise she'd been working on. Until she'd finished stitching together the baby quilt, she wasn't sure if it would turn out as well as she hoped.

The centerpiece was a picture of the land the baby would be born into with the Smoky Mountains cut out of blue-gray flannel and the trees, various shades of green. But best of all, high in the blue sky, were puffy clouds made from Abbey's old toddling blanket. Layla used materials from her mother's quilting basket – some fabric from before she was born, some added along the way.

As she sliced a butternut into thick circles of sunset orange, Layla was even more restless about the baby and Damian than she'd been a few days earlier when she wrote to Abbey.

Remember how the day I met Damian and Daddy made me tell him how all the logs in the woodpile got split and stacked? And then the next day, how I found out that Damian was Brian's sergeant? Well, I've tried for over two weeks to let all that go. My mind tells me to forget about him, to face up to facts. But my heart keeps flying the coop.

Do you believe in love at first sight? I know for you and Roy it was slow and gradual.

Jarred from her reverie by a powerful rustling behind the laurel bushes across the front yard, Layla stopped humming. She gripped her paring knife, wishing she could yell, *Who's there?* Or if it was a bear, *Get outta here!*

Just then the telephone rang. Layla dashed inside, bolted the front door and picked up the phone. Even though she stretched the cord so she could keep watching from the window, her view to the bushes was blocked, so the voice on the phone captured all her attention.

"Layla? Layla honey, is that you?" Auntie Avis's

voice sounded like people at the county fair riding on the roller coaster – thrilled and scared all at once. "Uh-huh."

"Abbey's gone into labor. Uncle Frank and I are just leaving to drive to Petersburg. We're gonna have us a baby before long. Think you can get the twelve-thirty bus?"

"Uh-huh."

"Good. Uncle Frank'll pick you up at the bus station in Petersburg and bring you over to the hospital. See you soon, honeybunch."

Layla tapped the receiver three quick times, hung up and dialed her father at work. They'd set up a special code and Ed already arranged to trade his lunch hour so he could pick up his daughter and take her to the bus when the time came.

Layla glanced out the window again. There was a broken branch lying near the laurels. She opened the door and grabbed the bowls of squash and peelings. In case it was a bear hankering for food, she didn't want to dance a do-si-do with it on the porch trying to get out to her father's truck.

Hey! she shouted, pausing to listen. But all was silent.

She was too excited to eat lunch, so she made a big thermos of her fortified drink to sip on the bus.

In the fifteen minutes it took Ed to drive home from the mill, Layla hastily added her toothbrush to her suitcase, closed it up, carried it to the kitchen door, peed, put away the squash, and rinsed the dishes.

She was drying her hands when she heard the truck horn toot.

"Got everything, Ducky?" Ed asked his daughter.

Blue eyes glinting, she climbed into the truck and nodded.

Ed started to back up.

"Waah!" Layla blurted, holding up her hand.

She bolted from the truck into the house, tore off the number from the notepad by the phone and ran back. If the bus was late or something went awry, she needed a way to contact Auntie Avis and Uncle Frank at the hospital in Petersburg.

On the ride down the mountain to Wayland, Ed handed his daughter a paper bag.

"For Mama Bear's baby," he said. They both smiled when Ed used the name Abbey earned the day she saved her brothers and cousin.

"Had to give it a final sandin' at the mill when I went in this mornin'."

Layla peeked in. "Aww," she said. She was delighted to find a wooden bear that could sit on a shelf like a figurine or be taken apart into pieces and puzzled together again.

When they arrived at the station, Ed swung out of the truck and handed Layla her suitcase. "Better get goin',

Ducky. Bus'll be here in ten minutes. I'll be down on Sunday." He hugged her.

Layla tucked the paper bag with the wooden bear into her tote sack right next to a pair of soft yellow booties she hoped to finish knitting on the eighty-five-mile trip from Wayland to Petersburg.

After she boarded the bus, Layla edged her way down the aisle to an empty seat in the back because it was too frustrating to explain her situation to someone trying to strike up a conversation. The soon-to-be godmother sat down and dug out a book of poems that Mrs. Phoebe gave her after learning about Damian and his penchant for Carl Sandburg.

A month away from her nineteenth birthday, the infatuated girl had pressed spring violets between the pages to mark her favorites in the same way she preserved images of Damian in the folds of her brain. The picture of Damian in the filtered light of the barn, big-pawed Clevis draped around his neck. Damian at the kitchen table, conveying by proxy, the pleasure of foods she could no longer eat. The high voltage of his tender touch.

On the bus, her long legs crossed and her foot jiggling as if it had to motor the Greyhound to Petersburg all on its own, Layla's thoughts darted like a hummingbird from Abbey to the baby to Damian, who came in a dream last night. In it, he called Layla's name and repeated the words, *Moon in the mud. Moon in the mud.* What kind of perplexity was that, Layla wondered?

The edgy girl opened her poetry anthology and the satiny pages purred as she ruffled through them. She was dumbfounded how a mere handful of words could capture something so fully and open her eyes to a whole new way of seeing.

Too antsy to read, Layla closed the book and, unable to focus on poems or knitting, watched the blur of trees and rocks and the glimpsed valley below as the bus wound down the mountain. She tried not to worry about Abbey.

Almost-sisters. That's how the cousins thought of each other. The two talked about everything – even "the deep and the dark" that they shared with nobody else. Though Abbey was bossy and overly maternal to her cousin when they were younger, they were on equal footing now.

Once, when they were trying to figure out how their opposite temperaments got along so well together, Abbey said, "Well, you know how they say opposites attract."

More like opposites show the other more clearly, Layla wrote.

"How?" asked Abbey.

A crow against a bright sky is twice as black as it is in a fir tree. You don't think about your pee being warm till you go to the bathroom on a freezing cold morning. When you bite into a sour apple it makes a ripe one twice as sweet – at least that's how I remember it. Gladness is so much deeper when you've known sorrow.

The night before, Abbey phoned. "The baby's dropped and the doctor says it'll be any day now. It better be or my toenails will grow through my shoes before I can bend over to cut them. 'Almost an eight-pounder,' the doctor said to me. 'But if you want to know if it's a boy or a girl, I only get that right fifty percent of the time.'"

Layla laughed.

"Everyone is predicting the baby is a boy because I'm carrying low and craving pickles. You promise to come, Layla? I don't know if I can make it if you're not there helping to take the pain away. Mama will call soon as I go into labor."

Abbey and Roy had attended natural childbirth class together. A lot of folks on the mountain didn't know what that was. Natural childbirth sounded like business as usual. But after Layla's own mother hemorrhaged to death from complications, Abbey and Roy, a nurse and newspaperman who knew the nitty-gritty from hospital admissions to obituaries, were determined to cover all bases.

The smell of diesel and stale air discouraged Layla's notion of drinking from her thermos. Looking out of the window, a wavy, narrow face startled her until she realized it was her own reflection staring back, full of questions.

When the Greyhound pulled into the station in Petersburg, Layla couldn't fathom how two hours had passed without doing a thing except spinning her thoughts into wool enough to cover a full-grown sheep.

Uncle Frank was already there. The cowlick that he usually flattened with hair cream was sticking up and wobbling like the top feathers of a quail and the feedbags under his eyes made it clear he was anxious about what his only daughter was going through.

Most men in an about-to-be-born baby's life were still relegated to driving, fetching, readying the cigars, and pacing the periphery. But times were changing. Some fathers, like Roy, began to take on the role of Lamaze coach.

By and large, birth still played out in an inner sanctum of women who, steeped in blood and tidal moons, remembered lonely Eve as they ushered the most sacred of gifts through the most primal of places, urging, in the body's own language to *push. Push.*

"Layla, honey. Here, let me take your suitcase. Abbey's been calling for you. The doctor says she's coming along but I think she's waiting on you to have that baby."

Once Layla was in the car, Uncle Frank gunned the motor and pressed his luck at the traffic lights like Layla was the one about to have a baby.

The rubber soles of Layla's sneakers squished on the

shiny linoleum of the maternity corridor as she followed the hurry-up pace of her uncle.

Avis jumped up to hug her niece as soon as she saw Layla. Abbey beamed pure relief, her stomach under the sheet resembling one of the giant white balls the cousins had rolled up for snowmen when they were little.

Roy, who looked like the labor pains were harder on him than Abbey, rose from the side of the bed to kiss Layla. Roy's mother, Edna, came over to hug Layla, even though they'd only been in each other's company a few times.

"Here comes another one," Abbey said, scrunching up her face. Roy gripped his wife's hand.

"Okay honey," he said. "Take a real big breath and blow out. One, two ..."

"Layla," Abbey grunted.

Layla moved close and laid her hands on her cousin's belly steeled tight with contraction.

Immediately, Layla felt something wasn't right – felt it down to the pit of her empty stomach.

Avis bent over to wipe Abbey's face with a damp washcloth.

"How are we doing?" asked a nurse who came in. "Excuse us for a minute while I check how much progress we've made." The nurse drew a privacy curtain around Abbey's bed, leaving the rest of family on the other side.

"Mrs. Brooks," the nurse said, checking the chart. "My name is Miss Hiller. I'm going to check you now and see how close you are to pushing." Behind the curtain, the nurse pulled on rubber gloves. *Snap!*

"Just relax, dear. Good for you! You're at nine centimeters, almost ready to push."

"Thank heavens," said Abbey.

"Let's check the baby's heartbeat." The nurse placed the stethoscope on Abbey's belly. She repositioned the disk on various spots, back and forth, up and down, stopping to adjust the tips more firmly in her ears.

"I'm having a little trouble locating the heartbeat," she said. "Could you roll on your side for me?"

"What's the matter?" Abbey asked. "Is something wrong?"

"Your baby is just playing a little hide-and-seek. Roll to the other side, now," the nurse said.

Abbey panicked. "Can't you hear anything?"

"Don't worry, dear," said the nurse. "I'm sure it's just the baby's position." The nurse pushed the call button beside the bed and lifted Abbey's wrist to take her pulse. She was listening to Abbey's heart when the head nurse came in and whisked through the closed curtain.

"What's going on?" Avis asked. The family looked at one another with frozen faces. Layla was already sick with worry.

From behind the curtain, they heard nurse Hiller. "I'm not getting a fetal heartbeat. BP is elevated. One-sixty over one hundred."

"Turn onto your back for me," said the head nurse, swiftly positioning the stethoscope earpieces. After listening in various positions, she checked Abbey's pulse. "Mrs. Brooks, I'm going to get the doctor. Meantime, were going to prep you for a C-section and get this baby out. Nurse Hiller is going to clear an operating room and get a gurney." The head nurse gave a brisk nod indicating there was no time to waste.

"Can't we wait?" Abbey asked.

"Your baby is in distress," said the head nurse. "You don't want that, do you?"

"No, but –" Abbey was verging on hysteria.

"You hold tight, dear. I'm going to get the doctor." Her nurse-white rubber-soled shoes squished double-time as she yanked the curtain open, nodded a tight smile to the family, and sped down the hallway.

"Layla," Abbey screamed. "Come help!"

Layla rushed into the curtained area, Avis and Roy right behind.

Quickly, Layla placed her hands on Abbey's belly and closed her eyes to better pick up sensations. The young healer felt an absence. Something that should have been there but wasn't.

Roy squeezed his wife's hand and tried to cheer her

on. Avis, petrified by memories of her sister's delivery, stroked Abbey's forehead and tried to hold back tears.

Layla was no stranger to the hover of imminent death. But not Abbey. Not this baby! Experienced as she was, Layla knew that when someone was dying there was nothing she could do but to try and bring peace. The young healer's mind raced, grasping for possible remedy. All she could think to do was hold her hands on Abbey in prayer. Pray to the Almighty – *beg* the Almighty – to help her cousin. To not let Abbey or her baby die.

Not my will, Thy will, Layla reminded herself. But in the same breath, she implored God to see and grant the absolute necessity of her petition.

*Surrender... Surrender... Surrender...*Layla repeated to herself, trying to clear the way for Spirit to flow through her hands.

The room started to blur. Everything dissolved, fading into white vapor – the people, the beds in the room, even Abbey. Layla was immersed in an ocean of light. Floating. Serene. Untroubled.

A short time later, the head nurse flew in with the doctor.

"We need everyone out," the doctor said.

"Layla, stay!" Abbey cried. "Keep going. I feel –"

"Out of the way, young lady," the doctor said, pushing Layla aside.

"Don't please," Abbey said. "Give her another minute."

"We might not have another minute." The doctor was curt. "You don't want anything to happen to your baby, do you?"

Roy, Avis, Frank, and Roy's mother, Edna, stood against the wall to make room for nurse Hiller and two orderlies who rolled a gimp-wheeled gurney through the door.

"Wait!" Abbey yelled. "I feel something."

"Let's all quiet down so I can listen." The doctor bent over and placed his stethoscope on Abbey's abdomen.

"Well... Yes. There we are..." He listened in another place. "Loud and clear. I think you're back in business, young lady. Let's check you out." He closed the curtain.

While the doctor examined Abbey, Layla saw her own apprehension mirrored in the faces of the gathered family. Sometimes, Layla thought, death wasn't the worst thing. Living life in the claws of fear was worse because whatever time you did have was ruined.

Fear could be so ravaging that taking your next breath was just the fierceness to survive, or else, an act of pure faith – especially knowing death was like a person's shadow you could never outrun. Layla thought that everybody who took another breath in the face of pain and death deserved a hero's medal for bravery every bit as much as Mrs. Phoebe's husband.

"She's ready to push," said the doctor, sliding open the curtain and peeling off his gloves. "I'll go prep. Your baby is ready to be born."

Strained faces, tensed necks, locked shoulders began to relax a little as the doctor hustled out of the room.

Layla put her hands back on Abbey.

"You did it, Layla," Abbey sobbed. "Whatever was wrong, you fixed it."

"I know," Layla thought, squeezing Abbey's hand. "I felt God's power flowing though my hands to save your baby." Whatever caused the baby's heart to stop, the fact that it restarted when she laid her hands on Abbey was the sign Layla was waiting for. God's confirmation that she was, without a doubt, a healer. She was sure now. Reviving Samson was real. So were thousands of other healings.

Everyone in the room breathed easier.

"They don't call this *labor* for nothing," Abbey said, panting with a contraction. "It's hard work... *unnnnnnnggghhhhh*."

"Deep breath, sweetie," Roy said, poking back the black frame of his glasses that, like his heart, slid downward.

"Six hours of laboring for a first baby!" Avis said. "You always were at the head of the pack, Abbey. Guess that's because you were the oldest," she said.

Layla remembered the constancy of her aunt's encouragement throughout the years. Not just to her own children, but to Layla as well. Yet beyond Avis's supportive words, there was something Layla treasured even more.

It was the way her aunt lit up whenever she saw her. That was the gift Layla most wanted to give Abbey's baby as it grew, because Layla knew – more than toys or clothes or money – it was the shine of pure love that put a sun in your world to grow by.

At ten minutes after four, thirty-five minutes after Abbey went into the delivery room, Dr. Granville came out. Until he lowered the surgical mask over his face, the family was anxious with all the unknowns.

"It's a boy," Dr. Granville said, pumping Roy's hand. "Eight pounds, two ounces. Everyone's doing fine. Healthy mama. Healthy baby."

"Thank you doctor," Roy said. His voice shook with emotion.

"You can see the baby in the nursery. Your wife is being wheeled to her room. Sorry I have to rush off but I've got another delivery."

"I'm going to kiss my wife and then go meet Christopher Franklin Brooks," Roy said.

Auntie Avis grabbed Layla's hand. "While Roy is having a private minute with Abbey, let's us go see the baby. Then I'm gonna run and call the boys and tell 'em they're uncles."

Layla had to sprint to keep up with her excited aunt. Edna and Uncle Frank followed closely as they hurried to the nursery.

It's not right, thought Layla, for the mother to be going one way, the baby the other, and everyone running in between. Evidently, Abbey felt the same way, because when the radiant foursome went to hug the new mother after extolling the beauty of the baby through the nursery window, Abbey said, "I want my baby!"

"The nurse says you need to rest," Roy explained.

"I want my baby now!" Abbey said.

"Sweetie, they'll bring him at feeding time," Auntie Avis said, smoothing Abbey's hair. "You rest now and get your strength back."

"I'm a nurse in this hospital," Abbey said. "If I have to, I'm going to march in and take him myself."

"Settle down, Mama Bear," Uncle Frank said. "Nobody's gonna come between you and your cub." Everybody laughed as he disappeared.

A few minutes later Uncle Frank came back into the room followed by a nurse carrying little Christopher all wrapped up like a store-bought roast.

"Ten fingers. Ten toes," the nurse said, starting to undo the white, pink-and-blue striped blanket. Abbey grabbed her baby out of the nurse's arms and hugged him. Right then she wouldn't have cared if Christopher had nine fingers and eight toes. She needed to reclaim the weight she'd been carrying in her body for nine months.

"You can't hold all that expectation and hope inside

you day and night and have someone just cart it off without a by-your-leave," she said, hugging Christopher for the longest time.

Abbey cradled Christopher in her arms and the family leaned in, cooing and commenting, when the nurse came in with a bottle.

"Here's a bottle for his first feeding. I'll show you how to test to make sure it's not too hot."

"I've got all the food my baby needs," Abbey said. "And it's always the right temperature."

"Just until your milk comes in," the nurse said, offering the bottle.

Without taking her eyes off Christopher, Abbey held up her hand in refusal. As the nurse walked out, lips pursed, shaking her head, little Christopher took to suckling natural as a pup.

"Why don't all of you go back to the house," said Avis. "Edna, I know you brought a feast of food. Then you can come back after everyone gets some rest and a bite to eat. I'll stay here with Abbey. Go on now, all of you go back to the house."

"Why do parents always say everything twice?" Abbey asked.

"You'll find out soon enough," Avis said, leaning over to stroke the baby's head.

"Here. Go to your godmother," said Abbey after a few minutes, handing Layla a diaper and the floppy little body of Christopher. "She'll burp you while I hug my men good-bye."

Layla had coaxed plenty of burps out of Jake and Micah Yeagley, but holding her cousin was different. There was a kinship of blood – a line of love that ran through their veins that spanned countries and oceans and years.

Layla patted Christopher's tiny back and wondered how so many lives and journeys and struggles could flow in such a little body.

"Burrup!"

Everyone laughed at the big sound that came out of such a wee thing.

"A good eater and a good burper. Can't start out better than that." Edna Brooks beamed.

Abbey took her baby son back into her arms. As Layla looked at mother and child staring into each other's eyes, she nodded. *Can't start out better than that.*

Layla's heart was full of love and her hands, full of healing.

Miracles. That's what it was. A day of miracles.

CHAPTER TWENTY-NINE

FOLLOWING Christopher's birth, Layla got an indication of how busy and how exhausted her father must have been after she was born. Abbey had so many hands pitching in to help, but poor Ed was sole mama, papa, and breadwinner for his newborn. It must have been, Layla realized, overwhelming. And having just experienced how near Christopher was to death, Layla grasped a deeper sense of Ed's devastation when her mother died. How worry must have dragged his heart down every time his daughter got sick, especially when she lost her tongue.

"It's a real shame you have to live life forwards," Layla

thought, "but you can only grasp it fully when you look backwards."

For five days, Layla was too busy to journal. Finally, just before her father came for the weekend, she tried to catch up.

Abbey came home the day after giving birth. She groused that she couldn't get any rest because the nurses kept coming in to check her pulse and because she was so worried about Christopher when they took him back to the nursery.

I've been helping fix meals, rubbing Abbey's back and feet and taking Christopher when he is done nursing to change his diaper. I thank God every day for using me to save him.

Ed came that morning. Except for the time she knocked the mixing bowl off the top of the refrigerator and the piece of her tongue fell onto the floor, Layla never saw her father cry. But when he laid his eyes on the baby, she saw tears well up in his eyes.

"Well, aren't you the finest little gopher," he said, stroking Christopher's hair.

Daddy, Layla wanted to say. *Don't start calling him gopher.*

"Topher the gopher," Roy said. "You'll not be Chris. You'll be Topher, thanks to your Uncle Ed."

So everyone started calling the baby Topher. That's when they weren't calling him punkin' or sweetie or pudding pie. With all those food names it was no wonder folks say to babies, "*I could just eat you up.*"

Before Ed and Layla left, Avis made a big Sunday dinner for the family. Only Uncle Frank was absent. "Want to save some of my vacation days for another visit," he said, when he left to go back to the plant in Shady Grove.

Layla hated to pack her suitcase and leave even though she'd be coming back to visit in a few weeks. She was already missing everyone. The only thing she wouldn't miss was the sound of the television at night. After Abbey fed Topher, Roy got up to change him. Then he'd sit down in front of the television for a few minutes, but he was so tired from work and a new baby, he'd fall asleep on the living-room sofa.

In the spare bedroom, Layla jolted from sleep, her heart pounding out of her chest during the terrifying seconds it took to realize that the station had signed off for the night and there was nothing but a screen full of jiggling black-and-white dots in a sea of static hiss. It sounded like millions of grasshoppers. It sounded like a serpent.

It was late when Layla and her father got back home from Petersburg. "Got to be up early for work. I'm going to head to bed," Ed said, stifling a yawn that set off a spate of coughing. "Night, Ducky."

Before she unpacked, Layla went outside to sit on

the porch swing. The waning moon reminded her of the white crescents in each of Topher's tiny fingernails. Abbey's baby opened up such a powerful yearning in Layla it made her want to weep.

Ever since Layla could remember, she was plagued by hungers she couldn't seem to satisfy. Wishing for solid food was the most definable. She tried to push her baby-hunger aside because, in the words of her aunt, "wishes don't wash dishes."

Whenever Layla had a strong desire for something, something not likely to ever happen, like meeting the queen of England or having a baby, she resorted to her *thankful* alphabet.

A... She couldn't remember a time when her *A* gratitude hadn't been *Auntie Avis*.

B... *B* was for *baby* Christopher, no question about it.

C...tonight *C* was for *chamomile* tea – a big cup before bed to settle her down.

D...That was always the same,too... *Daddy*.

E... *E* – Elation to be Christopher's godmother. Layla felt she earned the name godmother in the truest sense by saving his life. And elation that God sent her the sign she'd been praying for. A sign that erased all her doubts. Now, she knew with certainty what God's purpose was for her.

Sitting under the stars and listening to the insistent call of a hoot owl, Layla lettered her way through to *zinnias.* A month ago, in April, she planted seeds in the damp loam for a bright patch beside her mother's rose trellis. She loved the hardy flower's autumnal vibrancy before winter's restful browns and grays took hold. By the time Layla finished her alphabet she didn't need tea.

Tiptoeing back to her room with her suitcase, she unpacked, climbed into bed, and pulled up the comforter made by her mother.

One quilt square was cut from the blue overalls Ed wore the day her mother came into the sawmill to get another slat made for a broken chair.

"Those were my lucky overalls," her father told her. "I knew your mama from the bank. She could count out ones, fives, and tens faster than a card shark could deal a hand of poker."

There was a square of yellow-checked tablecloth from the early days of her parents' marriage that amassed too many mustard stains for decent use. Her mother cut off the one good corner to piece next to a white square of blanket that belonged to cousin Abbey when she was a toddler. Abbey towed that blanket around for so many years and it had to be washed so many times, it was mostly scraps and holes.

"I had visions of Abbey dragging that blanket up the aisle on her weddin' day," Avis said, handing a large swatch to her sister for her quilting basket and folding one into her own.

There was a light blue square with a smattering of flowers made from a scrap of one of her mama's old dresses. Whenever she covered up, Layla carefully arranged the flowered patch so it centered on her chest. That way she could rest her hand on it, imagining that she touched a little piece of her mother.

Layla thought about how baby Christopher would learn about each piece of the quilt she made for him – all the stories that covered him in love.

With a full heart, she drifted off in a sea of lovely feelings. And a deep, longing ache.

CHAPTER THIRTY

THE weeks after Topher's birth sped by with chores, spring planting, and a full schedule of healing work. Much as Layla missed being with Abbey, Roy, and her godson, she loved the quiet of the woods. Like the big easy chair by the fireplace that held the shape of her father even when he wasn't there, Layla's heart held the curves and hollows of her mountain – its colors, its sounds, its smells.

She decided to walk down the lane to the mailbox. Ed usually picked up the mail on his way home, but Layla had been pickling new beets all morning and craved fresh air instead of vinegar up her nose.

"Onward with vinegar!" She smiled, remembering Wolfy's battle cry when he was little. And she remembered Abbey's exasperation. "V*igor*, Wolfy! Vigor!"

The squirrels tumbled and mated, chasing each other around like they were on a caffeine high. In the middle of the road, a large rat snake soaked up the gravel's warmth. The once bitten, twice shy young woman skirted the snake respectfully. She still hadn't "handled" in church, though she still felt she was being moved in that direction.

The black metal of the mailbox was hot to the touch when she opened it. With May's end-of-the-month bills, several catalogues, and two magazines, the stack of mail had some heft as she shuffled through it.

One of the magazines, *Reader's Digest*, was a Father's Day gift she gave to Ed – a luxury he would never have allowed himself. Her father didn't have time or energy to get through a whole book, but he took pleasure in spot-reading the magazine's jokes and stories throughout the month.

And last year, Auntie Avis gifted Layla with a subscription to *Ladies' Home Journal*. "It's chock-full of news, ideas, and tips about everything under the sun. You're so holed up in that mountain, honeybunch, it'll keep you up to date."

All the glossy magazine pages and articles were a treat. But Layla was amused when she read about the latest color or style of clothing as if it were something nature hadn't already thought of. No matter how attractive an outfit was to Layla, none of it compared to an ordinary mallard. If a fashion designer combined the flickered green of the duck's head, the butter yellow of its bill, the bright orange of its webbed feet, the soft brown and gray of its breast feathers, the chocolate brown on its neck and back, and the deep purple blue under its wing, people would deem it too outlandish.

Once more giving berth to the snake's glistening black coils, Layla ambled back, breathing in the incense of the woods. Bathed in fragrance-induced well-being, she mounted the porch steps, eased onto the swing, and began to leaf through the new issue of *Ladies' Home Journal.*

On the cover was the dazzling Elizabeth Taylor, living a celebrity's life of diamonds, limousines, mansions, and yachts. But inside was the story of her divorce. It saddened Layla to think of the unspoken pain beneath that crimson, lipsticky smile. She wished she could invite the woman underneath all those Hollywood trappings to sit on the porch swing with a glass of sweet tea and drink in the peace of the mountain.

Sorting through the mail, Layla's hand froze when she spied an envelope stuck between a farm and tractor supply ad and a catalog from Montgomery Ward.

It was addressed in a hand that wasn't Auntie Avis's or Abbey's or any known to Layla, and bore no return address in the corner or on the back flap.

She opened up the envelope and unfolded the lined notebook paper inside.

May 21, 1974

Dear Layla,

I hope you don't mind my writing to you. I call Brian once in a while to check in on him and he gave me your address. He told me how he knew you. And why. It doesn't surprise me.

The night I met you, I had a dream. A DREAM, Layla! An unspeakably beautiful dream about you. That might not seem out of the ordinary, but I can't remember having a dream for four years. I stopped having dreams a few months after I went to 'Nam. Plenty of nightmares, though.

First, let me thank you again for being an angel of help and hope. My bike is good and I'll never forget the feast you served. I didn't know that a forkful of food could feed so many hungers.

I felt terrible leaving the way I did. But the last thing in the world I wanted to do was inflict more hurt. Since I got home from 'Nam eight months ago, I'm all razor blades, inside and out. That's why I left Chicago.

A few nights ago, I wrote this poem.

I am lost
I am lost
Lost in direction
Abandoned by protection
Cursed by my mind's recollection
Of misconception
It is time to begin again
I am lost
It is time to begin again.

Part of what drives me crazy is that, finally, against all odds, I got out of 'Nam. But I can't manage to get 'Nam out of me.

Some day I hope to visit you again, Layla. I hope that will be okay. I wish I had an address where you could write back to me if you wanted to. But right now, I'm a moving target. No clue where I'm heading.

Be well, angel of my dreams.

Damian

The porch swing was barely swaying. In her secret heart, Layla always hoped to see Damian again. But she didn't know if he wanted to see her too.

She reread the words again, lifting the paper to her nose for the scent of Damian. There were traces of mildew, ink, and wood smoke. Closing the pages, gently smoothing across the folds, Layla started to slip the pages into the envelope, but instead straightened out the notebook paper and read it again, lingering over every word.

A squawking jaybird brought her back to the needs of the day.

Frustrated that there was no way she could write back to Damian, Layla refolded the letter.

She wondered if she should show the letter to her father or just divulge selected information. If so, how much? It would be awful if a long-haired, tattooed stranger showed up on their doorstep when she was off visiting Abbey. Or on some dark night.

In the kitchen, Layla wiped off and labeled the mason jars of cooled-down beets, knowing she had to tell her father something.

She wondered why embracing new people, even desired ones like a baby, brought so many complications. It meant your heart and brain had to hold more of everything. Love, worry, problems, joy, the fear of losing. The hours of the day needed to make room, as well.

Layla hoped that the particulars of how and what to tell her father about Damian would solidify like the lemon Jell-O she mixed up for dessert that evening. But even after the dishes were done and her father was already on the porch chuckling over the humor section in his *Reader's Digest*, she was still at a loss.

When Ed wavered over a decision, he'd say, "I'll have to sleep on that."

Layla guessed that if she didn't burn to ash like a Fourth of July sparkler, Damian's letter could wait until tomorrow. Ordinarily, it would have been an uneasy way to go to bed. But with Damian's words tucked under her pillow, she dreamed impossible dreams even before she fell asleep.

CHAPTER THIRTY-ONE

ON a sultry late-August morning, Ed left for the mill carrying a lunch pail packed by his daughter.

Not fully awake, Layla smiled and waved good-bye to her father. The night before, she dreamed about Damian. *Carnal dreams.*

In July, two months after his first letter, Layla received a postcard from Damian with a picture of the Canadian Rockies on the front. On the flip side of the card that, luckily, Layla retrieved from the mailbox before her father, Damian's message read:

Dear Layla,
Heading for Alaska. Wild landscapes. Raw nature. Still trying to sort things out, but have to go underground for a while longer. Make my way through the dark where shadow has no meaning.

You are always in my deepest dreaming.
Be well, D.

Lost in mental swoon from her dream, moving languidly because of the heat, Layla was less attentive than she usually was to her surroundings.

Before sweeping the front porch, she took the sawdust-laden doormat that her father stomped on every evening and went down the steps to shake it, eyes closed and head turned away from the flying debris as she flapped. When she stopped shaking and opened her eyes, there he stood.

"Don't you move none," Zeb Yeagley said. He held a deer rifle leveled straight at her, not twenty feet away

Thin as barbed wire, hair matted, and with a mangy beard and the stagger of drink in his step, Zeb moved toward Layla, snarling like a mad dog.

At the Yeagleys', when she was a young girl, Layla stood up to Zeb's threats. But now his eyes had that glassy look that people under the influence get. Layla's gut told her not to laugh him off, not to turn away, and not to break for the house.

The adrenaline-pumped nineteen-year-old smelled the stink of alcohol and unwashed body odor as Zeb edged closer. Then swift as a striking viper, Zeb dropped his rifle and threw her reed-slim body to the ground. Layla fell so hard it took a minute to see the blade of his hunting knife, poised above her head.

Layla twisted and struggled to get up, but Zeb slammed her back again. He climbed on top of her and straddled each of her arms with a knee.

With one hand Zeb mashed the knife blade against her neck. With the other, he unzipped the fly of his stained, rank trousers. Shifting his weight from one knee to the other he reached in and whipped out his stiff red rod. Gagging from the ammonia smell of old urine and spoiled cheese, Layla's head jerked to the side.

"Open up your mouth you slit slug." Zeb's voice was hoarse and slurred. He dug the knife deeper until she could feel warm trickle running down her neck. Tears ran into her ears as she turned her head and looked into his distorted face.

"Open up!" he said, as he rammed his wood against her clenched lips. He pressed down on the knife blade until she screamed. When she opened her mouth to yell, Zeb jammed his penis in, thrusting in and out, bucking and groaning.

Gasping, choking, Layla struggled to get air.

"Shhhh," Zeb hissed. *"Sssshhh."*

That sound.

That sound!

Fast as lightning, slow as time in the midst of a car crash, Layla recognized that hiss; the pitch of it; the explosive force.

As she gagged on the hot spurts, she remembered all those years ago. Her choking. His shushes. Fighting for breath.

Zeb slumped forward and the knife slipped from his open hand. His weight on her chest allowed Layla only the shallowest intake of air.

It happened all at once, though Layla could never imagine that the body and the mind could accomplish two such monumental tasks at the same time.

She had a vision. Clear as the creek on a sunny day when every pebble on the bottom is visible, Layla saw what happened fourteen years ago when she was five. It wasn't a serpent that took her tongue. It was Zeb Yeagley.

And in the same instant that her mind realized it was Zeb, she felt the welling up of animal instinct that her father told her to trust. Her jaws widened and her teeth clamped together as hard as she could.

Zeb went mad with pain. He howled and grabbed himself. Layla jerked out from underneath him, but stumbled backward.

He reached out and grabbed her leg. With her free foot, she kicked with all her might, bashing him in the eye with her heel.

Righting herself, Layla seized the rifle and fled to the house. As she looked back, she saw Zeb, half crawling, half dragging after her.

On the porch steps, her knees threatened to give way. She tripped, heaved forward, catapulted through the door, and bolted the lock.

Her heart hammered so loudly in her ears, she couldn't hear if Zeb was still following or not. She knew she needed to call the operator and give the prearranged signal in case of an emergency. But before she could reach for the phone, a lead ball in her stomach started rolling upwards, up to her chest, into her throat. She barely made it to the kitchen sink before she vomited bile and Zeb spew. In the midst of choking heaves, she heard Zeb at the kitchen door, feet and fists banging.

"I'm gonna kill you you gawdam bitch," Zeb screamed. Though Layla had heard animals meeting their death in the woods – the high-pitched cry of a rabbit, the yelp of a coon-slashed dog, and the snarl of a shot bear – none ever pierced her the way Zeb's moaning shrieks did as he tried to break down the door.

Then everything went silent. Layla ran to the phone just as a big rock smashed through the window of the kitchen door. Zeb's hand reached through the jagged glass and groped around for the lock.

Layla dropped to the floor and scrambled toward the rifle. To steel her shaking body, she sat with her back propped against the refrigerator. Her mind raced through escape routes. She could run into the bedroom, shut the door, and shove the dresser up against it.

No! Something inside raged. Don't hide!

She wasn't skilled with guns, but she wasn't new to them either. Her father taught her to aim true, hold steady, brace for the kick, and squeeze smoothly.

By the time Zeb's hand found the lock and twisted it open, Layla had the safety released and was looking through the sight.

When the door opened, Layla fired low. Zeb stopped and staggered backwards, his bleeding pecker hanging out of his pants. White spittle foamed from his mouth and the look in his eyes was nothing Layla had ever seen or hoped to see again.

Suddenly, he lurched forward through the door. A strange calm came over her. She looked at Zeb as if she were at the grocery store examining a package of ground meat. She raised the barrel of the gun a little higher and shot again.

Zeb jerked and groaned. Dark ooze reddened the puncture hole on the thigh of his trousers. Zeb teetered as the red bloomed outward and began to drip onto the green linoleum. With cool calculation, Layla pulled the bolt back for another shot just as Zeb crumpled and fell amid shattered window glass near the area where her tongue had flipped out of the mixing bowl fourteen years earlier.

Layla got up and wrenched the knife out of Zeb's hand. Staring down at him, she felt cold. Robotic.

She went to the phone and dialed the emergency number.

"Eehh! Eehh! Eehh!"

"Layla Tompkin, is that you?

"Uhhuh!"

"Fire?"

Two short sounds.

"Ambulance?"

One short sound.

"Police?"

One short sound.

"Okay, Layla. Help is coming. You hang on, okay."

One short sound.

"I'm gonna call your father and neighbors now. Stay on the phone, now, Layla."

"Not the Yeagleys," Layla thought. "Don't call the Yeagleys." She remembered the time Ida Mae nearly went into cardiac arrest when she saw Samson alive and walking. She'd have an attack for sure if she saw her Zeb bleeding to death on the kitchen floor.

Layla spread a kitchen towel over the bloody, limp, chewed-up thing hanging out of Zeb's pants. Then she took the broom by the door and swept the broken glass to the side. She took the cast-iron frying pan off the stove and set it close by in case Zeb regained consciousness and she needed to knock him out again. Kneeling beside Zeb, she put her hand on his leg where it bled. She had no idea why; it just seemed the right thing to do.

Zeb's eyes were shut, his jaw slack. Without the twist of cruel malice on his face, Zeb looked sickly. Layla sat there like a bear in hibernation, everything at a standstill. Soon, the sound of tires rolled up the gravel drive.

"Layla! Layla!" Mrs. Gilly called out. "Oh my sweet Jesus, help us," Emiline said, creeping through the blood and glass on the porch.

Layla knew she should call back. That Mrs. Gilly would think the worse if she didn't reply, but she just couldn't rouse herself.

Mrs. Gilly stood in the doorway dumbstruck at the bleeding body of Zeb Yeagley lying on the kitchen floor and Ed Tompkin's daughter next to him, one hand on his leg, the other on a frying pan.

Of all the people to aid in a crisis, Emiline Gilly wouldn't come to mind as first or second choice. Not even tenth. There probably wasn't a sweeter soul in Fox Hollow but Emiline was emotionally frail. She often took to bed for what she called "a case of the nerves." Ever since her husband died in a coal-mining accident, Emiline had dwindled in mind and body to no more than a sliver of a woman. But besides the Yeagleys, Mrs. Gilly lived closest to the Tompkins' on the other side and the operator thought if help was needed, fast was better than nothing.

"Layla," Mrs. Gilly said. Her voice quavered as she spoke. "Layla, come on outta there, sweetie."

Layla smiled up at Mrs. Gilly as if she just asked the silliest thing in the world. She was frozen into place and couldn't move even if she wanted. Everything seemed to move in slow motion.

Mrs. Gilly grabbed onto the door frame to steady herself. "Come on now, sweet girl..."

A siren was closing in. Vehicles screeched to the front of the house and car doors slammed.

Sheriff Dones came striding in, hand poised on the butt of his holstered gun. The Sheriff nudged Zeb's foot like he was testing a killed rattler to see if it was really dead. "Okay, Layla," he said, leaning over his bulging belly to help her up. "Are you hurt anywhere?"

"How do I answer that?" Layla thought, as if the question was as mysterious as the universe. With glazed eyes, she smiled at Sheriff Dones as if he was speaking a foreign language...Greek or Urdu.

An ambulance siren neared as Sheriff Dones lifted up Layla and walked her out to the porch like a puppet that couldn't move without his manipulating her limbs.

Two EMTs rushed up the porch.

"Inside the house," Sheriff Dones said to one of them. "The Yeagley boy."

One of the technicians came over and took Layla's wrist.

"Layla Tompkin," the sheriff said. "Ed Tompkin's girl. She's a mute."

"Are you hurt anywhere?" the EMT asked, feeling up and down the length of her arms and legs, along her back and around her ribs.

Layla shook her head.

Layla flinched as the EMT probed her neck where Zeb dug the knife in.

There was a rumble coming up the lane so fast it sounded like a rockslide.

Ed skidded to a stop, leapt out of his truck, and came running over.

"Is she hurt? Is she hurt?"

Her father knelt down by the front of the swing and took his daughter's hand. "Are you hurt, honey?"

"She's in shock," the EMT said, taking the stethoscope out of his ears. "Some bruising and a pretty deep gash. We'll take her into Petersburg and get her checked out."

Suddenly, Layla started to shake. Shake so hard her teeth clacked. Ed ran in to get a blanket. When he came out his face was so red it looked like a stick of dynamite about to blow. He'd seen Zeb with his towel-covered privates and was reeling with the unimaginable implications.

"We better get him to the hospital," said the EMT.

Ed sat with his arm around his daughter on the swing while they loaded Zeb Yeagley onto a stretcher and into the ambulance.

Sheriff Dones called the shaken father aside to talk but when the ambulance driver went to take Layla, Ed stopped him.

"Layla'll ride with me. We'll follow you as far as Wayland and see Doc Fredericks. If Doc says we need to, we'll go on over to Petersburg."

"I've got to go fill out some paperwork," said the sheriff. "After Layla sees the doctor and has a chance to settle down, we'll all sit down and try to figure out just what happened. Meantime, I'd appreciate if you left everything as is until my deputy has a chance to write up a report. Shouldn't take more'n an hour." He shook hands with Ed, patted Layla's shoulder, and left.

Ed wrapped the blanket more tightly around his daughter. "Do you want anything, honey? A drink of water, maybe?"

Layla nodded, her mouth filled with bitter.

Her father brought a glass of water and Layla sat on the swing, filling her mouth and spitting like some hornet-mad whiskey swiller. She tried to rid herself of the sick dirtiness that adhered to her skin. She wanted to purge the shame and fury that slimed between her teeth and clung to the curled-up places of her brain.

Layla threw off the blanket and ran to the bathroom. She turned on the shower and tore off her yellow blouse sullied with spew and dirt and blood. She yanked off her skirt. Pulled off undergarments, every stitch she was wearing except her gold-chained heart, and stumbled into the shower. She let the water pelt down on her as she rubbed and scrubbed like she'd gotten into a mess of poison ivy.

"Layla. Layla...you okay, honey?" Ed's voice called into the bathroom but the sound of it dimmed into the background until all Layla could hear was the hard rain of shower water. She scrubbed with soap, she scrubbed with a washcloth, she scrubbed with the brush her father used to get the sawdust from his skin, but she couldn't get clean.

Abruptly, the water stopped. Obsessed with eradicating the foul abomination from her body, it took a moment for the drenched girl, fair skin scoured red, to figure out what had happened. The curtain slid open and her father was standing there with a towel.

"Come on out now, Ducky," he said. His voice was barely audible. He wrapped the towel around his dripping nineteen-year-old daughter, averting his eyes from her lithe womanliness, pragmatism trouncing embarrassment. "You're safe now. We're gonna get through this.

Sit down over here and let's get you dried off."

Layla sat, towel-wrapped on the commode, while Ed took another towel and put it over her hair, blotting and squeezing. Layla saw particles of wood and dust on his clothes and skin; no time to brush it off.

"I'm gonna bring you in some clothes now, Ducky. We need to get you over to Doc Fredericks. Think you could get dressed now?"

Layla nodded blankly.

On the drive down the mountain to Wayland, Ed broke the silence every few minutes, asking, "Are you all right, Ducky? Are you all right?"

When Ed and Layla arrived, Brian was sitting in his wheelchair, a grim sentry. The sheriff had radioed ahead with news of the attack.

"Hello," Brian said, looking from father to daughter with questioning eyes. Ed bustled his daughter inside. Even though there were patients in the waiting room, Doc Fredericks took Layla right away.

"Ed, why don't you take a breather out on the porch. I know Brian would be pleased to have your company. We'll all talk together after I've had a chance to look Layla over." As Ed turned toward the porch, Doc Fredericks held out a gown. "Undress all the way down to your skin, Layla, and put this on. I'll be back in a minute."

When Doc Fredericks returned, he put a pencil and paper on the white sheet of the examination table where

Layla sat slumped in the faded cotton gown. "I'm going to go over you from head to toe, Layla. You let me know if anything hurts."

Gently, Doc Fredericks started parting Layla's still wet hair, looking at her scalp and touching all around like it was a melon he was feeling for ripeness.

"Do you remember how you got this?" he asked, removing the gauze pad that the EMT put over her neck.

A knife, Layla wrote.

"I'll dress it in a minute," Doc said, covering the wound with fresh gauze. "I think we can get it closed up with butterfly closures instead of stitches. Then you'll need to keep antibiotic ointment on it. Better give you a tetanus shot too."

Will Zeb live? Layla asked.

"By all rights, Zeb should have bled to death from the bullet wound to his femoral artery. That's what the EMT told the sheriff. For some reason he didn't. He'll probably spend enough years behind bars wishing he had. But it doesn't take a Sherlock Holmes to figure out what went on. You've got a strong bite, Layla, but you only dented him."

A flush of red rose in Layla's face, spreading until her whole body burned with shame.

Doc Fredericks put his hand under her chin and lifted her bent head. "You did a brave thing, Layla, you've nothing to regret."

As he inspected Layla's mouth with a tongue depressor and flashlight, he kept a steady line of conversation going.

"This wasn't the first time, was it, Layla? Zeb did the same thing when you were little. Right?"

While Zeb was violating her she had the same revelation. But to hear it spoken out loud, was shocking.

"Years ago, I notified the sheriff with my suspicion that it was no serpent that took your tongue. Nothing ever came of it, though." Doc shook his head with frustration. "Were there any other times?"

Layla shook her head, though she knew there almost were.

"Right from the beginning I had doubts. You, know, Layla, medicine and the law follow particular signs to figure out what's going on. Religion follows another kind. They all have power if you believe in them."

Doc Fredericks told Layla to lie down. He thumped three or four times over her various internals – chest, ribs, liver, kidneys – listening to the sound.

"I can't figure out how you can ease Brian's pain when I can't. But you do. Does that make it any less real than a bona fide prescription?"

As he began to examine her lower abdomen, Doc asked, "Layla, did Zeb penetrate you vaginally?"

Woodenly, she shook her head.

"We're all just chemistry sets inside," Doc Fredericks

said, flexing the knee of one leg up to her chest and straightening it again. "We doctors are like kids playing around in the basement with our test tubes." He rotated her ankle round and pressed on her foot. "Adding chemicals together and mixing them up until we get things to change this way or that."

Doc Fredericks took her other leg and started rotating clockwise. "A pretty girl can change a man's chemistry faster than any pill. And a hug can sometimes cure more ailments than a hundred visits to a doctor.

"You can sit up now, Layla." Doc took a moment to clear his throat. "You know, Layla, everything that happens in this room is between you and me. That's a promise. Not your father. Not the police. Nobody else in the world unless you choose to tell them."

Doc Fredericks handed her the pencil and paper. "Is there anything else you want to tell me, Layla? Anything that happened. Anything at all that you want to say? Or ask?"

Layla brooded. As Doc Fredericks tended to the gash on her neck, the cold numbness inside her began to unfreeze. In the thaw, questions flooded into her mind. *"If I wasn't serpent bitten,"* she thought, *"was it God who caused my tongue to be cut out by Zeb? Was it so I could learn new tongues like Pastor Simpson said?"*

With each new question, she was more confused. *"What about my gift of healing? Maybe that isn't from*

God either. Maybe it's just in the heads of folks who believe I can heal." Her brain was totally muddled.

"You don't have to work out what happened or what it all means right now, Layla," Doc Fredericks said. Because Doc suspected, all along, that human wrongdoing was the cause of Layla's severed tongue, he was well aware of the roller coaster of ramifications, religious and otherwise, which would surely follow.

The doctor swabbed Layla's arm and administered a quick jab of vaccine. "You can ask me questions anytime. And no matter what questions or conclusions you come to, I hope you keep visiting for Brian's sake. I can't begin to explain what you do or how you do it, but I know it's real. And it's a precious gift to our family. For now, why don't you get dressed and then you and your dad and I will talk for a few minutes."

"If Doc Fredericks doesn't understand what happens when I lay my hands on people, maybe I don't have to understand either," Layla thought as she slipped on her bra and panties. *"But what'll happen when people find that it wasn't a serpent that bit out my tongue? When they find out the healing power is not a sign from God the way they think it is, will I still be able to help them?"* Her thoughts careened and collided as she buttoned up her blouse.

"It's deceitful, though, letting folks think something about you that isn't true." She fastened her skirt. *"But*

Doc Fredericks said the healing was real. If something is real, isn't it true?" She felt bruised and aching on the outside. Her insides were revulsed. And now her mind was feeling beat up too.

The unspoken motto in the Smoky Mountains was, "Resilience trumps the hand you're dealt." Time and time again, Layla made those words visible. But like elastic that finally gives out, Layla, frayed with shame, unraveling with fury and doubt, felt herself slipping irrevocably downward.

CHAPTER THIRTY-TWO

AFTER coming back from Doc Fredericks on Friday, Layla stayed in bed, glassy-eyed and unreachable. When she finally fell asleep, Ed made a call he dreaded. There was no whitewashing the guilt he felt – all the misjudgments he'd made through the years by continuing to leave his daughter in the care of the Yeagleys. But, even so, he needed to notify Avis out of duty and desperation.

"Noooo! Nooo!" Avis screamed as if Zeb had managed to reach out from his jail cell across the miles and was twisting his knife back and forth in her heart.

She sobbed as Ed related the details that he knew.

"I'll see what I can work out to help, Ed. Right now

the only thing I can think of is to hug her and love her, but I'm so upset, I can't think straight. I'll call tomorrow, first thing."

The next morning, Ed walked down the drive to retrieve the *Smoky Mountain Gazette* from the mailbox. When he saw the headlines, his jaws clenched down so hard his molars hurt. No way was he going to let Layla read the paper.

Minutes after Ed got back from the mailbox, Pastor Simpson, hat in hand, came knocking. Ed, in no mood to be cordial, nodded curtly and stood at the screen door without opening it.

"We're all prayin' for your daughter, Mr. Tompkin."

When Ed made no reply, the pastor reached into the breast pocket of his coat and held out an envelope in the awkward silence. "The Yeagley family wanted Layla to have this. Due to the –" he cleared his throat –"*unfortunate situation*, they asked if I'd deliver it."

Ed opened the screen, took the envelope, said "thank you for your trouble," closed the screen, and walked away. Though Ed knew he had no right to open the envelope, his daughter fully of age, he opened it anyway, justifying that he had every right to protect her. Inside was a get-well card that somebody had gone to Herman's drugstore in Wayland to pick out. The message was pure Hallmark, religious with a peaceful nature scene. The only personal touch was inside where it was signed *the Yeagley family*. Ed left the card on the kitchen table.

It didn't take long for the phone to start ringing. Friends, neighbors, and sympathetic townsfolk called or stopped by, saying they'd read the terrible news, how shocking it was, how was Layla doing, and how long would it be until she was back to her healing work?

When Ed brought a bowl of soup into Layla's bedroom, she'd overheard enough snatches of conversation to figure out that the story was spreading like mushroom spores.

I want to read what the paper said, she wrote.

Reluctantly, Ed brought his daughter the *Gazette* and then was dismissed from the room with a forceful wave of her Ace-bandaged hand. Head down, Ed plodded back to the kitchen. Since the attack, he was barely managing to hold together his emotions. Far worse though, was how to help his daughter through her pain.

Layla sat up in bed, bumping her nightstand where the soup sat untouched. She opened the pages of the newspaper that Ed had folded up and stashed inside his desk, and began to read.

Faith Healer Victim of Violent Attack

By Nick Josephs

Wayland, Tennessee

Nineteen-year-old Layla Tompkin, well-known local faith healer, was raped at knifepoint yesterday morning, August 30, 1974, in front of her mountain home eight miles east of Wayland. Zebidiah Yeagley, the alleged attacker, is the oldest son of a neighboring family.

The injured woman was transported to Wayland where she was treated for shock, multiple contusions and a knife wound to the neck.

Because the victim is mute and must communicate in writing, Sheriff Ronald Dones has postponed interrogation until later today. The alleged rapist, also injured in the attack, was taken by ambulance to Mercy hospital in Petersburg and will be remanded over to the county prison after treatment until further investigation.

Due to the fact that Miss Tompkin is a revered figure in the area, emotions are running high. Community outrage has citizens calling for a lifetime behind bars for the perpetrator and inquiry into why this known felon, previously incarcerated for armed robbery, was granted an early release from prison.

Layla Tompkin is expected to make a full recovery.

Full recovery.

Post-rape, that was the expectation for her printed in black-and-white on the front page of the *Smoky Mountain Gazette.*

"How is that possible?" she thought. "That stomach-turning Zeb smell penetrates every cell of my body. My skin smells like Zeb; water, food, air, everything has his stink. It's so far down there's no way I'll ever get it out."

Layla's recuperation proved to be a lot easier in column inches than in the not-so- newsworthy aftermath. At first, the nineteen-year-old could count her wounds. As she revolved in front of the hallway mirror, straining to view her back, she saw nine abrasions from the driveway's sharp gravel. Ten bruises from Zeb's bucking and grinding. Three fingernails ripped below the quick. Both wrists sprained so badly she could hardly lift a glass of water. And a single knife slash on her neck, opening the flesh into a shallow mouth as mute as the one above her chin. She could tally her injuries like the score of one of Frankie's baseball games. But emotionally, there was no such tidy measure.

The aftershocks of the attack were impossible to compute. On the heels of that first stunned day, her perception became skewed like a stone-struck windshield. Everything she looked at was seen through shatter. Firm footing vanished. So did the way forward, her former compass magnetized by a darker pull.

She was a healer. God's chosen vessel. Yet, when she failed to be protected by a life devoted to service, a back-door deadbolt and an easy-to-reach rifle, her notions of safety and rock-solid beliefs crumbled.

In her journal Layla wrote, *I feel like the archeologists at Indian Grave Gap, sifting through the rubble of everything that's ruined. But there's not enough glue in the world to put the brokenness back together.*

Meanwhile, the rape continued to burrow deeper and deeper into her mind and body. Time had two divisions. Before August 30, 1974. And afterwards.

Like Brian and Damian, Layla joined the ranks of survivors.

Faith carries some people through. But for Layla, it had fled the scene like a burglar who makes off with everything valuable. Motivation can go a long way, assuming a person's will to live stays intact. The importance of will was never more plainly stated than by a Vietnamese woman Brian told Layla about during one of their healing sessions.

"I was in the jungle," he said, "when I came to a clearing and saw this emaciated woman squatting in the debris of her torched home. The bloated bodies of her husband and children, full of bullet holes, lay nearby. I stooped down to give her a drink from my canteen. Then I dug out a granola bar from my pocket and handed it to her. She refused. 'What good is food if no reason left to eat,' she said. I left the bar anyway. I really didn't know what else to do."

Layla saw, firsthand, what Brian went through. Initially, he was patched together in hopes that some of the smashed and detached might come back on board – at least enough to ambulate with prosthetics, make love or, minimally, live without bedpans. After that, attention turned to other vitals. Intangibles that were equally destroyed but were not mentioned in any of Doc's anatomy books, never illustrated with a reference to "see figure *a*."

Now Layla wondered, as she often did during her healing sessions with Brian, on what bone, to what nerve do you attach severed trust? Belief? Hope? Especially when, like transplanted organs, they no longer recognize they belong. Maybe the starfish she'd read about in biology were able to regenerate from limb loss because shell and soft tissue are less mysterious than the biochemistry of conviction. The synaptic leap of purpose. The DNA of meaning. The rape of every good thing you know.

According to the local folklore on the ridges and in the gaps of the Smokies, "when you enter the world, as baby Layla did, with your feet pawing the air before your eyes can see where to put them, it's a strong sign you'll lose your way from time to time."

Right from the get-go there was more truth than myth

in the prediction about the new child's path. For without a mother, the little girl's way forward was already full of detours.

But the prophecy's full import didn't come home to roost until that stifling August day. Being a healer defined Layla. She ministered to others from childhood to the brink of her twenties, accepting that much was taken from her so she could become worthy of God's gift. She'd grappled with doubt and become more faithful. Her life had meaning and her days had purpose until that August morning so muggy that a light scent of lavender dusting powder rose from the armpits of her cotton blouse and from the dampish underclothes beneath her skirt.

Abruptly, in less time than it took to sneeze or snuff a candle, everything changed.

Everything.

Nothing made sense. *Why did God let Zeb cut out my tongue?* she wrote in her journal. *Take away my ability to speak? Take away my taste of peaches and chocolate pie? Why did God let Zeb hunt me down and rape me? Why did my mama die? What kind of God would cause so much pain and devastation?*

The more questions Layla asked, the more lost and despondent she became. The troubled nineteen-year-old could no longer sleep. She couldn't drink more than a few swallows. She could hardly breathe. Hopelessness moved through her body like blood.

When she saw an ant on the windowsill, she crushed it, grinding its body under her thumb with a fury that scared her. "What difference does it make?" she thought. "God already hates me."

Suddenly, she realized what she must do. *No more!* she vowed. Like someone possessed, she began to ransack drawers and cupboards, gathering up the materials she needed.

The smell of permanent marker turned her stomach as she scrawled the oversized letters onto the cardboard. She went outside to hammer one sign onto the house and stormed down the lane to tape another sign on the mailbox.

Two days later, on September 5, 1974, an article appeared in the newspaper.

Hands Off for Local Faith Healer

By Nick Josephs

Wayland, Tennessee

Nineteen-year-old faith healer, Layla Tompkin, victim of a recent attack, has suddenly withdrawn her therapeutic services. Area residents are in a quandary.

"Losing Layla Tompkin's healin' is a blow to us all," said Wilma Hensley, distraught mother of four. "What are the injured and ailing to do? The

nearest hospital is two hours away. The clinic's in the next county. Only one doctor for all Wayland. How are we all supposed to manage?" When asked for his reaction, Earl Bass replied, "That girl fixed my wry neck good as new."

Another regular of the young healer's assistance who asked to remain anonymous said, "Gift like that...well, in my book it's a sin not to use it no matter what happened to the girl herself."

Signs have been posted on the mailbox and near the door of the faith healer's residence. Layla Tompkin is no longer making house calls or offering her services at home or at church.

When contacted as to if or when she would resume sessions, Miss Tompkin, mute since the age of five, offered no comment, written or otherwise.

This time, when Ed saw the article, he didn't try to hide the newspaper from Layla. Even if he wanted to, he wasn't sure there was a cubby or a crevice that wasn't already stuffed with unspoken feelings and something else. He couldn't say what that *something* was, but he could feel the weight of it thickening the air into a substance that made it difficult to breathe.

CHAPTER THIRTY-THREE

LAYLA restrained the urge to dig her nails into her itching neck. "Starting to heal up," Doc Fredericks pronounced, examining the wound. But what Doc couldn't see was the slow creep of Zeb's venom infecting Layla from within – the shame; the smoldering fury; the secret about who took her tongue that she was hiding from her father, her family, from all the people who thought she had the power of healing.

A week since the attack, Layla wrote in her journal. *Like those who get viper-struck at church, I feel burning as the poison works its way through my blood. Some drink buttermilk so their stomach won't be empty when the heaves come. Some die.*

For me, death would be a welcome relief from all the pain.

At supper, Ed could no longer bear to see his daughter eat two bites of soup and set down her spoon. "Ducky, you've got to eat." He plunked down his fork and looked at her.

"Is there somethin' that would go down easier? Ice cream?"

Looking down at the table, Layla shook her head.

"It's hard to eat when somethin's eating at you," said Ed. "Anything you want to talk about?"

His daughter clenched her jaw muscles.

"We've always trusted each other," he said. "Always told each other the truth."

A snake didn't take my tongue. Zeb did, she wanted to write. A few pencil strokes and she could purge her poisonous secret. But then what? She wouldn't put it past her father to take his rifle and go shoot Zeb. She knew he put very little stock in the courts ever since the ruling that allowed strip-mining onto the mountain. "Fried-egg justice," Ed called it. "Comes down to greased palms or what the judge ate for breakfast."

If her father shot Zeb, they'd put Ed in jail too, and that would be calamitous. Locking her father away from the sky and the earth, the birds and trees, would kill him quicker than any electric chair.

After supper, Ed dried the dishes to ease Layla's load. He kept looking from the paring knife he was drying to the wound on her neck. Layla saw him glancing at her the same way he did when she was five and drew the picture of the snake. She was fuzzy from morphine back then, but she remembered everything. "Strange," she thought, "how pain and tribulation remain like a photograph in your brain. In your bones too."

They listened to the news on the radio while they cleaned up. Some crazy person tried to jump his motorcycle over Snake River Canyon in Idaho and had to parachute down. And President Ford pardoned Richard Nixon for the lying scandal of Watergate. Layla wished she could be that forgiving.

"Ducky," Ed said, after she scrubbed out a cooking pot for the third time. "That pot's plenty clean now. Your rubbin' so fierce your gonna turn it into a sieve."

"A sieve," she thought. "That's what I am. Eaten away by lies."

When she was little, Layla learned about white lies – holding back a portion of the truth that could bruise someone's feelings. But what about *gray* lies? Information certain to inflict grave and lasting damage?

Ed was fond of saying, "If your mind's fixed on seein'

what's done and gone, or looking at what's on the road ahead, you lose sight of all the good that's right in front of your nose."

Layla knew there was truth in what her father said, but presently, she was so full of knots she couldn't see straight. And she learned the hard way that even when you're looking at what's in front of you, you're likely missing something else.

Maybe it's only a small shift from where your eyes are focused. Like shaking out a rug and not seeing what's behind the bushes.

As she mulled over her troubles, Layla began to see how particular beliefs had started to grow. A lost tongue; altered speech; Samson, jolted by her fall on his chest, then risen; comforting Rachel's wrist pain. Before long, the smallest root traveled underground, propagating itself like kudzu. Still, that didn't wholly explain the multiple times she brought relief and healing, especially saving Abbey's little Topher.

Remembering what happened to Samson so many years ago made Layla think of the saying, "Seeing is believing."

But looking back, she could see the reverse was true too. When you believe something, it changes how you see – like a pair of prescription eyeglasses.

She wondered how she never grasped that fact till now.

CHAPTER THIRTY-FOUR

ABBEY'S letter laid on the table for two days before Layla could bring herself to open it.

September 9, 1974

Dear Layla,
You're scaring me. Mama said you wouldn't come to the phone when she called a few days ago. And Uncle Ed said you weren't up to coming to the phone when I called. And that you didn't want anyone to visit right now. I know you must be feeling battered up beyond belief.

One time I was caring for a woman at the hospital who had been raped and I could tell that besides her body being violated, she felt a heavy load of shame. The way she mumbled or whispered when I talked to her and the way she couldn't raise her eyes to look at me or the doctor was so sad. You sure wouldn't blame a person for their own appendicitis. But there are some who make the victim feel like they're the guilty ones, at least partly. I'm hoping that's not how you feel, Layla. It's not the least bit true. I know you are loyal to the Yeagleys, but Zeb has been trouble from day one. It's a good thing he'll be taken off the streets.

Please write how you are doing. What's going on inside. You know there's nothing you could ever say that would be wrong in my book. And nothing we've ever kept from each other.

You need to get away from where all that awfulness happened. Roy will come there Saturday morning, pick you up and bring you here. We'll have time to talk about anything you want to. And besides, Topher misses his Layla. He's growing so fast now. Only three months old and he's rolling over.

A change of scenery will do you a world of good. And I'd be glad for the company.

Know that we are all wrapping our hands and hearts around you.

Your Abbey

That night Layla told Ed to call Abbey and say no.

"Should I tell her you'll visit soon?" Ed asked.

Layla averted her eyes and shook her head. There was no way to say when. No way to say why.

CHAPTER THIRTY-FIVE

LAYLA woke in a sweat. Another fitful night.

"What a terrible dream," she thought. But when she realized she wasn't dreaming her heart plummeted.

Past 7:30, she dragged out of bed realizing her father had already left for the mill.

Lately, Ed sensed that more than his daughter's sleep was disturbed. He had a strong eye for symptom – corn blight, wood rot, fusarium wilt, and his daughter's equilibrium. Unquestionably, the attack had brutalized her.

But something deeper lingered that he couldn't put his finger on. And, added to the guilt of not being there to protect her, what troubled his daughter, troubled Ed.

The worried father felt duty-bound to address a difficult subject with Layla that he deemed as vital to her healing as Doc Fredericks' antibiotics. Certainly, Avis would have a heart-to-heart with Layla, but Ed was too concerned for his daughter's future to let the deep implications of the rape slide by. Just as there are primitive forest people far away from civilization who have no word for *war*, the word *shirk* didn't exist in Ed's vocabulary.

For Ed, much was at stake. He was comforted that when he died, Layla would have a paid-off house and enough to live on. Yet Ed dared to hope that Layla wouldn't end up some old maid that people referred to as "the mute on the mountain." Someday, he prayed, she would find love. So, the night before, he asked Layla if she would join him on the porch for a little while.

"Ducky," he said, feeling heat creep up his neck and face, "what Zeb did to you was a vile, ugly thing. I know you know rape is despicable. A terrible wickedness."

In the twilight, Ed swallowed hard as he looked at his daughter's anguished face. "Someday, some man is gonna fall head over heals in love with you, same as I did with your mama. And when that time comes, I don't want you fearful on account of what Zeb did. The closeness of a man and a woman who love each other feels right and good and true. You know how the song of a wood thrush is so beautiful it breaks your heart and heals it at the same time?"

Almost imperceptibly, Layla nodded.

"Well, it's like that. So don't you be thinkin' it's anything to be afraid of." Patting his daughter's hand ever so gently, he said, "You'll remember that now, won't you, Ducky?'

Layla nodded again.

If she wasn't tormented by her secret about the rape, she might have broached the barest beginnings of another secret – her hidden feelings about Damian. The reveries and dreams that possessed her thoughts before the rape. Her fierce longings and secret attempts to *will* Damian to come back. The day after she received Damian's letter in May, she'd tested the waters by casually mentioning it to her father, surprised by how unperturbed he was to hear the news. But now, even Damian had become a shadowy dream.

Layla brushed her teeth on the morning of her tardy waking. Weeks ago, her mind and body were as receptive and yielding as ripe fruit, juicy with assurance that life was as preordained as the structure of a leaf or the number of legs on a millipede. Now, her father's words from the night before were trying to find a place in her brain to sink into that wasn't full of gangrene.

The phone rang. Auntie Avis had been calling every

day to offer consolation, asking if Layla would be up for a visit soon.

"I understand, sweet girl...sometimes you have to work things out yourself. But just you say the word and I'll be there. Or I'll come get you and bring you here while you get back on your feet."

Thank you. Layla tapped four times on the telephone receiver. *I love you*...three distinct taps. And despite the unarguable comfort it would be to have her aunt nearby, in her secret mind, Layla tapped, *relief.* The angst-ridden nineteen-year-old couldn't begin to imagine the devastation her secret would bring to Auntie Avis any more than her father.

There was a knock at the door.

"Can't people read?" Layla thought. With the boldly lettered sign tacked to the door in plain sight and word of mouth, how could anyone be confused about her no longer offering healing.

Most folks knew that Layla had, as the newspaper said, "withdrawn her therapeutic services" and were giving the injured girl time to recuperate. Some of her regulars, though, persisted in their requests for help. A peculiar situation cropped up, as well. The editor of the *Wayland Gazette* notified Ed of a number of long-distance inquiries about Layla's healing abilities, asking how to get in touch. Layla refused to follow up.

Again, knocking, this time louder. Cautiously, Layla

peeked through the newly installed café curtains, drawn together day and night over the re-paned glass on the kitchen door. It was Doc Fredericks. In her preoccupation, Layla forgot the doctor was going to stop by to look at the wound on her neck that had reddened with infection.

"Morning, Layla," Doc said, with more gravitas than cheer. The odor of Ed's burnt-toast breakfast permeated the airless room. The doctor was disheartened to see his patient no closer to healing on the inside than externally.

"Let's take a look," he said, setting his medical bag on the kitchen table. As Doc palpated the glands under Layla's neck, her brows knitted together.

"Tender?" Doc asked, lifting her wrist to take her pulse.

Layla shook her head *no* and rubbed at her temple with her free hand.

"Headache?"

Yes, Layla nodded.

"Bad night?"

She nodded.

"How's your appetite?"

Layla looked down.

"It's important not to miss your meals. You need nourishment to heal."

Doc opened his bag and set out alcohol, swabs, a

stainless-steel box of scalpels, and antibiotic. "Anything you want to talk about?"

Layla shook her head.

"Have you told your father about Zeb, yet?"

Layla shook her head.

"Sometimes takes longer to heal than we'd like," Doc said, as he gently lanced several small pockets of pus.

Doc cleaned off the thick ooze. "Brian asked if you'd come as soon as you're up to it."

Layla averted her eyes and pressed her lips together in tight refusal.

"I wouldn't even mention it, but lately, he's having a very rough go. Please think about it, Layla." Only the thinnest veneer of professionalism, vanishing by the day, saved Doc from outright begging Layla to help his suffering son. He applied a thick smear of ointment over the wound.

"That should do it for today." Doc disposed of the refuse in the wastebasket by the kitchen sink and repacked his medical supplies. "Let me know if you don't see improvement in a day or so. Or if there's anything else you need."

Layla nodded and mouthed, *thank you.*

"Bye now." Doc squeezed her shoulder. "Give my regards to your father." He paused a moment, hoping she might reciprocate with a message for Brian. But with no response, he opened the door and left.

Breakfast was a few sips of fortified milk. As she forced down each swallow, she vowed to catch up with all the chores she'd neglected.

One foot in front of the other. That's how you move forward.

It was a hollow persuasion countered by hard fact that, even in a bottomless pit, dust, dishes, and dirty laundry continued to accumulate.

"The worst, first," she thought. Tackling the chore she most dreaded, everything that followed would be mindless. Though she could hardly bear to touch it, Layla began by hand-washing the blouse she was wearing the day of the attack. She scrubbed the yellow material, salting it with tears, trying to get out the blood and spew. One part of her wanted to burn it. But another part fought back. Zeb had already taken too much. Though nothing short of salvation could wash the stain from her insides, with enough elbow grease, she might be able to reclaim her blouse.

Hands red with borax, she pummeled the fabric in scalding water, wiping her tear-drenched cheeks first on one shoulder, then the other.

Though Layla was continually amazed at the variations of laughter from giggles to guffaws so contagious they set others to laughing, she never realized how many forms of crying there were. She was bosom buddies with the big, oily tears that gave release to physical pain. And familiar with despair's gut-wrenching heaves and sobs so bottomless her eyeballs ached. But lately she was becoming familiar with another kind of weeping. Acid tears that burned with rage. Secrets. Shame.

Rubbing on the blouse stain with enough friction to spark fire, Layla held the thin cotton up to the light to see how it was coming. No visible stain remained, though she swore she could see its ghost. She wrung out the excess water and added the blouse to the rest of the wash, ready to be dried.

Furtively, Layla peeked through the curtains to make sure the coast was clear of would-be customers or curiosity seekers before she ventured outside to hang up the laundry. With a heaped-up basket of damp clothes, she nearly knocked over a mason jar that someone left near the door. She stooped to look at the note that was fastened to a quart of soup. On it was a Bible verse written in a hand she recognized. *Bear with each other and forgive whatever grievances you may have against one another. Colossians 3:13.*

Evidently, the act of forgiveness chafed at Ida Mae Yeagley's heart too. As grief-stricken as the mother was about her son getting shot, she was equally distraught about what happened to the girl she helped rear from infancy.

Just a few days before, Ed came back from the Piggly Wiggly and while Layla helped him unload the groceries, he said, "Saw Ida Mae Yeagley today." Ed sounded like a man with lockjaw, hardly able to get the words through his gritted teeth.

Layla turned from the cupboard where she was shelving a box of corn starch to look at her father, afraid of what happened, but needing to find out.

"She shook her head, all apologetic and then it was a race to see which of us could go to another aisle quicker."

"Bear with each other," Layla thought, shoving the jar out of the way with her foot, not caring if it toppled and broke. Layla had twice as many grievances to bear as Ida Mae.

Layla clothespinned the garments to the line, wishing she could shake out the secrets in the folds of her brain as sharply as she snapped Ed's work shirts before she hung them.

Usually the outdoors buoyed Layla. But just as surely as she lost all but the taste of bitter when she lost her tongue, she'd lost all sense of joy. She didn't know how to fix her broken spirit because she didn't know how to find it. Or where to start looking. Somehow, she couldn't help thinking that's what happened to Damian too.

Layla grabbed the jar of soup and darted back into the house, wary of visitors. Before she put the soup in the refrigerator, she wadded up the note and threw it in the trash. She hoped someday she would see Petey again. And her childhood friends and schoolmates, Sarah Jane,

Rachel and Lizzie. But if she didn't see Ida Mae until the end of time, it would still be too soon.

Exhausted from lack of sleep, Layla wanted to take a nap. But she was too scared to close her eyes. She didn't know which was worse: Dreading that while sleeping she would die from the devastation and lies. Or that she might wake up again.

CHAPTER THIRTY-SIX

"A LETTER for you, Ducky." Ed slid an envelope onto the kitchen table as he shuffled through the scant handful of mail. Layla hadn't bothered to go to the mailbox that afternoon or any other day since the attack. At first she was too shaken and sick. And afterwards, she was afraid she'd be waylaid by a photographer or one of the growing number of people who'd found out where she lived and were looking for a miracle. Wanting to be left alone, she became a prisoner in her own house. When Ed was at home, he fended off the strangers and persistent clients who hoped Layla would make an exception.

When a bus from a church two states away lumbered up the drive and a crowd of hopefuls disembarked and stood in silent vigil in front of the house holding signs that read, *Heal the Sick* and *Freely You have Received, Freely Give*, Ed called the sheriff.

Though there was no return address, Ed suspected he knew the author of the letter on the kitchen table. He glanced at his daughter, looking for a reaction. But, except for a slight startle, her downcast face remained as impassive as it had been for a number of weeks.

"From the fella who chopped the wood?"

Layla shrugged, so Ed let it drop.

"Don't interfere," Avis said, when Ed mentioned about Damian coming to the house and his letter that followed. "Long as she seems healthy and happy."

"Going out to do chores, now," Ed said, removing his shoes and pulling on his barn boots. "Be back for supper in about an hour."

Layla's heart pounded when she saw the handwriting. She hadn't heard from Damian in months. It was maddening not to have any contact from him and maddening that she couldn't write back. Now she dreaded what would happen if he found out about the rape.

As soon as her father left, she worked open the flap of the envelope and trembled as she removed the pages.

October 6, 1974

Dear Layla,

Last night, I called Brian, to see how things were going. When he told me what happened to you, I exploded. If I'd been there, that pervert would have wished for a pleasant disemboweling, instead. God, Layla. I wish I could do something or say something that would help but no words seem right.

Right now, I'm in a village of less than a thousand people in Alaska waiting for some Harley parts to come in. (Nothing so simple as a cracked fork and a blowtorch. But nothing as mysterious as meeting you either.)

According to the locals, I was lucky it was just my cycle that got chewed up by a pavement break. It could have been me for bear meat, instead. Out here at the end of time and landmass, they call motorcycles "meals on wheels."

I wish you could have seen some of the scenery on the highway to Alaska. Maybe it would help ease your pain. I know it's been a good antidote for mine. Watching a moose lumber toward me on my side of the road, its antlers stretched to the side like huge upturned hands, blots out everything else. The beast is so immense its tongue alone could knock me over. Ditto for one of the grizzlies I encountered who could carry (not drag, carry) that ton of moose in its mouth at an alarming speed. A man on a motorcycle would be an after-dinner snack.

Distraction while riding the Alcan is foolhardy but unavoidable. Mountains the color of distance and dream. Blue lakes mirroring the clouds, the trees and mountains with such clarity and depth, you wonder if you're right-side up or upside down. Mountain goats that look like cotton bales on white pegs with that clueless "who turned out the lights" look in their eyes. Lungs full of road dust. Rain sheeting off my face as I plow through mud-pudding after a heavy storm. There's more than a little irony in having escaped a bullet in 'Nam, only to get shrapnel in my shin from loose gravel just out of Dawson Creek. It gives "road warrior" new meaning.

In the meantime, I'm gutting halibut at a local cannery and hoping the Harley parts get here before my posterior freezes on the permafrost as the nights get colder. A fellow at the cannery offered me his couch – another irony. All those nights I spent facedown in jungle scum, I longed for a decent bed. But I find no comfort in them now. Anything I can't carry with me feels like a distraction. My carcass alone, feels like overload. Too much baggage banging around in my sack of skin.

I did take up his offer, though, when he said I could take his sea kayak out and paddle around an inlet. What a trip, Layla! Giant bull kelp. Purple starfish the color of grape jam. And a seal that followed my boat like a play toy beckoning me out farther from shore and then coming to a standstill in the water, only its head visible above the ripples.

I stopped about fifteen feet away and we stared at each other. And suddenly, I noticed another seal to the right of it. And then another head popped up to the seal's left. I looked around and saw that I was encircled by seals. All motionless. All equidistant from each other, with me at the center. A compass couldn't have drawn a more perfect circle.

I was spellbound. Couldn't tell you how long the seals stayed. It felt like what eternity must feel like. Then, the seals disappeared as silently as they had gathered and I was totally alone.

Can't begin to explain it, except that somehow I felt you were there too. Usually, most of what I know about a thing is from what I can see. But there is so much more. All the invisible beneath the visible. Unrealized possibilities. The unspoken. The unspeakable.

Autumn is already turning the trees gold here. No reds of the Northeast. These days, I gird myself for all that the seasons strip away as if somehow it will lessen the loss. Stupid, huhhh?

I'm sure most people are trying to cheer you up, Layla. Their words and pats on the back urge you to buck up. Get on. Get over it. But in the mysterious way I felt we connected last spring, I hope you trust that whatever you're feeling has a purpose. I know that's hard to believe. I'm still not sure what that purpose is for me. I don't know why the good and the innocent have to suffer and die young. It makes me question God, myself, the whole meaning of life. But, since I'm the one who keeps asking the questions, I guess I'm the one who has to figure out the answers, at least for myself. No epiphanies yet. Somehow though, keeping in touch with the men I was with in 'Nam gives me a reason to get up in the morning. I don't know why it makes a difference, it just does. When you've been holed up that long together, trying to save your own skin and each other, you bond in ways no one can understand except others who've been there.

And I know this sounds crazy but I have come to a conclusion – the smallest beginning of coming to terms about the way I am now. To see what goes on in war, to have done the things I've done, the only sane response is to go insane.

I know Doc Fredericks is seeing to your physical wounds. Let those you love help you heal the rest. (Not something I'm particularly good at.) I know I push people away. Guilt is a big reason – it's why I got all my tattoos after the war. Another is that I've discovered a new enemy – me.

I'm the wrong person to be spouting off about anything and I don't even know what I'm trying to say, other than I wish I could undo what happened to you and what you must be going through now.

Stay strong, Layla,
Damian

Layla sat unmoving as she finished the letter. Tears rolled down her cheeks. She cried because she felt a connection with the one person who might fully understand her shame and her secrets and there was no way to communicate with him.

If he really cared, why didn't he call? Why didn't he, at least, give her an address so she could write back?

CHAPTER THIRTY-SEVEN

MORE than a month after the rape, Layla awakened with a sense of foreboding. "A high-jinx day ripe for misery," she thought. She pulled on the previous day's clothes, feeling the kind of residual cold that makes snow linger in the depressions of ground and shadows of trees after all the rest has melted.

Wary of the approach of unwelcome visitors, Layla sat on the front porch peeling vegetables for her father's supper and, usually, to puree for soup for herself too, but lately she couldn't muster up the added energy.

The wisp-clouded sky was the milky blue of old Mr. Gus's eyes. Before the rape, Mrs. Gus had Layla come to their cabin on the other side of Fox Hollow to bring relief to her husband's back that seized up from heavy lifting and overdoing things in general. While Layla's hands peeled carrots, her mind flayed off layers of argument about whether or not to reveal the whole truth about how she lost her tongue.

Piece by piece, with the precision that Clevis ate a mouse, leaving only a whiskery nub of nose and the pea-sized gall bladder, Layla searched for how her childish misperceptions took root and transformed into what she believed. And how those beliefs shaped her thoughts and actions and, over time, who she became. She couldn't begin to unsnarl the reality of her healing powers – if, indeed, they were real – from the delusions about how she came to have them.

Uncertainty ate at Layla like venom.

She used to be able to go through her day with pure intention. Whether she was picking apples, hanging laundry or cooking up mush, she could hear the secret speech of a thing. Not in words. But the whisper of its spirit. As she stirred the cornmeal in the pot, she felt the presence of the ear of corn that made the meal and the crows that tried to steal its gold and the sun that grew the corn. She guessed that was why folks in the church spoke in tongues. Ordinary words couldn't contain the vastness of the Spirit – the Spirit that was in flesh and flowers and cooking pots.

This past month, though, all she could hear was her own turmoil. She kept praying for a sign to show her what to do, but she was so distracted, she didn't know if she'd recognize a sign unless it was stretched across the sky with her name on it. So she tried to keep to the every-dayness of things, busying her hands with dusting and cooking and taking care of what was within her reach.

People still called for healing. Or, worse, just showed up. But she felt too fraudulent to offer it to anyone, even Brian.

She couldn't bring herself to go to church, either. "Can't face all those folks," she thought, "staring at me and seeing straight through to the falsehoods. And if I say Zeb was the one who took my tongue, it will bring a mountain of added shame to the Yeagleys."

Part of Layla's predicament was she had nobody to share her troubles with except Doc Fredericks. But she wasn't easy talking to him about her spiritual turmoil. The doctor still went to church, but when Brian got his legs blown off, Doc told her he had a lot of doubts about God.

Damian, with what he went through, might understand, but he might as well be on the moon he was so out of touch.

Drowning in her own doubts, Layla couldn't burden her father or Auntie Avis or anyone else with the mind-wracking implications of the rape.

It was too much. Too much confusion and no good answers.

Completely depleted, with no way to claw her way out of the abyss, Layla decided to let go. Let God figure out what she was supposed to do next because she couldn't. But the trouble was, since the rape, she was so soul-sick that her concept of God didn't have any more meaning than the words *Layla* or *healer* or *life purpose*. They were senseless sounds like words that kids say over and over until they're no more than noisy clatter.

"There are them that preach and them that practice," Ed liked to say.

"I'll try praying," Layla thought. Even if the words are empty shells like worm-eaten nuts, all the meat gone. She knew she could pray sitting, standing, sideways or upside down. She didn't think it really mattered how she let go of her sorry state and let God take over, but thought it might work better if she bent her knees as a sign she was ready to bend her will to God.

Did God, she wondered, look for signs that people were following His spirit as much as people looked for signs from God?

Layla set the bowl of vegetables next to the bucket of compost peelings, walked down the porch steps, and knelt down on the ground. She stretched her arms wide, palms uplifted to the sky, and began.

God,

There's such a load on my mind and soul, such dark hate and perplexity in my heart, I don't know what to do. I know when a thought comes in my mind it sways how I do things. On account of You being all-knowing, You know how low and vengeful my thoughts are towards Zeb Yeagley.

Every time I think about what happened it's like someone who got serpent bit at church. The venom is working its way through my limbs and innards. Now it's lodged in my heart.

I know there are a thousand thousand signs of goodness and miracle all around me but it's like I've been struck blind and deaf as well as tongueless.

Please help me to know what I'm supposed to do. And whatever it is, help me to have the strength to do it because I get the feeling from the way things sometimes go that, even though I know my burdens are meant for good, not evil, the road ahead could be full of more struggles.

I'm sick to death of listening to my hateful self and my fearful thinking. I lay my failings in Your hands. Help me to know Your will. I'm ready to be filled with Your spirit or struck dead by a thunderbolt.

Amen.

Kneeling there, arms outstretched, the early October sun had a fine blaze to it that pierced her fair skin and bored deep inside. Layla could feel the gold of her locket heat up underneath her blouse. She kept hoping for some sign that God heard her and that help was on the way. But the only thing she felt was the digging pain of a little stone under her left knee. She got up, brushed the dirt off her skirt, and climbed back up the steps of the porch.

She picked up the bowl of vegetables and the paring knife, and heaved a heavy sigh.

Patience, she kept repeating. *Patience.*

But as she continued to peel vegetables, Layla wondered if she might be as lost to God as God was to her.

CHAPTER THIRTY-EIGHT

MORE than two months had elapsed since the rape. Zeb, released from the hospital, was now incarcerated in the Wayland city jail.

Ed was increasingly worried about his daughter. Before work one morning, he stopped by Doc Fredericks' office to report Layla's insomnia, weight loss, frequent headaches, and her persistent despondency.

"Come on in," Doc said, alarmed at Ed's sallow skin tone and the dark circles under his eyes.

"Anytime you can get Layla in, I'll see what I can do. Maybe a vitamin B12 shot would give her a boost.

Meanwhile, I'm concerned about you." He took Ed's pulse.

While Doc listened to Ed's chest and back with his stethoscope, the troubled father broached a question brewing in his mind over the past eight weeks. "Doc, I've been puttin' two and two together and I don't like the answer I'm comin' up with."

"How do you mean?" Doc asked, wrapping a blood pressure cuff around Ed's arm.

"You know how you always questioned Layla's tongue wound? How it was so clean-cut?"

"Yes," Doc said, attempting evenness.

"That snake story never did sit right. But nothing else ever did surfaced. And most folks were so sure it was true, 'specially after finding out Layla had the gift of healing. So I guess I let it pass. But when that bastard violated her..." Ed trembled.

Doc stopped pumping and loosened the cuff.

"When he used that knife of his on her neck... it got me thinking. You think her tongue was cut out?"

"Certainly would go along with the appearance of the wound." Doc answered, carefully.

"Was Zeb the one who took it?"

"Possible," Doc said.

"If it is him, I'm goin' over to the jail and castrate him with my bare hands."

"Can't blame you a bit, Ed," Doc said, interrupting.

"But there's nothing to be gained by working yourself into a state." Doc laid a steadying hand on Ed's shoulder.

"Did Layla say anything?"

Doc, sworn to professional confidentiality, shrugged and shook his head in a quandary. But he looked directly into Ed's eyes, father to father, with a pain that spoke volumes.

Ed rose abruptly. "I aim to find out."

"Hold on a minute, Ed." The doctor stalled, hoping to diffuse any rash behavior. "I want to write you a prescription for some supplements."

"Later, Doc." With a handshake, Ed flew out of the door.

As Doc Fredericks watched from the clinic window, Ed gunned the motor of his truck and peeled wheels down the street. Not knowing what the agitated father planned, the doctor wondered if he should alert the sheriff.

Already traumatized from the rape and with people wanting healing still showing up to see if she was home, Layla was hem-stitching a pair of heavy privacy drapes to replace the thin curtains in her bedroom. She heard a slamming door that sounded like their truck. Unable to fathom why her father would come home in the middle of the day, she ran to the kitchen window and peeked out.

Ed stormed through the kitchen door so fast he came close to knocking her down.

"Have a seat, Layla. We're gonna have us a talk."

Layla was scared to see her father so fired up.

"I want the truth from you, you hear?" He got a pencil and the spiral-bound writing tablet from the counter, smacked them onto on the kitchen table, and motioned for his daughter to have a seat. He sat down opposite her, immoveable as the front yard boulder.

Layla nodded, swallowing hard.

"How did your tongue get taken?"

I thought it was a snake, Layla wrote. *I heard it hiss.*

"Is that what you still think?"

No.

"Then what?"

Gnawing on her lip, Layla repetitively thumped the rubber tip of the pencil on the writing pad as if she could, somehow, erase the past. Forestall the future.

Ed pressed. "I asked you what happened?"

Tears spilled from Layla's eyes. She flipped the pencil point down and took a deep breath. *Zeb*, she scribbled.

"Why didn't you tell me?"

I didn't know till he raped me. When he said Sshhussh, Ssshussh.

"The hissing that makes you jump so?" Ed said, the full realization of another mystery falling into place.

Weeping, Layla nodded.

"Why'd you keep it secret?"

I was scared.

"Of what?"

What you'd do to Zeb. What would happen to you.

"Lucky he's behind bars," her father said, through clenched teeth, though it sounded like iron bars would be no match for Ed's wrath.

Scared what I believed for so many years that wasn't true.

"It's the rest of us should have known better. You were five, Layla."

People still believe it's all signs – *the snake, my tongue, my healing.*

Bludgeoned by the confirmation that it was Zeb – monstrosity upon monstrosity– Ed sat barely breathing, caught in the stranglehold of complications.

"It's a mess all right.... an almighty stinkin' mess." He banged his fist on the table.

"Never should have left you with that family," he said. "Should have let Avis keep you from the beginning and none of this would've happened. You'd still have speech. Wouldn't be tormented all these years. Or raped." Ed hammered his fist on the table with such ferocity that Layla jumped.

When she reached over to comfort him, Ed leapt up, grabbed the shotgun from the corner and charged out, nearly ripping the door from its hinges. Layla was too shocked to move. She'd never seen her father like this before. Never fathomed the deep-seated doubts he'd kept hidden all these years. Fearing the worst, Layla took off after him, hoping to stop him before he got to the jail.

When she saw he hadn't gone to his truck, she was confused. Then, the quicksand of her own despair, vivid in her mind, triggered another possibility.

"Aahheeee...Aaahheeee," she screamed. She raced to the barn. The door was shut. She unlatched it and dashed into the barnyard and back again, yelling into the hayloft, into the stalls.

Not knowing where to start looking, she ran outside. As she shut the barn door, momentarily catching her breath, she frantically surveyed the road and the yard. *Don't let there be a gunshot,* she prayed, so full of dread that she jumped at the sound of a disgruntled crow.

There was nothing in the front yard except a squirrel, digging in the dirt beneath the laurel bushes, burying a cheekful of booty. In the side yard, the maple leaves, tinged in autumn reds and golds, were full of whispers. The ropes of the swing shivered. Suddenly Layla was running.

Her father was there, under the maple tree, hunched over his wife's grave, clutching her headstone.

"Aaheee," Layla cried, moving the rifle well beyond reach so she could kneel beside him.

"Shouldn't have let it happen," he said, the words catching in his throat. "Never should have... Never..." he moaned. Anguished tears flooded his eyes.

Layla, sobbing quietly, laid her head and her hands on

her father's back. It seemed even the birds were silent as father and daughter remained motionless on top of the buried body that connected them both. As the minutes elapsed, a calm resolve seemed to seep into them. At last, Ed straightened up by increments and pressed his fingers against his wife's name on the polished marble. He lifted one of his daughter's hands from his back, squeezing so tightly she winced. Then he stood, half-stumbling backwards.

Wiping his eyes with the back of his hands, Ed took out his handkerchief, mopped his cheeks, blew his nose and, with a deep breath, tried to regain some semblance of composure. As Ed checked his watch, Layla saw the carpentry of her father's mind making calculations. "I want you to go pack some things, Ducky. I think you should go stay with your aunt for the time being. We can make the next bus if you hurry."

Layla shook her head. No way was she able to face confession to anyone else. She just wanted to be alone.

Ed was at an impasse. He started to say something, but the vehemence in his daughter's eyes stopped him. "We'll talk about it tonight, then. Have to get to work, now." He hadn't told Layla how close he was to getting laid off. Even though his boss was sympathetic, Ed had been late to work or missing it completely too many times since Layla's rape.

Two days later, Layla rode to work with her father so he could drop her at Doc Fredericks before he went to the mill – her half of the bargain. She promised she'd go for a checkup if her father let her stay at home. Besides, she was determined to find out if Doc betrayed her secret about Zeb to her father.

The drive down the mountain felt strange and unfamiliar, as if she were an alien looking at everything with otherworldly detachment. In a way she was. For two months, Layla was seldom outside the yard of her own home, much less anywhere else. Wayland seemed smaller and shabbier than she remembered. As Ed drove Layla to the doctor's office, she slouched in her seat, head lowered, hoping nobody would recognize her. And once at Doc Fredericks', she ran inside. Since it was early, she was relieved that no one was in waiting room yet.

Doc gave Layla a shot of B12, and an earful about eating more and isolating herself less.

Layla fished for a piece of paper folded in her pocket, the accusatory question already written. *Did you tell my father about Zeb being the one who took my tongue?*

"No," Doc said. "I didn't divulge your secret about Zeb, Layla. I wouldn't do that. Your dad figured it out all by himself."

Layla nodded, wanting to believe him. She tried to

slip out from the clinic without encountering anyone, but Eileen Fredericks intercepted her on the front porch.

"Layla, honey. Come have a cup of tea with me."

Layla shook her head, pointing to an imaginary wristwatch as if she had a pressing engagement.

"Tea's already steeping," Eileen insisted, guiding the frail young woman into the kitchen.

What did the doctor's wife know? Layla wondered. Did her husband tell her anything?

To fill the awkward silence, each stared into their steaming cup of swirling sediment. Layla was surprised at how old Eileen looked. Haggard. As if the force of gravity dragged on her matronly bones and fleshy folds more forcefully than it did on others.

Eileen hesitated. "Layla, honey, I washed your body when you were five. I've watched you grow, face the unimaginable...and now this last awfulness. I've no right to ask you. God forgive me..." She gulped back tears. "But I'm a mother doing what mothers do."

Layla thought back to her own mother's love, finding a way through six feet of root-bound earth to comfort her father and her in the midst of crisis.

"I'm begging you to help Brian." Eileen said, without a shred of pride to mask the helplessness she felt. "He's desperate for relief...most days he pumps himself so full of painkillers, he's somewhere else – just wasting away."

Layla's hands dropped from her teacup into her lap

and balled into tight fists. *I'm a fraud,* she wanted to scream. *It's a lie. All lies.*

Trapped by what Mrs. Fredericks was asking, Layla bolted up, snatched her tote bag, and fled from the kitchen, wagging her head in despair. Eileen ran after her, apologizing.

Halfway down the hall, Layla heard a muffled scream, as if someone whose mouth was stuffed with rags was being skinned alive.

"Eeeahuuuugggh." The sound pitchforked into every cell of her body.

She would never forget the unbearable pain she felt the night her tongue was severed.

Brian! Layla turned on her heels and raced toward his room.

You're a charlatan, her brain sniped. *Don't you dare!* But before she could stop herself, Layla entered the room without even knocking.

In the throes of agony, Brian's body convulsed, one hand clawed into his thigh, the other, fist-crammed in his mouth. A syringe, with the needle plunged into a vial of morphine, lay on his lap.

Layla dropped her tote, transferred the syringe to the night table, stooped down, and laid her hands on Brian. Or more accurately, on the part of Brian that refused to accept that it was no longer there.

Gripping the arms of his wheelchair, Brian tried to

resist the spasms that rocked his body.

Suddenly realizing the consequence of her impulsiveness, her brain lashed out. *What do you think you're doing?*

How can I not? raged another voice.

Then, the quiet message. *Let it be. Just let it be. You don't have to ask questions or get answers.*

Brian twisted and jerked, barely stifling the gut-wrenching cries that escaped with each new jolt of pain.

As the spasms came less and less frequently, Brian's words dry-heaved from his throat. "It drives mad. Just when I think I'm beginning to lick this, it comes back like a sledgehammer."

Layla kept working on him. Slowly, Brian's seizing diminished.

In the silence, Layla's griddle-hot hands floated to their familiar healing points as she plowed through walls of doubt and self-loathing, trying to let it be. She was finishing the treatment, smoothing waves of energy over Brian's missing and remaining body as if she were flattening out the wrinkles on a bedcover, when she looked up and saw that he was looking at her.

"Still hurting?" he asked.

Perturbed that she was so transparent, Layla nodded.

"A couple weeks ago, Damian called and asked about you. When I told him what happened, he said he'd write. Did he?"

Layla nodded.

"Said he felt like rat scum for not writing more. And that he wanted to call, but thought it might be awkward. Afraid he might say the wrong thing."

Layla's breathing accelerated.

"You two sure made an impression on each other, didn't you?"

Still kneeling at the foot of Brian's wheelchair, Layla kept her eyes downcast.

"If I didn't owe him my life, I'd be more jealous." Brian stroked the top of Layla's head, ending with a playful tug on her hair. "You know that, don't you?"

A half-smile flickered over Layla's face.

"Better," Brian said, with a big exhalation, when Layla finished her treatment. "Much better.

"We're gonna get through this, kiddo," Brian assured her, as they hugged. "We've got to. What other choice do we have?"

Brian, almost a licensed doctor himself, marveled at the relief he felt – relief that no medical book had the formula to duplicate. He marveled at the restoration of hope. It wasn't that the pain was worse than it had been. It was the erosion of trying to cope, day after day, without an end in sight.

Layla was in amazement herself. Something inside her shifted. Like the changing angle of the sun after winter is over, she felt the barest beginnings of light and warmth.

CHAPTER THIRTY-NINE

AIMING to return home from Doc Fredericks' on the late-morning bus so she could finish her chores and get supper ready, Layla walked down the main street of Wayland to the station.

It didn't take long to cover the central part of town. She passed the Piggly Wiggly, Herman's drugstore, the bowling alley, and Effie's Fine Dress and Bridal Boutique. She passed the sheriff's office where Zeb Yeagley awaited sentencing before being transferred to the state penitentiary. And then, she had no earthly idea why, her feet changed direction and walked her right up to the sheriff's door. She reached out to turn the knob and stopped cold.

Don't be a crazy person. But her slender hand opened the door of its own volition and she walked in.

Sheriff Dones looked up from some papers he was working on.

"Layla Tompkin. What a surprise." He tilted back on his big wooden chair and folded his hands over his considerable belly.

Layla picked up a pencil off the desk and reached for the notepad in her pocket.

"Here. You can use this," Sheriff Dones said. He licked his finger with his beefy tongue and lifted a square from a stack of scrap paper at the side of the desk.

I want to visit Zeb Yeagley, she wrote.

The sheriff raised his eyebrows and cleared his throat. "Well, this is one for the books," he said, not knowing what to do.

Layla stood, quietly.

He cleared his throat again. "I can't let you do that, Layla."

I have to, Layla wrote.

"Does your daddy know about this?" the sheriff asked.

I'm nineteen, she wrote back. *Old enough to get married.*

"I guess I can't deny you your rights. But I think it's a dang fool idea."

It's important, Layla scribbled.

"Well, it's against my better judgment."

A few minutes. Please.

"All right. But I'm not leaving you two alone, together."

They walked into a room behind the front office. As Layla followed the sheriff, she felt like she had cat whiskers extending upright and sideways relaying information about a passage too narrow for escape. In the back there was a small kitchen alcove, a bathroom, and two cells. Zeb was the only one behind bars. He was stretched out in his bunk staring up at the bottom of the bed above him.

"Zebidiah, you have a visitor," Dones said, unlocking the door of the cell from a big bunch of keys. "I'm gonna shackle your hands and feet, Zeb."

Zeb, unshaven, his skin the same grimy white of the bedsheet, slowly sat up, wincing slightly. When he saw Layla, he froze. After a long, stone-cold stare straight at Layla, he looked down.

The sheriff slipped the silver rings off his belt and locked them onto Zeb. "Considering the circumstances, I'll be standing over here on the side while you visit. Anything funny and I'll be on you faster than greased lightning."

Dones exited the cell and let Layla enter. Hand resting lightly on his gun, the sheriff stationed himself close by.

Zeb stared at his feet, refusing to look at the girl whose tongue he cut out with a hunting knife and the young woman he violated again just months ago.

In the cell, constructed from cement blocks, life was

pared down to bare basics – a cup to drink from, a place to sleep and go to the toilet, and iron bars. There was no music or preaching in that jail cell. No feeling of Sunday hallelujah. But the same power that walked Layla's feet into the sheriff's office was in possession of her.

Layla knelt down on one knee in front of Zeb and attempted to make eye contact with the grim, head-lowered man she knew all her life. Her hands began to tingle the way they did when she was healing and a white hush enveloped the cement and metal cell.

Many times, people in the Holiness church offered her vipers. A big five-foot canebrake rattler fat as a man's arm. Copperheads. Cottonmouths. But she never felt anointed to handle serpents so she didn't take them up. She'd been anointed to lay on healing or sometimes speak in tongues, even though all she could do was make sound. But that's mostly how the tongued-folks sounded too, as they let the strange and wondrous vibrations of the Spirit come through them.

But now, the Holy Spirit was in her heart anointing her, leading her to pick up the hands of the serpent that took her tongue. The anointing was so strong Zeb had no power to harm her. She lifted Zeb's shackled hands to her bowed forehead and held them, mentally asking forgiveness for having done him physical violence. Zeb didn't pull his hands away, but he didn't raise his head to look at her either.

There's no way I can ever forget what you did to me, Zebidiah Yeagley. But I forgive you. For the torment. For taking my tongue. For violating me. I don't know what made you do it. Drink? Demon? Whatever it was, I forgive you. I pray for your healing, Zeb. And I'll keep praying for you.

Uncertain how much time lapsed, Layla became aware of Zeb's roughly calloused hands, felt their flesh touching and the beginnings of cold sweat – a sign that the Holy Spirit was ebbing away. The dazed healer placed Zeb's hands back in his lap and tried to make eye contact one more time, but Zeb, inscrutable and unmoving, kept staring at the floor.

Suddenly, Layla was filled with apprehension. She got up and nodded a quick thanks to Sheriff Dones and exited. As she left, she heard the clanking of shackles and keys and the sheriff mumbling. "Definitely, one for the books."

Outside, the autumn sun blazed. Dankness from the cement cell dissipated from her bones in an instant and she felt feather-light. The constriction, strangling Layla's heart since the rape, uncoiled. Miraculously, after months of half-breaths – grudging little spurts of necessary air – Layla was able to take a full, easy breath, filling her lungs as big as party balloons and letting it whoosh out again.

Thank you, God, she said, as she hurried to catch the bus. *I never could have done that myself.*

Thankyouthankyouthankyou...

CHAPTER FORTY

LAYLA continued to treat Brian out of friendship, not conviction. She didn't have the heart to withhold whatever relief – real or perceived – that he believed she imparted.

So much had happened just before the rape: Meeting Damian in April; Topher's birth in May; her nineteenth birthday in June when the whole family came to celebrate. Those events were incised into her brain like the letters on the big maple tree that anchored the rope swing and shaded her mother's grave.

Ed told his daughter, "Before we started buildin' this house, I carved *E+L 1952* on the tree trunk so your mama and me would always remember where our roots were."

Along with Damian's occasional letters and postcards, prior memories fortified Layla and gave her strength to grapple with what remained unanswered: Whether or not she had the power to heal. Now that her father knew about Zeb, she still wrestled with whether or not to tell others.

What should I do, Daddy? People believe the snake is why I have healing.

"Some things you can get to fixing right away. Some things you never can fix," he said, a hard stone of blame still lodged in his heart. "And difficult as it is, some things take time. Can't hurry change any more than you can make the leaves fall quicker by raking them out of the tree. You'll know the right thing to do and the right time to do it when it comes."

Layla's doubt came in surges. Sometimes it was as dense as the mountain fog obliterating all visibility, blind trust the only assurance there was ground below her feet.

This fall, the wooly bears that hung from the leaves bore hairy bands of red-brown, wider than she'd ever seen. In the caterpillar's opinion that meant the coming winter would be milder than usual, a prospect Layla welcomed. These days, she felt the cold and heat more keenly, as if a protecting layer had been stripped from her body.

Layla was just returning from a visit with Topher. She could hardly keep from squeezing his little arms and legs, pudgy as piglets. "Abbey's milk must be mostly cream," she thought.

There was a load of chores to catch up with, but Layla felt the urge to write in her journal. She hadn't made daily entries even though the hours-long bus ride on either side of her journey gave her plenty of time. Instead, she continued to knit a scarf for her father.

His old scarf, the one she made a few years earlier, was snagged and frayed beyond decent wear. Wanting to make sure her father had protection around his neck against the coming chill, she was knitting the soft brown yarn in tight stitches, and extra-wide so he could pull it up over his mouth and nose. The cold air set off his cough so much worse this year than last.

Mr. Roble, the bus driver, let Layla disembark at the Tompkins' lane before continuing on to Blue Springs. Balanced by an overnight case in one hand and a shopping bag in the other, Layla walked up the gravel road toward home. After Petersburg, breathing the mountain air was pure pleasure.

What would be the harm, she thought, if she detoured to her private thinking rock by the side of the creek?

The early November day was perfection. Azure sky. A warm breeze with a cool edge that said, *soon. Soon.*

Filled with melodious birdsong, the day felt twin to those exquisite first days of spring, except the air was pungent with fermentation, and the sound of the rustling leaves sent shivers up Layla's spine.

As Layla made her way across the overgrown footpath, the autumn leaves underfoot snapped, crackled, and popped just like the breakfast cereal she saw advertised on Abbey and Roy's television set. Knowing how the particulars of most days faded quickly, new experiences shoving present tense into past, Layla was anxious to write about how Topher was rolling over and sitting up now. And how, since the rape, she hadn't figured out what to tell people about who took her tongue. Or whether or not she was still a healer since she had no idea, either. But after her visit to Zeb's prison cell and her talk with her father, she had, if not clarity, a little more ease.

She got to the familiar rock, set down her bags and climbed onto the warm brown surface big enough for a bed. With her journal opened to a blank page, Layla held her pencil in readiness, waiting like a bird to see the wiggle of something it could peck at. But she couldn't concentrate. Her clothes and hair smelled like cigarette smoke, butt-stuffed ashtrays, and the restroom deodorizer in the Petersburg bus station.

The combined stink in the sweet air kept distracting her. With fresh clothes in her suitcase, Layla decided to change. Trying to rid herself of reek, she stripped to her skin.

With the same joy that drew Layla to Topher when he gurgled, the creek lured her to its dancing ripples. Slowly, she waded in among the darting minnows, shrieking and shrieking because it was so cold. Finally, she plunged in completely and laid back in the water to let the swirling current wash her hair free from stench.

Out of her periphery, she saw something dark glide into the water across the creek. Probably a muskrat, by the size of it.

Stretched out and floating in the water, one side up to the sun and then otter-rolling so her other side warmed, Layla felt scoured clean inside and out. The whole world seemed to shine. Not the usual squint-bright of the sun. This shine made every leaf and weed – even the water strider bugs – glow as if they were illuminated from within.

Stream babble filled her ears, drowning out other sounds, so by the time she heard the branches cracking under whatever was approaching, it was too late to run.

There was no way the heavy thuds could be deer. Silently, the petrified girl half-swam, half-waded over to the side of the bank where the roots of a huge sycamore bunched into the creek like giant, gnarled hands. Hovering low in the water to mask her scent, she squatted behind the trunk, shivering.

She picked up several good-sized stones from the creek bottom, keeping one in her hand and setting the rest on the bank for reserve. If it was a bear or mountain cat, she might get a good enough shot to convince it to leave. The footfalls stopped. With her view blocked by the tree, she risked being discovered if she peeked out. So she stayed hidden, quaking with cold.

Nothing happened.

No sound.

No movement.

Then, over the tumble of the creek, she heard steps coming closer. Closer...

From the opposite side of the tree where she was hunkered, she heard a heart-stopping sound.

"Hellooo..."

It was a man's voice.

Layla froze. Naked, out in the middle of the woods, no one within earshot, she was virtually cornered by whoever it was. Someone coming to fish? Lyman Jeeter? Zeb escaped and on the run, making his way back home for a meal and some money?

"Hellooo." Sharper this time. Deeper.

"Layla...Layla?"

It couldn't be.

"Layla?"

"Oh my God," thought Layla. "It is!"

It was *his* voice. On the heels of relief came the fire of thrill. The man she dreamed about asleep or awake, unsure she would ever see him again, was finally here.

And chasing right behind her heart-pounding elation was the terrible timing of it all.

After five months of yearning to see Damian, she couldn't let him see her covered in gooseflesh, her limbs turning blue, and her hair like wet riverweed.

"Layla, Layla, are you all right?"

His voice sounded so anxious she was about to reply.

"Layla," he called out, louder. "I need to know if you're okay."

She peeked over a gnarl of sycamore root that anchored into the water and saw Damian's dilapidated black boots not five feet away. She was too shaky to trust any sound she could make, so she knocked on the tree root with one of the rocks in her hand.

Damian's whole body jerked at the sound.

"Oh my God. Layla, Layla," he said, kneeling down and leaning forward over the sycamore's thick outcropping.

"Look at you; you're so beautiful. God, you're shivering." He pulled off his leather jacket and held it out. "Here. Take this."

Behind the tree, Layla dragged her stiff body out of the water and wrapped up in his coat. The black leather radiated heat like a woodstove. Damian came around the wide, mottled trunk and guided the trembling young woman into the sun.

"Come over and sit down," he said. "Get warmed up."

The rock warmed her underside. The jacket warmed her topside.

"I'll be right back," he said. His inked skin was more startling than she remembered.

Layla nodded.

Damian dashed off toward the road and, in minutes, was back carrying a bedroll and a saddlebag. He untied his sleeping bag and blanket and wrapped them around Layla, cocooning her like caterpillar. Then he sat on the rock and made himself into a big chair, pulling Layla's covered-up body against him, rocking and rubbing along the blankets to warm her slender arms.

Gradually, Layla stopped shaking. Even after her shivering ceased, the two sat on the rock for the longest time, her back leaning against his chest, his arms tight around her, both of them staring at the creek, not saying a word.

"Are you okay?" he asked, gently running his finger over the scar on her neck.

Layla nodded.

"After I got my bike fixed, I came back as fast as I could.

"Did you know you were a famous faith healer all the way to the Pacific Ocean?"

Layla shook her head.

"I picked up a paper in Seattle and there was an Associated Press article about you – about what happened. You're really okay? You sure?"

Layla nodded, scarcely able to breathe.

"When I arrived at your lane, I got off my bike to walk, trying to slow down my thoughts, thinking of what I would say. Then I heard yells coming from over here. It sounded like you and I thought you might be in trouble. When I saw clothes on the rock and looked at the journal, I knew you had to be nearby." His arms tightened around her. "God, I'm glad you're all right."

Layla pushed the blanket off her head to look at him. He was browner than she remembered. Leaner.

Damian brushed a few wet strands off of her face and let her head sink back against his chest again until she could hear his heart beating through the bones of her skull.

Without his jacket, Damian's arms were bare up to the sleeves of his T-shirt. Where her wet hair and face touched the skin of his upper arms, he could feel how cold she was. He cupped a hand over each of her ears. Layla heard the sea in the warm shell of his palms.

"Two ears," he said, gently pressing. He cupped his palms over her closed eyes until orangey-gold glowed beneath her lids. "Two eyes." He wrapped his arms back around her body. "Two arms," he said hugging her. "We're all so symmetrical...people, animals, flowers, trees. Like the world was created by some child-god cutting out paper dolls."

They sat silent again.

"I wrote you a poem," Damian finally said.

Layla turned her head and, extricating an arm from the blankets, tapped her ear.

Damian fumbled through his saddlebag and produced his notebook. He thumbed through the battered pages and held it open for her to read.

Layla turned, and pointed to Damian.

Damian hesitated, started to read, then stopped.

He gave a little half-laugh. "There's something profoundly absurd about using words to express silence."

Again, Layla tapped her ear.

"Stubborn, aren't you." Damian smiled. "I like that." He took a deep breath and began.

Why do we close our eyes
to that we cannot see
An eclipse is just a moment
for the moon to be free

My shadow is my bond
to the sun's energy
My ego is an alias
who calls himself me

As my mind tries to document
continual imagery
Silence is the language
that speaks infinity.

"You're like the silence that speaks infinity, Layla." Damian closed the curled pages.

Layla had never heard such a tender voice come from such a bull-strong body.

Damian bent his face down and kissed the top of her head.

"God, I missed you." Layla felt his arms tighten. "You're the most beautiful thing I ever laid my eyes on." He laid his cheek on her wet head.

"I know it doesn't seem reasonable, Layla. To meet someone by chance. To meet them once and be so sure. I was such a fool to leave....not writing more...not knowing if you felt the same way."

Turning around to face him, Layla put her finger to Damian's lips. They looked into each other's eyes. Searched behind the sheen and color and tunneled through the black hole to the wordless core of being.

Their heads came closer until their lips met. Instantly, the moment they touched, Layla felt a rush of sweetness. Sweet that was missing since she was five. Sweetness that entered her lips and traveled directly into her blood and body. Her toes tasted that sweetness like they were ten little tongues, each one lapping up nectar till they swooned in pleasure.

She had no concept of how long she and Damian kissed. When they finally drew apart, her bones had melted. Shrugging off the blankets, she sat there in

Damian's black leather jacket, her bare legs, and nothing underneath, except her gold chain locket. She wondered if she should feel embarrassed, but all she could do was laugh. They both laughed. Laughed and hugged and kissed again. It felt so natural. Worlds away from the fashions in *Ladies' Home Journal* that could never compare to the raiment of her heart.

Layla reached up and touched the fanged serpent on Damian's cheek, asking with her eyes the meaning of it.

"I got tattooed after I came home from 'Nam. I'm a two-tongued lying snake, Layla. People say first impressions are important, so I want everyone to know that up front."

Layla shook her head, *no*.

She picked up her journal that was lying nearby on the rock and scribbled, *That's not the deep-down truth.*

"But it's a big part of the truth, Layla. I can't get around it. I believed my government and did what I thought was right. If I don't own up that I killed innocent people, and stood by while children got killed, then I'm dead to human decency."

Layla ran her fingers, tracing along the serpent's scales.

"I can't change my past, Layla. I'm still trying to figure out how to live with it. But I want to change today and tomorrow and the next day. I'll find a job. I'll go back to school. I don't know exactly what yet. The only thing I know for certain is that I want to be with you."

Me too, she nodded. Damian hugged her tight against him and she hugged back.

"All these years I've waited," he said, his chin resting on top of her head.

"Waited for two thoughts in a row not tainted by doubt or despair. I've found it, Layla. Right here on this rock with you. Not that the doubt has disappeared. It's that you matter more."

The two stayed close against each other for the longest time. Layla reached up and put her hands on either side of Damian's face. She felt her healing flowing into his troubled brain. But she felt his healing flowing back into her, as well.

Her fingers ran over the curved fangs of the snake on Damian's cheek, following down the reptile's scaled body. As she traced along the tail that wound around his neck, the familiar words sounded in her head. *And these signs shall follow them.*

She was led to speak in new tongues. Tongues of silence and the heart. To lay hands on the sick. And now, finally, she was led to take up serpents.

God anointed her to touch both the serpent that took her tongue and the serpent that bedded in Damian's skin and heart. At last, after losing her way for so long, Layla understood what she could not see before. That all paths lead to one place. And, wherever she went, she would meet the snake.

As she touched Damian's cheek, rapture surged through her hands into that yearning place inside she was never able to fill before.

She felt connected to everything on the planet – united in a place beyond time and sensible thinking where her mother and Thomas Alva Edison and Jesus lived alongside of everyone who was and is and ever will be. A place where loss turns into gift.

Half-tranced, she wondered if she was dreaming.

"I don't want to leave you, Layla," Damian said. "Ever again."

Me neither, Layla worded with her eyes.

"Get dressed and I'll walk you home."

When they got to the front porch, Layla motioned for Damian to come in.

"No. It wouldn't look right. I'll stay out here until your father comes home."

Will you eat supper with us? Layla gestured.

"Let's see how this goes, first," Damian said. He and Layla kissed. With his arms around her waist, foreheads touching, Damian half-whispered, "But, no matter what, we'll find a way to be together. I promise."

As Layla took her suitcase and went inside, Damian sat down on the porch steps at the end of a gravel lane he had happened upon by chance.

He gazed at the trees and the mountains beyond and waited.

EPILOGUE

THE attic feels different. Smaller, dustier. *Welcoming*. I set down the huge cardboard box I've just lugged up and sit in the dim light thinking about the vow I made on that rainy day when I was thirteen.

For the next decade, I pieced together the story behind those news clippings the same way my mother pieced together the quilt she made for me before I was born. Scraps from the past. Journal entries, letters, and countless interviews with family members about what they knew. I talked to old Doc Fredericks, Sheriff Dones, neighbors, everyone who might know something, badgering them with questions – a trait my parents praise as curiosity but others call nosiness.

Before going back downstairs, I open the box and go

through the contents, recalling the steps of my ten-year journey. Dozens of journals make up the bulk of the box – daily diaries Mama kept from the time she was seven. Hefty stacks of letters she wrote and received, and five notebooks detailing my sleuth work, blow by blow.

I ease out an album and page through the plastic-protected articles from the *Smoky Mountain Gazette*. Faith Healer Victim of Violent Attack; articles about the trial, Hands Off For Local Faith Healer; the AP article that spread the news cross-country; news that the faith healer had resumed her work.

Following the articles are pages filled with all the photographs I managed to duplicate or finagle from extra copies. Layla as a baby. Barefoot Layla at five, needing a good hair-brushing, swinging under the maple tree, looking skyward. School pictures. Family photos through the years. Photos of Layla and Damian, taken during the eleven months of their courtship, looking like any love-struck couple – well, not quite like any other couple if you add in the tattoos, ponytail, and Layla's otherworldly blue eyes.

I turn the page and see the photographs I loved hearing about over and over – *their wedding*.

With my finger, I trace the images of the loving faces of all who were gathered in that holiest of churches – the rock by the creek where Layla and Damian's lips first touched. Abbey is on the left, stunning Abbey, in her maid of honor dress. To the right of Abbey, standing in his three-piece suit, is best man Brian, who navigated the uneven terrain with his prosthetic legs. (Brian had recently joined his father's practice. About the time I was six, I remember when Doc Fredericks retired and Doc Brian was the one who took out my tonsils and stitched me up when I fell out of the trees. He could always make me laugh, even when he was giving shots.)

And there, walking down the path to the creek is a picture of what "goodness from sorrow" looks like. Four-year-old An Linh is strewing fistfuls of red petals from a basketful of porch trellis roses. The child's uncertain brown eyes dart back and forth as she walks past the onlookers, backtracking whenever she misses a spot. When diminutive An passes Topher, he toddles out to pick up a dropped petal and tries to give it back to her, until Roy reigns him in.

Halfway to the rock, the child sees Mrs. Phoebe, puts down her basket and runs to her. Mrs. Phoebe lifts little An, kisses her, and goes to retrieve the basket. With her adopted daughter in her arms, the child named Peace who came from Saigon on Operation Babylift, Mrs. Phoebe holds the basket so An can scatter petals as they both finish the walk to the big brown rock.

On cue, with only the babble of the stream as accompaniment, Avis warbles out the first notes of "Here Comes the Bride."

Everyone joins in. Doc Fredericks in his deep bass, Damian's parents, friends, and family singing together as Ed and his daughter walk out from behind the big sycamore.

All dressed in white...

Dressed in the simple white gown her mother had worn, with a wreath of ox-eyed daisies in her hair and carrying a bouquet of wildflowers, Layla and her father make their way past the beaming faces.

Sweetly, serenely in soft glowing light.

Lovely to see, marching to thee,

Layla barely hears the singing. Her eyes are locked onto Damian's and his onto hers. Their beam of love is as visible as the September sun.

Sweet love united for eternity.

I turn the page and see pictures of Damian and Layla hammering nails into the home they built. At Ed's bidding, they chose a spot on the family property, close to the creek's ripple and splash. The next sequence of pictures shows the walls going up, the roof, the stone fireplace, Damian carrying Layla over the threshold, the newly-dug front garden with its twiggy rosebushes.

Then, a handful of photos, two years' worth of moments that race by when you're young and in love. Layla a busy homemaker and healer. Damian, a part-time construction worker, another pair of hands helping Ed with the animals and field work, and a published writer with a well-received first book under his belt.

Next comes one of my favorite photos: Layla stretched out in bed with a beatific smile, a sleeping cat curled on the enormous round of her pregnant belly. And then, a picture of Layla and Damian and their only child, Grace.

Me.

In my mother's journal, she wrote this shortly after I was born.

Even though I'm plagued by weak-leggedness on ledges, whenever I look upon the Smoky Mountains and the valley below, the sight of it fills me with such piercing beauty that I become a new creation. Changed like sugar in water where the hard of the sugar dissolves until you can't tell which part is sugar and which part water. A whole new thing. A sweet elixir. That's how I feel when I hold baby Grace.

As I grew, my mother and father instilled in me language as rich and varied as each season's bounty. My mother, Layla, through touch, through palpable energy, taught me the tongues of trees and water and light. The sound of silence. The syntax of negative space – those interstices between words where, mole-blind, we grope our way forward.

My father, Damian, gave me poetry, encouraging me to write the same way he prodded other veterans to set down their experiences.

Dad started a magazine, *Broken We Stand,* for vets to share their common pain. A place to release the emotions they keep locked up just so they can get out of bed each morning and make it through another day. Stories and poems about the incomprehensible ways people can behave to other people. About how brutality sits like a predatory bird, talons sunk into the soft meat of their brain – a presence that coexists with whatever they see. *Even beauty*. Whatever they feel. *Even love.* As the soldiers write about their grief and guilt – about their missing limbs, shot nerves, seeped-out souls, and obliterated dreams – by some strange transmutation, their losses become sacred.

All these years, Mother has continued to minister to those who seek her healing. After she and my father started courting, she confessed her secret first to him and later to everyone else. Compelled to set the record straight, she revealed that Zebidiah Yeagley, not a serpent, took her tongue.

The signs at the Tompkins' house that she put up after the rape in early September were taken down after Christmas.

Though there was no rational explanation for why she could ease people's pain, regulars flocked back and new folks came.

Now that I am a year older than my mother when she gave birth to me, and have just graduated with my

Master's degree from a school far from home, the least I can do is to return the gifts I've been given.

From my grandfather, Edward Tompkin, my earliest gift was a lullaby. He intoned *hush little baby* so many times that whenever I hear the words *mockingbird* or *diamond ring*, Rorschachs appear of a porch swing and the smell of sawdust. Paw-paw, who put bits of honeycomb into my mouth with his rough-ridged fingers. Who sanded and hammered together my cradle that sits nearby on its dusty rockers. Who built a new wooden swing to replace the splintered one on the maple tree, and, just before I left for college in Boston, made the wooden frame that sat on my dorm-room desk with a picture of us all.

It was the last project he worked on before his death a year ago when he finally succumbed to a respiratory infection. Paw-paw Ed taught me that if you watch the sunrise each morning, you are given a new beginning. And each evening's sunset offers respite from whatever trials the day may bring.

Before I close the box, I lift out one last item, the gift I'm about to take downstairs and give to my parents. It's a leather-bound copy of my thesis project – the story I've been working on all these years: *The Healer of Fox Hollow.*

I smell the cover – the rich, leathery scent of a pair of new shoes made to walk wherever you need to go – and think how my mother's right foot will probably go a mile a minute when she sits down to read these pages.

Reaching up to touch the heart-shaped locket at my throat, I open the book and read the dedication, one more time.

This story is for my family. All of them. Especially for my father, Damian, who taught me endurance and a stubborn yearning for wholeness in a shattered world. And for my mother, Layla.

Here, at last, is your voice.

ACKNOWLEDGEMENTS

There are countless forms of healing from pharmaceuticals to hugs and, in this case, the intensely busy people who so generously shared their time and talents. Among those I thank with full heart are: Janette Deihl, Marian Dornell, Phyllis Gardener, Irene Harvey, Becky Lawrence, Joshua Leonard, Helen Manfull, Annie McGregor, Rev. Glenn Mitchell, Pamela Monk, Lisa Roney, George Rose, Laurie Ross, Sue Smith, and Lorena Waselinko.

Immense gratitude to Jonathan Leonard for not only allowing me to use poetry from his book, *Abstraxions*, written in his early twenties, but also to excerpt the poems out of full measure and attribute the words to Damian.

There were several specialists who administered life-saving, critical care to this story.

Unspeakable gratitude to Laney Katz Becker at Markson Thoma. I couldn't dream up an agent like

Laney – consummate professional, tireless champion of her authors, compassionate to the core. Time and time again, her diagnostic writer's eye zeroed in on blood and bone and administered editorial gold. In the most seminal ways, Laney ushered this story into life.

Profound thanks to Joseph Pittman, Editorial Director/head wizard at Vantage Point Books, who manages, in the midst of schedule overload, to put out the welcome mat, and as an author himself, focus his laser-like writer's sensibilities on the what ailed the story and offer inspired ideas to heal it.

Last, first, and always, I have no adequate words to thank my husband, Bob, who read this story chapter by chapter through more versions than I care to remember – season after season of sharing insights, identifying missteps and mistakes, brainstorming solutions, and cheering me on. For the past forty years, he has provided me with the continuous physical, emotional, and spiritual healing that allows me to write, to live, to love.

Reader's Guide

The Healer of Fox Hollow began as a personal exploration. To better understand what unifies us as well as what separates us, I imagined myself with radically different mindsets from my own. Guided by the all-too-real, this story pushed me to places where ordinary language fails. Places of darkness and the horrific. Places of doubt where we stand naked in our fear, loneliness, suffering. Places of healing and light where we experience heartbreaking human kindness, forgiveness, grace, love, and ultimate mystery.

In the end, writing this story left me with more questions than answers. But it widened the doors of my understanding in ways that I'm working to translate into meaningful action. Here are some questions that clarified my explorations. I hope they are helpful on your journey, as well.

1. *How do you communicate unspeakable subjects and emotions in your own life?*
2. *Doc Fredericks calls faith healing a placebo. Yet when Layla relieves his son's pain, he has no satisfactory explanation. Is Layla's healing real? Have you had personal experience with alternative healing? Was it effective?*
3. *What beliefs do you, or others you know, hold that change the way you see? That change how you act? Have you ever believed something that you never questioned until later in life?*
4. *What role does doubt play in the story for each of the characters? Does doubt play a negative or positive force in the story?*
5. *How does having the story set in the Smoky Mountains of Tennessee influence the characters? Discuss how the "mountain folk" and their beliefs, ethics, and history color this story. What is the role of nature in the novel?*
6. *Are there any signs, prophecies or omens that you pay attention to in your own life? What is the significance of the snake?*
7. *Brian has a sign in his room, One Should Love Some Things More Than Life And Fear Some Things More Than Death. Do you agree? Why or why not?*

8. *What helped each of the main characters to survive the unthinkable? What sustains you?*
9. *What motivated Layla to turn down a college education in favor of remaining on the mountain? Have you ever faced a difficult decision that changed the direction of your life's path?*
10. *What do you think the statement, "here, at last, is your voice," means? Was Layla really voiceless? What external and internal circumstances silence a person's voice?*
11. *Layla, Petey, Brian, and Damian are wounded physically and/or mentally. Can someone be healed but not cured? Cured but not healed?*